Chapter 1: A Stitch in Time

The hum of the city vibrated through the cracked window of my tiny studio, a discordant symphony of honking horns and distant laughter mingling with the scent of fresh coffee from the café below. I had long surrendered any notion of space, letting bolts of fabric and scraps of tulle claim every corner of the room. My design table, once a proud, polished surface, now resembled a battleground—traced patterns lying haphazardly beside half-finished sketches, a chaotic testament to the passion that drove me.

Today, though, the excitement that usually accompanied the birth of a new creation felt like a fragile thread, fraying at the edges. My fingers worked on autopilot as I threaded the needle, the fabric a silken reminder of the magic I once wielded with ease. But even as I coaxed the thread through the eye, my mind flickered back to Jason. The way he'd leaned against the doorframe last night, arms crossed, his gaze sliding away as I had excitedly shared my latest design idea. The warmth in his eyes had been replaced by a stormy cloud, and I wondered if it was my creations he no longer admired or if he'd grown tired of the girl behind the sketches.

"Another wedding dress?" he had muttered, the edge of sarcasm slicing through the air like the sharpest shears.

"What's wrong with that?" I had replied, forcing a smile that didn't quite reach my eyes. "It's not just a dress; it's a dream. It's the beginning of a lifetime."

But he had simply shrugged, the distance between us widening as he retreated into the shadows of the hallway. That moment lingered like a ghost in my mind, haunting me as I carefully pinned the fabric, trying to ignore the heavy weight settling on my chest. I was losing him, and with each stitch I made, I felt a piece of myself unraveling, caught in a tangle of insecurities.

The doorbell chimed, a melodic interruption to my spiraling thoughts. I set my work aside, wiping my hands on my apron, smudged with remnants of thread and remnants of hope. "Coming!" I called, bracing myself for whatever awaited me on the other side of the door.

When I opened it, the sun streamed into the dim space, illuminating a whirlwind of energy: my best friend, Mia, her hair bouncing with every step like a wild flame. "Surprise!" she exclaimed, her arms overflowing with a rainbow of fabric swatches.

"Mia, what are you doing here?" I laughed, my heart lifting just a little as her exuberance cut through the gloom.

"I brought inspiration!" she declared, flinging the swatches onto my design table like confetti. "I thought you might need a little push to reignite that creative spark of yours."

"Or maybe I just need a nap," I quipped, eyeing the explosion of colors that now cluttered my workspace. "How am I supposed to design a wedding dress with this circus?"

"Trust me, it'll work. Sometimes all it takes is a little chaos to see the beauty." She plopped down on the floor, surrounded by the colorful chaos she'd created.

With a reluctant smile, I joined her, sifting through the vibrant fabrics. "So, what's new in your world? Any hot dates with the new guy?"

Mia's eyes sparkled. "Actually, yes! We went to that new Italian place on West 14th. You know the one with the cute outdoor seating? Luca is charming, and he has this passion for food that is infectious."

I couldn't help but grin at her enthusiasm. "Sounds like someone's smitten."

Her cheeks flushed, and she waved her hand dismissively. "Okay, maybe a little. But enough about me. What's up with you and Mister Broody? You two are like a soap opera I can't look away from."

I sighed, the weight of her observation sinking in. "It's just... I don't know. He used to be so supportive, and now it feels like my dreams are too much for him. I can't help but feel like I'm dragging him down."

Mia's expression softened, and she reached out, squeezing my hand. "You're not dragging him down. You're building something beautiful here, and if he can't see that, then he's the one who needs to step up."

As I stared into her earnest eyes, the flicker of hope ignited once more within me. "You really think so?"

"Absolutely! Now, let's see what magic we can create with these fabrics." She dove headfirst into the pile, rifling through the materials with glee.

As we began to layer textures and colors, the atmosphere in the room shifted. Ideas flowed like the vibrant threads slipping between my fingers. The wedding dress I'd envisioned began to take form in my mind, a dance of elegance and passion, as though my dreams were weaving themselves into reality. For the first time in days, the thrill of creation wrapped around me like a warm embrace, chasing away the chill that had settled in my heart.

"Look at this!" Mia held up a delicate lace overlay, its intricate patterns catching the light like delicate whispers of a love story waiting to unfold. "This could be the centerpiece!"

I could feel my heart racing, a sudden rush of inspiration flooding through me. "Yes! With a satin underlay and a cascading train, it could embody the very essence of romance."

Together, we dove deeper into the sea of fabric, ideas flowing freely as we bounced concepts off one another. With every stitch, every snip of the scissors, the shadows of doubt and heartache faded, replaced by the vibrant tapestry of hope and creativity. But amid the joy, a nagging question remained: Could I truly mend what felt broken in my relationship? Or would the threads of my heart unravel in the pursuit of my dreams?

As Mia and I sank deeper into the creative whirlwind, the fabrics began to sing with possibilities. Each hue held a promise, and every stitch whispered a tale of love waiting to be told. I felt a surge of energy, a newfound spark ignited by her enthusiasm, making the cluttered space come alive with vibrancy.

"Okay, let's name this dress!" Mia exclaimed, holding a shimmering piece of satin against her chest as if it were a trophy. "Something that captures the essence of what we're creating here. It needs to reflect dreams and love."

"Like a secret garden in spring?" I suggested, envisioning the delicate flowers that would weave through the layers, the petals brushing against the fabric like soft caresses.

Mia beamed, her eyes twinkling. "Exactly! The Garden of Whimsy! It's perfect!"

With that, the name felt like a charm that breathed life into our design process. Hours melted away as we tossed ideas back and forth, piecing together our vision. The laughter that filled the room was infectious, drowning out the nagging worries that had plagued me just moments before.

"Okay, now for the embellishments," I said, rummaging through a drawer bursting with buttons, sequins, and trimmings. "What if we added pearls to accentuate the neckline?"

Mia's face lit up like a New Year's Eve firework. "Or some vintage brooches! Something unexpected that tells a story. Like an heirloom that the bride can pass down!"

"Brilliant! Something that connects the past with the future. I love it!"

Just as I began sketching the final details, a loud crash echoed from outside. I jumped, my heart racing, and we exchanged wide-eyed glances. "What was that?"

"Maybe a New York pigeon got into a street fight?" Mia joked, but her laughter was strained, an undercurrent of concern threading through it.

"Or maybe the world is just colliding outside my window," I muttered, trying to shake off the uneasy feeling creeping up my spine. I walked over to the window, peering down at the street below, where a crowd had gathered.

"What's happening?" Mia joined me, her curiosity piqued.

A small group of people had formed around a street performer who was struggling with a tangled microphone cord while a jazz band played a lively tune nearby. The scene was chaotic yet joyful, the kind of moment that perfectly encapsulated the pulse of the city. I smiled, the energy lifting my spirits slightly.

"See? Life is full of surprises," Mia said, nudging me playfully. "It's all about how you handle them."

"You're right," I replied, stepping back from the window. "Maybe I should take a page from their book and embrace the chaos a bit more. Maybe even create a wedding dress that celebrates spontaneity."

"Now you're talking! 'The Dress of Unexpected Twists!'" she exclaimed, her voice an octave higher in excitement. "A gown that reflects the ups and downs of love itself!"

As we laughed and brainstormed, the door swung open, and in walked Jason, his brow furrowed. The sight of him sent a cascade of emotions crashing over me—relief, confusion, hope—but mostly a tight knot of anxiety.

"What's with all the noise?" he asked, glancing around at the colorful disarray.

"Mia's here, bringing inspiration!" I replied, forcing a brightness into my tone that felt a little too strained. "We've been creating something magical."

He looked at Mia, then back at me, his eyes holding a mix of skepticism and something else—disappointment? "Is this what you call magic now?"

The jab stung more than I wanted to admit, and Mia's eyes flicked to me, concerned. I swallowed hard, sensing the familiar tension tightening between us like a noose.

"Jason, it's not just mess; it's—"

"Creativity? Sure," he interrupted, his tone clipped. "But you know you have a deadline to meet. High-profile clients don't wait around for your whims."

I could feel the heat rising to my cheeks, a mixture of indignation and hurt flooding through me. "This isn't whimsy; this is my work! It's my passion!"

Mia wisely stepped back, her presence suddenly feeling like an unwelcome third wheel in a rapidly deteriorating situation. "Maybe I should leave you two to talk," she said, her voice soft but firm. "I can come back later?"

"No!" I protested, but she had already gathered her swatches and was making her way toward the door.

"Let's talk when things calm down," she said over her shoulder, leaving me alone with Jason.

As the door clicked shut, the air between us thickened, heavy with unspoken words. "You shouldn't have done that," I said, crossing my arms, trying to shield myself from the brewing storm.

"Done what? Defended your time?" he shot back, running a hand through his tousled hair, his frustration palpable. "You're lost in your little fabric world, and it's like I'm standing on the outside looking in."

"Maybe that's because you're choosing to stay on the outside!" I countered, my voice rising. "I've shared everything with you—the sketches, the ideas, the late nights. But lately, you're just... not here."

His expression softened momentarily, but the distance lingered. "I'm here, but I'm also trying to keep this relationship grounded. You can't just float away on your creative cloud without considering how it affects us."

"I need my creativity, Jason! It's not just a hobby; it's my life!"

He stepped closer, his frustration morphing into something deeper, a yearning that echoed in the space between us. "And I'm scared that this passion of yours is going to consume you. What if it takes you away from me?"

I opened my mouth to argue, but his words struck a chord within me. The reality of his fears lingered like a stubborn shadow, a reminder that my dreams might come at a cost. My heart raced, and for the first time, I questioned whether our love could withstand the weight of my ambitions.

"Jason, I—"

Before I could finish, the door swung open again, and Mia reappeared, her face flushed. "You'll never believe this! I just saw a man proposing right outside! With the most extravagant ring!"

Jason's demeanor shifted, a glimmer of curiosity breaking through the tension. "A proposal?"

"Yeah! It was so romantic! They must have been tourists, but it was pure magic."

Mia's excitement wrapped around us like a lifeline, and as she recounted the details, I watched Jason's expression change. The storm cloud above us began to dissipate, revealing glimpses of a brighter sky.

Perhaps there was hope after all—hope that we could find a way to weave our dreams together instead of allowing them to tear us apart. As Mia continued to share the enchanting scene, I caught Jason's eye, and in that brief moment, I knew we were both searching for the same thing: a way to bridge the gap between our worlds, to stitch together our passions, love, and ambition into a single fabric that would define our future.

The energy in the room shifted as Mia continued to recount the details of the street proposal. Her animated gestures and bright laughter created a comforting bubble, one that briefly shielded me from the lingering tension with Jason. The way she described the couple—her eyes sparkling as she mentioned the bride-to-be's gasp of joy and the onlookers' cheers—made me yearn for that kind of unabashed happiness, the kind that felt so distant in my own life.

"Seriously, it was like a scene from a movie!" Mia exclaimed, clasping her hands together, her excitement infectious. "The way he knelt, the ring glinting in the sunlight—pure magic! You should've seen her face; it was like a thousand fireworks went off in her heart."

Jason chuckled, his initial irritation dissipating under the weight of Mia's enthusiasm. "That's what proposals should feel like, right? A spectacle. I mean, who wouldn't want a crowd cheering as they commit to a lifetime?"

"Exactly! That's how love should be—loud, messy, and unapologetic." Mia waved her arms as if conducting an orchestra, and I couldn't help but smile at her spiritedness.

But as the momentary levity wrapped around us like a warm blanket, I felt the undeniable pull of reality. The joyful image of a couple beginning their journey stood in stark contrast to the tangled threads of my own relationship.

"What would you do if you were proposed to right here, right now?" Mia asked, turning her gaze toward me with a playful glint in her eye.

I paused, letting the question linger in the air like the scent of freshly brewed coffee. "Well, if it were done right—with love, creativity, and maybe a surprise flash mob—then I'd say yes without a second thought." I shot Jason a playful look. "But only if it included a grand gesture!"

"Grand gestures are overrated," Jason interjected, a slight smirk on his lips. "Sometimes, it's the quiet moments that hold the most meaning. Like that time we—"

"Don't," I warned, raising a hand. "I know exactly where that story leads, and I'm not sure it's the right path for us right now."

Mia, sensing the impending shift in the atmosphere, leaned in closer, her curiosity piqued. "You two have a history, huh? What's the best story? Come on, spill it!"

"No, no, we're not digging into the past," I said, waving my hands as if to clear the air. "Let's stick to dreams, fashion, and the magic of street proposals."

"Okay, but I want details later," Mia said, a teasing smile on her face.

Just then, my phone buzzed on the table, interrupting the moment. I grabbed it, half-expecting a message from a client. Instead, it was a notification that made my heart race—a new email from a bridal magazine. My breath hitched as I opened it, my fingers trembling slightly. The subject line read, "Your Submission: Next Steps."

"Is it good news?" Jason asked, leaning closer, the playful banter forgotten as curiosity replaced the earlier tension.

"Yes! I submitted designs for a feature in their next issue. They want to discuss the possibilities!"

Mia squealed, jumping up and down in delight. "See? This is what I'm talking about! This is your moment!"

As the excitement swirled in the room, Jason's expression shifted, clouded by a hint of concern. "But you have a lot on your plate already, don't you? You're balancing work, me, and... this sudden fame."

"It's not sudden!" I countered, my voice a mix of determination and frustration. "This is years in the making, Jason. I've been working hard to get recognized in this industry. I can't let fear stop me now."

His gaze softened, but doubt lingered. "I just don't want you to lose yourself in the process."

"I won't! I promise," I said, my voice steadier than I felt. "This is part of who I am, and I need you to support me, not pull away."

Before he could respond, a loud thud reverberated from the other side of the wall, startling us all. I shot a look at Mia, who raised an eyebrow, both of us exchanging puzzled glances.

"What was that?" she whispered, instinctively inching closer to me.

"I have no idea," I replied, moving to the door. With my heart pounding, I creaked it open slightly, peeking into the dimly lit hallway. The flickering light above cast eerie shadows, and the hum of distant voices filtered through. "It sounded like it came from the stairs."

"Should we check?" Mia asked, her eyes wide with a mix of curiosity and trepidation.

"Maybe it's just a neighbor moving furniture," Jason suggested, but his voice lacked conviction, echoing my own unease.

But curiosity gnawed at me, and I nodded, pulling the door open wider. "Let's see."

Mia stepped out first, followed by Jason, and together we ventured down the narrow hall. Each step echoed, and the air grew thick with anticipation. As we approached the stairwell, the sounds grew clearer—a mix of scuffling and low murmurs, almost like a struggle.

"What if it's a fight?" Mia whispered, her voice barely audible, laced with both fear and excitement.

"Or a robbery," Jason replied, scanning the area with a serious expression.

We paused at the top of the stairs, straining to hear more clearly. Then, just as I was about to turn back, a sharp cry pierced the air, sending chills racing down my spine. "Help!"

Instinct kicked in, and I rushed forward, pulling Jason and Mia along. We hurried down the stairs, hearts racing, as the sounds grew louder—a desperate plea mingled with the noise of scuffling feet.

When we reached the landing, we stopped short. A small crowd had gathered near the front door, all eyes trained on something just beyond our view. I felt a surge of adrenaline, the rush of fear and determination colliding within me.

"What's going on?" I asked a stranger standing nearby, a man with a worried frown.

"Someone's been attacked!" he said, his voice tense. "I don't know who they are, but it's bad!"

My heart raced as dread washed over me. "We need to help!" I said, instinctively moving closer to the source of the commotion.

Jason grabbed my arm, a mix of concern and protectiveness in his gaze. "Wait, we don't know what we're walking into!"

But before I could respond, the door burst open, and a figure stumbled into view—a woman, her clothes torn, face bruised and streaked with dirt. Panic danced in her wide eyes as she caught sight of us, her voice trembling. "Please, they're coming! You have to help me!"

The room fell silent as we processed her words, the air heavy with uncertainty.

Before I could respond, a sound echoed from the street outside, shattering the moment. A car revved loudly, tires screeching against the pavement. In the distance, shadows flickered, moving closer, their intentions unknown.

I took a step forward, my heart racing as I faced the chaos unfolding before us. The vibrant world of fabric and dreams faded into the background, replaced by the urgency of the moment. And as the realization hit me that everything I held dear might be about to change, I braced myself for whatever lay ahead, knowing that this was only the beginning.

Chapter 2: The Inevitable Fracture

The air in my studio was thick with the scent of cotton and a hint of regret, a potent mix that clung to the walls like an unwelcome guest. Rolls of fabric, each more vibrant than the last, lay scattered across the floor, the remnants of my relentless pursuit for perfection. Each swath was a testament to countless late nights, fueled by caffeine and a feverish desire to impress, yet now they felt like shackles, binding me to a world I'd begun to resent. My fingers, once deft and inspired, now trembled with anxiety as I tried to shape ideas that seemed to flit away like the fluttering butterflies I longed to capture in silk.

I stepped back, surveying the chaos around me. A smattering of sketches littered my worktable, crumpled and abandoned in the whirlwind of creativity turned sour. The designs that had once sparked joy now seemed like ghosts of dreams long forgotten. My heart sank further when I remembered the fashion show looming on the horizon, a shining beacon that felt more like a storm cloud. All I could think about was the disappointment that awaited me if I didn't meet my own impossible standards.

Jason's voice echoed in my mind, sharp and cutting through the haze of fabric and thread. His words had stung like a fresh wound, a reminder that while I was drowning in the depths of my work, he felt like a distant memory, something I was clinging to while letting everything else slip away. I could still see his expression, that mixture of hurt and anger that danced across his handsome features when he confronted me earlier. "You're obsessed, Anna. It's like I don't even exist in your world anymore," he had said, his voice strained with frustration.

A laugh had bubbled up in my throat, bitter and disbelieving. "Obsessed? You call passion obsession?" I shot back, my heart racing with indignation. "This is my life, Jason. You knew that when we started this."

"Passion doesn't come at the expense of the people you love!" he countered, his eyes blazing.

I could feel the fissures forming between us, widening with every word, every accusation. I had let the fear of failure seep into our relationship, pushing him away while I swam deeper into my artistic abyss.

"Maybe I'm just too busy to babysit your feelings," I spat, the heat of the moment clouding my judgment. It felt like a cheap shot, one that was below the belt, and yet the satisfaction of saying it was almost too intoxicating to resist.

The silence that followed was deafening, filled only with the sound of our heavy breathing, a war of wills being fought in the charged space between us. He had taken a step back, eyes wide, as if my words were daggers cutting through the bond we had carefully woven over the years. In that moment, I saw him—the man I loved, the man I was destroying with every selfish choice.

When he turned to leave, the door slamming behind him echoed like a gunshot, leaving me standing in the wreckage of my own making. My heart plummeted into the pit of my stomach, a sickening realization washing over me. I had crossed a line, and now I was left alone in a studio full of creations that felt tainted, cursed by the weight of my own choices.

I sank to the floor, surrounded by the fabric that had once been my escape, my muse. The vibrant colors seemed muted in the dim light, shadows creeping in like the doubts that clawed at my mind. My designs, which had sparked with life and possibility, now looked like remnants of a dream that had shattered into a thousand unrecognizable pieces. I buried my face in my hands, the reality of my actions crashing over me like an unforgiving wave.

Each breath felt heavier, laden with regret as I thought of Jason, his kindness overshadowed by the brashness of my ambition. I had let my need to succeed overshadow the love we had built, neglecting the foundation that had once felt so solid. It was an unbearable truth that gnawed at me, the understanding that I might have lost the most important part of my life in the pursuit of a fleeting vision.

The studio, once a sanctuary of creativity, had transformed into a cage of despair. I could feel the walls closing in, fabric draping like the shroud of my crumbling hopes. In the distance, the world moved on—cars honked, pedestrians chatted, life thrummed with an energy that I no longer felt connected to. The vibrant city outside my window seemed like a different universe, a place where laughter and love thrived, while I remained trapped in my bubble of artistic despair.

As I stared into the chaos surrounding me, I suddenly saw something glimmering among the disarray. One of the sketches I had crumpled in my frustration was peeking out, its edges curling like petals of a wilting flower. I picked it up, recognizing it immediately. It was the design that had sparked the initial excitement for my collection, a gown that danced with possibility.

With a newfound determination, I pushed myself off the floor, wiping away the remnants of tears and self-pity. The world was still there, waiting for me to find my place within it again. Jason's absence felt like a gaping wound, but I realized I couldn't heal what was broken until I rediscovered the joy that had led me here in the first place. I had to find a way to merge my passion for design with the love that was still waiting for me, flickering in the shadows like a candle fighting against the wind.

The realization washed over me like a refreshing breeze, stirring something deep within. I had to reclaim my creativity, breathe life back into the fabrics, and weave them together not just for a show, but to remind myself of the love I had nearly let slip away. It wouldn't be easy, but I owed it to Jason, to myself, and to the vibrant dreams that had led me to this moment. With resolve, I began to sketch anew, pouring everything I had into the designs that would mend not just my heart but the fragile threads of my life, one stitch at a time.

The days that followed felt like a somber waltz through the remnants of my shattered reality. Each morning, I rose to the same muted light filtering through the grime on my studio window, a harsh reminder of the choices that had led me here. My sketches lay scattered like fallen leaves in an autumn storm, remnants of a passion now tinged with regret. Every fabric I touched whispered of memories—memories of laughter shared with Jason, of the warmth of his presence, now replaced by a cold echo in the stillness of the room.

I tried to lose myself in the rhythm of work, diving headfirst into the chaos of sewing machines and swathes of silk, hoping the hum of creativity would drown out the ache in my chest. But every stitch I made felt heavy, laden with the weight of my failure. My colleagues buzzed around me, oblivious to the turmoil churning within. "You okay?" a friend asked one afternoon, her brow furrowed in concern as she watched me fuss with a particularly stubborn piece of fabric.

I forced a smile, the kind that didn't quite reach my eyes. "Just perfect. Living the dream, you know?" My voice dripped with sarcasm, a defense mechanism against the flood of emotions threatening to spill over.

She raised an eyebrow, clearly not convinced. "You're about as perfect as a dress with a hidden zipper. What's really going on?"

I opened my mouth to offer a dismissive reply, but the words caught in my throat. Instead, I let out a sigh that felt like it could deflate my entire world. "It's just... everything." The honesty surprised me, the admission of vulnerability slipping through my carefully crafted façade.

"Everything? Sounds like you need to take a break, go out, have a drink or something. Maybe a cute guy will distract you from the fabric crisis."

I chuckled, the sound feeling foreign and hollow. "Cute guys? In this town? You mean the ones that come with a side of drama? No thanks. I've had my fill."

"Come on! It's like that saying—'there are plenty of fish in the sea,'" she teased, nudging me playfully.

"I think I'm allergic to fish," I muttered, turning back to my work as the conversation lingered in the air, an uncomfortable reminder of the warmth I'd lost.

As the week crawled by, my attempts to regain control felt futile. I busied myself with last-minute alterations, counting down the days until the fashion show as if it were a prison sentence. Each night, I returned to an empty apartment, the silence wrapping around me like a shroud, reminding me of everything that had unraveled. My phone buzzed sporadically with messages from my friends, inviting me out, encouraging me to socialize, but I declined them all, preferring the solitude that tasted bitter yet oddly comforting.

Then, one particularly dreary evening, as I fought to thread a needle with shaking hands, a soft knock broke the tension that had enveloped me. I glanced up, half-expecting it to be one of my well-meaning friends, but instead, there stood Jason, looking as torn as I felt. His presence ignited a flurry of emotions—relief, anger, longing—all tangled into one chaotic ball in my chest.

"Hey," he said, his voice low, almost tentative.

"Hey," I replied, the word barely escaping my lips. I didn't move, rooted to my spot as a million questions ricocheted in my mind. What was he doing here? Hadn't he walked out for good?

"I thought I'd check in," he said, stepping further into the studio. The fabric strewn around us seemed to amplify the awkwardness of the moment, each roll and scrap a silent witness to our unravelling.

I swallowed hard, trying to decipher the look on his face. "Check in? After a week of silence?"

His eyes dropped, shame flashing across his features. "I was... angry. And I still am. But I didn't want to leave things like that."

I studied him, the way his hands shoved deep into his pockets, the slight tremor in his voice. There was a vulnerability there that pulled at my heartstrings, even as my anger simmered just beneath the surface. "You're not here to yell at me again, are you?"

He shook his head vehemently. "No. I'm not here to argue. I just... I miss you, Anna."

I felt the air shift, the gravity of his words pressing down on me. "Miss me? Or miss the version of me who was completely devoted to you?" I couldn't help but lash out, bitterness creeping into my tone.

"That's not fair," he replied, his voice rising slightly. "I love your passion. I just wish you could balance it with us, with me. I don't want to compete with fabric and thread."

My breath hitched at the truth buried in his statement. "It wasn't supposed to be a competition. I thought you understood that I had to make this show a success."

"I do, but at what cost?" His frustration was palpable, and I could see the weariness etched into his features. "You're drowning in this, Anna, and I'm standing on the sidelines watching you sink."

The accusation stung, a truth I had been too scared to confront. "What do you want me to do? Give up on my dreams? Let this all go?"

"No! I want you to realize that there's more to life than just work," he said, his voice softening. "I want you to fight for us, for the love we had before this took over."

My heart raced at his words, a flicker of hope igniting within me, even as doubt nagged at the edges of my mind. Could we really navigate this maze we'd created? The tension was palpable, hanging thick in the air between us as I searched for the right words to bridge the chasm that had opened so violently.

"I don't know if I can," I admitted, the admission feeling like a surrender.

Jason stepped closer, the warmth of his presence enveloping me. "You can. We can."

For a moment, the chaos of my studio faded into the background, and all that remained was the intensity of his gaze and the flickering possibility of hope. But beneath the surface, the reality of our situation loomed like an uninvited specter, a reminder that trust, once fractured, takes time to heal.

And so, we stood there, caught in a fragile web of uncertainty, the weight of our unspoken fears mingling with the soft light of the evening filtering through the window. It was a moment that felt like both a beginning and an end, the space between us charged with the potential for healing—or further heartache. The choice was ours to make, but in that moment, I dared to believe that maybe, just maybe, love could stitch together what work had unraveled.

The days melted into each other like watercolor paint left in the rain, each moment bleeding into the next, blurring the edges of reality. I found myself engulfed in the relentless hum of sewing machines and the soft rustle of fabric, but the comfort they once provided felt elusive, slipping through my fingers like grains of sand. I worked tirelessly, trying to lose myself in the fabric, pouring over designs with a fervor that bordered on obsession. Yet, the thrill had evaporated, leaving only the remnants of my dreams swirling in a storm of self-doubt.

One evening, as the golden light of the setting sun filtered through the dusty window, casting long shadows across the floor, I noticed a flicker of movement outside. It was Mia, my best friend, standing on the threshold, her vibrant energy like a breath of fresh air against the stagnation that enveloped me. "There you are, the hermit of haute couture," she teased, stepping inside with an exaggerated flourish, her wild curls bouncing as she moved.

"Did you come to rescue me from my own fabric prison?" I replied, forcing a smile, my voice tinged with a playful sarcasm I didn't truly feel.

She surveyed the chaos, her eyes widening. "It looks like the sewing machine had a nervous breakdown. How about we take a break? You need some fresh air."

"Fresh air? In this city? You're asking me to breathe in car exhaust and the scent of regret."

Mia rolled her eyes, crossing her arms defiantly. "Trust me, a little air won't kill you. It might even make you feel alive again."

With a reluctant sigh, I set down my shears, the weight of the day clinging to my shoulders like a heavy coat. "Fine, but I can't promise I won't start drafting a new gown while we're out."

"That's the spirit! Let's get out of here before you create a whole new collection of heartbreak designs." She laughed, her eyes sparkling with mischief, and I couldn't help but feel a flicker of hope as I followed her out, away from the chaos that had consumed my mind.

We wandered through the bustling streets, the energy of the city wrapping around me like a warm blanket. The golden hour cast everything in a soft glow, and I marveled at the life pulsating around me—the street vendors shouting, children laughing, and couples strolling hand in hand, blissfully unaware of the storms brewing within their hearts. As we strolled, I found myself laughing at Mia's incessant chatter, the familiar cadence soothing my frayed nerves.

"You know, you really should think about getting out more. I swear, the only person you interact with besides your fabric is your sewing machine," she quipped, nudging me playfully.

"Don't underestimate the connection I have with my sewing machine. It's always there for me when I need it," I shot back, my lips curving into a grin.

"Right, because a machine totally understands the complexities of human emotion."

We shared a laugh, and for a moment, the shadows of my troubles receded, allowing the sunlight to dance through my heart. I allowed myself to forget the chaos back in my studio, the painful silence that had replaced Jason's laughter. Instead, I focused on the rhythm of the city and the comfort of my friend's presence, my mind free from the suffocating weight of my decisions.

Later, as we settled into a cozy café, the rich aroma of coffee enveloped us, wrapping around us like a hug. Mia's eyes sparkled with mischief as she leaned across the table, her voice low and conspiratorial. "So, spill. What's going on with you and Mr. Broody?"

I sighed, the heaviness creeping back into my chest. "I don't even know, Mia. Everything feels like a mess, and I can't seem to find my way back."

"Have you talked to him since that day?"

"No. I'm not even sure what I would say."

She raised an eyebrow, a knowing smile playing on her lips. "You could start with an apology. It tends to help."

"An apology? For what? Wanting to pursue my dreams? For choosing my passion over...over whatever it is we have?" I felt a spark of indignation flare up, but deep down, I knew she was right.

"Or for yelling things you didn't mean in the heat of the moment," she countered gently.

"Touché," I muttered, stirring my coffee absently.

"Look, Anna, I get that you're passionate about your work, but passion shouldn't mean you throw away the people who care about you. You don't have to choose."

Her words settled over me like a thick fog, both comforting and stifling. The truth was like a weight pressing against my chest, and the thought of reaching out to Jason filled me with a mix of dread and longing. I had to face the music sooner or later, but the fear of what awaited on the other side held me back, like a marionette tangled in its own strings.

Mia continued, "I think you're just scared. Scared of failing at your show and scared of failing at love. But you have to take that leap, even if it feels like you're jumping into the deep end."

I let her words swirl around me, contemplating the truth behind them. As the sun dipped lower in the sky, casting the café in warm, golden hues, a sense of determination began to form. Maybe it was time to put aside my fears and reach out, not just to Jason, but to reclaim the love and the dreams that had begun to drift away.

After we finished our coffee, I stepped outside, my heart pounding in my chest as I pulled out my phone, the screen lighting up in the fading light. I hesitated, my fingers hovering over Jason's name. It felt monumental, a decision that could either build a bridge or widen the chasm between us.

Before I could second-guess myself, I hit the call button. The ringing echoed in my ears, each tone amplifying the uncertainty bubbling within me. Just as I opened my mouth to speak, a voice broke through the static. "Hey, it's Jason. Leave a message after the beep."

The sound of his voice, even through the voicemail, sent a shiver of longing through me. I took a deep breath, feeling the warmth of the sun on my skin. "Hey, it's me. I just wanted to talk. Can you call me back?"

I hung up, my heart racing as I stared at the screen. What if he didn't call back? What if I'd pushed him too far?

Mia squeezed my arm, pulling me back to reality. "See? That wasn't so hard, was it?"

"Hard? No. Terrifying? Yes."

Just then, my phone vibrated in my hand, a sudden jolt of electricity surging through me. I looked down, heart pounding as I read the name on the screen: Jason.

"Speak of the devil!" Mia exclaimed, her eyes wide with excitement.

I stared at the phone, a mix of hope and anxiety swirling within me. "What do I say?"

"Just be honest. You've got this," she encouraged, a reassuring smile illuminating her face.

With a deep breath, I answered the call, my voice trembling as I greeted him. "Hey."

"Hey," he replied, his tone cautious yet warm, the familiar cadence stirring something deep within me.

We fell into a tentative rhythm, our conversation weaving through the awkwardness of the past days, each word building a fragile bridge between our hearts. But just as I began to feel a glimmer of hope, a loud crash shattered the moment, echoing in the background.

"What was that?" I asked, panic creeping into my voice.

"Anna, I—" he started, but the line abruptly went dead, cutting off the promise of what could have been. My heart dropped into the pit of my stomach as dread washed over me, a chilling realization sinking in.

"Jason?" I called, but the silence hung heavy in the air, swallowing my words. I looked at Mia, who wore a mask of concern, her brows knitted tightly.

"What just happened?" she asked, her voice tense.

"I don't know. He was just about to say something…"

I glanced back at my phone, the call having ended without warning, leaving a gaping void where our connection had just been. My pulse raced as an uneasy feeling curled in my gut, whispering that something was very wrong. I couldn't shake the sense that whatever had happened in that moment had the potential to change everything, and as uncertainty wrapped around me like a dark cloud, I realized I had to act quickly.

"What do I do?" I whispered, the gravity of the situation crashing over me.

"Let's go. We need to check on him," Mia urged, her eyes fierce with determination.

With no time to waste, we dashed into the chaos of the city streets, my heart pounding as I raced towards the unknown, a storm brewing within me, ready to confront whatever awaited us on the other side.

Chapter 3: Threads of Change

The moment I pulled into the heart of Maplewood, the world felt different. The air, imbued with the sweet scent of fallen leaves mingling with a hint of woodsmoke, wrapped around me like a warm blanket. I parked my car, the engine sputtering into silence, and stepped out into a kaleidoscope of color. The trees, draped in fiery reds and shimmering golds, swayed gently in the crisp breeze, as if inviting me to join their dance. This town, with its cobblestone streets and charming storefronts, exuded a cozy familiarity that momentarily eased the heaviness in my chest.

Clutching my worn leather satchel, I made my way down Main Street, where every shop seemed to offer a glimpse into a life less complicated than my own. My heels clicked against the pavement, a stark contrast to the soft rustle of nature around me. In the distance, the bell tower of the old church chimed the hour, its sound echoing through the streets like a gentle reminder that time had not stopped, even if my life felt suspended.

The bridal boutique stood out with its pastel-hued awning and whimsical window display, adorned with cascading flowers and delicate lace. I hesitated at the entrance, a mixture of excitement and trepidation swirling within me. The bell jingled as I stepped inside, a soothing chime that heralded my arrival. Inside, the atmosphere shifted. The air was scented with lavender and fresh fabric, a concoction that instantly soothed my frazzled nerves.

"Welcome!" A cheerful voice broke through my musings. Clara, the owner of the boutique, stood behind the counter, her apron dusted with threads of fabric. She was a whirlwind of energy, her bright smile lighting up the room like a ray of sunshine piercing through a cloudy sky. "I don't believe I've seen you around here before. You must be new to town!"

"I'm just visiting for the weekend," I replied, my voice soft but curious. "I needed a little escape."

"Oh, I completely understand!" Clara exclaimed, her eyes sparkling with genuine enthusiasm. "This town is perfect for unwinding. The hustle and bustle of city life can be a bit overwhelming, can't it? I'm Clara, by the way."

"Nice to meet you, Clara. I'm Emma." I extended my hand, and she clasped it warmly, as if sealing a pact of friendship right then and there.

As we exchanged pleasantries, I noticed the walls adorned with breathtaking gowns, each telling a story of love and dreams. Intricate beadwork glimmered under the soft lighting, and the rich fabrics whispered of fairy-tale moments waiting to happen. Clara caught my gaze and grinned.

"Want to take a closer look? I promise you won't be disappointed," she said, leading me further into the shop.

With each step, I felt the weight of my worries lift, replaced by an intoxicating sense of inspiration. Clara's passion for her craft bubbled over as she shared stories of brides who had walked through her doors, each one carrying hopes and wishes that felt almost palpable in the air.

"Every dress has a personality," she mused, holding up a flowing silk gown. "This one is for the romantic, the dreamer. I can already picture her twirling under twinkling lights, lost in her own world."

I laughed, the sound spilling out before I could contain it. "And what about the ones that scream 'I need caffeine and a plan'?"

Clara threw her head back, the sound of her laughter ringing like bells. "Oh, honey, I have just the dress for that! It's the one I call 'The Last-Minute Wonder.' It's for brides who decide to get married tomorrow and need to look fabulous doing it!"

As we shared banter and laughter, I realized how easily I slipped into this new rhythm. Clara was infectious, her energy igniting something dormant within me. We shifted from dresses to life stories, each thread revealing a little more of ourselves. I found myself recounting snippets of my own journey—how I'd once been a vibrant designer, filled with visions and sketches, before the world had dulled my colors.

"Everyone goes through rough patches, Emma," Clara said gently, her gaze steady and understanding. "But it's never too late to reignite that spark. You just need the right inspiration."

In that moment, I wanted nothing more than to believe her. Perhaps this retreat was more than just an escape; perhaps it was a catalyst for change.

Later that afternoon, Clara invited me to join her for a cup of coffee at a local café. The warmth of the sun filtering through the trees provided a perfect backdrop as we settled on a patio surrounded by colorful flowers. The café buzzed with laughter and conversation, the air thick with the rich aroma of freshly brewed coffee and baked goods.

"So, what did you do before you came here?" Clara asked, her eyes twinkling with curiosity.

"I was a designer in the city," I admitted, a twinge of nostalgia creeping in. "But life got... complicated. I sort of lost my way."

"Ah, the classic tale," she said, her tone playful. "But here's the thing: sometimes you need to get lost to find your true self again. It's like a bad haircut—painful at first, but it usually leads to something better."

I chuckled, appreciating her wry perspective. "You have a way of making bad situations sound charming."

"Just call me the silver lining fairy," she winked, lifting her coffee cup in a toast. "Here's to finding ourselves—one thread at a time."

As we clinked our cups together, I felt an unexpected surge of hope. Perhaps this quaint town, with its warm community and charming characters, was precisely what I needed to weave my life back together.

The next morning dawned with a soft light spilling through my window, casting a golden hue across the cozy room I had rented in a charming bed-and-breakfast. I inhaled deeply, savoring the sweet scent of maple syrup wafting from the kitchen below. The sounds of laughter and clinking dishes stirred an unexpected joy within me. It felt like the town itself was welcoming me, coaxing me into its warm embrace.

After a leisurely breakfast of fluffy pancakes drizzled with syrup and sprinkled with fresh blueberries, I decided to explore more of Maplewood. The streets were quiet, the sun casting long shadows that danced playfully across the cobblestones. I passed quaint shops, each window a portal into another world. A bookshop caught my eye, its shelves teeming with volumes that promised adventure and romance, so I stepped inside, the bell tinkling above me as I crossed the threshold.

The shop was dimly lit, with wooden shelves crammed full of books that lined the walls. The air was thick with the musty scent of paper, a smell that felt comforting and familiar. As I wandered deeper, my fingers brushing against the spines of novels, I could hear the soft rustle of pages being turned somewhere in the back. Following the sound, I entered a small nook where an elderly man was immersed in a book, a pair of reading glasses perched precariously on the tip of his nose.

"Excuse me," I said, feeling slightly intrusive. "What are you reading that has you so captivated?"

He looked up, his eyes twinkling behind his glasses. "Ah, a delightful tale of love and redemption. Just what this town needs more of, wouldn't you say?"

I chuckled, leaning against the wall. "I think that's what we all need sometimes. A good story to remind us of what's possible."

"Indeed!" he declared, closing the book with a soft thud. "Stories have a way of unearthing our buried dreams, don't they? You seem like someone on the brink of a new chapter. Care to share?"

I hesitated, caught off guard by his perceptiveness. There was something warm and inviting about his demeanor, so I found myself divulging snippets of my recent struggles. The man listened intently, nodding with understanding, his brow furrowed in empathy.

"Change can be daunting, but it can also be the spark that ignites our passions," he said thoughtfully. "You must embrace the chaos. After all, some of the best stories come from a little turbulence."

With a newfound sense of clarity, I thanked him for his insight and stepped back into the sunlight, ready to embrace whatever the day might bring. The vibrant energy of Maplewood seemed to pulse around me, urging me to explore its nooks and crannies. I meandered through the town square, where a farmers' market was setting up. Stalls overflowed with pumpkins, apples, and homemade jams, a feast for the senses. The vibrant colors and cheerful chatter were irresistible.

As I wandered from stall to stall, I caught sight of Clara at a booth adorned with delicate fabric swatches and sewing tools. She was animatedly chatting with a group of women, her laughter ringing through the air like a melody. I couldn't help but feel drawn to her magnetic energy.

"Emma!" Clara exclaimed as she spotted me, her smile radiant. "Come over! I was just telling them about the new fabric collection I'm working with. You have to see this!"

I joined her, the warmth of her presence wrapping around me like a hug. She eagerly displayed various textiles, each one more beautiful than the last. "This one is called 'Autumn Whispers,' and it feels like wearing a piece of the season," she said, letting the fabric flow through her fingers like water.

"It's stunning," I said, genuinely impressed. "You have such an eye for design."

"Thank you! But it's not just about the fabric; it's about the stories behind each piece," Clara explained, her enthusiasm palpable. "Each dress we create has a narrative—a love story waiting to unfold. You understand that, don't you?"

I nodded, my heart swelling with excitement. "I used to create designs with that same passion, but somewhere along the way, I forgot the magic of storytelling through fabric."

"Well, it's never too late to pick up those threads again," she said, her voice laced with encouragement. "Why not help me out today? I could use an extra pair of hands, and it might reignite that creative spark of yours!"

The idea was both exhilarating and terrifying. But the thrill of collaboration outweighed my apprehension. "I'd love to!" I replied, unable to suppress my excitement.

We spent the morning arranging fabric swatches, chatting with locals, and exchanging ideas. Clara introduced me to her friends—each woman a tapestry of stories and experiences. They welcomed me with open arms, their laughter weaving a sense of belonging that I hadn't felt in a long time.

"Tell us about your designs," one woman asked, her eyes bright with curiosity.

"Well, I haven't really designed anything recently," I admitted, glancing at Clara, who nodded encouragingly. "But I used to love creating pieces that told a story, pieces that made people feel something—joy, love, hope."

"Those are the best kinds of designs!" Clara chimed in. "And I bet you still have that creativity bubbling beneath the surface. You just need the right opportunity to unleash it."

As the sun climbed higher, casting a warm glow over the market, I felt the whispers of inspiration begin to swirl within me. The laughter, the connection, the vibrant energy around me began to awaken something that had long been dormant. In the midst of fabric and friends, I realized I was standing at the precipice of change, and I was ready to leap.

In the early afternoon, Clara gathered everyone for a mini fashion show, showcasing her latest creations. The women donned stunning dresses that swirled and twirled, their laughter echoing as they strutted down the makeshift runway, the leaves crunching underfoot as they celebrated each moment. The joy in their eyes reminded me of why I had fallen in love with design in the first place.

Clara turned to me, her expression filled with mischief. "You should totally try one on! Let's show these ladies how it's done!"

I hesitated, but her infectious enthusiasm swept me up. "Alright, why not?" I laughed, the thrill of spontaneity sending a delightful shiver down my spine.

As I slipped into a flowing dress that danced around my legs, I caught a glimpse of myself in the mirror. The fabric hugged my figure just right, and for a brief moment, I felt as if I could take on the world. Clara beamed with pride, and the applause of the women filled the air, wrapping around me like a warm embrace.

In that moment, under the clear blue sky with laughter ringing around me, I began to believe that maybe, just maybe, I could rediscover my passion for design—and perhaps even the woman I had once been.

The fashion show wrapped up with a flourish, a delightful cacophony of laughter and applause ringing through the market. I stepped out of the dress, my heart still racing from the thrill of it all. Clara's infectious spirit had drawn me into a world I had long thought was lost to me. She clapped me on the back as I rejoined her, a grin splitting her face.

"You looked fabulous! I think we've found your new calling: model-slash-designer extraordinaire!" she teased, her eyes dancing with mischief.

"Just what I always dreamed of," I replied, rolling my eyes playfully. "Strutting my stuff in a small-town market. Next, I'll be signing autographs."

But Clara wasn't finished. "Oh, I'd be your number one fan! And you know what? We should definitely collaborate on something—design a dress together! You can use all those ideas you have locked away in your mind."

The suggestion sent a thrill of excitement coursing through me, though an undercurrent of anxiety tugged at my thoughts. "I don't know, Clara. It's been a while since I've designed anything," I confessed, my voice wavering slightly. "What if I've lost it?"

"Sweetheart, you haven't lost a thing! You just need to be reminded of your own brilliance. Think of it as a creative detox." She clasped my hands, her sincerity evident. "Besides, I know we can make something beautiful together. I see it in you."

Her confidence sparked something deep inside me—a flicker of the passion I thought had extinguished. "Alright," I said, a grin creeping onto my face. "Let's do it."

The following days blurred together in a flurry of fabric swatches and sketches. Clara's boutique became my sanctuary, a vibrant space where I could feel my creativity blossoming anew. The laughter and camaraderie of the other women added warmth to each day, and the shared meals became a ritual of connection. We swapped stories over coffee and pastries, our lives intertwining in ways I had never anticipated.

One afternoon, as the sunlight filtered through the windows, casting golden patterns on the floor, Clara and I worked intently at a sewing machine. I was stitching the hem of a whimsical design we had crafted together, the fabric flowing like a gentle stream.

"This is it!" Clara exclaimed suddenly, her eyes wide with excitement. "We need to showcase our creation at the Maplewood Fall Festival next week!"

I stopped, the needle suspended mid-stitch. "The festival? But that's so soon! What if it's not ready?"

She waved her hand dismissively, a gleam of mischief in her eyes. "That's the beauty of spontaneity! We'll be the stars of the show. Just imagine it—our dress draping down the runway, the crowd gasping in awe!"

I couldn't help but be swept up in her enthusiasm, yet a small voice of doubt lingered. "What if they don't like it? What if I mess it up?"

"Emma, darling," Clara said, her tone softening, "it's not about perfection. It's about expression. Besides, the more we put ourselves out there, the more we grow."

Her words resonated within me, and I nodded slowly. "Okay, let's do it. Let's show Maplewood what we can create!"

As the days passed, our efforts intensified. We poured ourselves into the design, the fabric blossoming under our fingertips, taking on a life of its own. With each stitch, my confidence grew, but a twinge of anxiety still lurked in the shadows. I hadn't showcased my work in years, and the thought of stepping back into that world both thrilled and terrified me.

On the day of the festival, the town square transformed into a vibrant spectacle of autumn colors and festive decorations. Stalls lined the streets, filled with local crafts, baked goods, and the unmistakable aroma of cider wafting through the air. I could feel the energy buzzing around me, a blend of excitement and anticipation that set my heart racing.

Clara and I arrived early, our carefully crafted dress safely tucked in a garment bag. As we set up our small display, I marveled at the sheer number of people milling about, each face filled with joy and laughter. It felt surreal to be part of this community—a community that had embraced me so quickly.

"Here we go!" Clara said, her eyes alight with enthusiasm. "Time to unveil our masterpiece!"

With trembling hands, I helped her pull the dress from the bag. The fabric shimmered in the sunlight, a swirling blend of deep burgundy and gold. As we draped it over a mannequin, I felt a swell of pride. This wasn't just a dress; it was a piece of my heart woven into every stitch.

The crowd began to gather, drawn by the spectacle of colors and the promise of something beautiful. Clara adjusted the dress, her excitement contagious as she beckoned me closer. "Just look at them! They love it already!"

As the first model stepped onto the makeshift runway, the crowd erupted in applause. My breath caught in my throat, a mix of pride and anxiety as I watched her glide down the path, the dress flowing around her like a waterfall of fabric. I could feel the energy shift, the anticipation palpable in the air.

One after another, models paraded before the crowd, each one showcasing a different aspect of our design. My heart raced, the thrill of seeing our creation come to life igniting a fire within me. Laughter and applause filled the air, wrapping around me like a warm hug.

And then, as the last model stepped off the stage, a sudden hush fell over the crowd. My heart sank. Had we missed the mark? I exchanged a worried glance with Clara, who looked equally bewildered.

Then, like a bolt from the blue, a familiar figure emerged from the throng. It was my ex, Alex. My heart plummeted.

"What are you doing here?" I blurted out, my voice barely above a whisper.

His gaze was fixed on me, and the look in his eyes was a mixture of surprise and something deeper. "I heard about the festival and thought I'd check it out. Didn't expect to see you here."

With the weight of his presence looming over me, I felt the ground shift beneath my feet. Clara stood beside me, her expression a mixture of confusion and concern.

"Emma, are you okay?" she asked softly, sensing the tension that had suddenly engulfed the moment.

I opened my mouth to respond, but the words caught in my throat. This wasn't how I envisioned this day would go. With Alex in the audience, everything I had worked for felt precarious, as if it could unravel at any moment. The exhilaration of the festival began to fade, replaced by a gnawing anxiety that twisted in my stomach.

As I tried to steady my breathing, I felt Clara's reassuring presence beside me. "You've got this, Emma," she whispered, her voice a soothing balm. "Just remember why you're here. Focus on your art."

I took a deep breath, trying to ground myself in the moment, but my heart raced as I caught Alex's gaze again. I could feel the crowd around us, their excitement palpable, but all I could focus on was the tension coiling in the air between us.

With a hesitant smile, I approached the edge of the crowd, prepared to face whatever awaited me, but the moment I stepped forward, a sudden commotion erupted. A loud crash echoed through the square, sending the crowd into a frenzy.

Panic swept through me as I turned to see a vendor's table collapse, scattering jars of homemade jams and sauces across the ground. Shouts filled the air as chaos erupted, and I felt a jolt of adrenaline surge through me.

I looked back at Alex, whose eyes were wide with surprise, and I realized this festival had turned into something entirely unexpected. I was left standing there, caught between the past I thought I had left behind and the future I was beginning to reclaim, and as I glanced back at Clara, I knew that whatever came next would define not just this moment but the threads of change woven into my life.

Chapter 4: Unraveled Ties

The scent of fresh fabric lingered in the air of Clara's boutique, mingling with the subtle sweetness of blooming lavender from the window boxes. As I stepped through the door, the tiny bell chimed—a sound that seemed to echo with the whispers of hopes and dreams stitched into every seam. Clara was hunched over a pile of fabric swatches, her brow furrowed with concentration. Sunlight streamed through the window, casting a golden hue on her auburn hair, illuminating the vibrant patterns that surrounded her like a kaleidoscope of creativity.

"Hey, you," I greeted, leaning against the doorframe, arms crossed, trying to catch her attention without disturbing her flow. "Got a minute?"

She looked up, her blue eyes sparkling with surprise and a hint of relief. "Of course! I always have time for you." Clara straightened, pushing aside the swatches as if they were obstacles rather than sources of inspiration. "I was just thinking about how to make my line more appealing. This new chain has put the squeeze on me. It's like trying to compete with a lion when you're just a little lamb."

I stepped further inside, letting the door close softly behind me. "More like a lion with a giant marketing budget and a ferocious team of fashionistas." My heart ached for her. I knew what it felt like to fight an uphill battle against overwhelming odds. "What if we revamped some designs together? You know, give them a fresh twist?"

Her lips curled into a tentative smile, one that flickered with both hope and skepticism. "Really? You'd want to help?"

"Absolutely. Your pieces have character, but I think we can add a touch of flair that'll make them pop." I grinned, recalling our late-night conversations filled with laughter and dreams, where Clara had shared her passion for fashion like a lover revealing secrets.

"Think of it as a creative partnership. You design, and I'll... well, I'll sprinkle some fairy dust over it."

Clara chuckled, her laughter lightening the heaviness that had settled between us. "Fairy dust? I'm all in. But let's be real. I could use a miracle."

With newfound energy, we dove into the realm of fabrics and sketches. The room transformed from a simple boutique into a vibrant workshop, filled with laughter and the occasional playful banter as we flung ideas back and forth. I sifted through her collection of swatches, my fingers dancing over textures, feeling each fabric as if it were an extension of Clara herself. Together, we brainstormed designs that combined her classic style with my contemporary flair.

"Imagine this," I suggested, holding up a shimmering teal fabric that caught the light just right, "as an elegant evening dress with a plunging neckline and delicate lace overlay. Perfect for the kind of woman who wants to turn heads and break hearts."

"Or for the kind of woman who wants to disappear into the shadows after stealing the spotlight," Clara teased, her eyes twinkling mischievously. "But I love it. It's bold and daring. We could even add some asymmetrical details to really set it apart."

As we worked, the phone in my pocket buzzed incessantly. I could feel Jason's messages vibrating against my thigh, insistent little reminders of a life that felt like a different world—one filled with uncertainty and shadows of past decisions. With every buzz, my thoughts drifted back to him. But every time I considered reaching for my phone, Clara's laughter pulled me back to the present.

The creative energy surged between us, and with it came a sense of liberation. I lost track of time, finding solace in the vibrant colors and textures that surrounded us, in the laughter shared over an assortment of sketches littering the floor. Clara, too, seemed revitalized, her worry momentarily eclipsed by the joy of our collaboration.

"What about this?" I proposed, flipping a sketch onto the table. "A flowing maxi dress that transitions from day to night with a simple change of accessories. Easy, breezy, and perfect for any occasion."

Clara squinted at it, her lips pursed in thought. "I like it, but let's add a twist. Maybe a deep back with some intricate lacing? Something to surprise and delight."

Our creative session continued like that, each suggestion leading us deeper into a labyrinth of ideas, each more vibrant and exciting than the last. As the sun dipped lower in the sky, the boutique filled with a warm, golden glow, the atmosphere heavy with the scent of freshly brewed coffee wafting from the café across the street.

"Okay, let's take a break," Clara declared, wiping her brow. "I need caffeine if we're going to conquer the world of fashion."

"Agreed," I laughed, stretching my arms above my head and feeling every ache and thrill of the day. We stepped outside, the warm breeze wrapping around us like an embrace, lifting the spirits that had been heavy just hours before.

"Look at this place," I said, gesturing to the quaint street lined with twinkling fairy lights. "It feels alive. How can we make your boutique reflect that energy?"

"By refusing to let the bigger stores crush our spirits," Clara replied, her voice firm yet hopeful. "Let's create something that makes people stop in their tracks, something they can't find anywhere else."

As we strolled, the soft chatter of passersby and the laughter from nearby tables blended into a symphony of community. I felt the weight of Jason's messages fade into the background, replaced by the sweet promise of new beginnings and the excitement of building something meaningful with Clara. The day had unraveled into something beautiful, a tapestry woven with friendship, creativity, and the unyielding spirit of resilience.

The next few weeks flew by in a whirlwind of sketches, fabrics, and laughter. Clara and I transformed the boutique into a sanctuary of creativity, breathing life into every corner. The store buzzed with energy as we showcased our revamped designs—a kaleidoscope of colors and patterns that seemed to dance under the warm glow of the chandeliers. Each piece told a story, each stitch a testament to our friendship and shared determination.

As I adjusted a display of floral dresses, I caught a glimpse of Clara in the mirror. Her hands moved deftly, arranging accessories with an artist's precision. "Do you think we should offer discounts for the first few customers?" she mused, her brow slightly furrowed in thought. "I want people to experience the magic we've created, but I also can't afford to give everything away."

"Maybe a special launch event instead?" I suggested, turning to face her. "You know, something that feels like a celebration. People love an experience." The idea sparked a glimmer of hope in her eyes, and I could see the gears turning in her mind.

"A launch party?" she echoed, enthusiasm blossoming. "That could draw in a crowd! Music, snacks, a fashion show—" Her voice grew more animated as she rattled off ideas, her natural charisma shining through. "We could invite local influencers, give away gift bags! Oh, this could be huge!"

Her excitement was contagious, and I couldn't help but smile. "Let's make it happen. We'll create a buzz so loud that even the big chain store will hear it!"

As we brainstormed, the air thickened with possibility. But just as I was getting lost in Clara's vision, my phone buzzed again—another message from Jason. I glanced down, the screen lighting up with his name, and my heart did that irritating little flip it always seemed to do. I could practically hear his voice in my head, that familiar mix of charm and uncertainty, and I felt the pull of our shared past.

"Something on your mind?" Clara asked, her expression shifting to one of concern. She caught me at a moment when my thoughts had wandered. "You've been distracted lately."

"It's nothing," I replied quickly, but she arched an eyebrow, not buying it for a second. "Really, just a friend from the past trying to check in."

"Is that all?" she pressed, crossing her arms. "Because it sounds like more than that. You've been avoiding responding, which means he's probably not just a 'friend.'"

I sighed, running a hand through my hair, a gesture of defeat. "Okay, fine. It's complicated. He's my ex, and he just keeps messaging me. I don't know why I'm hesitating to reply." I leaned against the counter, allowing the weight of my thoughts to settle between us. "We had our moments, but... we also had a lot of mess. I guess I'm not ready to untangle that."

"Yikes. Sounds like you're caught in a web of unresolved feelings." Clara chuckled, trying to lighten the mood. "But listen, you can't let someone else's past dictate your present, right? You've got a new chapter starting here."

"True." I pushed the phone deeper into my pocket, letting the fabric of my feelings hang in the air like the scent of the jasmine blooming outside the window. "I just... I want to focus on this. I don't want to get pulled back into something that could derail everything we've built."

Clara nodded, her expression softening as she assessed my turmoil. "And you're right to protect this space. Just remember, the past is a door. You can choose to leave it closed or open it, but make sure you're ready for whatever comes through."

Her words sank in, their weight grounding me. It was refreshing to have someone who understood not just my creative struggles but my emotional ones, too. We made a pact that day: to focus on our passions and dreams, to keep pushing forward, and to make the boutique a reflection of the vibrant lives we wanted to lead.

With Clara at my side, planning the launch party became an exhilarating adventure. We transformed her boutique into a haven of excitement, pulling together the best local vendors, securing a lively DJ, and crafting a menu filled with delicious treats that made the taste buds sing. Clara even found a local artist willing to showcase their work in the store, further weaving the community into our plans.

On the day of the event, the sun dipped low in the sky, painting everything in hues of pink and gold. Clara and I hustled through the boutique, our hearts racing with anticipation. As the first guests began to trickle in, I felt a buzz of excitement crackling through the air, a mixture of nerves and hope that seemed to pulse in rhythm with the music.

"Look at this place!" Clara beamed, her eyes sparkling as she surveyed the scene. "I can't believe we pulled it off!"

"And it's only going to get better," I said, trying to mask my own mounting anxiety. I caught sight of familiar faces—friends, neighbors, and even a few curious newcomers drawn in by the festivities. Each person brought a wave of energy that made my heart soar, reminding me of how interconnected we all were.

Just as I began to breathe in the atmosphere, my phone buzzed again. I glanced down, half-expecting to see another message from Jason, but instead, it was Clara's brother, Mike. He was standing just outside the door, a wide grin on his face, looking every bit the handsome charmer I'd grown up with. His arrival sent a jolt of unexpected tension through the air, shifting my focus in a way that made my stomach flip.

"Am I too late for the fashion show?" he called, stepping inside and drawing the attention of a few nearby guests.

"Not at all!" Clara exclaimed, rushing over to greet him. "We're just getting started. Come help us with these last-minute touches!"

I lingered back, observing as Clara and Mike shared a lighthearted banter, their laughter mingling with the cheerful music. There was an undeniable chemistry between them, a spark that ignited something deep within me—a flicker of jealousy mixed with a warm glow of happiness for Clara. It was strange how emotions could be so tangled, especially when all I wanted was for her to succeed.

"Hey there, party planner," Mike said, glancing my way as he helped arrange some decorations. "You did an incredible job putting all of this together. I can't believe how many people showed up!"

"Just trying to keep up with Clara's grand ideas," I replied, mustering a smile that felt genuine enough. "She's the mastermind behind this transformation."

He chuckled, the sound deep and rich. "Well, you've both created something special. I can't wait to see how everyone reacts to the new designs."

His praise wrapped around me, creating a sense of belonging I hadn't expected. Maybe, just maybe, I was finally finding my place in this new world. As the evening unfolded, I felt the threads of our lives weaving together, creating a fabric richer and more vibrant than I could have imagined. The boutique transformed into a kaleidoscope of laughter, creativity, and connection—a sanctuary of dreams stitched together by friendship and hope.

The boutique pulsed with life as the launch party unfolded, a whirlwind of colors and sounds that made my heart race with excitement. Guests mingled, their laughter mingling with the beats of the DJ's music, creating a backdrop of joy that enveloped the evening. Clara flitted around the space like a whirlwind, her eyes shining as she chatted with patrons, her natural charisma turning casual interactions into moments of connection.

"Look at this crowd!" she exclaimed, her cheeks flushed with happiness as she handed me a glass of sparkling lemonade. "I never imagined so many people would show up."

"Neither did I," I replied, taking a sip that sparkled on my tongue. "It's like the whole town decided to come together."

"Or maybe it's just your charm," Clara teased, nudging my shoulder playfully. "Whatever it is, we should bottle it up and sell it. Who wouldn't want a little extra charisma in their lives?"

"Let's not get ahead of ourselves," I laughed, glancing around the room. I could see the soft glow of the lights reflecting off the fabrics we had painstakingly chosen. Each dress on display shimmered under the twinkling lights, the designs we had collaborated on finally brought to life. "But I wouldn't mind a few more people noticing us."

As the night progressed, the energy in the boutique shifted. Clara had set up a mini fashion show to showcase our best designs, and as I helped her arrange the makeshift runway, I could feel the anticipation buzzing in the air. It was exhilarating to think that all our hard work was about to pay off.

"Alright, let's get this show on the road!" Clara clapped her hands together, her voice commanding attention. The crowd hushed, their eyes drawn to her as she stepped onto the small stage we had created. "Welcome, everyone! Thank you so much for being here tonight. We're thrilled to share our new collection with you."

The applause that followed filled the room, a tangible wave of support that made my heart swell with pride. Clara took a deep breath, visibly energizing herself for the presentation. "Without further ado, let's kick things off with our first look!"

As the first model stepped onto the runway, adorned in a flowy, asymmetrical dress in vibrant hues, I felt a sense of pride swell within me. Clara's designs were not just clothes; they were stories, woven together with threads of passion and creativity. Each step the model took felt like a dance, embodying everything Clara had dreamed about.

"Did you see that?" I whispered to Clara as the applause erupted again. "She looks stunning!"

"Of course! That's our vision," Clara beamed, her eyes sparkling. "We're not just selling clothes; we're selling a lifestyle."

"More like a revolution," I quipped, unable to contain my excitement. "Who needs those corporate giants when we have creativity and community?"

The show continued, and with each model, Clara's designs gained momentum. I felt my own doubts about the past and the messages from Jason fade into the background. The crowd's energy propelled me forward, infusing me with a sense of purpose I hadn't felt in ages.

But just as I was starting to believe everything was coming together, I spotted a familiar face lurking at the edge of the boutique. It was Jason, his expression a mix of uncertainty and determination as he scanned the crowd. My heart raced, a familiar knot forming in my stomach. Why now?

"Everything okay?" Clara noticed my change in demeanor and followed my gaze, her brow furrowing. "Do you know him?"

I opened my mouth to respond, but the words caught in my throat. "Uh, it's just... an old friend," I managed to say, though the weight of the truth lingered uncomfortably between us. Clara's eyes darted back to Jason, her curiosity piqued.

"You should go talk to him," she encouraged, nudging me gently. "If he's here, it must be important. Just be honest."

"Easy for you to say," I replied, my voice low. "What if he throws my life into chaos again?"

"Then let him!" Clara replied, fierce determination in her eyes. "You deserve to confront your past. Besides, this night is about new beginnings, right? You're in a different place now."

Before I could protest, Clara turned her attention back to the show, leaving me standing there, heart pounding as I watched Jason approach. His handsome face held an expression of concern mixed with longing, and I felt a flicker of nostalgia creep in. Memories flooded back—our late-night conversations, the laughter, the connection that once felt unbreakable.

"Hey," he said, his voice cutting through the noise of the crowd. "I didn't expect to see you here."

"Neither did I," I replied, my heart racing as I tried to maintain a casual tone. "This is Clara's event. We've been working on it for weeks."

"I know," he said, glancing around the boutique, the pride in his voice evident. "I saw the posters around town. You've done an incredible job."

"Thanks," I said, attempting to keep the conversation light, though the weight of his presence hung heavily in the air. "It feels good to create something positive for once."

His gaze locked onto mine, a hint of vulnerability flickering in his eyes. "Look, I know things ended on a rough note between us, and I'm really sorry for how everything played out. I've been trying to reach you because I want to explain."

My stomach churned as memories of our breakup resurfaced, each one sharper than the last. "You didn't need to reach out. I've moved on."

"Have you?" His question hung in the air, heavy with implications, and I felt a flicker of uncertainty creep in. "Because you don't seem like someone who's moved on. You look... well, amazing. But you also look like you're still carrying something."

My defenses bristled at his observation. "Maybe I am. But I'm figuring it out without you." I glanced away, my gaze landing on Clara, who was now posing proudly beside the models, her joy evident as she absorbed the positive energy from the crowd.

"Look," Jason continued, his voice steady yet tinged with urgency, "I'm not here to disrupt your life or throw you off course. But I need you to understand that I've changed. I'm not the same person I was when we broke up."

The sincerity in his eyes pulled at something deep within me, but I pushed it aside. "That's great, really. But I'm not looking to revisit the past. This is about my future, and I'm finally building something for myself." I meant every word, but his presence stirred up a storm of conflicting emotions I had thought I had buried.

Before Jason could respond, the crowd erupted into cheers, and I turned just in time to see the final model strut down the runway in a breathtaking gown that cascaded like a waterfall of colors. Clara joined the applause, her expression radiant, and I felt the warmth of the moment wrap around me.

As the excitement settled, I caught Jason's gaze again. "You need to go," I said firmly, though the quiver in my voice betrayed my confidence. "I can't do this right now."

"Just think about what I said," he urged, his expression a mixture of hope and regret. "Please. I'll always be here if you need me."

With that, he stepped back, blending into the crowd as if he were just another face in a sea of color and noise. My heart raced, uncertainty flooding my veins as I turned to see Clara approaching, a whirlwind of energy and excitement.

"Did you talk to him?" she asked, her eyes wide with curiosity.

"Yeah," I said, forcing a smile as I tried to mask the turmoil swirling within me. "It was... interesting."

"Interesting?" Clara echoed, her tone teasing yet concerned. "Interesting doesn't sound like you're ready to throw him out of your life."

"Maybe I'm not," I admitted, my voice barely a whisper. "But I need to focus on this—on us."

Just then, the lights dimmed, and the DJ's voice boomed over the speakers, announcing the afterparty. The crowd surged forward, laughter and music blending into a festive cacophony. Clara's eyes sparkled with excitement as she pulled me toward the dance floor, but the weight of Jason's words lingered in my mind, pulling me in two directions.

As we danced, I tried to shake off the unease, losing myself in the moment. The rhythm thrummed through me, the music wrapping around us like a warm embrace. But just when I thought I had found my groove, a text notification flashed across my phone, drawing me back into the chaos. I glanced down, my heart dropping as I read the words that shattered the fragile peace I had built.

I need to talk. It's urgent.

My breath caught in my throat as I stared at the screen, the weight of my past crashing into my present with the force of a tidal wave. I looked up to find Clara watching me, her expression shifting from excitement to concern.

"What is it?" she asked, her voice steady yet laced with worry.

I hesitated, caught in a moment where everything seemed to hang in the balance—the party, my dreams, my friendship, and the unresolved feelings that tied me to Jason. "It's... nothing."

But as the music pulsed around us, I knew the truth: nothing would ever be the same again.

Chapter 5: The Unexpected Encounter

The clock ticked on the wall, the steady rhythm a comforting backdrop to the chaotic world swirling outside my window. The faint hum of the sewing machine filled the room, a steady companion as I fed the fabric through, each stitch binding not just threads but fragments of my scattered thoughts. The late hour cast a soft glow, the lamp's light bathing the room in a warm embrace. It was during one of these solitary sewing sessions that I first noticed the flicker of movement outside, a shadow passing by the garden.

Curiosity pricked at me, but I dismissed it, focusing instead on the fabric in my hands—a rich emerald green that whispered promises of transformation. The cloth was meant for Clara, an attempt to surprise her with a dress that danced in the wind like the leaves in spring. I had poured my heart into the design, each seam a testament to my affection for her and my hope for a better tomorrow. The stitches, however, were no match for the soft creak of the front door swinging open.

"Anyone home?" a familiar voice called out, echoing through the house. I froze, half-stitched dress held limply in my hands. It was Ethan. Clara's brother had returned from the city, and his presence filled the air with an unfamiliar energy, as intoxicating as the scent of fresh coffee on a brisk morning. He sauntered into the room, hair tousled as if he'd just woken from a dream, eyes sparkling with the mischief of someone who had spent far too long in the city lights.

"Thought I might find you in here, playing dressmaker." He leaned against the doorframe, a half-smile dancing on his lips, and in that moment, the chaos of my world seemed to still. The shadows of my past lurked in the corners, but the warmth radiating from Ethan pushed them back, even if just for a moment.

"More like drowning in fabric," I shot back, my tone lighter than I intended. "But if you're offering fashion advice, I'll take that over the silence any day." I managed a grin, and his laughter rang out like music, filling the room and disarming the heavy weight I had been carrying.

He stepped closer, the light catching the angles of his face, revealing the boyish charm that had always made him an enigma in my life. "You look like you could use a break. How about a cup of coffee? Or something stronger?" His eyebrow arched, a playful challenge hidden in his gaze.

"Is that your way of asking me to join you in your late-night adventures?" I raised an eyebrow, contemplating the depths of that offer. The image of us together flitted through my mind like a moth to a flame. "Because I really should finish this dress. Clara will have my head if I don't."

"Ah, the loyal friend archetype," he mused, tilting his head slightly as he studied me. "What if I told you that the real adventure is right here, in this moment? You could have all the time in the world to sew tomorrow. Tonight, though, you have the chance to unwind."

He was relentless, his charm seeping into my reservations, and I found myself hesitating. Was it so wrong to step away from my self-imposed isolation for a moment? I set the dress aside, the fabric whispering a silent protest, and joined him in the kitchen.

The coffee pot gurgled ominously as I flicked the switch, the warm aroma filling the air like a long-forgotten memory, and as we waited, he filled the silence with tales of his recent escapades. Each story was laced with a sense of adventure that ignited something dormant within me, and I couldn't help but laugh at the ridiculousness of a broken subway car and an impromptu karaoke night that had apparently ended with him singing an off-key rendition of an old classic.

"I'm pretty sure my neighbors are still recovering from that," he quipped, his eyes sparkling with mischief.

"What a gift you've given them," I replied, leaning against the counter, the warmth from the coffee pot radiating through the room. The playful banter flowed effortlessly between us, a rhythm that felt as natural as the sewing I had just abandoned. It was in these moments, under the soft glow of the kitchen lights, that I felt a strange familiarity blossoming between us, a connection that went beyond the bounds of friendship.

As we sipped our steaming mugs, the world outside faded into a backdrop of muffled sounds. The weight of my past lurked like an uninvited guest, but Ethan's laughter chased away the shadows, bringing with it the promise of possibilities I had long since buried. The guilt, however, was a constant companion, reminding me of the fractures in my heart that I couldn't yet mend.

"Why do you always carry the weight of the world on your shoulders?" he asked suddenly, his voice low and serious, breaking through the playful facade we had built. The laughter faded, replaced by a flicker of vulnerability that startled me.

"I guess I've always felt responsible," I replied, the words spilling out before I could filter them. "For Clara, for our little world here... it can be exhausting."

Ethan's gaze softened, and I could see a flicker of understanding in his eyes. "You deserve to have fun too, you know. Love shouldn't be a burden; it should be something that lifts you."

Those words hung in the air between us, heavy with meaning. They resonated deeply, pulling at the frayed edges of my heart, challenging everything I had come to accept about love and relationships. But how could I indulge in that sentiment when my past was a constant reminder of heartache?

In that moment, I could feel the tension coiling between us, electric and palpable. The chemistry was undeniable, a spark igniting the air around us, but I felt the familiar tendrils of guilt wrap around my heart. I had worked so hard to bury my feelings, to protect myself from the vulnerability of love. But here was Ethan, with his soulful eyes and charming demeanor, offering a glimpse of what could be.

And just like that, as the clock continued its relentless march toward the dawn, I found myself at a crossroads, one where the past and future collided in a whirlwind of uncertainty.

The tension hung in the air like the remnants of a thunderstorm, charged and electric, as we stood in the warm kitchen light, our mugs half-full, thoughts swirling like the steam rising between us. I could almost hear my heart echoing in the silence, a chaotic drumbeat underscoring the delicate balance of emotions that teetered at the edge of our conversation. Ethan leaned against the counter, his casual posture a stark contrast to the intensity of our moment, and I was suddenly aware of how much I wanted to bridge that chasm between us, to dissolve the boundaries I had painstakingly built.

"Love should enrich our lives, not drain them," he repeated, his eyes piercing into mine as if trying to unravel the knot of fears tightly wound within me. "But you act like you've been carrying a boulder on your back, and I have to ask, what's really stopping you from enjoying the moment?"

"Maybe I'm just a natural pessimist," I replied, half-joking but feeling the weight of truth in my words. I was adept at guarding my heart, at wrapping it in layers of practicality and caution. The world had taught me that every soft moment could be ripped away in an instant, and I wasn't ready to take that risk again.

"Pessimism is just optimism with experience," he said, a hint of laughter dancing in his voice. "Trust me, I've seen the world beyond this sleepy town. There are worse things than taking a leap of faith."

His words lingered in the air like the aroma of fresh coffee, wrapping around me in a warm embrace. I could feel the edges of my resolve starting to fray, and just then, a playful challenge flickered in his eyes. "You want to make something real tonight? Prove me wrong."

"Is that your idea of a good time?" I asked, feigning indignation while suppressing a grin. "Challenging my deep-seated fears in the middle of the night?"

"Absolutely," he replied, his enthusiasm infectious. "Let's make a pact. For the next hour, no worries, no past, just us. Let's do something ridiculous. What do you say?"

"Ridiculous, huh?" I mused, contemplating the prospect. I had spent so much time in my bubble of responsibility that the idea of unshackling myself, even for a moment, felt both liberating and terrifying. "You know, 'ridiculous' could lead to all sorts of trouble."

"Trouble is exactly what I'm hoping for," he teased, the playful glimmer in his eyes igniting something adventurous within me. "Let's just have some fun. Come on, I dare you!"

With a mock sigh of resignation, I set my coffee mug down. "Fine, but if we end up on a police report, I'm blaming you."

His laughter filled the room again, a melodic sound that felt like a breath of fresh air. "I'll take full responsibility for any shenanigans. You've got my word."

He grabbed my hand, and just like that, we were racing out the door, the night air wrapping around us like a cool blanket. The stars twinkled above, mocking the mundane rhythm of my life. The scent of damp earth and blooming wildflowers swirled in the breeze, carrying the promise of something exhilarating.

"Okay, what's the plan, oh daring leader?" I asked, trying to keep pace with his long strides.

"Let's start with a midnight adventure to the old bridge," he declared, grinning like a child caught in the thrill of a secret. "I've heard it's a great place to stargaze."

"The old bridge?" I scoffed, pretending to be shocked. "That's where the town's ghost is said to lurk. You're not afraid of ghosts, are you?"

"Not afraid of ghosts, but I'm terrified of not living life to the fullest," he shot back, the seriousness of his words clashing beautifully with the mischief dancing in his eyes.

As we reached the bridge, its weathered wooden beams creaked underfoot, the echoes of our laughter mingling with the whispers of the night. The moon cast a silver glow across the water below, creating a shimmering path that seemed to beckon us forward. Ethan leaned against the railing, his gaze fixed on the horizon, where the stars twinkled like scattered diamonds.

"Beautiful, isn't it?" he said, his voice softer now, almost reverent.

"It really is," I admitted, feeling the weight of the moment settle over us like a warm embrace. "I can't remember the last time I looked at the stars this closely."

"Funny how life can make us forget to pause and just breathe." He turned to face me, his expression serious yet inviting. "What do you see when you look up?"

"Just a bunch of shiny dots, really," I replied, attempting to downplay the deepening connection. But as I spoke, the truth bubbled up inside me. "No, I see... possibilities. I see dreams I've shelved for too long."

"Then let's take them off the shelf," he urged, stepping closer. The space between us crackled with an undeniable energy, and I could feel my heart racing in a way that was both exhilarating and terrifying. "What's stopping you from reaching for those dreams?"

"I guess... I'm afraid of falling," I whispered, the admission slipping out before I could censor it. "I've fallen before, Ethan. Hard. And it's left marks."

His eyes softened, filled with an understanding that made my chest tighten. "Falling is part of living, though. Every stumble brings you closer to what you really want."

For a moment, silence enveloped us, the gentle lapping of the water below punctuating our thoughts. The world felt infinite, each star overhead a reminder that we were just tiny specks in a vast universe. Yet here we were, two souls seeking solace in the night.

Ethan's gaze didn't waver, and I felt an undeniable pull, as if the gravity between us was stronger than any fear I had harbored. "What if we take that leap together?" he asked, his voice barely above a whisper, yet it felt like a shout in the stillness.

The question hung between us, the night air thick with anticipation. What would it mean to leap? To let go of the weight I had carried for so long? I could feel the walls I had built start to tremble, the foundation of my heart quaking at the thought of letting someone in again.

But then again, Ethan was different. He was not just Clara's brother; he was a bright light in the shadows of my doubts, a challenge to my long-held beliefs. Perhaps the leap wouldn't lead to the abyss but to something breathtakingly beautiful.

And as I gazed into his soulful eyes, a flicker of hope ignited within me, promising the possibility of a new beginning, one where laughter echoed through the shadows and love could thrive, unburdened by the weight of the past.

The moon hung low in the sky, casting a silver sheen over the old bridge, transforming the mundane into something ethereal. The water beneath us rippled softly, reflecting the starlit canvas above. I stood beside Ethan, the warmth of his presence radiating through the cool night air, and I couldn't shake the feeling that this moment was significant—an intersection of my past and the future I had been too afraid to embrace.

"Have you ever really looked at the stars?" he asked, leaning against the railing with a casual confidence that made my heart flutter. "I mean, truly looked at them? They tell stories, you know."

I turned my gaze to the sky, the constellations twinkling like distant whispers. "What kind of stories?" I asked, curious.

"Every star has its own history, its own journey. Some are ancient, others are newborn. But together, they create a tapestry, something bigger than themselves." He paused, glancing at me with an intensity that sent a shiver down my spine. "Just like us."

"Wow, you really are a romantic, aren't you?" I teased, trying to keep the mood light.

"Romantic? Or just someone who knows how to appreciate life's mysteries?" His tone was playful, but there was an undercurrent of sincerity that made my stomach flip. "Life is too short to let fear dictate our choices, don't you think?"

As I contemplated his words, a sudden breeze swept through, rustling the leaves around us and sending a chill racing down my arms. "You make it sound so easy," I replied, attempting to mask the turmoil bubbling beneath my calm exterior. "Just let go and leap into the unknown."

"Easy? No. Worth it? Absolutely." He turned to face me fully, his gaze unyielding. "The unknown is where all the magic happens."

A flutter of uncertainty danced in my chest, the shadows of my past creeping in again. I wanted to believe him, to toss my fears to the wind, but they were heavy chains that clanked loudly in my mind. "What if I fall?"

"What if you fly?" His voice was low, almost hypnotic. "Imagine the view."

I opened my mouth to respond, but before I could gather my thoughts, a sudden rustling interrupted us. The sound came from the trees lining the path leading to the bridge, sharp and unsettling, like something—or someone—was approaching. My heart raced, and I instinctively took a step closer to Ethan. "Did you hear that?"

"Yeah, I did," he replied, his expression shifting from playful to alert. "Stay close."

The moment felt charged with an unexpected thrill, the kind you only find in suspenseful movies. I could feel the adrenaline pumping through my veins, heightening every sense as we both turned our heads toward the trees. The shadows danced, and I half-expected a deer or a raccoon to emerge, but the tension felt too palpable, too... alive.

"Maybe it's just an animal," I suggested, though my voice trembled slightly.

Ethan nodded but didn't look away from the thicket. "Maybe. But let's be cautious."

We stood together, a fragile fortress of two against the encroaching night. As the rustling grew louder, a figure stepped into the dim light filtering from the moon. My heart dropped into my stomach. It wasn't a harmless animal at all.

"Clara?" The voice that called out was familiar yet jarring, echoing through the stillness. My sister's silhouette emerged, outlined by the soft glow of the moon, but there was something off about her. Her usually vibrant aura was muted, her eyes darting with an intensity that made my stomach knot.

"Clara!" I called, relief flooding me even as confusion mingled with concern. "What are you doing out here?"

Her breath came in quick bursts, and as she stepped closer, I could see the glimmer of something urgent in her eyes. "I was looking for you! I've been trying to call you!"

"Call me?" I echoed, bewildered. "Why didn't you just come home?"

"Because—" she hesitated, her gaze flicking nervously between Ethan and me. "Because I didn't know who else to turn to. I needed you."

"What's going on?" I demanded, a lump forming in my throat as fear pricked at my chest. "You look like you've seen a ghost."

"Not a ghost, but I wish it were that simple," she replied, her voice dropping to a whisper. "I found something... something I think you need to see."

Ethan took a step back, his expression shifting from concern to protective as he placed a hand on my shoulder. "What are you talking about?"

Clara's eyes darted around, as if she expected someone—or something—to jump out at any moment. "We can't talk here. It's not safe."

"Not safe?" The words felt like a punch to the gut, a jolt that sent my heart racing. "Clara, you're scaring me. What do you mean?"

"Please, just trust me," she implored, her voice barely above a whisper. "I need you to come with me."

Ethan's grip tightened on my shoulder, grounding me as uncertainty flooded my mind. I glanced at him, searching for a sign, a nod, something that might help me decide between my sister and the boy whose presence had just begun to feel like home.

"Okay," I said slowly, my heart thudding in my chest. "But where are we going?"

"Just follow me," Clara insisted, her eyes wide with urgency. Without another word, she turned and started down the path. I hesitated, torn between the thrill of adventure and the dread coiling in my gut.

Ethan squeezed my shoulder one last time, and I took a deep breath, summoning the courage to follow my sister into the unknown. But just as I took my first step, the trees behind us rustled again, louder this time, sending a chill down my spine.

"Wait," Ethan whispered, his voice taut with tension.

Before I could respond, a dark figure burst from the shadows, racing toward us with blinding speed. My heart dropped as instinct kicked in, and I knew—whatever awaited us was not just the shadows of our past but something much darker, something that threatened to consume everything we had just begun to understand about love, trust, and the fragile ties that bind us all.

Chapter 6: Patterns of the Heart

The soft hum of the sewing machine mingled with the rustle of fabric as I stepped into Clara's boutique, the scent of fresh linen and a hint of lavender enveloping me like a comforting embrace. Sunlight streamed through the tall windows, casting playful patterns on the polished wooden floor, illuminating the stacks of vibrant fabric swatches that lined the walls like a kaleidoscope of possibilities. Each piece called out to me, whispering secrets of potential designs, of visions yet to be realized.

Ethan was already there, his broad shoulders hunched over a sketchbook, his brow furrowed in concentration. The light caught the subtle waves of his dark hair, giving it a halo-like glow that made my heart flutter unexpectedly. I leaned against the doorframe, watching him for a moment, absorbing the way he immersed himself in his craft. There was something undeniably magnetic about him—a blend of passion and precision that pulled me in like a moth to a flame.

"Hey there, artist," I said, stepping into the room, my voice light yet laced with the undercurrents of nervous energy that sparked between us. "What masterpiece are you conjuring up today?"

He glanced up, his green eyes brightening as they met mine. "Just trying to breathe new life into some of Clara's classic pieces," he replied, a playful smirk tugging at the corners of his mouth. "You know, make them a bit less... grandmotherly."

I laughed, shaking my head. "Careful, or you'll find yourself on the receiving end of a knitting circle's wrath."

"Bring it on. I'll take on an army of grandmothers if it means you'll help me bring this vision to life." His confidence was intoxicating, the way he leaned back slightly, challenging me with a playful glint in his eye.

A warmth spread through me at the thought of collaborating with him, each idea building upon the last, sparking a creative fire that I hadn't felt in what felt like ages. I walked over to the table where he had laid out sketches of fitted blazers and flowing skirts, vibrant patterns dancing across the pages. "You've really captured Clara's essence here," I said, studying his designs. "It's elegant yet fresh."

"Much like you," he quipped, his tone light, but I caught a glimpse of something deeper in his gaze—a flicker of sincerity that sent a delightful shiver down my spine.

Before I could reply, my phone buzzed ominously in my pocket, pulling me from the moment. I glanced at the screen, and my heart sank. Jason. Just the name sent a familiar chill racing through me, a reminder of the past I'd tried to shake off like an old coat.

Ethan noticed my expression, his brow furrowing in concern. "Everything okay?"

"Yeah, just—" I hesitated, weighing my words. "It's just my ex. He's... persistent."

"Persistent how?" There was a hint of protectiveness in his voice, an edge that intrigued me.

"Let's just say he's not one to take 'no' for an answer." I attempted to brush it off, but my voice wavered, revealing more than I intended.

"Do you want me to deal with him?" Ethan's gaze was steady, his lips a thin line of determination.

I felt a wave of gratitude wash over me, but I also recognized the absurdity of the offer. "No, it's fine. I can handle it." But even as I said it, my heart didn't quite believe me.

Before I could dwell on it, Ethan pushed back from the table, his eyes sparkling with mischief. "Alright, then let's show Jason what he's missing out on." He grabbed a nearby fabric swatch, tossing it over his shoulder as he walked toward the door. "Come on. We're taking this to the next level."

"Wait, where are we going?"

"To make the world jealous of our creativity." He winked, and my breath caught. The thought of being out in the world with him, showcasing our designs, ignited a thrill within me.

We stepped out into the warm afternoon sun, the bustling street alive with the sounds of laughter and chatter. The aroma of freshly baked pastries wafted from a nearby café, mingling with the scent of blooming flowers from the market stalls. As we walked side by side, I could feel the energy of the city echoing the pulse of our budding partnership.

"So, what's the plan, O Fashionista Extraordinaire?" I teased, nudging him playfully.

He grinned, his expression playful yet serious. "We need to find some inspiration—something that screams 'us.'"

"'Us?'" I echoed, the word hanging in the air, laden with possibilities.

"Yeah. I mean, we're creating something fresh, something that reflects both of our styles. It's like mixing the best ingredients in a recipe."

His enthusiasm was infectious, and I found myself caught up in his vision. "Okay, then let's hit the fabric market! We need to find something that truly embodies this fusion."

As we navigated through the vibrant streets, our conversation flowed easily, punctuated by laughter and banter. With each passing moment, I felt the barriers I had meticulously constructed around my heart begin to crumble. Ethan's presence was intoxicating, filling the gaps that loneliness had carved in my life.

But just as the thrill of possibilities began to weave itself into the fabric of my reality, my phone buzzed again. I glanced down, and my stomach dropped. Another message from Jason, demanding to see me.

I hesitated, the weight of his persistent presence pressing down on me like a dark cloud, threatening to overshadow the vibrant light that Ethan had ignited within me.

"What's wrong?" Ethan's voice pulled me from my thoughts, concern etching lines across his forehead.

"Just... Jason again," I muttered, my fingers curling around the phone like a lifeline.

"Forget him," he urged, his voice low and steady, like a promise that made my heart race. "You deserve to be free of that. Let's focus on what we're creating together."

In that moment, standing in the sunlit street with Ethan by my side, I felt the tug of two worlds—the familiar pull of my past, and the exhilarating unknown that lay ahead.

The vibrant hum of the city enveloped us as Ethan and I strolled through the market, his laughter intertwining with the melodies of street musicians and the clatter of shoppers exchanging pleasantries. Stalls brimmed with a riot of colors, fabrics draping over wooden tables like spilled paint. The air was thick with the sweet aroma of baked goods, mingling with the earthy scent of fresh flowers, a sensory overload that invigorated me. It felt like a fresh start, a new palette waiting to be painted.

"What do you think?" Ethan asked, halting before a stall adorned with shimmering silk in hues of deep emerald and midnight blue. "This could add a touch of drama to our collection." He held up a swatch, the light catching it in a way that made it appear almost alive.

"Drama? Or just a little too 'Oscar-winning actress' for a boutique line?" I countered, teasing, though I felt my heart quicken at the thought of transforming Clara's classic designs into something bold and daring.

He feigned offense, clutching the fabric to his chest as if I'd insulted a beloved pet. "There's no such thing as too much drama in fashion! It's all about making statements, after all." His eyes sparkled with playful rebellion, and I felt a rush of admiration for his fearless creativity.

"Alright, Mr. Fashionista, let's get dramatic. But let's also remember who we're designing for. Clara's clientele might not be ready for a full-on avant-garde experience." I laughed, shaking my head as I snatched the silk from him, my fingers brushing against his in a moment that felt electric, a tiny spark in a world filled with chaos.

Our banter continued, flowing as effortlessly as the fabric we selected. We moved from stall to stall, gathering materials, sketching out ideas, and filling my mind with visions of what could be. The more we collaborated, the more I felt the remnants of my past—of Jason and his relentless attempts to pull me back into his orbit—fade into the background.

Ethan was a breath of fresh air, a reminder that creativity could blossom unexpectedly, like wildflowers breaking through concrete. But as the sun dipped lower in the sky, casting golden hues over the market, an unsettling thought gnawed at the edges of my excitement. What if my past came crashing back into this beautiful moment, darkening everything we'd built together?

Just as I was lost in the wonder of new designs and the thrill of collaboration, my phone buzzed again, a sharp reminder of reality. I glanced at the screen, my heart sinking as I saw Jason's name flash before me, a sinister reminder that I couldn't entirely escape my past.

"Dare I ask?" Ethan's voice broke through my thoughts, his gaze narrowing with concern as he caught the flicker of distress on my face.

"It's Jason again," I said, trying to keep my voice light but failing miserably. "He wants to talk."

"Talk or lecture?" Ethan raised an eyebrow, his expression a mix of concern and protectiveness that made my heart race.

"Probably a bit of both," I admitted, running a hand through my hair in frustration. "He thinks I'm just going to—what, welcome him back with open arms? Like I'm some sort of emotional doormat?"

"Not happening on my watch," he declared, his voice firm, almost protective. "You're better than that, and you deserve more than to be swept back into a past that didn't serve you."

His conviction sparked a warmth inside me, and for a moment, the tension of Jason's persistent messages faded. "I appreciate that. I really do." I felt my voice soften, an unexpected vulnerability slipping through. "But it's complicated."

"Complicated doesn't mean unmanageable," Ethan replied, a hint of mischief dancing in his eyes. "We can tackle this together. Why don't we take the fight to him?"

"Take the fight to him? You're kidding, right?" I laughed, though the absurdity of it ignited a flicker of exhilaration within me. "What are we going to do, storm his apartment like fashion warriors?"

"Exactly! We'll burst in wearing our best designs, and I'll challenge him to a duel—an epic battle of fashion prowess," he said, his tone serious but the grin on his face betraying the humor behind his words.

I couldn't help but laugh again, feeling lighter with every passing moment. "I can just picture it now: 'En garde! My silk is stronger than your shallow charm!'"

"Precisely! And I'll wear the emerald silk to really set the mood." He twirled dramatically, and I couldn't suppress my laughter, the tension dissolving into the playful atmosphere we had created.

But then, my laughter faded slightly as the weight of my situation seeped back in. "As entertaining as that sounds, I doubt my heart can handle a confrontation right now. I want to focus on what we're creating, on the possibilities between us."

Ethan's smile softened, the warmth in his eyes making my heart flutter. "Then let's focus on that. We'll keep working on our collection, and if he shows up, we'll deal with it then. Together."

I nodded, feeling a swell of gratitude wash over me. The idea of facing Jason alone felt daunting, but knowing I had Ethan by my side gave me a glimmer of confidence. "You're right. I'm ready to let the past fade away."

We continued our shopping spree, our laughter ringing through the market as we layered our vision with swatches of color and texture, transforming our ideas into tangible possibilities. The way Ethan interacted with the vendors, charming them with quick wit and genuine interest, only deepened my admiration. He was more than just a talented designer; he had a way of bringing joy to everything he touched, making even the mundane seem magical.

As the sky began to darken and the market started to quiet down, we found ourselves in a small café, sharing a slice of decadent chocolate cake. The rich flavors melted on my tongue, and I couldn't help but smile at the absurdity of it all. Here I was, in the company of someone who brought out the best in me, indulging in sweet confections while my past loomed like a storm cloud just outside.

Ethan leaned back in his chair, his eyes sparkling with mischief. "So, what do you think? Will our new line send shockwaves through the fashion world?"

"Absolutely," I said, unable to hide my grin. "We're about to revolutionize Clara's boutique."

He raised his glass of sparkling water, a glimmer of triumph in his gaze. "To revolutionizing boutiques and sending exes running!"

"Cheers to that!" I clinked my glass against his, feeling the laughter bubbling inside me, a sense of freedom unfurling like the petals of a blooming flower.

But just as we began to relax into our shared moment, the café door swung open, and in walked Jason. My heart dropped like a stone, a chill sweeping over me as his gaze locked onto mine. The moment froze, the laughter and warmth of the café fading into a distant echo as I faced the reality I had tried to evade.

The moment Jason stepped through the café door, time seemed to stretch like taffy, thickening the air with an unwelcome tension. His presence sliced through the warm buzz of laughter and the rich scent of chocolate cake, and my heart dropped into my stomach like a stone. I could feel the color drain from my cheeks as if he had siphoned the light from the room.

"Of all the places to run into you," he said, his voice smooth, an unsettling familiarity washing over me. "I thought you'd be hiding out somewhere less... public."

I felt Ethan stiffen beside me, the casual ease of our earlier conversation evaporating into the ether. "What a coincidence," I managed, forcing a smile that felt more like a grimace. "I didn't know you were a regular here."

"Just passing through," he replied, his eyes darting to Ethan, assessing, calculating. "Looks like I'm interrupting something important."

Ethan shot me a quick glance, his expression a mixture of concern and challenge. "Not at all," he said, his tone steady but edged with a hint of defiance. "We were just enjoying some cake. What brings you here, Jason?"

"Just wanted to see if I could catch up with my favorite ex," Jason said, a charming grin plastered on his face, though the sparkle in his eyes held a darker undertone that made me uneasy. "You know how it is—always nice to check in on old flames."

The double entendre sent a shiver down my spine. I felt caught in a crossfire, my past colliding violently with my present. I didn't want to be here, sharing a space with someone who had once made me feel so small. "Jason, this isn't a good time," I said, trying to keep my voice firm but calm, though I felt a tremor creeping in.

"Oh, come on," he pressed, taking a step closer. "Let's not pretend like we don't have unfinished business."

"Unfinished?" I echoed, incredulity lacing my words. "You mean like the time you left in the middle of a conversation without even saying goodbye? Is that what you call unfinished?"

He waved a hand dismissively, a condescending smirk curving his lips. "You know that was just a momentary lapse. We were young, caught up in the whirlwind of life."

Ethan's eyes narrowed, and the protective energy radiating from him felt like a shield I desperately needed. "Seems like some things are better left in the past," he interjected, his voice low but firm.

I caught the glint of defiance in Ethan's gaze as he leaned slightly forward, positioning himself between me and Jason, the tension coiling like a tightly wound spring. "We've moved on. I've moved on. You should too."

Jason laughed, a sound devoid of warmth. "Moved on? Really? Because it looks to me like you're just playing house with a pretty little designer who can't even stand up for herself."

I bristled at his words, the insult cutting deeper than I cared to admit. "This isn't about you, Jason," I snapped, my voice rising, fueled by anger and hurt. "You don't get to dictate my life or how I feel."

"Is that so?" he challenged, a glint of amusement flashing in his eyes. "And what about us? You're just going to pretend those feelings didn't exist? That everything we had can be so easily swept under the rug?"

"Enough!" I felt the heat of emotion flooding my cheeks, the room tilting on its axis as I wrestled with my past and present. "I don't want to revisit old wounds. I'm happy now."

"Happy?" He arched an eyebrow, stepping closer, invading my space, and I could feel the remnants of our shared history clawing their way to the surface. "With him? The two of you look like a magazine ad gone wrong."

Before I could respond, Ethan's hand found mine under the table, his touch grounding me amid the storm swirling around us. "You're right about one thing, Jason. She is happy. And if you think you can just waltz back into her life with empty promises and charm, you've got another thing coming."

Jason turned his attention to Ethan, a mix of surprise and disdain crossing his features. "And who are you? The boyfriend? The new knight in shining armor? This is all very cute, but it doesn't change anything."

"Call it what you want," Ethan replied, his voice unwavering, "but I'm here for her in a way you clearly never were. It's time you understand that."

"Is that right?" Jason shot back, his gaze flicking between us, searching for cracks in our defenses. "What makes you think you know her better than I do?"

The atmosphere crackled with tension, and I felt like I was standing on a precipice, caught in a storm. I had to say something. "I know what I want," I stated firmly, surprised by the strength in my voice. "And it's not you, Jason. I've moved on, and I'm ready to embrace what's next in my life."

His expression hardened, a flicker of anger flashing across his face. "You think you can just erase our history? All those memories we made? That's cute. But let me remind you, the heart doesn't forget so easily."

Ethan squeezed my hand tighter, his presence a steady anchor amid the tumult. "We're not here to reminisce. We're here to create something new," he said, glancing at me with an encouraging smile that reignited the fire within me.

The heat of Jason's anger was palpable, and I felt a shift in the air, the tension thickening around us like a heavy blanket. "You're making a big mistake, and one day, you're going to regret turning your back on me," he warned, his tone dripping with an unsettling mix of charm and menace.

"Do your worst," I replied, my heart racing but my voice steady. "I'm not afraid of you anymore."

Jason's lips twisted into a smile that didn't reach his eyes, a storm brewing beneath the surface. "We'll see about that," he said, his words hanging ominously in the air as he turned to leave.

As the café door swung shut behind him, I felt a wave of relief wash over me, followed by an unsettling realization of how close I'd come to being pulled back into a web I thought I'd escaped.

Ethan's grip on my hand relaxed, but the worry etched on his face was evident. "Are you okay?"

"I... I think so." My voice trembled slightly, adrenaline coursing through my veins. "That was intense."

"Intense doesn't even begin to cover it." He leaned closer, his expression softening. "You handled yourself incredibly well. I'm proud of you."

A warmth blossomed in my chest at his words, the validation igniting a spark of courage within me. "I didn't want to let him win. I want to move forward, not backwards."

"Good," he said, his voice steady. "Because you deserve someone who lifts you up, not someone who keeps dragging you down."

But just as I began to breathe again, my phone buzzed once more, and I instinctively reached for it, heart racing at the thought of another message. The screen lit up, revealing a text from Jason that made my blood run cold: "This isn't over. I'll be watching."

My breath hitched, the realization crashing over me like a wave—this was just the beginning of a battle I hadn't anticipated. And as Ethan's hand found mine again, the warmth of his touch felt like a lifeline against the storm brewing on the horizon.

Chapter 7: Tangled Emotions

The boutique was alive with chatter, laughter, and the soft clink of glasses, creating a symphony of celebration that wrapped around me like a warm blanket. Clara's launch party was meant to be a night of joy, yet the atmosphere buzzed with something far more complex, a current of emotion that left me feeling unmoored. I leaned against a wall, my gaze drifting toward the center of the room where Clara animatedly showcased her new collection. The vibrant fabrics flowed around her like an ocean of color, each piece telling a story of its own. She was the queen of her kingdom, and I was just a loyal subject, lost in the tides of my own thoughts.

Jason stood at the bar, his presence magnetic yet suffocating. He flashed that familiar smile, the one that had once made my heart flutter, but now it felt like a distant echo. I could see the effort in his eyes as he tried to bridge the gap that had widened between us during our time apart. "You remember how to drink, right?" he joked, his voice playful yet tinged with an undercurrent of sincerity. I managed a smile, though it felt like wearing a mask, a facade that hid the turmoil roiling beneath.

But as I forced myself to engage in small talk, I couldn't shake the feeling that my heart was somewhere else entirely. Ethan was across the room, his laughter ringing out like music, drawing my attention like a moth to a flame. He stood with Clara's brother, a playful debate over the merits of high fashion versus comfort fashion unfolding between them. I couldn't help but admire the way his dark hair fell just above his brow, the way he ran his hand through it when he was animated, the effortless charm that made him seem like the sun in a world of shadows.

"Are you going to keep staring, or do I have to rescue you from your thoughts?" Jason's voice pulled me back, a teasing lilt in his tone that was meant to lighten the mood, but all it did was highlight the chasm between us.

"Just... admiring Clara's designs," I replied, though my eyes were still drawn to Ethan, who had just flashed a grin that seemed to brighten the entire room. "She's really outdone herself this time."

"Sure, sure. Just don't forget the guy who's standing right in front of you," Jason said, a hint of frustration creeping into his voice.

I turned back to him, an awkward smile plastered on my face. He was trying so hard, but the spark that had once ignited our relationship felt like a dying ember, while the flame ignited by Ethan was roaring, unpredictable and exhilarating. The two of us stood like strangers on a bridge, and I was frozen, unsure which direction to take.

A flurry of activity interrupted my thoughts as Clara beckoned everyone to gather around for her official launch announcement. I glanced at Ethan, hoping for one last moment of eye contact, a silent acknowledgment of what had been brewing between us. He caught my gaze, a knowing smile playing on his lips that sent a bolt of warmth coursing through me, igniting a nerve I had forgotten existed.

As Clara spoke, her words faded into background noise, and I found myself drawn deeper into my thoughts. Memories of Jason flooded my mind—road trips filled with laughter, lazy Sunday mornings spent in a tangle of sheets, the promise of a future that seemed so bright. But now, standing here, it felt like a faded photograph, the colors blurred and the edges fraying. Jason's efforts to reconnect felt like trying to fit a square peg into a round hole. I couldn't deny the history we shared, but there was a dissonance that rang louder than the memories.

As Clara finished her speech, applause erupted around the room, jolting me back to reality. "So, are we celebrating or what?" Jason's voice pulled me from my reverie, but I could see the uncertainty lurking in his eyes, the subtle way he searched my face for reassurance.

"I just... need a moment," I murmured, stepping away from him. I felt the weight of his gaze on my back as I made my way toward the balcony, seeking fresh air and clarity. The night air was cool against my skin, a welcome contrast to the stifling emotions that had taken root inside me.

Leaning against the railing, I closed my eyes and took a deep breath, letting the chaos of the party fade away. The stars glittered above me, and I let my mind wander, tangled in the memories of two very different men. Jason had been my anchor, my safe harbor, but with Ethan, the winds felt like they were pushing me toward uncharted waters.

"Are you okay?" Ethan's voice broke through the quiet, rich and smooth like a fine whiskey, grounding me in the moment. I opened my eyes, surprised to see him leaning against the doorframe, his expression a mixture of concern and curiosity.

"I just needed some air," I admitted, the truth spilling from my lips before I could consider the implications. "It's a little... overwhelming in there."

He stepped closer, his presence warm and inviting. "Clara really knows how to throw a party. But I can see that it's more than just the crowd." His gaze held mine, piercing yet soft, as if he could read the tempest raging within me.

"Maybe I'm just not ready to be back in the spotlight," I replied, the words slipping out before I could filter them. I wasn't entirely sure I was talking about the party anymore.

Ethan took a step forward, the tension between us crackling like static. "You know, I think it's okay to feel a little lost sometimes. It's part of being human."

"Or maybe it's just me being indecisive," I said, forcing a laugh that fell flat.

"Indecisive, or just figuring it all out?" he countered, a teasing smile tugging at his lips. "There's a difference, you know. One sounds like a problem, the other sounds like growth."

His words lingered in the air, sparking something within me. For the first time that night, I felt understood, unguarded. But just as I was about to delve deeper into the conversation, the door burst open, and Clara's brother stumbled out, laughter spilling into the night like champagne.

"Ethan! Come on, man! We're about to play a game inside!" he called, oblivious to the tension that hung between us.

Ethan hesitated, glancing back at me, a silent question in his eyes. The moment hung heavy in the air, a fragile thread ready to snap under the weight of unspoken feelings. I wanted to call him back, to extend this moment just a little longer, but my heart felt like a fortress—protected, yet achingly lonely.

"Go have fun," I said, forcing a smile that felt genuine but was laced with an undercurrent of regret. "I'll catch up later."

With one last lingering look, he turned and followed Clara's brother inside, leaving me on the balcony, feeling the weight of two worlds colliding. I could hear the laughter and the chatter drift through the open door, but all I could feel was the quiet thrum of uncertainty pulsing through me.

As I stood alone, I realized that whatever was brewing inside me was not merely a conflict of feelings—it was a reckoning of the heart.

The vibrant cacophony of voices and laughter echoed from inside the boutique, yet here on the balcony, the world felt serene. The moon hung low in the sky, casting a silvery glow over everything it touched. The air was crisp, and I breathed it in deeply, attempting to clear the confusion swirling in my mind. Jason had always been my comfort, but comfort was starting to feel a lot like stagnation, while my thoughts kept drifting to Ethan, whose presence was like a breath of fresh air, invigorating and wild.

Just as I began to settle into this strange duality of feeling both rooted and lost, the door swung open again. Clara appeared, a whirlwind of energy and enthusiasm, as if she had just emerged from her own celebratory bubble. "There you are! I was beginning to think you'd vanished!" Her eyes sparkled with mischief, oblivious to the internal storm brewing within me.

"Just getting some air," I replied, offering a smile that felt more genuine now. Clara had an uncanny ability to lift spirits, her exuberance infectious. "How's the party? Did the fashion gods smile upon your launch?"

"They smiled, and then they threw a little shade. I think I saw a couple of my designs getting side-eye from the critics," she laughed, the sound like music. "But that's part of the game, right? If you're not making waves, are you really making fashion?"

"Definitely making waves," I said, my spirits lifting. Clara's passion was contagious, and I couldn't help but feel my heart warm at her resilience. "You've outdone yourself. The collection is stunning."

"Thanks! But enough about me. What's going on with you?" She leaned against the railing beside me, her expression shifting to one of genuine curiosity. "You seemed... distant, like you were somewhere else entirely."

"Just caught in a whirlwind of emotions," I admitted, allowing myself to be vulnerable for a moment. "Jason's back, and I'm trying to figure out where I stand with him—and with someone else."

Clara raised an eyebrow, her interest piqued. "Someone else? Do tell! Is it the brooding guy I saw you with earlier?"

"Ethan," I said, the name slipping from my lips like a secret. "We have this... connection, and it feels like it's pulling me in a direction I didn't see coming. But with Jason here, everything gets complicated."

"Complicated is an understatement. It's like a soap opera waiting to happen." Clara smirked, her eyes twinkling. "You're the star, and I'm here for the drama."

"Trust me, I'd prefer a quiet life without the telenovela twists," I retorted, but laughter bubbled up despite the weight of my thoughts. "It's just that Jason and I have so much history, and I don't want to throw that away."

"But is holding onto history worth sacrificing potential happiness?" Clara challenged gently, her tone softening. "You have to follow what feels right. Your heart knows the way, even if your mind is doing cartwheels."

Before I could respond, Clara's brother sauntered out, his expression a mix of curiosity and mischief. "Are we planning a secret heist on the party, or are you two just gossiping about my wardrobe?" he quipped, a playful smirk on his lips.

"Just plotting how to take over the fashion world, obviously," Clara replied, rolling her eyes theatrically.

"Good luck with that," he laughed, then turned to me. "What's this about a complicated love life? Are you in a love triangle? Because I might need popcorn for that."

"More of a love pentagon, if we're being technical," I shot back, earning a chuckle from Clara and a puzzled look from her brother.

"Okay, now I need to know everything. Spill it!" he demanded, leaning in closer as if this was the most pressing matter in the universe.

I chuckled but found myself caught between wanting to share and the instinct to protect the delicate nature of my feelings. "It's not as exciting as it sounds," I said, waving a hand dismissively. "Just trying to figure things out."

"Pffft, figuring things out is the worst. Just go with your gut!" Clara chimed in, nodding enthusiastically. "That's what I do, and look where it's gotten me!"

"Exactly!" her brother said, grinning. "A thriving boutique and a serious fashionista status. You can't argue with that kind of success."

"Sure, but my 'gut' is screaming confusion," I replied, feeling a hint of frustration creeping in. "What if I make the wrong choice?"

"That's life, my friend! Choices, regrets, and the occasional pizza at 2 a.m. to numb the pain," Clara said, her voice bright and encouraging. "But let's focus on the present. Jason's here now, and you need to confront that. Maybe he's grown up too."

"Or maybe he's still the same guy who thinks a romantic dinner consists of takeout and Netflix," I countered, the thought flaring up with unwelcome clarity.

"I wouldn't rule him out just yet," Clara said, a teasing glint in her eye. "Besides, what's the worst that could happen? You might even remember why you liked him in the first place!"

Just as I was about to retort, the door swung open again, and this time it was Jason himself, a drink in hand and an apologetic smile on his face. "Hey, there you are! I was looking for you," he said, glancing from me to Clara with a slightly sheepish look.

"Just discussing the nuances of love triangles and my questionable life choices," I said, unable to resist the opportunity to poke fun at the absurdity of it all.

"Ah, classic party talk. So, how do you feel about love triangles? Or pentagons, apparently?" He raised an eyebrow, his tone light but laced with something deeper, something that hinted at the weight of his own unresolved feelings.

"Like I said, it's complicated," I replied, meeting his gaze with a steadiness I didn't feel. "But I think it's time to face some of that complexity head-on."

Jason's expression shifted, a flicker of understanding passing through his eyes. "I get that. Look, I know things haven't been easy between us, and I'm not expecting a fairy tale. I just want a chance to explain."

"Explain what? How you waltzed back into my life expecting everything to pick up where we left off?" I challenged, the edge of frustration sharpening my words.

"I know it seems that way, but I've changed," he insisted, his voice steady, the sincerity clear. "I've had time to think about us—about me—and I don't want to just assume you'll take me back. I want to earn it."

"You're asking me to let go of the past, Jason. That's not an easy task."

"Then let's start with one step at a time," he proposed, the earnestness in his eyes softening my resolve, even if only a fraction. "Let's just enjoy tonight. We can talk later, figure things out. No pressure."

The sincerity in his voice was both a balm and a thorn, soothing yet unsettling. "I'll think about it," I said, and I could tell by the way he nodded that he was taking it as a yes, which was both comforting and disconcerting.

As the party swirled back into focus, I felt the tension in my chest ease slightly, though it was still there, lurking. Jason's presence pulled me in one direction while thoughts of Ethan lingered at the edges, like a beautiful sunset fighting against the night. Clara and her brother drifted back into the throng of guests, leaving me standing there, adrift in a sea of uncertainty, torn between the past I knew and the potential for something new.

It was a delicate balance, a tightrope walk between love and loyalty, and I found myself inching forward, unsure which way to leap.

The chatter in the boutique had swelled into a delightful cacophony as the evening wore on. Laughter floated through the air like confetti, and the scent of Clara's signature candle wafted around me, mingling with the rich aroma of red wine. I clutched my glass, the smooth surface cool against my palm, trying to focus on the moments unfolding around me instead of the tension coiling within. Clara moved gracefully among her guests, her smile radiant, the undeniable queen of the evening, while I felt like a pawn caught between two kings.

Ethan had disappeared into the crowd, swept away by Clara's brother, who was charming everyone with exaggerated stories of their childhood mischief. I felt an undeniable pang of longing, a gravitational pull that seemed to tug at my very core. I turned back to Jason, who stood nearby, watching me with an intensity that made my skin tingle. His easy smile was back, but there was an earnestness in his expression that hinted he was still seeking something deeper from me.

"Do you want to dance?" he asked, extending a hand toward me. The invitation was casual, but I sensed the weight behind it. There was a rhythm in his voice, a subtle plea that sent an electric thrill coursing through me.

"Here?" I raised an eyebrow, glancing at the swirling crowd. "I don't think this place was built for impromptu dancing."

"Every place is a dance floor if you're brave enough," Jason replied, a charming lopsided grin spreading across his face. "Besides, I could use a little more of your company to convince me to stay."

His words were both a challenge and a comfort, but I hesitated, the decision weighing heavily on my heart. "What about Ethan?" I said, my voice quieter than I intended, though the thought hung in the air like a lead balloon.

"Ethan will understand," Jason replied, his confidence unwavering. "This is about us—whatever this is. We need to figure it out."

The moment stretched between us, filled with unspoken promises and fears. Finally, I took his hand, allowing him to lead me toward the makeshift dance floor, a small area cleared near the boutique's entrance. The music shifted to a softer melody, and the surrounding laughter dimmed into a comforting backdrop as we swayed together. I felt the heat of his body next to mine, a familiar warmth that sparked memories of us dancing in our college days, lost in our own world.

"See? This isn't so bad," he murmured, his voice low, sending a flutter through my chest. "Just like old times."

I couldn't shake the feeling that while some moments felt familiar, they were tinged with a new layer of uncertainty. "It's different now," I admitted, my voice barely a whisper as I looked into his eyes. "We're different."

He studied me for a moment, the playfulness fading from his expression, replaced by something earnest and raw. "I know I've made mistakes, and I don't expect everything to go back to how it was. But I want to be here for you. I want to try again."

The sincerity in his voice tugged at my heart, but the thought of Ethan lingered in the corners of my mind like a shadow. Just then, the door swung open again, and Ethan stepped back onto the balcony, his laughter echoing like a bell, bright and inviting. I caught his eye, and for a brief moment, it felt as if the world had narrowed to just the two of us, the rest of the party fading into insignificance.

"Hey, you two! Are we having a secret dance party without me?" Ethan called out, a playful glint in his eye.

Jason's grip tightened slightly on my waist, and I sensed a tension ripple between the three of us. I forced a smile, my heart racing as I was torn between two worlds, two emotions fighting for dominance.

"Not a secret party, just a moment," I replied, attempting to diffuse the sudden strain in the air.

"Oh, I see how it is! Just because I didn't don my dancing shoes doesn't mean I can't join!" Ethan sauntered over, his confidence radiating like the moonlight glimmering on the boutique's glass facade.

"Come on then," Jason challenged, his voice laced with playful defiance. "Join us. Show us what you've got."

Ethan laughed, his smile infectious, as he stepped forward and took my other hand, creating a makeshift circle. "Alright, let's see if I can remind you of how to really dance."

I glanced between the two of them, the palpable tension humming in the air as the music swelled. Jason and Ethan stood on either side of me, and it felt like I was being pulled in two different directions, my heart teetering on a precipice.

As we began to sway together, the rhythm intertwining our movements, I couldn't help but notice the heat emanating from both men, their energies colliding in a dazzling display of rivalry and camaraderie. Each beat of the music resonated in my chest, amplifying the emotions swirling inside me. Laughter erupted around us, the other guests joining in, and suddenly, it felt like the whole world had turned into a swirling dance of possibilities.

But as I lost myself in the music, I noticed Jason stealing glances at Ethan, his expression shifting subtly. There was something deeper brewing beneath the surface—an unspoken challenge, a silent competition that was as thrilling as it was unnerving. I could sense the rivalry blossoming between them, and the awareness prickled at my skin.

"Let's see who can impress her more," Jason declared, his competitive spirit ignited, eyes glinting with mischief. "How about a little dance-off?"

Ethan raised an eyebrow, an amused smirk forming on his lips. "You're on! But fair warning: I've got some moves that could make you reconsider your life choices."

The playful banter set the stage for something electric, and I felt my heart race, caught in the storm of anticipation. I was trapped in the center of their contest, and every moment only heightened the stakes.

"Okay, okay! But let's keep it friendly!" I laughed, though my stomach fluttered at the thought of being the prize in their playful duel.

Jason kicked off the dance-off with a goofy spin that sent laughter rippling through the crowd. Ethan followed suit, his moves slick and confident, drawing cheers from the onlookers. I couldn't help but laugh, feeling the tension shift slightly as the energy in the room transformed into something lighter.

But as the playful energy soared, I caught sight of Clara standing at the edge of the crowd, her smile wavering slightly. It was a fleeting expression, almost as if she sensed something amiss, a crack in the joyful facade. My heart skipped a beat, and I couldn't shake the feeling that the joy of the moment was just a thin veil over the complications that lay beneath.

Ethan's laughter echoed as he showcased a series of playful twirls, pulling me into the dance with a confident ease. "See? You can't resist my charm!"

As I spun away from him, laughter spilling from my lips, I glanced back at Jason, whose expression was a blend of admiration and jealousy. Suddenly, the weight of my decision pressed down on me again, and I felt myself falter. What was I doing? It was supposed to be a carefree night, but it felt like a tightrope act, and I was inching closer to the edge.

In the midst of the laughter, I felt my phone buzz in my pocket, a disruption that sent a ripple of anxiety through me. I pulled it out, glancing at the screen, and my heart dropped. A message from my mother, words flashing before my eyes like a warning siren: We need to talk. It's important.

The world around me blurred, the laughter fading into silence. I could sense both Jason and Ethan waiting for me to respond, the atmosphere charged with unspoken words and unresolved feelings.

"Hey, I—" I started, but the sudden weight of my mother's message pressed down on me, knotting my stomach in a way that felt all too familiar.

But before I could gather my thoughts, Clara pushed through the crowd, her eyes wide, urgency etched on her face. "We need to talk. Now."

And in that moment, as the music played on and the laughter swirled around us, I felt everything shift, like the ground had opened beneath my feet. The choices I thought I had were suddenly clouded by a new revelation, one that threatened to change everything I thought I understood.

"Wait, what's going on?" I asked, my voice shaky as the uncertainty loomed large, pulling me under.

"Just come with me," Clara urged, her tone leaving no room for debate.

And as I followed her, leaving behind Jason and Ethan, I couldn't shake the feeling that I was stepping into the unknown, where the tangled web of emotions awaited me, ready to ensnare me in its grasp.

Chapter 8: A Needle and Thread

The remnants of the party still linger in the air, a sweet mix of champagne bubbles and half-forgotten laughter echoing through my mind. I step into my studio, my sanctuary, where the walls are lined with fabrics in hues that speak to me like old friends. Here, the world outside falls away, replaced by the soft rustle of material and the whisper of creative possibility. The floor is a patchwork of sketches, crumpled papers, and swatches, each a testament to my chaotic thoughts.

The light filters through the large windows, casting a warm glow that ignites the colors around me. I grab a pencil, my fingers trembling slightly. My heart races as I begin to sketch—curves and lines flowing like the thoughts tumbling in my head. Each stroke feels cathartic, a release of the pent-up emotions that have been bubbling beneath the surface. I can almost hear the echoes of my insecurities, taunting me, reminding me of every time I hesitated, every time I allowed fear to dictate my decisions.

There's a small mirror hanging on the wall, reflecting not just my face but my struggles. I catch a glimpse of my own wide eyes—eyes that once sparkled with unguarded ambition, now clouded with doubt. How had I allowed a single evening to rattle me so thoroughly? It was a party, not a judgment day. Yet, as I sketch, I can almost see Ethan's expression flash before me, that moment of confusion when I recoiled from his touch, a mixture of fear and longing dancing in the air between us.

"Get it together, Elise," I murmur to myself, my voice a soothing balm against the inner turmoil. I pick up a piece of vibrant turquoise fabric, its texture soft and inviting, as if it were daring me to embrace its beauty. This fabric could become something breathtaking; it could be a part of a new beginning. I fold it, draping it over a sketch, allowing the colors to meld in my mind, creating a tapestry of potential that feels electrifying.

Hours slip by as I lose myself in the rhythm of creation. My fingers glide over the fabric, pinning, folding, draping, each movement soothing my frayed nerves. With every snip of the scissors, every jab of the needle, I feel the weight of my fears begin to lighten. I'm reminded of the first dress I ever designed, a kaleidoscope of colors that defied convention—a piece that whispered to the world that I was here, that I mattered. That dress had transformed me from a wallflower into someone vibrant, someone who dared to dream.

Just as I finish the latest sketch—a flowing gown that embodies both freedom and vulnerability—my phone buzzes on the workbench. The screen lights up with a text from Clara. Ethan's been waiting for you. He wants to talk. A knot tightens in my stomach. I had left the boutique in such a rush, a whirlwind of emotions and unresolved tension. What could we possibly say to each other that would bridge the chasm my doubts had carved?

I take a deep breath, grounding myself in the moment. It's time to face the music. I slip into a comfortable pair of jeans and a soft sweater, brushing my fingers through my hair, catching my reflection one last time. The girl staring back is familiar yet different, forged anew from the ashes of the night before. With a resolute heart, I step out of my sanctuary, the door clicking shut behind me like a seal on my fears.

The walk to Clara's boutique feels longer than usual, the streets buzzing with life yet strangely muted as I navigate my thoughts. A gentle breeze tousles my hair, carrying with it the faint scent of blooming flowers from a nearby garden. I let it fill my lungs, trying to draw in courage with each breath. The world continues spinning, yet here I am, ready to reclaim my narrative.

Upon entering the boutique, the familiar bell chimes, and the air is saturated with the comforting scent of fabric softener and floral notes from the displays. Clara stands behind the counter, her brow furrowed with concern that eases into a warm smile upon seeing me. "There you are! He's in the back," she gestures, her voice laced with gentle encouragement.

I swallow hard, the knot in my stomach tightening as I approach the back room. Each step feels monumental, as if I'm walking the plank. Ethan is leaning against the wall, arms crossed, his expression one of mixed apprehension and hope. The moment our eyes meet, the world narrows down to just the two of us, the background noise fading into oblivion.

"Hey," I say, the word sounding weaker than I intended, but it hangs in the air like an unspoken invitation.

"Hey," he replies, his voice steady, but I can see the flicker of uncertainty in his eyes. "I was worried you wouldn't come."

"Honestly? So was I," I admit, a hint of laughter in my tone, attempting to break the tension. "But here I am, ready to face the music—or, you know, whatever this is."

"Can we talk?" he asks, shifting slightly, his posture now open, vulnerable. "I don't want to lose what we have, but I can't pretend that what happened at the party didn't shake me."

"Me too," I confess, my heart racing as I step closer. The distance between us feels electric, charged with possibility. "I've been... wrestling with my fears, Ethan. I don't want to let my past dictate my future anymore."

His gaze softens, and for a moment, the weight of the world lifts, revealing a flicker of hope. "Then let's embrace the uncertainty together. We don't have to figure everything out right now. Just... can we take it one step at a time?"

As I nod, a rush of warmth floods through me, and in that moment, I realize that maybe, just maybe, the future isn't something to dread but to anticipate with a heart wide open.

The atmosphere in Clara's boutique crackles with unspoken tension, a fragile thread stretching taut between us. I stand there, caught between fear and hope, the weight of our conversation hovering in the air like a perfume I can't quite place. Ethan's presence feels both comforting and electrifying, as if he's an anchor to the chaos swirling inside me. I can't help but notice the way his shirt clings to him, the fabric straining slightly across his shoulders, and it distracts me momentarily.

"Okay, let's talk," I say, injecting a lightness into my tone that I don't quite feel. "But I need to warn you: I'm a master at overthinking. If I seem a bit scattered, just remember it's part of my charm."

He chuckles, and the sound washes over me, melting away some of my anxiety. "I think scattered can be charming in small doses. Otherwise, it's just chaotic."

"Touché," I respond, crossing my arms, pretending to weigh the merits of chaos versus charm. "So, what's first? The awkward silence, or do we dive right into the emotional wreckage?"

"Let's skip the silence," he replies, a hint of mischief dancing in his eyes. "I'd rather not start our conversation with you internally berating yourself."

His playful tone eases the tension a little more, and I take a deep breath. "Right, then. Here goes nothing. I've been thinking... a lot. About us. About how I reacted at the party. I wish I could go back and handle it differently, but I can't. And I'm sorry."

Ethan shifts closer, the warmth radiating from him drawing me in. "Apologies aside, why did you pull away? Was it just the fear of what we might become?"

"It's a little more complicated than that," I admit, my gaze dropping to the floor. "I've always struggled with letting people in. When I saw the look on your face, it was like a door opened, and I panicked. I thought I'd let my past dictate my future, and that terrified me."

"Why do you think your past has to dictate anything?" he asks, his voice gentle but firm. "Your history is a part of you, but it doesn't have to be your present."

I glance up, meeting his steady gaze, a flicker of understanding igniting within me. "You're right. But I've spent so long guarding my heart that the thought of letting someone in feels like stepping off a cliff. It's exhilarating and terrifying all at once."

"Then maybe we can figure out how to fly together," he suggests, his smile disarming and hopeful. "It doesn't have to be all or nothing. We can take it slow. No pressure."

"Easier said than done," I murmur, fighting back the wave of doubt. But deep down, I can feel the tiny embers of hope beginning to stir. "What if we take one step forward and two steps back?"

"Then we dance." Ethan's grin is infectious, and I can't help but laugh, the sound echoing in the small space like the first drops of rain after a long drought. "Let's promise to keep it real. If something feels off, we'll talk about it. No more running."

"Deal," I reply, warmth spreading through me as we seal the promise with a tentative smile. "Just no two-stepping into the realm of melodrama. I'm allergic to that."

"Melodrama, noted," he replies, holding up his hands in mock surrender. "I can't promise I won't inject a little humor along the way, though. Can't have a serious heart-to-heart without a few bad jokes."

"Great, I've always wanted a comedian in my life," I tease, my spirits lifting. "You'll have to work on your timing, though. The last joke I heard fell flat."

"Challenge accepted," he says, crossing his arms, a playful glint in his eyes. "Now, let's take this next step. What do you want?"

The question hangs in the air, heavy with possibility. What do I want? It's a question I've avoided for far too long. "I want... I want to feel free to explore this connection between us without the shadows of my past creeping in," I say, the words tumbling out before I can second-guess myself.

Ethan nods, his expression sincere. "That's a start. And what about your designs? You mentioned at the party that you felt stuck."

"I did, didn't I?" I smile at the memory of my overly dramatic proclamation, the one that had led to me retreating like a startled deer. "My designs are my lifeline, my way of expressing what I can't say. But sometimes it feels like I'm trying to piece together a puzzle without all the pieces. I want to create something bold, something that feels authentic to me."

"Then let's work on it together," he says, his voice filled with genuine enthusiasm. "I can help you brainstorm. Besides, I'm pretty good at color palettes. Not to brag, but I once color-coordinated a whole wardrobe for my sister. She still raves about it."

"Is that your secret talent? Color coordination?" I ask, raising an eyebrow. "Should I expect you to start a side hustle as a stylist?"

"Only if you pay me in fabric," he replies, his smirk playful. "So, what's your vision for this next collection? Let's make sure you channel all that creative energy."

As I explain my ideas, a surge of excitement floods through me. I've always believed that creativity thrives in collaboration, and sharing my vision with Ethan feels exhilarating. We bounce ideas back and forth, the conversation flowing easily, a dance of imagination and inspiration. His enthusiasm is contagious, and I find myself smiling more, laughter bubbling to the surface as we brainstorm.

"We should do a showcase," he suggests, his eyes lighting up with the idea. "A small event where you can unveil your designs to the world. Nothing big, just a gathering of friends and a chance to see what you've been working on."

"A showcase?" The idea is thrilling and terrifying all at once. "You think anyone would care?"

"Absolutely," he says, his conviction unwavering. "You've got something special, Elise. People will want to see it. Besides, we can call it a 'soft launch'—sounds fancy, doesn't it?"

"Very fancy," I say, warming to the idea. "But what if it flops?"

"Then we'll just eat cupcakes and laugh about it," he replies, unfazed. "What's the worst that could happen?"

With a newfound sense of courage, I nod slowly, my heart racing at the thought of stepping into the spotlight. "Okay, let's do it. Let's make it happen."

Ethan's grin widens, and I can't help but feel a surge of excitement coursing through me, a flicker of possibility igniting in the air. Maybe this time, I'll let myself be seen. And for the first time in a long while, it feels like I might just be ready to embrace whatever comes next.

The air in Clara's boutique hums with excitement as we plot our showcase, and I feel a wave of anticipation crashing over me like a tide of vibrant colors. Ethan leans back against the wall, his expression a mix of mischief and sincerity, his dark hair falling charmingly across his forehead. "So, cupcakes and a fashion reveal," he says, smirking as if he's concocting a secret recipe. "What could possibly go wrong?"

"Famous last words," I counter, rolling my eyes playfully. "But I like your optimism. At least we'll have sugar to cushion the blow if it flops spectacularly."

He laughs, a sound that dances in the air, light and infectious. "Trust me, Elise, it won't flop. You're too talented for that. And besides, cupcakes are always a hit. Even if the designs are a disaster, we'll just call it 'avant-garde.'"

"Ah, the classic 'pretentious art' approach," I say, crossing my arms and feigning contemplation. "Maybe I'll wear a beret and sip espresso while I explain my 'vision.'"

"Perfect! Just don't forget the existential crisis that comes with it," he adds, his eyes twinkling with humor. "But seriously, let's nail down the details. When do you want to do this?"

I hesitate, caught between the thrill of sharing my creations and the gnawing fear of judgment. "How about in a month? That gives me time to finalize the designs and make everything perfect."

"Month it is! And I'll help you every step of the way." His tone is earnest, and I can see the determination etched in his features. "Let's do some planning now. What's first on your list?"

The conversation flows effortlessly, ideas sparking like fireflies in the twilight. We bounce back and forth, sketching out a loose agenda filled with deliciously vague phrases like "design aesthetics" and "thematic elements," while also mentally preparing for a plethora of cupcakes. Each suggestion is met with a playful retort, as if we were engaged in a flirtatious game of tennis.

"Do we need a guest list?" I ask, feeling a sense of urgency creep in as I consider the logistics.

"Definitely. We want to fill the room with the right vibe. Let's invite Clara, a few close friends, maybe some local influencers. You know, people who'll appreciate the artistry behind the designs rather than just the end product."

"Influencers? Now you're speaking my language," I respond, my excitement building. "I've always wanted to mingle with the Instagram elite. Maybe I can borrow their followers. But can we get some people who can appreciate art beyond just likes?"

"Challenge accepted," he winks, jotting down notes. "Let's make sure we include people who understand that fashion can be a form of expression, not just a commodity. And while we're at it, how about we throw in a little live music?"

"Live music?" I exclaim, my heart racing at the idea. "That could set the mood perfectly. But... do you think we can pull that off in a month?"

"Why not? We'll make it happen," Ethan assures me, his confidence a warm blanket against my doubts. "What's a little spontaneous planning between friends? Besides, I have a cousin who plays guitar. I'll just bribe him with pizza. Works every time."

"Who knew the secret to live music was a good slice?" I muse, feeling lighter with each passing moment.

Just as we dive deeper into planning, Clara emerges from the back, her arms laden with fabric swatches and a radiant smile on her face. "You two look like you're hatching a plan for world domination," she teases, glancing between us with a knowing look.

"More like a cupcake-filled fashion showcase, but close enough," Ethan replies, throwing an arm around my shoulders. "We're going to set the world on fire with Elise's designs!"

"Flame on!" Clara grins, dropping the fabric swatches on the counter, sending a few cascading to the floor. "What can I do to help? I'm all in for this adventure."

I can't help but smile at the camaraderie brewing among us, a warm sense of belonging washing over me. "We could use a bit of help with the logistics—maybe your connections for the venue and the music?"

"Absolutely," Clara says, already pulling out her phone. "I know just the place—a cozy little café with a great vibe for showcasing art. And the owner is a total sweetheart. I'm sure she'll love your designs."

Ethan and I exchange glances, the thrill of potential igniting the air around us. We're building something together, crafting a world where my dreams can unfurl like the delicate petals of a blooming flower.

But amidst the excitement, a small voice whispers warnings in the back of my mind, reminding me of my past failures and the fears that still lurk. What if I'm not good enough? What if the designs don't resonate? The thought gnaws at me like a persistent itch I can't quite scratch.

"Okay, then," I say, forcing my voice to sound casual, even as my heart races. "Let's get this planning underway. We'll figure out the rest as we go."

The three of us dive into the details, weaving plans like threads in a tapestry. Time slips away as we throw around ideas, laughter mingling with anticipation. Clara handles the venue arrangements, while Ethan takes charge of the music. And I... I focus on creating the designs that will define this moment, the culmination of my hopes and dreams.

The days pass in a blur of fabric, sketches, and a surprising amount of cupcakes, each one a tiny token of our blossoming friendship. With every stitch I make, I feel the tension ease slightly, and I find myself pouring more of my heart into each design, infusing them with color and life. It feels liberating, and for the first time in ages, I find joy in my craft again.

As the date of the showcase approaches, excitement thrums through me, yet the shadows of doubt loom larger than ever. I'd worked hard to leave my past behind, but the echoes of old fears whisper relentlessly. On the day of the event, I stand in front of my mirror, heart racing as I scrutinize my reflection. The dress I wear is one of my latest designs, the fabric draping perfectly over my curves, but the insecurity is still there, lingering like an uninvited guest.

"Just breathe," I tell myself, drawing in a deep breath. "You're here to share your work, not to impress everyone."

But as I arrive at the café, the warm light spilling from the windows and the soft hum of conversation greeting me, I can't shake the feeling that the ground beneath me might give way at any moment. I take a deep breath, scanning the room filled with familiar faces—friends, Clara's loyal customers, and a few local influencers I recognize from social media. The buzz of excitement is palpable.

Ethan approaches, his eyes gleaming with anticipation. "You ready for this?"

"I think so," I reply, my voice barely above a whisper.

He steps closer, his gaze steadying me. "No pressure. Just remember, it's about sharing your passion. The rest will follow."

With a nod, I manage a small smile, feeling slightly more grounded. The evening unfolds like a dream, the warmth of camaraderie wrapping around us as laughter echoes through the café. Clara organizes the seating while Ethan adjusts the lights, creating a cozy atmosphere that feels just right.

As the first notes of music fill the air, I take my place in front of the gathering, my heart pounding like a drum in my chest. I can feel the weight of everyone's eyes on me, and for a moment, time stands still.

And then it happens. As I begin to speak, a sudden commotion erupts at the door, drawing everyone's attention. A figure bursts into the room, breathless and wide-eyed, and my heart drops as recognition dawns.

It's someone from my past, someone I had never expected to see again, and the realization hits me like a cold wave. I freeze, the words dying on my lips, and suddenly, the air feels thick with tension.

Chapter 9: Breaking the Mold

The air crackled with anticipation as I stood backstage, a kaleidoscope of fabrics and emotions swirling around me. Clara's boutique, a treasure trove of style nestled on the bustling streets of our small town, had transformed into a hive of creativity, laughter, and a hint of chaos. Models flitted about in a flurry of sequins and silk, each one embodying a piece of my heart, a snippet of my journey toward self-acceptance. The scent of fresh-cut flowers mingled with the sharp tang of hairspray, forming a heady concoction that left me both dizzy and exhilarated.

With every passing moment, the adrenaline coursing through my veins seemed to pulse louder than the beat of the music thumping from the speakers. I glanced at the clock on the wall, its hands creeping closer to showtime. My collection, a celebration of individuality and love in all its forms, was ready to take center stage. Each piece I designed whispered secrets of my past, stitched together with threads of resilience and a sprinkle of audacity. I had poured not only my skill into these garments but also my heart, reflecting the essence of who I was and who I dared to become.

As I peered through the curtain, I caught sight of Ethan across the room. He stood there, tall and reassuring, his presence a lighthouse guiding me through the fog of anxiety that threatened to envelop me. His gaze met mine, and a warm smile broke across his face, effortlessly melting away the tension that coiled around my chest. "You look incredible," he mouthed, the words traveling through the air like a lifeline, grounding me amidst the storm of butterflies fluttering in my stomach.

"Thanks," I replied, my voice barely a whisper but imbued with gratitude. His support had been my anchor throughout this journey, lifting me when self-doubt threatened to drown me. We had spent countless nights sketching designs together, his laughter a soothing balm to my frayed nerves as we brainstormed ideas. "You should probably start calling me a fashion genius," I added playfully, nudging him gently as I adjusted the hem of a sequined dress that danced like stars in the twilight.

"Let's not get ahead of ourselves," Ethan teased, rolling his eyes with exaggerated flair. "Genius is a strong word. How about 'talented designer' with a penchant for dramatics?" His laughter echoed like a melody in the cacophony of preparations, wrapping around me like a comforting embrace.

"Deal." I chuckled, the lightness of our banter infusing me with a renewed sense of purpose. I had spent years shaping my identity, battling insecurities like shadows lurking at the edges of my mind. But tonight was different. Tonight, I was ready to break free from the molds society had cast around me. The vibrant colors of my collection mirrored the vivid hues of my emotions, each outfit a statement, a declaration of self-love.

"Alright, everyone, let's get ready for the first look!" Clara's voice sliced through the chatter, commanding attention like a maestro. She bustled around, her energy contagious as she directed the models and stylists with the authority of a seasoned conductor. The room buzzed with an electric thrill, a mix of nerves and excitement. My heart raced, not from fear, but from the sheer exhilaration of finally being seen, of showcasing my journey and passion on that runway.

As the lights dimmed, the spotlight flickered to life, illuminating the path ahead. I took a deep breath, letting the weight of my dreams settle into my bones. This was not just about fashion; it was about reclaiming my narrative, about standing tall in my truth. With one last glance at Ethan, I stepped into the fray, my heart a drumbeat of courage echoing within me.

The moment my heels clicked against the runway, the world shifted. I could feel the energy of the audience, a blend of familiar faces and curious onlookers, weaving through the air like a fine silk thread. Each step was a bold proclamation, a claim staked on my identity. The fabric of my designs flowed around me, billowing like the wings of a butterfly emerging from its cocoon, vibrant and unashamed.

The first model strode forward, wearing a flowing gown that shimmered like the night sky. It was adorned with delicate embroidery that told a story of late-night conversations and laughter shared over countless cups of coffee. As she twirled, the fabric danced in a symphony of colors, each hue representing a facet of my growth. The audience gasped, and I felt a surge of pride swell within me, as if each gasp were a gentle wave of affirmation washing over my insecurities.

The second look followed, a chic ensemble that exuded confidence and flair. It was a reflection of my tenacity, a blend of softness and strength. I could almost hear the whispers of my past, urging me to embrace every wrinkle, every flaw, as part of my tapestry. The applause that erupted with each model was a chorus of validation, echoing my journey back to me—a reminder that I was not alone in this dance of life.

With every piece showcased, I felt the weight of expectations begin to crumble, revealing the vibrant tapestry of my identity beneath. I was no longer a reflection of what others wanted me to be; I was a fierce woman who had crafted her path, piece by piece, stitch by stitch. As the finale approached, I took a moment to soak it all in—the lights, the cheers, the thrill of being unapologetically myself.

And then, the final model stepped onto the runway, adorned in my masterpiece: a gown that encapsulated my essence, a bold declaration of love in its most authentic form. The fabric shimmered under the bright lights, flowing with an ethereal grace. As she glided forward, I felt a connection to each heartbeat in the room, a shared understanding of the struggles that had brought us to this moment.

This was not merely a showcase of fabric and thread; it was a celebration of transformation, a testament to the strength found in vulnerability. I could almost hear the collective sigh of relief, the whispers of "Finally" mingling in the air, as if the audience recognized a piece of themselves within my journey.

The applause cascaded around me like a gentle wave, pulling me into its embrace, washing away the remnants of doubt that had clung stubbornly to my skin. I stood there, soaking in the energy of the moment, my heart racing in rhythm with the thrumming bass of the music pulsing through the air. Each clap, each cheer, was a reminder of the journey I had embarked upon, the fierce battle I had fought against the expectations that had wrapped around me like a vine, choking my creativity. This was my moment, the culmination of sleepless nights and endless revisions, and I intended to savor every fleeting second.

As the lights dimmed and the audience settled into a hushed anticipation, I caught sight of Ethan at the edge of the runway, his eyes sparkling with pride. He leaned against the wall, arms crossed, exuding an air of nonchalant charm that made my heart flutter. "You did it," he mouthed, his expression a mixture of disbelief and awe. It was a sentiment I shared, for a year ago, I wouldn't have dared to dream this big. The journey from timid designer to a voice in the fashion world felt as surreal as a sunrise over the ocean—beautiful, terrifying, and utterly transformative.

"Ready for the next act?" Clara's voice cut through my reverie, her excitement infectious as she nudged me toward the backstage area. "You're about to meet some buyers who can make or break this collection, so put on that charm of yours!" Her tone was a blend of urgency and encouragement, a reminder that the show was just the beginning. The realization hit me like a lightning bolt: this wasn't merely a showcase of my creations but an opportunity to forge connections and let my story unfold beyond the runway.

I took a deep breath, inhaling the floral scent of the bouquets decorating the backstage area, grounding myself. "Alright, let's do this," I said, summoning a confidence I didn't fully feel but desperately needed. I followed Clara as she led me through the bustling hive of stylists, models, and assistants, each one an essential piece in this colorful puzzle.

As I stepped into the main room, I was greeted by a throng of people chatting animatedly, drinks in hand, and eyes sparkling with the thrill of the event. I could see familiar faces—friends and family who had supported me from the start—but it was the buyers mingling near the front that caught my attention. They wore expressions of curiosity, their tailored suits a stark contrast to the free-spirited essence of my designs.

"Let me introduce you to Marissa," Clara said, guiding me toward a woman with impeccably styled hair and a clipboard that seemed more like an extension of her arm than a mere tool. "She's a big player in the fashion industry. If anyone can get your collection into the right stores, it's her."

I approached Marissa, forcing my legs to move forward as if they were made of lead. "Hi, I'm—"

"Yara, the designer behind this stunning collection," she cut me off, her eyes assessing me with an intensity that made me squirm. "I've heard quite a bit about your work. Impressive, I must say."

"Thank you," I replied, a mix of pride and trepidation bubbling up. "I wanted to create something that speaks to individuality, love, and, well, embracing who we really are."

"Good pitch," she nodded, her pen scribbling furiously on her clipboard. "But let's see if your collection matches your words." With that, she motioned for me to lead the way.

As I guided her through the pieces, showcasing the intricate details and unique silhouettes, I felt the energy shift. Marissa leaned in closer, her skepticism melting into intrigue as I described the inspiration behind each outfit—the late nights sketching in my tiny apartment, the countless rejections that had only fueled my fire, and the love that had driven me to push beyond my limits.

"Passion," she mused, her eyes sparkling with realization. "That's what fashion needs more of. Everyone's playing it safe these days."

"Exactly!" I exclaimed, the spark of connection igniting between us. "Fashion should be a reflection of who we are, not just a trend to follow."

Just as we finished discussing the final piece, a model emerged from the crowd, her expression one of surprise and confusion. "Yara, you need to see this," she said, urgency lacing her voice. "There's a problem backstage."

I felt my heart lurch. "What kind of problem?"

"Some of the outfits are missing. I overheard a couple of girls talking about it."

My stomach twisted in knots. "What do you mean missing? They can't be missing."

Ethan appeared at my side, his brow furrowed in concern. "What's going on?"

"Some outfits—" I started, but before I could finish, Clara's voice rang out, slicing through the rising tide of panic.

"Yara! We need you!"

I exchanged a quick look with Ethan before following Clara back through the throngs of people, my heart pounding with every step. What if the missing outfits were crucial pieces? What if this was the twist I didn't see coming, the wrench thrown into my carefully orchestrated plan?

Clara led me to the chaos backstage, where models stood fidgeting in half-finished looks, the stylists racing against the clock. "We need to buy time," Clara said, her voice steady despite the frenzy around us. "Can you handle a quick speech?"

"A speech?" I asked, bewildered.

"Just a few words to keep the audience engaged while we figure this out. You're the heart of this show, Yara. They want to hear from you."

With a swift nod, I steeled myself. "Alright, let's do it."

I took a deep breath, the chaotic energy of the backstage flooding my senses, and stepped out into the spotlight once again. The audience turned their attention toward me, their eyes a blend of curiosity and concern.

"Hello again!" I said, injecting a dose of enthusiasm into my voice, even as my heart raced. "I'm here to share a little more about my collection and the inspiration behind it while we make a few adjustments back there."

The words flowed, fueled by the passion that had ignited within me during the show. I talked about love, about resilience, and the power of embracing who we truly are. The audience hung on to my every word, their faces reflecting the same hope and courage that had pushed me forward.

And in that moment, I realized that even amidst the chaos, I had the power to reclaim the narrative. This wasn't just about the clothes; it was about the story behind them, about each individual who wore them and the journey they embarked upon. I was not merely presenting a collection; I was inviting everyone into a world where self-expression reigned supreme, a world where love and individuality flourished.

As I finished my impromptu speech, the applause roared through the air, wrapping around me like a warm embrace. Ethan's proud smile beckoned from the crowd, grounding me as I navigated the storm of uncertainty. Together, we would weather whatever challenge lay ahead.

The applause settled like a comforting blanket around my shoulders, but it was quickly followed by a weight that pressed down upon me as I stood there, basking in the afterglow of my speech.

Clara was still behind the scenes, orchestrating the chaos with a poise I wished I could emulate. As I scanned the audience, I saw the expressions of surprise morphing into admiration. It felt like magic, but the undercurrent of tension tugged at me, reminding me that magic was often only a thin veneer over reality.

"Yara, can I steal you for a minute?" Ethan's voice broke through the haze, his warm presence a beacon in the sea of strangers. He stepped closer, concern etched on his handsome features. "I heard about the missing outfits. What's the plan?"

"Honestly, I don't know," I admitted, my heart fluttering in response to the uncertainty. "Clara is handling it, but I just gave an impromptu speech to buy us some time. I'm hoping it worked."

"Your charm can work wonders," he said, a teasing smile playing on his lips. "But let's not underestimate the power of a well-timed distraction. What if I help Clara keep the crowd engaged while you make sure everything is okay backstage?"

"Good idea! You're always two steps ahead of me," I said, my heart swelling with gratitude. It was moments like this that reminded me how fortunate I was to have him in my corner. "You always know how to handle a crowd."

"Flattery will get you everywhere," he replied with a wink, and my insides twisted pleasantly.

As he slipped into the backstage fray, I turned back to the audience, still buzzing with the energy of the moment. I knew I had to make sure everything was under control, but a pang of apprehension gripped me. What if the missing outfits were more than just wardrobe malfunctions? What if someone had deliberately sabotaged my collection? A wave of anxiety washed over me, but I shook it off. This was my moment, and I wasn't about to let shadows from the past dim my light.

Navigating through the sea of fabric and stylists, I reached the heart of the chaos. Models were clustered around, some looking anxious, others frustrated, and the atmosphere buzzed with whispers and hurried movements. Clara was at the center, her hands gesturing emphatically as she spoke with a few of the stylists. "We can do this! Just keep calm. Yara's collection is incredible, and we can fix this," she assured everyone, her confidence infectious.

"What's the situation?" I asked, stepping closer.

"Two dresses are missing. They didn't make it back from the laundry," Clara replied, her eyes narrowing as she assessed the models around her. "One of them is the centerpiece of your collection—the one with the floral embroidery."

Panic clawed at my throat. "That dress was the heart of my message! It spoke to everything I've worked for."

"I know, I know," Clara said, a hand on my shoulder. "But don't panic. We can improvise. You've created so much beauty here. Let's focus on what we do have."

I inhaled deeply, trying to channel her calm. "You're right. Let's adjust the lineup and make sure the audience knows how special this collection is."

Just then, a model rushed up to us, her eyes wide with urgency. "Yara, I think I saw someone with the missing dresses!"

My heart raced. "What do you mean? Who?"

"I don't know, but she was wearing this distinctive hat and had a messenger bag," the model explained, glancing nervously at Clara. "She looked... suspicious."

The image of a figure with a hat and bag flitted through my mind, merging with the dread creeping up my spine. I could only think of one person it might be: Veronica, my former friend turned rival who had always believed I didn't deserve the spotlight. The thought chilled me to my core. "Where did she go?"

"Outside. She said something about needing to cool off, but it didn't feel right," the model continued, her voice trembling.

"Clara, I need to check on this," I said, urgency propelling me forward. "I can't let anyone ruin this for me."

"Go!" Clara urged. "I'll keep things moving here."

With a nod, I dashed outside, the cool air hitting my face like a splash of cold water. My heart raced as I scanned the area, seeking any sign of the elusive figure. The buzzing from inside faded, replaced by the hum of the city beyond the boutique's doors. I stepped further into the night, hoping to catch a glimpse of the dresses or, better yet, of Veronica.

As I rounded the corner, I spotted a familiar silhouette by the alley, her back turned to me. The dim light illuminated the edge of a wide-brimmed hat that obscured her features. My pulse quickened as I crept closer, each step echoing in my ears. This was it. This was the confrontation I hadn't anticipated but knew I had to face.

"Veronica!" I called out, my voice sharper than I intended.

She turned slowly, a sly smile creeping onto her face. "Well, if it isn't my favorite designer. How's the show going?"

"Cut the pleasantries. Where are my dresses?" I demanded, the weight of my fear transforming into anger.

"Oh, those?" she said, feigning innocence as she tugged at the bag slung over her shoulder. "You really think you can just waltz in and claim all the glory? You should have known better."

"Is this really about the dresses, or is it about you trying to sabotage my success?" I pressed, taking a step closer.

"Success? You think you've succeeded? You've just stumbled into a moment. It won't last," she scoffed, a flicker of bitterness in her eyes. "But I do enjoy watching you squirm. It's quite the entertainment."

Fury boiled within me. "You think I'm just going to let you take that away from me? This is my moment!"

"Moments are fleeting, dear," she replied, her tone dripping with sarcasm. "But if you're willing to make a deal, perhaps we can both walk away happy."

Before I could respond, a figure emerged from the shadows—a stranger, tall and imposing, stepping between us with an air of authority. "What's going on here?"

I felt my heart skip a beat as I recognized the tension in the air shift once more. The stranger's presence was ominous, a wild card in a game I thought I understood.

"I was just having a little chat with my friend," Veronica said, her demeanor shifting from defiance to coyness.

"Friend?" the stranger echoed, scrutinizing both of us.

I glanced at Veronica, her smile faltering, and suddenly I knew we were in deeper waters than I had anticipated. The stakes were rising, and my moment in the spotlight felt like it was slipping away once again.

"What are you really after?" I demanded, feeling a shiver of fear creep down my spine as the stranger stepped closer, the air thickening with unspoken threats and lingering shadows.

The stranger's smile widened, and I realized in that moment that the game was only just beginning.

Chapter 10: Stitches in Time

Fabric draped over tables, the hum of sewing machines, and the distant chatter of stylists were the soundtrack to my life these days. The air was heavy with the scents of cotton and silk, mingling like old friends. Each day I stepped into Clara's boutique, it felt like entering a world where dreams were spun into reality. I could almost hear the whispers of the gowns, urging me to unveil their secrets. A palette of colors greeted me—soft ivories, blush pinks, and the deep midnight blues that reminded me of summer nights. The dresses hung like silent sentinels, each one a tapestry of emotions, waiting for their moment under the spotlight.

Ethan was there, a constant presence amidst the whirlwind. His brow furrowed in concentration as he meticulously pinned fabric into shape, his hands deftly maneuvering as if the fabric were alive beneath his fingers. I loved how his passion seeped into every stitch, his dedication contagious. In those late hours, surrounded by bolts of fabric and spools of thread, I felt the tension of the upcoming fashion show fade away, replaced by something richer, deeper.

"Do you think the lace on this gown says 'timeless elegance' or just 'I've watched too many rom-coms?'" I asked, holding up a delicate piece adorned with intricate floral patterns. The lace caught the light, shimmering like memories caught in a daydream.

Ethan chuckled, the sound warm and rich. "It says you've got good taste. Besides, a little rom-com influence never hurt anyone. It's all about the story, right?" His eyes sparkled with mischief, a glint that always ignited something within me.

"True. But let's not forget the bride. She'll be living her own rom-com that day." I returned to my work, my fingers deftly stitching the lace onto the bodice. Each movement was like a dance, a rhythm I had come to know intimately.

Ethan's fingers brushed against mine as he adjusted the fabric draping over a mannequin. "So what's the story for this one?" he asked, nodding at the gown taking shape.

"A small-town girl, dreaming big but afraid of losing herself along the way. She meets a guy, a whirlwind romance ensues, and she realizes love doesn't mean sacrificing who you are," I replied, my heart racing as I spoke.

"Sounds like the perfect plot twist for a wedding," he mused, his voice low and thoughtful. "But what about the ending? Does she end up with the guy?"

"That depends on her. Sometimes love is about choosing yourself," I said, my voice softer now.

A comfortable silence enveloped us, punctuated only by the rhythmic whir of sewing machines. I lost myself in the moment, letting the fabric and the stories weave around me, wrapping me in warmth. Yet, underneath the camaraderie, there was an undeniable current—an electric tension that crackled whenever we were close.

Just then, Clara burst into the studio, her energy filling the space like a burst of sunlight. "You two! Have you seen the latest shipment from Paris?" she exclaimed, her excitement contagious.

"More fabric?" I asked, trying to keep the grin from my face. The thought of adding new elements to our collection was like candy to a child.

"Not just fabric, but the latest trends!" Clara said, her eyes wide with enthusiasm. "You have to see it. We can't let the competition outshine us."

Ethan raised an eyebrow, leaning against the table with an easy confidence that made my heart race. "Competition? Is that really what we're worried about?"

Clara rolled her eyes playfully. "Absolutely! We're not just making dresses; we're crafting experiences. We want brides to walk away feeling like they're stepping out of a fairy tale."

"Or a rom-com," I added, sharing a conspiratorial smile with Ethan.

"Exactly!" Clara laughed. "Now, come on. Let's see what magic we can create."

As we ventured into the back room, a vibrant array of fabrics greeted us—rich silks, playful tulles, and ethereal organzas. My hands brushed against a fabric the color of freshly bloomed lavender, and a rush of inspiration hit me like a tidal wave. I could already envision a gown that would encapsulate the essence of spring, delicate and romantic.

Ethan stood beside me, peering over my shoulder, his breath warm against my neck. "You're imagining something grand, aren't you?"

"Something that sings of new beginnings," I said, unable to keep the excitement from my voice. "Like a bride stepping into a new chapter of her life."

"Then let's give her a gown that shouts it," he replied, a playful challenge glimmering in his eyes.

The room buzzed with creativity as we explored the endless possibilities. Hours slipped away as we draped, pinned, and played with textures. The laughter echoed off the walls, mingling with the clatter of tools and the murmur of dreams being crafted.

But in the midst of this vibrant chaos, a shadow lingered, flickering just at the edge of my consciousness. The looming fashion show, with all its promises and uncertainties, awaited us like an impending storm. And while the gowns would dazzle, I couldn't shake the feeling that something deeper was stirring beneath the surface, a hidden tension woven into the very fabric of our collaboration.

As days slipped into nights, the boutique transformed into a realm of possibility, where every stitch held the weight of a promise. The fashion show loomed closer, an event that felt like both an exhilarating leap and a precarious tightrope walk. The buzz of anticipation was electric, but so was the creeping sense of vulnerability that swirled within me.

"Okay, I'm thinking this gown needs something daring. A daring silhouette," I declared, twirling around a mannequin draped in a cascade of satin. The fabric fell like water, pooling at its feet, yet I felt a spark of revolution was missing.

Ethan glanced up from his sewing machine, a smirk playing at the corner of his lips. "Daring? Last week, you thought 'daring' meant not using a petticoat."

"Hey, it's a classic!" I shot back, feigning indignation, but a smile tugged at my mouth. "And now I think we need something that stops the show. A moment where every eye in the room turns and gasps."

"Let's start with the fear of looking like a cupcake," he replied, laughter lighting up his blue eyes. "What if we add a dramatic train? A splash of color—maybe emerald green? That could be both daring and elegant."

I loved how easily our ideas intertwined, sparking new thoughts like a wildfire. "Emerald could work," I mused, leaning closer, allowing the fabric to drape over my hands, feeling its coolness against my skin. "But we need to make sure it tells a story. I want the brides to see themselves in it, to feel the magic."

"Then how about we weave in some elements that symbolize growth?" he suggested, gesturing animatedly, as though the gown itself were alive, capable of transformation. "Maybe lace motifs that echo leaves, a journey from bud to bloom."

The image ignited something within me—a vision of resilience. "Yes! A gown that represents the journey, the struggles, and the joy. Every bride deserves to wear a piece that feels like it was crafted just for her."

As we brainstormed, time blurred around us. Outside, the world carried on, but within our boutique, it felt as if we had created our own universe—one where fabric and thread became words, telling tales of joy and heartache. The soft glow of fairy lights danced off the walls, wrapping us in a cocoon of creativity and camaraderie.

"Have you ever wondered what it would be like to wear one of our gowns?" I asked, curious to explore his thoughts beyond the fabric and design.

Ethan paused, his fingers stilling over the fabric he was working on. "Not really. I mean, a tux is more my style, and honestly, I think I'd look ridiculous in a wedding dress."

"Oh come on, you'd be fabulous," I insisted, playfully nudging him. "We could even give you a flowing train. You'd be the most stunning bride!"

His laughter erupted, filling the space with warmth. "I can see it now—a dashing groom making a daring entrance in a wedding gown. Talk about stealing the spotlight."

"Hey, maybe that's the twist we need for our show," I said, my eyes lighting up at the idea. "A groom in a gown to remind everyone that love knows no boundaries!"

"Perfect. We can charge extra for the drama," he replied, his tone teasing but his expression thoughtful.

As we continued to bounce ideas off each other, the atmosphere shifted subtly. The jokes, once lighthearted, began to carry a weight I hadn't anticipated. I caught myself stealing glances at him, tracing the contours of his face, the way his hair fell into his eyes when he leaned over his work. The chemistry between us crackled, an unspoken acknowledgment of the attraction simmering just beneath the surface.

"Okay, but seriously," he said, breaking the moment, "we have to focus. The show is in a week, and we need these gowns to be the best they can be."

"Right," I said, forcing my mind back to the task at hand, though my heart raced with the implications of his words. "What about this—let's finish the emerald gown, and then we can focus on the other designs. We need a cohesive look for the show."

He nodded, determination replacing the playful banter. "Agreed. Let's make every piece a statement."

The rest of the evening slipped into a rhythm of sewing, laughter, and creativity. Yet, despite the camaraderie, a subtle tension clung to the air, as if our surroundings were charged with the thrill of unsaid words.

As the clock ticked closer to midnight, Clara wandered back into the studio, her presence a breath of fresh air. "What have you two been scheming about? I can feel the energy from halfway down the street!"

"Just plotting to take over the fashion world," Ethan replied, his tone light, but his gaze met mine with a knowing look that sent butterflies fluttering in my stomach.

"Good. I expect nothing less from you two," Clara said, a twinkle in her eye. "But seriously, have you finished the sketches for the show? We need to finalize everything soon."

"Almost there," I said, gesturing to the sketches scattered across the table. "Just a few more tweaks."

"Then we need to discuss the models. I've got a couple of names in mind, but I want your input. You both know what works for the vision."

With Clara's interruption, the moment shifted once again. We dived into discussions about models, styles, and how best to present our creations. The conversation flowed easily, but even amidst the planning, I couldn't shake the sense of change lingering in the air.

That night, as I packed up to leave, I felt a sense of purpose intertwine with something else—an undeniable pull toward Ethan that made my heart race and my mind swirl with possibilities. The fashion show was a mere week away, but it felt like the real spectacle was unfolding right there between us, cloaked in layers of fabric, laughter, and unspoken dreams.

As the final days before the fashion show dwindled, the boutique pulsed with a vibrant urgency, the air thick with creativity and the faint smell of jasmine from the flowers Clara kept on the window sill. Each morning, I arrived early, my heart racing with excitement and a hint of trepidation. The gowns we were crafting were more than mere garments; they were encapsulations of dreams, hopes, and the transformative power of love. But beneath the surface, I felt a tension brewing, an undercurrent that promised change.

"Okay, how about this—let's add a touch of gold threading to the emerald gown?" I suggested one afternoon, studying the rich fabric as it shimmered under the studio lights. "It could create a sense of depth, something that glows when it catches the light."

Ethan leaned back, arms crossed, his eyes glinting with mischief. "You know what that sounds like? An opportunity for me to blind the audience. How can I possibly compete with a gown that practically radiates sunshine?"

"Oh please, the only thing blinding is your fashion sense," I shot back, unable to hide my grin.

His laughter rang out, a rich sound that mingled with the soft music playing in the background. "Touché. But seriously, I'm all in for the gold. It adds an unexpected flair, like a plot twist in a good novel."

"Exactly! Every gown should have its own narrative," I replied, enthusiasm bubbling up within me. "And just think how stunning it will look under the runway lights. It will be like the bride is walking through a magical garden."

As we worked, our banter became a rhythm, a dance of words that flowed easily between us. But even as we filled the room with laughter, my heart was a tumult of emotions. Each touch of his hand on mine as he reached for fabric sent a jolt through me. I tried to brush it off as mere excitement for the show, but deep down, I knew it was something else. Something unspoken that hung between us like the flickering fairy lights illuminating our workspace.

Clara burst in one afternoon, holding her phone with the urgency of someone about to deliver earth-shattering news. "You guys! You won't believe who's attending the fashion show!"

Ethan raised an eyebrow, feigning indifference. "Let me guess—Anna Wintour? Because I think I'd faint if that were true."

"Close! It's Aiden Calloway!" Clara's voice crescendoed with excitement. "He's a fashion mogul—like, the fashion mogul! If he sees our collection, it could change everything for us!"

My stomach flipped at the thought. Aiden Calloway was a name synonymous with high fashion, a man whose endorsements could launch careers. "What does he want with our little corner of the world?"

"He's scouting for fresh talent, looking for the next big thing," Clara replied, eyes sparkling. "And he's known for giving rising designers a chance—if he likes what he sees."

Ethan's gaze met mine, and for a fleeting moment, the gravity of the situation hung heavily between us. "No pressure, right?" he joked, but I could see the seriousness behind his eyes.

As the countdown to the show continued, the boutique became a hub of frenetic energy. Models were fitted, hair and makeup trials commenced, and the air buzzed with the anticipation of new beginnings. Yet, amid the flurry, I felt a growing sense of unease. The weight of expectations pressed down on me, morphing my creative excitement into anxiety.

One evening, while we were sewing the final touches on the emerald gown, I broke the silence. "Ethan, what if it all goes wrong? What if Aiden sees our collection and thinks it's not good enough?"

He paused, looking at me intently. "Hey, we've poured our hearts into this. It's not just about impressing him; it's about the stories we're telling. If he doesn't get that, it's his loss."

"Right, but what if we've misread the audience? What if they don't see the beauty we're trying to create?"

"Stop right there." His voice was firm yet gentle, grounding me amidst the chaos. "You're an artist. You can't control how others perceive your work. Just stay true to yourself and your vision. That's what will resonate."

His words soothed me, even as the anxiety lingered like an unwelcome guest. We worked late into the night, and I found comfort in our shared silence, a bond that deepened with each passing moment.

The day of the fashion show arrived, cloaked in a haze of nerves and excitement. Clara was a whirlwind, directing models and ensuring every detail was perfect. I stood backstage, the final piece of the emerald gown held in my hands like a precious secret.

"Are you ready?" Ethan asked, leaning against the wall, looking impossibly handsome in his tailored suit. The contrast of his attire against the backdrop of chaos made my heart flutter.

"Ready as I'll ever be," I replied, my voice barely above a whisper.

"You'll be amazing," he said, confidence pouring from him like sunlight breaking through clouds.

As the show began, the room filled with the murmur of anticipation. I stood backstage, peeking through the curtains, heart racing as the first model stepped onto the runway, clad in one of our creations. The fabric flowed like water, the audience holding its breath as if enchanted.

Each gown that followed was met with applause, a symphony of appreciation echoing through the space. But as the emerald gown neared its turn, I felt a mix of pride and dread, unsure if it would capture the essence of what we had envisioned.

When the moment arrived, I took a deep breath, my heart pounding as the model stepped out. The gown seemed to come alive under the lights, the gold threading catching the glimmer and reflecting it back tenfold. The audience gasped, a sound of awe that sent a thrill racing through me.

But just as I began to relax, the unthinkable happened. The model stumbled, a small misstep that sent her careening off balance. My breath caught as I watched the gown twist in an alarming way, the fabric catching on her heels. Time slowed as I reached out instinctively, but it was too late.

A moment later, the gown tore—a violent rip that echoed like a gunshot through the room, sending a shockwave of silence crashing over the audience. My heart sank, a hollow feeling spreading through my chest as gasps filled the air.

Ethan rushed to my side, concern etched across his face. "Is she okay? What just happened?"

"Nothing! I mean—everything! The gown—" I stammered, watching in horror as the model regained her footing but the magic of the moment shattered like glass.

The runway felt like a battlefield, every eye turning toward us, every whisper a knife in my side. I wanted to disappear, to curl up in a corner and hide from the judgment that loomed like dark clouds overhead.

And then, amidst the chaos, I heard a familiar voice ring out from the crowd, sharp and cutting through the murmurs. "What a disappointing display! Where's the talent?"

I turned, my heart sinking further as I recognized the voice—the very person I had hoped to impress more than anyone else in the room. Aiden Calloway stood there, arms crossed, a disdainful look etched on his features. The weight of his gaze felt like an anchor, pulling me into the depths of my fears.

With my dreams hanging in the balance, the air around us crackled with tension, and I couldn't help but wonder if this was the end—or just the beginning of something far more complex.

Chapter 11: The Ties That Bind

The sun crested over the skyline, painting the boutique's storefront with hues of soft gold, while a gentle breeze whispered through the city streets, hinting at a day that promised transformation. Clara's boutique was a riot of color and life, the kind of place that felt like a dream woven from the fabric of ambition and artistry. Twinkling fairy lights draped like stars across the ceiling, their warm glow dancing off the polished wooden floor, reflecting a kaleidoscope of floral arrangements that swayed gently, as if keeping time to an unheard melody. It was an enchanting scene that could charm even the most discerning critic, and yet, as I stood backstage, the weight of anticipation pressed heavily on my chest.

This was the day I had been preparing for—my designs would finally take center stage, showcased in the boutique that had become my sanctuary. The scent of fresh blooms mingled with the faint aroma of fabric softener, wrapping around me like a comforting embrace. I took a deep breath, inhaling the essence of hope and creativity that filled the air, yet underneath it all, I felt a familiar knot of anxiety unfurling in my stomach.

Clara, a whirlwind of energy and enthusiasm, flitted around the backstage area, her laughter brightening the tense atmosphere. "You're going to knock their socks off, Amelia! Just remember to breathe. It's just a show, not a colonoscopy!" Her words sliced through the tension, and I couldn't help but chuckle, grateful for her relentless optimism.

"Right, no pressure," I said, my voice barely a whisper as I fiddled with the hem of my dress, a piece I had created from a vision sparked months ago. Its fabric shimmered under the fluorescent lights, catching the eye in the most delightful way.

As I stepped away from the mirror, adjusting the sleeves that flowed like gentle waves, I was pulled from my thoughts by the sound of heels clicking sharply against the floor. Turning, I found Jason leaning against the doorframe, a devil-may-care grin plastered across his face. His hair was tousled just enough to make it look like he had rolled out of bed and walked straight into my heart.

"Fancy seeing you here," he quipped, his voice smooth like the finest silk.

"Thought I'd give my designs a little air of mystery," I replied, trying to sound breezy but betraying the flutter of nerves in my stomach.

Jason stepped closer, the scent of his cologne—a mix of cedar and something citrusy—invading my senses, both intoxicating and grounding. "You're going to be amazing. Just look at you. The dress is stunning. And you? Wow."

My cheeks warmed under his gaze, and I couldn't suppress the smile that tugged at my lips. "Thanks, but you might want to reserve your compliments for when I actually step out on the runway. I might trip and faceplant. It wouldn't be the first time."

"Or it could be a statement piece. 'The Art of Falling Gracefully,'" he teased, his eyes sparkling with mischief.

We shared a laugh that echoed off the walls, lightening the atmosphere around us, but as the minutes ticked away, my heart raced with a mix of excitement and dread. The runway beckoned, promising both success and vulnerability, and with it, the uncharted territory of my feelings for Jason. Just as I found myself getting lost in that thought, the moment shattered like glass when Ethan walked through the backstage doors, his presence commanding the attention of everyone around him.

He was dressed sharply, a tailored suit that hugged his shoulders perfectly, enhancing the chiseled lines of his jaw. His gaze swept the room before landing on me, and for a heartbeat, it felt as if time had paused. There was a warmth in his eyes, a silent acknowledgment of the journey we had embarked on together, the late-night conversations, the shared dreams, and the quiet understanding that danced between us like fireflies on a summer evening.

"Amelia," he said, his voice a low murmur that sent shivers down my spine. "You look incredible."

"Thanks," I managed, trying to mask the whirlwind of emotions that surged within me.

"Are you ready for this?" he asked, stepping closer, the air crackling with unspoken tension.

"As ready as I'll ever be," I replied, forcing a confidence I didn't entirely feel.

He smiled, a genuine warmth that made my heart skip a beat. "Just remember, it's your moment. Own it."

With a nod, I turned back to the mirror, adjusting the delicate lace at my neckline, but I could feel Ethan's gaze lingering on me, a warm presence that provided a steadying anchor amidst the chaos of the day. As the lights dimmed, signaling the beginning of the show, a mixture of exhilaration and anxiety surged through me. I was about to step into a world where dreams were spun into reality, yet with every thud of my heart, the unmistakable truth settled within me—I was about to walk into a spotlight that could either illuminate the way to my aspirations or cast shadows over my tangled emotions.

As I stepped onto the runway, the lights bathing me in a warm glow, I felt the applause wash over me like a tidal wave, powerful and exhilarating. My designs came to life under the bright lights, flowing and billowing like whispers of creativity. The audience leaned forward, captivated, and in that moment, everything else faded away—the nerves, the uncertainties, the weight of expectations. It was just me and the fabric, entwined in a dance of artistry and passion.

But as I glanced down the runway, my eyes locked onto Ethan, who stood in the front row, his expression a blend of admiration and something deeper. My heart swelled, and it hit me like a thunderbolt:

this was more than a fashion show. This was a declaration, a moment where I had the chance to show not just the world but myself who I truly was. And in that clarity, amidst the applause and the flashing lights, I realized my heart belonged to someone who truly saw me, not just as a designer or a dreamer, but as Amelia, the girl who was finally stepping into her light.

The applause washed over me in waves, each clap resonating like a heartbeat in a vast ocean of excitement. I walked the runway, my pulse racing in time with the rhythm of the crowd, the lights bright enough to melt the edges of reality into a soft blur. It felt as though the entire world had narrowed down to this single moment, a sweet convergence of creativity, confidence, and a flicker of vulnerability.

But just as I turned to strike my final pose, my gaze darted toward Ethan again. He was leaning forward, a proud smile illuminating his face, and for an instant, everything else faded. The crowd's cheers became a distant hum, and I found myself wishing for the chance to walk off the runway and into his arms, where the weight of the world would be lifted, and I could shed the persona I'd crafted for this show. I longed for the warmth of his gaze, the way he made me feel like I could fly, and yet here I was, caught in a whirlwind of silk and sequins, a storm of emotions swirling within me.

As I stepped off the runway, my heart was still dancing to the cadence of applause when Clara rushed toward me, her arms outstretched like a shield against the chaos. "You were magnificent!" she exclaimed, her excitement palpable. "I've never seen anything like it! The way the light caught your designs was pure magic!"

"Thanks, Clara," I replied, my voice barely rising above the excitement that buzzed around us. "It feels surreal."

Before she could respond, Jason appeared, a proud grin plastered across his face. "You stole the show, Amelia. Seriously, even I was thinking about trading my shirt for one of those dresses." His laughter rang out, a refreshing contrast to the adrenaline coursing through me.

"Please don't," I shot back, grinning. "The world isn't ready for that kind of fashion statement."

The banter flowed easily, a comforting layer amidst the excitement. But as I tried to immerse myself in the moment, I caught Ethan's gaze again, his eyes reflecting a different kind of depth, an intensity that suggested he understood the vulnerability that lingered beneath my bravado. It was then I realized that even amidst the joy, I felt a nagging sense of uncertainty. I was standing on the precipice of something monumental, yet my heart was pulling me in two different directions.

Clara's voice broke through my reverie. "Amelia, the press is here, and they want to speak with you. You ready for this?" Her eyes sparkled with enthusiasm and a hint of mischief.

"Ready or not, here I come," I joked, though my stomach twisted nervously. The thought of facing reporters sent a fresh wave of anxiety rippling through me.

As we approached the small gathering of reporters, I felt like I was slipping into a role I hadn't fully rehearsed. Cameras clicked like a flurry of angry cicadas, and I plastered on a smile that was becoming all too familiar.

One reporter leaned in, her notepad poised as if it were a weapon. "What inspired your latest collection?" she asked, her voice sharp and probing.

"Honestly, it was all about embracing vulnerability," I replied, trying to steady my thoughts. "Each piece represents a journey through fear and doubt, turning them into strength. I wanted to celebrate what it means to be both fragile and fierce."

The words flowed more easily than I expected, like water from a wellspring. I lost myself in the moment, sharing anecdotes of late-night sewing marathons, my grandmother's influence on my designs, and the way each thread carried a piece of my story. Laughter bubbled between us, the initial pressure easing as I connected with them on a level that felt genuine.

Just as the conversation deepened, a familiar voice cut through the chatter like a knife. "Amelia, can I steal you away for a moment?" Ethan's tone was playful yet earnest, his eyes glinting with mischief.

I turned to the reporters, offering them an apologetic smile. "I'll be right back," I promised before stepping away from the whirlwind of questions. The contrast between the buzzing crowd and the intimate connection I shared with Ethan was stark.

"Do I have your attention now?" he asked, his voice low and teasing, a smile playing at the corners of his lips.

"Always," I replied, unable to contain the warmth that spread through me at his presence.

"I just wanted to say how proud I am of you," he said, his sincerity grounding me. "You were stunning out there. The way you spoke about your collection was beautiful. You really poured your heart into it."

"Thank you," I breathed, my heart racing at his words. "It means a lot coming from you. You've always seen me for who I really am, beneath all the layers."

He took a step closer, the energy between us crackling like static electricity. "That's because I know you, Amelia. You're more than just your designs. You're..." He hesitated, his expression shifting as if he was grappling with a weighty thought.

"What?" I urged, caught in the tension that hung in the air.

"Never mind, it's not the right moment." His eyes darted back toward the bustling crowd, and I felt the connection we shared waver slightly.

Before I could press him, Clara appeared, her enthusiasm a palpable force. "Amelia! They're ready for you again! The editor from Style Savvy wants to do a feature piece on your collection!"

Ethan's gaze remained fixed on me, the unspoken words still hanging between us like an unfinished melody. "I guess you have to go," he said, his tone a mixture of pride and something I couldn't quite place.

I nodded, feeling a bittersweet pang in my chest. "I'll catch up with you in a bit?"

"Sure," he replied, but there was a hint of distance in his smile, like he was already retreating into his thoughts.

With a final glance, I turned to face the reporters again, but my mind was still tangled in the moment we had shared. I answered questions about my creative process and what lay ahead for me, yet my heart was drumming to a different beat, a rhythm underscored by Ethan's enigmatic presence.

The rest of the evening unfolded in a blur of flashing lights and buzzing conversations. I moved from one group to another, a whirlwind of fashion and fervor, but underneath it all, I felt a disquieting thread weaving through the tapestry of my night. Ethan's smile lingered in my mind, yet the weight of what remained unspoken hovered just beyond my reach.

As the show drew to a close and the last applause echoed in the boutique, I found myself searching for him amidst the throng of faces. But the crowd shifted, and in the frenzy, he slipped away, leaving me standing there, wrapped in the afterglow of my success and the lingering questions that swirled like confetti in the air. The night was still young, yet as I stared into the distance, I couldn't shake the feeling that this moment was a crossroads—one path leading to the bright lights of my aspirations, the other winding toward the heart of a connection that might change everything.

The afterglow of the fashion show clung to me like the faint scent of jasmine in the air, sweet yet bittersweet, reminding me of both triumph and the gaping void where Ethan had stood. I was caught in the vibrant chaos of congratulatory hugs and eager journalists, their questions swirling around me like confetti in a windstorm. Yet, despite the celebration, I felt a nagging emptiness that no amount of applause could fill.

"Amelia! That was legendary!" Clara's voice cut through the noise as she embraced me fiercely, her enthusiasm infectious. "You are a rock star. I mean, if there's any justice in the world, the fashion gods will be showering you with offers in no time."

"Thanks, Clara. I just wish I could shake this feeling that something is missing." I let out a small laugh, but the truth hung in the air like an unfinished note.

"Well, you know what they say about missing pieces. Sometimes they just need a little time to reveal themselves," she said, her eyes sparkling with a knowing light.

Before I could respond, Jason sauntered back into my periphery, his easy confidence a stark contrast to the heaviness I felt. "What's this? The queen of the runway is feeling blue? Someone should bring her a crown!" He grinned, leaning against a wall, a casual air about him that felt both comforting and familiar.

"Crown? More like a tiara made of stress and sequins," I shot back, forcing a laugh. "You'd think after such a successful night, I'd be over the moon."

"Maybe it's because you're too busy gazing at the stars to see the fireworks right in front of you," he replied, his tone playful yet somehow probing.

"What are you, my therapist now?" I teased, but my heart thudded at the truth behind his words. "Because I definitely need one."

"I'm not licensed, but I could take a crack at it. How about a nightcap instead?" He winked, and my pulse quickened at the thought. The idea of sharing a quiet moment with him felt both enticing and daunting.

"I don't think I'm in the right headspace for drinks right now, but thanks," I said, scanning the room, hoping to catch a glimpse of Ethan, but he was nowhere in sight.

Jason's eyes narrowed slightly, as if sensing my distraction. "Fair enough. Just remember, you don't have to carry the world on your shoulders alone, you know. I'm here."

"Thanks. That's... reassuring," I murmured, still preoccupied with the absence of Ethan. There was a comfort in Jason's presence, a sense of familiarity I had always cherished, but tonight, it felt like an incomplete puzzle.

The crowd began to thin, the excitement fading like the last notes of a song. Clara was swept away by a group of admirers, leaving me standing amid the remnants of a night that had once sparkled with promise. I wandered toward the back of the boutique, where the soft hum of conversation faded, and the world outside blurred into the background.

As I stepped outside, the cool night air wrapped around me like a balm, easing the weight of expectations. The stars twinkled overhead, a glittering reminder of all the possibilities that lay ahead. But my heart ached with the absence of Ethan, and I felt like a moth drawn to a flame, desperately seeking the warmth of his understanding.

I leaned against the wall, the brick cool beneath my palms, and let my mind wander. What had he wanted to say before Clara interrupted? That one moment felt heavy with unspoken words, and the uncertainty of it gnawed at me like a persistent itch.

Just as I was about to head back inside, I caught sight of him across the street. Ethan stood under the streetlight, his silhouette framed by the glow, his expression a mix of determination and hesitation. My heart leapt as I made my way toward him, weaving through the scattered patrons lingering outside the boutique, the weight of the moment electrifying.

"Ethan!" I called, my voice cutting through the cool night air. He turned, and the surprise in his eyes ignited a flicker of hope within me.

"Amelia," he said, stepping forward. "I thought I'd lost you in the chaos. You were incredible tonight."

"Thank you. But... I feel like we left something unfinished back there," I admitted, my heart racing. "You were about to say something, and then—"

"Yeah, I know. I didn't want to interrupt your moment," he replied, running a hand through his hair, the gesture revealing a vulnerability I had never seen before.

"Is it that you don't believe I can handle it? Because I'm not just a designer—I'm a whole person, and if I can walk that runway, I can certainly handle a conversation with you."

"Amelia," he began, his gaze steady and intense, "it's not that at all. It's just..." His voice trailed off, and for a moment, the world around us faded into silence.

"What?" I pressed, the tension in the air palpable.

He shifted, glancing around as if ensuring no one else was listening. "I care about you. A lot. But I'm not sure if you feel the same way or if you're just caught up in the moment."

"Of course I feel something! You know I do! I'm just—" I stumbled over my words, my frustration bubbling to the surface. "I'm trying to figure out how to navigate this, to balance my feelings for you with everything else that's happening in my life right now."

Ethan stepped closer, his expression earnest. "Then let's figure it out together. I want to be there for you, Amelia. Not just as a friend or a support system, but as something more."

The intensity of his words sent a thrill coursing through me, yet doubt crept in. "But what if I can't balance it all? What if I lose everything?"

"Life is unpredictable. All we can do is take the next step and trust it will lead us somewhere worthwhile," he said softly, reaching for my hand.

I could feel the heat radiating from him, the connection that had always been there but was now so much more potent. "What if I say yes? What if I decide to let you in?"

"Then I'd say we're on the brink of something beautiful."

Before I could respond, a commotion erupted from the boutique. A figure burst through the doors, breathless and frantic, cutting through our moment like a knife. "Amelia! Clara needs you inside! There's been a problem!"

Panic jolted through me, a stark reminder that life often had other plans. "What happened?" I asked, heart racing.

"There's an issue with one of the models, and Clara can't handle it alone!"

Without another word, I glanced at Ethan, his eyes reflecting a mix of concern and determination. "We'll talk later?" I urged, needing to hold on to that spark before it faded into the chaos.

"Absolutely. I'll be right here," he promised, his voice steady even as the urgency of the situation pulled us apart.

I dashed back toward the boutique, adrenaline flooding my system as the vibrant world around me shifted once more. The night had been filled with glimmers of hope and promise, but as I stepped back into the storm of voices and frantic movements, I couldn't shake the feeling that the real show was just beginning.

What awaited me inside felt like a tempest brewing, and deep down, I sensed that the ties binding me to this moment—and to Ethan—were about to be tested in ways I could never have anticipated.

Chapter 12: The Aftermath

The applause still echoed in my ears, a sweet symphony of approval that felt like a warm embrace. The stage lights had dimmed, the crowd dispersed, but the thrill of the show lingered in the air, thick with the scent of fresh paint and the remnants of stage smoke. I should have been soaring, untouchable, a queen on her throne, but the high of the moment began to wane, replaced by an unsettling sense of uncertainty that wrapped around me like a heavy cloak.

The days that followed the performance blurred together, each one an echo of the last. I found myself standing in front of the mirror, analyzing every inch of my reflection as if the woman staring back could offer clarity. My hair, still styled from the show, framed my face like a crown, and my eyes sparkled with the afterglow of accomplishment. Yet beneath that spark, there was a flicker of doubt, a tiny whisper that called my confidence into question.

It was during one of these reflections that Jason decided to reappear in my life like a ghost from a past I thought I had exorcised. His knock on the door was tentative, as if he feared the strength of the door he once believed he could walk through without consequence. When I opened it, there he stood, a lopsided grin plastered on his face, the same one that once made my heart race and my resolve crumble.

"Hey, stranger," he said, his voice smooth as honey, yet tinged with an unmistakable edge of arrogance that made my skin crawl.

"Jason." My tone was curt, the way you might greet a car alarm that had gone off in the middle of the night. "What do you want?"

His eyes flicked to the sketchbooks scattered on my living room table, the vibrant colors bleeding into one another, much like my emotions. "I saw the show. You were amazing. I mean, seriously, you stole the spotlight. I've never seen you shine like that."

"Thanks," I said, crossing my arms defensively. "But I'm not interested in revisiting the past."

He stepped inside, uninvited, and I felt a twinge of panic at the sudden intimacy of his presence. The familiar scent of his cologne, a mix of sandalwood and musk, enveloped me, dragging up memories of late-night talks and laughter that felt like a distant dream. It was a scent I had thought I could forget, but now it pulled me back into the tide of history we had shared.

"Is that what you really want?" he asked, tilting his head, that same lopsided grin transforming into something more genuine. "To forget everything we had?"

I wanted to tell him it was simple—easy, even—but my heart betrayed me. It fluttered in my chest, reminding me of our midnight drives and lazy Sunday mornings wrapped in sheets, two souls tangled together in a world that felt like ours alone. But the truth was more complicated than I wanted to admit.

"I don't know, Jason. Maybe it's easier this way," I said, my voice softer than I intended, each word a thread of vulnerability unraveling before me.

"Easier isn't always better. You should know that by now."

The tension in the room thickened, a palpable force that clung to us like the remnants of a summer storm. I could feel his eyes studying me, searching for a crack in my facade, but all he'd find was the reflection of my own confusion. Guilt washed over me as I thought of Ethan, who had been my anchor in this turbulent sea of emotions. He didn't deserve to be caught in the crossfire of my past, yet here I was, staring into the eyes of the very man who had left me adrift.

"Do you even care?" I challenged, the words slipping out before I could reel them back in. "About how this affects me? How I'm trying to move on?"

"Of course, I care," he replied, his expression earnest. "I wouldn't have come back if I didn't. I'm just trying to understand what happened, why you pushed me away."

I turned away, anger flaring like a match struck in the dark. "You really want to know? You left. You chose to walk away when things got hard. I had to figure things out on my own."

The air crackled between us, a storm gathering strength as my emotions collided. His silence hung in the room like a heavy curtain, and for a moment, I wondered if he truly understood the gravity of his choices.

"Maybe I was stupid," he finally said, his voice low. "Maybe I didn't appreciate you the way I should have. But I want a second chance. I want to make things right."

A second chance. The words fluttered in the air, and I grasped for them, but they slipped through my fingers like sand. My heart raced as I grappled with the implications. Did I even want a second chance? I could feel the guilt gnawing at me, a relentless tide threatening to drown the remnants of my joy.

Just then, my sketchbook caught my eye, its pages filled with color and chaos, a reflection of the turmoil within me. I stepped away from Jason, the need to create pulling me toward it like a moth to a flame.

"You know what?" I said, turning to face him, the resolve creeping back into my voice. "I need to process this. I need to think."

"Think?" he echoed, and I saw the flicker of hurt flash across his face. "You can't just run away every time things get complicated."

"I'm not running away. I'm trying to figure out what I really want," I shot back, frustration bubbling to the surface.

"Then let me help you."

His insistence filled the room, and for a moment, I felt my resolve waver. But there was a flicker in my mind—Ethan's laughter, his support, the way he listened without judgment. I couldn't deny that he had become my refuge, a safe harbor in a storm of feelings.

"I can't," I whispered, my voice barely audible over the chaos swirling in my head. "I can't keep juggling all these emotions."

Jason's expression shifted, a mixture of anger and sadness playing across his features. "So, what then? You're just going to walk away again?"

The question hung in the air, sharp and piercing, and I could feel my heart thudding in my chest, each beat a reminder of the decisions ahead of me. But amidst the turmoil, a flicker of clarity broke through. I couldn't afford to let guilt or nostalgia dictate my choices. I needed to confront my feelings honestly, not just for Jason, but for myself.

"Maybe," I said finally, a note of determination threading through my voice. "Maybe it's time I stop running and start facing the truth."

With that, I turned back to my sketchbook, the pages open to a fresh canvas, where I could pour my confusion into something tangible. As I began to draw, the colors swirling and mixing on the page, I felt a sense of calm washing over me. I might not have all the answers, but in this moment, I knew one thing for sure: I was ready to confront the tangled mess of my heart, to untangle the threads of my past and figure out how to weave a future that truly belonged to me.

As I filled the page with swirls of color, the world outside faded, leaving only the rhythmic scratching of my pencil against the paper. Each stroke was cathartic, a release of the emotions swirling within me like a storm. My thoughts drifted, unfurling like ribbons in the breeze, intertwining my past with my present. Jason's presence lingered in the back of my mind, an echo of laughter and heartache, while Ethan's unwavering support became a lifeline I clung to, grounding me as I navigated this chaotic terrain.

My apartment was awash in the soft glow of afternoon light, the sun filtering through the sheer curtains, casting playful shadows across my sketches. I leaned into the familiar comfort of my creative space, the clutter of my life sprawled around me—a mix of unfinished projects and half-formed ideas, each one a testament to my journey. But as I lost myself in my art, I couldn't escape the weight of Jason's return, the uncertainty it introduced into my carefully constructed world.

Suddenly, the doorbell chimed, jolting me from my reverie. I blinked, surprised at the abrupt interruption, my heart quickening in response. Hadn't I just resolved to push everyone away? With trepidation, I set my pencil down and padded over to the door, each step echoing my growing anxiety.

When I opened it, I was met with a face I hadn't expected. Standing there, a bundle of flowers in hand and a sheepish smile adorning his face, was Ethan. The moment felt suspended in time, as if the universe had conspired to throw my tangled emotions into sharper relief.

"Surprise!" he beamed, holding out the flowers like an offering. The vibrant blooms were a kaleidoscope of colors—yellows, pinks, and whites—all nestled together, their fragrance wafting into the air and wrapping around me like a warm hug. "I thought you might need a pick-me-up after all the excitement."

"Ethan, you didn't have to—" I began, but my words faltered as I took the bouquet. The blooms were alive with energy, much like the feelings he stirred within me.

He stepped inside, brushing past me with that comfortable ease that made my heart race. "I had a feeling you might be lost in your head right now. I figured flowers could help remind you of the beauty in the chaos."

I chuckled softly, the tension in my shoulders easing as I arranged the flowers in a vase. "Is that your secret weapon? Flowers and charm?"

"Only the best tactics for tackling emotional turmoil." He flashed a grin that could light up the darkest corners of my confusion. "Besides, I've seen you when you're lost in your thoughts. It's like watching a deer caught in headlights—adorable but a little concerning."

"Adorable?" I raised an eyebrow, playfully challenging him. "Is that really how you see me?"

"Absolutely. It's your natural state—equal parts bewilderment and brilliance." He leaned against the kitchen counter, arms crossed, watching me with an intensity that sent butterflies fluttering in my stomach.

A comfortable silence settled between us, filled with unspoken words and lingering glances. I knew what I felt for Ethan went beyond friendship. His presence anchored me, offering a steadiness I hadn't realized I craved. But the guilt from my unresolved feelings for Jason clawed at the edges of my consciousness, threatening to ruin this moment.

"Have you had a chance to think about what we talked about?" Ethan's voice broke through my thoughts, his expression shifting from playful to serious.

I hesitated, the knot in my stomach tightening. "You mean the possibility of...us?" I gestured vaguely, uncertain how to frame the enormity of my feelings.

He nodded, his gaze unwavering. "Yeah. I just want to know if you're open to it. I care about you, and I'm not afraid to say that."

His honesty made my heart swell and ache simultaneously. How could he make it sound so simple when my feelings felt like a tangled web? "It's complicated, Ethan. I've been through so much, and now with Jason back, it's like I'm being pulled in two directions."

"Then let's untangle it together," he suggested, stepping closer, his warmth wrapping around me like a cozy blanket. "You don't have to figure it all out alone."

I stared into his eyes, a pool of understanding and support. "I wish it were that easy. But it feels like I'm on a tightrope, balancing my past with my present, and every step is a risk."

"Life is full of risks. You can't let fear dictate your happiness." His words were gentle but firm, as if he was reaching deep into my soul, trying to anchor me to something solid.

"I don't want to hurt anyone," I admitted, the vulnerability in my voice palpable.

"Sometimes, we have to make tough choices, even if it means hurting someone we care about," he replied. "But you owe it to yourself to find out what truly makes you happy. Isn't that worth the risk?"

My breath caught in my throat as I considered his words. There was something undeniably intoxicating about the way he made me feel, like I was seen and valued in a way I had never experienced before. Yet, there was Jason, a ghost of my past who threatened to stir up all the old emotions I thought I had buried.

Ethan reached for my hand, his touch electric and grounding all at once. "What if we take it slow? No pressure, just getting to know each other in this new light?"

"Slow sounds...nice," I agreed, feeling a flicker of hope ignite within me. "I'd like that."

Just as I began to smile at the prospect of moving forward, my phone buzzed violently on the counter, shattering the moment. I snatched it up, the screen flashing Jason's name, and a wave of trepidation washed over me.

"I should probably—" I started, but Ethan's expression shifted, a mixture of amusement and curiosity dancing in his eyes.

"Want me to answer it for you?" he teased, raising an eyebrow playfully.

"Very funny," I replied, suppressing a smile. But the truth was, I was tempted. "Maybe I should just ignore it."

"Or you could face it head-on," he suggested, a sly smile creeping across his face. "You can't let him keep haunting you. Just answer it and see what he wants."

With a sigh, I pressed the green button, bracing myself as I held the phone to my ear. "Jason?"

"Hey, I was wondering if we could talk. I feel like we left things unresolved," his voice came through, smooth yet persistent, a reminder of the unresolved tension that still hung between us.

"I'm busy right now," I replied, glancing at Ethan, who was watching me with a knowing look.

"Busy? Or avoiding?" he challenged, and I felt a flash of irritation.

"Maybe a little of both," I admitted reluctantly.

"Can we meet? I need to explain myself, to clear the air," Jason pressed, his tone a mix of desperation and charm that had once lured me in effortlessly.

I hesitated, glancing at Ethan, whose gaze held an intensity that made my heart race. This was a moment of decision, a crossroads where I could either cling to the past or step boldly into the unknown future.

"I'll think about it," I finally said, cutting the conversation short. I hung up, the weight of my decision hanging in the air.

Ethan's eyes held a glimmer of admiration. "That was bold."

"I can't let him pull me back in. I need to figure this out," I said, my heart pounding in my chest.

"Exactly. Let's focus on what's in front of us." His hand found mine again, and this time, the connection felt electric, a promise of new beginnings.

With a sense of renewed determination, I looked into Ethan's eyes, ready to embrace the possibility of something beautiful and true.

The sun dipped below the horizon, casting a golden hue across my cluttered living room, where art supplies lay strewn about like remnants of a creative battlefield. Ethan had left an indelible mark on my heart, and as I sat there with my sketchbook open, I felt the weight of his presence lingering, filling the space with an unfamiliar warmth. The initial thrill of possibility that sparked between us ignited a fire I had forgotten existed.

I flipped through the pages, lost in the vibrant colors and chaotic designs that had poured out of me during my moments of uncertainty. Each stroke of my pencil was a step away from the emotional tug-of-war that Jason had reignited, and the more I drew, the clearer the lines of my heart began to take shape. The freedom to create became my solace, the only thing that could drown out the noise of my swirling thoughts.

The sound of my phone buzzing on the table broke the silence, dragging me back from my creative reverie. I picked it up, half-expecting another attempt from Jason, but the screen flashed Ethan's name. My heart did a little flip as I answered, an unexpected giddiness bubbling up inside me.

"Hey," he said, his voice a rich blend of warmth and mischief. "I was thinking we could do something spontaneous. How do you feel about a late-night ice cream run?"

"Is it even appropriate to eat ice cream this late?" I teased, unable to suppress my smile. "What will the neighbors think?"

"They'll think we're two adults making questionable life choices, and they'd be right. What do you say?"

I considered it for a moment, glancing at the disarray of my apartment, but the idea of stepping out into the night with Ethan, even for something as simple as ice cream, felt like the kind of adventure I desperately needed. "Alright, I'm in. But if we run into anyone I know, you're going to have to explain the whole 'adults making questionable choices' thing."

"Deal," he laughed, the sound bright and infectious. "I'll pick you up in ten."

The brief anticipation of our impromptu outing sent a flutter through me, a mix of excitement and nerves as I threw on a light jacket, my heart racing with the promise of laughter and shared secrets. The night felt electric, the air charged with possibility as I stepped outside to wait for him.

When his car pulled up, the glow of the headlights illuminated the street, and I could see him leaning against the driver's side window, that same charming grin spread across his face. "Ready for the best ice cream of your life?" he called, his eyes twinkling in the light.

"Only if you're paying!" I shot back, unable to resist the playful banter.

"Please, you think I'm not generous with my ice cream funds?" he said, feigning offense as I climbed into the passenger seat.

The drive was filled with light-hearted chatter, the kind that makes time fly. I reveled in the ease of our conversation, the way he made me feel at home even when the destination was still a mystery. As we drove through the city, the neon lights flickered past us like a cascade of dreams, illuminating the possibilities that lay ahead.

Ethan pulled into a quaint little ice cream shop, a hidden gem adorned with colorful murals and glowing string lights. "This place is legendary," he declared, hopping out of the car before I could even unbuckle my seatbelt.

The sweet aroma of waffle cones filled the air as we stepped inside, and I could feel my taste buds dancing in anticipation. A chalkboard behind the counter boasted an array of flavors that made my mouth water—lavender honey, cookie dough explosion, and the ever-mysterious midnight mint.

"I'm getting the lavender honey," Ethan announced, his eyes gleaming. "It's like eating a garden."

"Sounds fancy. I think I'll go for the cookie dough explosion," I replied, chuckling as I read the flavor name aloud. "Because who doesn't want an explosion in their mouth?"

We ordered our cones, and as we stepped outside to enjoy them, the cool night air felt refreshing against my skin. We found a small bench nearby, where the city's sounds faded into the background, allowing our conversation to flourish.

"Okay, so what's your go-to comfort food?" Ethan asked, licking his ice cream thoughtfully, his eyes narrowing as he pondered the question.

"Comfort food?" I mirrored, savoring the rich cookie dough flavor. "Definitely mac and cheese. There's something magical about a bowl of it after a long day."

"An excellent choice. I would have expected you to say something more sophisticated," he teased.

"Sophisticated is overrated!" I laughed. "Sometimes, you just need carbs to heal the soul."

Our laughter echoed into the night, and as we spoke, I felt the tension begin to ease. Each story we shared brought us closer, dissolving the invisible barriers I had erected around my heart. I was beginning to see a future with him, one filled with late-night ice cream runs and silly banter.

Just as I began to lose myself in the moment, my phone buzzed again, cutting through the warmth we had cultivated. I glanced down, my heart sinking as I read Jason's name flash across the screen once more.

"Everything okay?" Ethan asked, his brow furrowing slightly as he noticed my change in demeanor.

"Just... Jason," I said, my voice tinged with frustration. "He keeps trying to get in touch. I thought I made it clear that I need space."

Ethan's expression shifted, a mixture of concern and understanding. "Do you want to answer it?"

I hesitated, glancing at the phone, the incessant buzzing feeling like a tempest stirring within me. "No, I don't want to. But I don't know how to make him stop."

"Just be honest with him," Ethan suggested gently. "You're not obligated to entertain his feelings if you're not feeling the same way."

"Easier said than done," I muttered, frustration bubbling beneath the surface.

As I stared at the phone, I felt the weight of my decisions pressing down on me. Just then, a figure emerged from the shadows, a familiar silhouette that made my stomach drop. My breath caught as Jason stepped into the light, a frown etched on his face.

"What are you doing here?" I blurted, shock washing over me as I instinctively moved closer to Ethan, whose presence felt reassuring and grounding.

"I came to talk to you," Jason replied, his voice steady but laced with an urgency that sent shivers down my spine. "I've been trying to reach you."

Ethan stiffened beside me, the atmosphere suddenly thick with tension. "Now? You chose now to come by?"

"This is between us," Jason said, his gaze darting between us, a hint of defensiveness creeping into his tone.

I felt my heart racing, the confusion and guilt mixing with anger. "You can't just show up like this. I'm not ready to talk."

"Maybe you should be," he challenged, a determined glint in his eyes.

Ethan's jaw tightened, and I could sense the conflict brewing just beneath the surface. "This isn't the time or place," he interjected, his voice low and firm.

But Jason stepped closer, ignoring Ethan's presence entirely. "You need to hear me out. I'm not giving up on us."

My heart sank, a tempest of emotions surging within me. It was happening again—an entanglement I thought I could escape had just tightened its grip, and now I was left standing at a crossroads, the weight of my past and present colliding with a force I wasn't sure I could withstand.

"Stop!" I shouted, the word bursting from me like a dam breaking under pressure. "This isn't fair to either of us. You can't expect me to just forget everything."

Jason opened his mouth to respond, but I was done listening. My pulse raced as I faced the two men who represented both my past and my future. I could feel the tension crackling in the air, a moment pregnant with uncertainty. I had to choose, but the fear of making the wrong decision threatened to paralyze me.

"I need space to think," I finally managed, my voice trembling.

As I turned away, the sounds of the night faded, leaving a deafening silence in their wake. I felt their eyes on me, the weight of their expectations hanging heavy in the air. With my heart pounding, I took a deep breath, ready to carve out my own path, even as the world around me began to spin in unexpected directions.

Chapter 13: A Thread Unraveled

The warm, earthy aroma of chamomile wafted around the quaint café where Clara and I often retreated from the tumult of our lives. Today, the familiar clatter of cups and low murmur of conversations blended into a soothing backdrop, lulling me into a state of calm that felt both fragile and comforting. I cradled the delicate porcelain cup, watching the steam spiral upwards like my swirling thoughts, hoping the tea would work its magic and help me make sense of everything.

Clara had always been my confidante, a steady presence amidst the chaos. With her curly auburn hair framing her freckled face and a smile that seemed to chase away clouds, she had an innate ability to draw out the truth hidden within me, like a skilled fisherman reeling in a stubborn catch. Today, though, her usual sparkle was dimmed by the shadows of her own burdens, a reminder that we all carried our own secrets and scars.

"I can't believe I'm even considering it," I admitted, the words slipping out with a weight I hadn't anticipated. "I've never been good at confronting people, especially Jason. It feels... impossible."

Clara leaned in, her brow furrowed with empathy. "What's impossible is pretending everything is fine when it's not. You deserve to be happy, even if that means having a tough conversation."

I took a sip of my tea, the warmth spreading through me like a comforting embrace. "But what if he doesn't take it well? What if I hurt him? He's always been so... understanding."

"Understanding can turn into complacency," Clara replied, her voice steady. "You're not a placeholder in his life, and you shouldn't be in your own."

Her words pierced through my hesitation, forcing me to acknowledge the growing distance between Jason and me. It had started small—missed calls, late-night work excuses, the way he often seemed miles away even when sitting right beside me. I had brushed it off, convinced that love would find a way to bridge any gap, but love wasn't meant to be a series of silences filled with unspoken fears and half-hearted attempts.

"Have you ever been afraid to let go?" I asked, searching Clara's eyes for an answer that might help me understand my own hesitation.

She hesitated for a moment, as if the question stirred up memories she preferred to keep buried. "More than I care to admit," she finally replied, a distant look in her eyes. "Letting go means facing the unknown, and that's terrifying. But holding on when it's already over? That's a different kind of fear, one that can suffocate you."

I leaned back in my chair, allowing her words to settle like the tea leaves swirling at the bottom of my cup. The thought of facing Jason filled me with dread, but perhaps that dread was a sign that I needed to act, not retreat. The realization was as liberating as it was terrifying.

Clara reached across the table, her hand covering mine. "You're stronger than you think. Trust yourself. And if things don't go the way you hope, you'll have me to pick up the pieces."

Her unwavering support felt like a lifeline, tugging me gently toward clarity. I couldn't keep pretending that everything was fine; it was time to confront the tangled mess of my emotions and the reality of my relationship with Jason.

"Okay," I said, my voice steadier than I felt. "I'll do it. I'll talk to him."

The decision settled in my gut, heavy yet strangely freeing, like shedding an old coat that had become too tight and scratchy. The café around us continued to bustle, the world blissfully unaware of the turmoil brewing within me. I took a deep breath, letting the scent of chamomile wrap around me like a warm blanket.

Clara grinned, her eyes sparkling with pride. "Now, that's the spirit! Just remember, you're not just saying goodbye to him; you're also saying hello to yourself. To the person you want to be."

As I stepped out of the café, the chill of the evening air rushed to greet me, invigorating and sharp. I walked down the sidewalk, the city alive around me, streetlights flickering like stars above. Every step resonated with purpose, a growing determination igniting my heart.

When I finally stood outside Jason's apartment, my heart thudded a wild rhythm against my ribs, nerves dancing in my stomach. It was a small, unassuming building, the paint peeling and the windows foggy with the warmth of life within. I had spent countless hours inside, nestled in comfort and laughter, but now it felt like a foreign territory I was about to invade.

Taking a deep breath, I rang the bell, the sound echoing ominously in the silence of the hallway. Each second stretched out like an eternity until the door finally swung open, revealing Jason with his tousled hair and those bright, hopeful eyes that had once made me melt.

"Hey! I wasn't expecting you," he said, his voice warm yet puzzled.

"Can we talk?" I managed, my voice steadier than I expected.

His brow furrowed slightly, but he stepped aside, allowing me to enter. The familiar scent of his cologne and the lingering aroma of whatever he had cooked for dinner enveloped me, pulling at my heartstrings. I hesitated at the threshold, grappling with the gravity of what lay ahead.

Jason gestured toward the couch, and I perched at the edge, feeling like I was about to dive into a pool of ice-cold water. "What's up?" he asked, his casual tone belying the tension in the room.

I opened my mouth to speak, but the words clung stubbornly to my throat. Instead, I took a moment to observe him—his relaxed posture, the way he absently ran a hand through his hair, and the flicker of concern that crossed his face when he noticed my hesitation.

It was now or never. With a swift inhale, I steadied myself, ready to unravel the thread that had bound us together for so long.

The air in Jason's living room was thick with an unspoken tension, each breath felt heavier than the last. The walls, adorned with photographs of us—smiling in sunlit parks, laughing over dinner, moments frozen in time—seemed to loom around me, reminding me of everything we once were. I glanced at Jason, who was shifting his weight from one foot to the other, his curiosity battling with the uncertainty in his eyes.

"I've been thinking," I began, the words clumsy as they tumbled out. "About us." The phrase hung in the air, weighty and profound, like a stone dropped into still water, sending ripples through our previously tranquil surface.

Jason's expression shifted, a mixture of hope and trepidation flickering across his face. "Thinking is good, right? I mean, it means you care."

I forced a smile, but inside, my heart raced like a rabbit cornered by a fox. "Yes, but it's not that simple."

"Okay..." he said, frowning slightly. "I'm listening."

"Lately, it feels like we're living parallel lives. We're together, but somehow not. You're always busy, and when we are together, it feels... different." The words spilled out in a rush, as if my mouth was trying to outrun my fear. "I miss the connection we used to have, Jason. I miss us."

He took a step back, the moment hanging between us like a thick fog. "I didn't realize you felt that way. I thought things were... fine."

"Fine is a far cry from wonderful," I replied, frustration bubbling up inside me. "I've tried to ignore it, to push it away, but it keeps coming back. I can't keep pretending everything is okay when it feels like we're two ships passing in the night."

Jason ran a hand through his hair, a gesture I knew well. It was his way of processing, of trying to find clarity in the chaos. "I thought we were just going through a phase. Work has been crazy, and I figured we'd come out of it together."

"Maybe we're not meant to come out of it together," I said, each word falling heavier than the last. "I've been feeling so lonely in this relationship, like I'm just a chapter in your book rather than a co-author. And I'm starting to wonder if we're even on the same page anymore."

His face fell, the color draining slightly as if I had pulled the rug out from under him. "So, what are you saying? That you want to end this?"

The question lingered in the air, raw and brutal, sending a chill down my spine. I had dreaded this moment, the culmination of sleepless nights and restless thoughts, but there it was, laid bare between us. "I think it might be time for us to go our separate ways," I said, my voice softer but resolute. "It hurts to say that, but I think we both know it's true."

Silence enveloped us, thick and suffocating. Jason's gaze dropped to the floor, as if searching for words in the fibers of the rug beneath his feet. "I didn't see this coming," he finally admitted, his voice barely above a whisper.

"Neither did I," I said, my heart breaking for the both of us. "But sometimes, love isn't enough to keep two people together. We've grown in different directions, and I don't think we can bridge that gap anymore."

He nodded slowly, the realization settling in like a heavy mist. "I guess I've felt it too, but I didn't want to believe it. I thought we could just fix it."

"Maybe some things can't be fixed, only accepted," I replied, surprised by the clarity in my own words. "You deserve someone who can give you everything you need, just like I deserve the same. And right now, I don't think we're that for each other."

The air grew colder as I watched the flicker of hope die in his eyes, replaced by a grim acceptance. "So, what happens now?" he asked, his voice steadier but laden with sadness.

"I think we need to let each other go," I said, my heart heavy but my mind clear. "It doesn't erase the memories, the good times we had. I'll always cherish those, but clinging to what was will only hurt us both in the long run."

Jason took a deep breath, the weight of my words settling over him. "You're right. It's just... hard to let go of someone you care about."

"I know," I said softly. "But sometimes, letting go is the kindest thing you can do for each other."

We stood in silence, the echoes of laughter and love from the past fading into an uncertain future. Finally, Jason stepped forward, closing the distance between us. "I want you to be happy, even if it's without me," he said, his eyes glistening with unshed tears.

"Thank you," I murmured, feeling the ache of loss seep deeper into my bones. "I want the same for you."

He took a step back, the air between us crackling with unfulfilled potential and unspoken farewells. "You know, we can still be friends," he offered, a hopeful glimmer breaking through the sadness.

I shook my head gently. "Maybe someday, but not right now. We need space to heal and figure out who we are without each other."

He nodded, his expression resigned but understanding. "I get it. I just... I never expected it to end like this."

"Neither did I," I replied, my voice barely above a whisper. "But sometimes endings can lead to new beginnings."

As I turned to leave, I felt the weight of my decision settle into place, a bittersweet mixture of relief and sorrow. Each step toward the door felt like a small act of rebellion against the fears that had kept me shackled for so long. The door clicked shut behind me, sealing away a chapter that had once felt like a home.

Outside, the city thrummed with life, lights twinkling like stars against the darkening sky. I breathed in deeply, the crisp air filling my lungs with a renewed sense of purpose. It felt strange to be free, yet a thrilling rush of possibilities surged through me.

As I walked, my mind wandered to Ethan. Our time together had always felt electric, a connection that pulsed with energy and laughter, yet I had hesitated to explore it fully. Now, the thought of him sent butterflies dancing in my stomach. It was time to embrace what lay ahead, to uncover the joys of newfound connections without the weight of my past holding me back.

Each step felt lighter, as if the chains of expectation had fallen away, leaving me open to the potential of what was to come. The night air kissed my cheeks, and I could almost hear the universe whispering its encouragement, reminding me that sometimes, in letting go, we truly begin to find ourselves again.

The crisp night air felt electric against my skin as I walked away from Jason's apartment, the city alive with a vibrant pulse that matched the quickening beat of my heart. I reveled in the newfound freedom coursing through me, a sensation akin to shedding a heavy coat in the midst of a stifling summer. Each step seemed to carry away the weight of what had just transpired, replacing it with anticipation that danced in my veins. I had let go of what was no longer serving me, and now I was ready to explore what could be.

My phone buzzed in my pocket, pulling me back to reality. I glanced at the screen, and a smile crept across my face. Ethan's name glowed back at me, a beacon in the swirling chaos of my thoughts. I hesitated for a moment, the remnants of my conversation with Jason still echoing in my mind, but I was determined to embrace the joy that came with new beginnings. I hit "accept," my heart racing as if I were about to dive into the deep end of a pool after standing at the edge for far too long.

"Hey! I was just thinking about you," Ethan's voice flowed through the line, warm and inviting. "How are you?"

"I'm... good, actually," I replied, the word tasting foreign yet delicious on my tongue. "I just had a pretty intense conversation."

"Oh? Do tell," he said, the teasing lilt in his tone urging me to share more.

"It was about my relationship with Jason," I confessed, the words flowing easily now, a release I hadn't realized I needed. "I finally faced the truth, and it felt like pulling off a Band-Aid. It hurt, but now it's done."

"Good for you! That takes guts," he said, and I could almost hear the grin in his voice. "So, what's next for you?"

I paused, contemplating the question. What was next? I felt a strange mix of exhilaration and trepidation as I stood at this new crossroads. "I'm not sure yet. But I feel like I'm ready to explore some new possibilities."

There was a moment of silence on the other end, and I wondered if he was processing my words or simply enjoying the sound of the city in the background. Finally, he spoke, his voice lower, almost conspiratorial. "What if we explored together?"

The suggestion hung in the air, charged and enticing. I could picture us laughing over drinks, wandering through art galleries, or sharing secrets beneath the stars. "That sounds amazing," I said, a thrill shooting through me. "What do you have in mind?"

"I know this little place that has the best tacos in the city," he replied, the enthusiasm in his voice palpable. "And after that, there's a rooftop bar with a view that will knock your socks off. How does that sound?"

I couldn't help but laugh. "Tacos and rooftop views? You really know how to woo a girl."

"Just wait until you see the sunset from up there," he teased. "You'll be utterly enchanted."

With a quick exchange of details, we agreed to meet in an hour. I found myself walking with a spring in my step, anticipation thrumming in my chest. It felt refreshing, as if I were stepping into a new life—one filled with possibilities and adventure.

As I arrived at the taco spot, the faint sound of music wafted through the air, mingling with the rich scent of spices and sizzling meats. The place was bustling, a mix of laughter and conversation enveloping me as I stepped inside. I spotted Ethan at a corner table, his presence instantly grounding and familiar. He waved, a broad smile lighting up his face, and I couldn't help but grin back.

"You made it!" he exclaimed as I approached, his eyes sparkling with mischief. "I was starting to think you'd been swept away by a taco thief."

"Only if they were made with magical ingredients," I quipped, sliding into the seat across from him. "What's the secret to these tacos, anyway? Is it love or just really good guacamole?"

"Definitely love," he said, his tone mock-serious. "The guacamole just makes it better."

We shared stories and laughter over our food, the atmosphere wrapping around us like a warm blanket. Each bite of the spicy, flavorful tacos sent a jolt of joy through me, a delicious reminder that life was meant to be savored. The conversation flowed easily, touching on everything from childhood memories to our shared love of obscure indie films. With each passing moment, I felt myself leaning into this connection, the ghost of my past relationship fading like an old photograph.

After finishing our tacos, Ethan insisted we head to the rooftop bar. "Trust me, you won't regret it," he said, his excitement infectious.

As we climbed the narrow staircase, my heart raced, both from the thrill of the night and the undeniable chemistry crackling between us.

The rooftop was a hidden gem, adorned with twinkling lights that danced against the deepening twilight. The city sprawled out before us, a glittering tapestry of life, each light a story waiting to be told. I took a deep breath, the cool air filled with laughter and the distant sounds of music, feeling utterly alive in this moment.

"Wow," I breathed, taking in the view. "This is incredible."

Ethan stepped closer, his arm brushing against mine. "Just wait until the sun sets. It's something special."

As the horizon blushed with hues of orange and pink, the moment felt almost surreal. I turned to Ethan, his expression soft yet intense, as if he were seeing the world—and me—for the first time. "I'm really glad we're doing this," I said, my voice barely above a whisper.

"Me too," he replied, his gaze steady. "It feels... right."

Just then, a loud crash shattered the serene atmosphere, drawing our attention to the street below. A delivery truck had careened into a lamppost, sending debris flying and causing chaos in the bustling street. The muffled sounds of panic erupted, and my heart raced as I peered over the edge, the reality of the city below abruptly shattering our moment.

Ethan reached for my arm, his grip firm and reassuring. "Let's go check it out," he said, his voice steadying me in the whirlwind of commotion.

As we hurried down the stairs, adrenaline coursing through my veins, I felt a rush of uncertainty. What if this night turned into something more than just a delightful adventure? What if it exposed layers I wasn't prepared to confront? I glanced at Ethan, his expression filled with determination and concern, and something deep within me stirred. Maybe I was ready for whatever chaos life had in store for me, whether it was exhilarating or frightening.

We reached the street, where people had gathered around the scene, their faces a mix of curiosity and concern. My pulse quickened, caught between the energy of the crowd and the allure of the unknown. Just as I turned to Ethan, eager to share the rush of excitement and fear, a sudden shout pierced through the air.

"Everyone, step back! Call 911!"

My heart raced as I scanned the scene, and in that moment, I spotted a figure emerging from the shadows of the chaos—a familiar silhouette that sent a shiver down my spine. It was Jason, his face contorted with distress, locking eyes with me across the throng of bodies.

The world around me faded into a blur as the realization hit, heavy and unavoidable. This night, which had begun as a promise of new beginnings, was now entwined with the past I had tried to leave behind. I took a step back, torn between the exhilarating possibilities of the future and the haunting shadows of what had just ended.

Chapter 14: The Space Between

The aroma of fresh coffee filled the air as I stepped into a hidden café, the kind you could easily miss if you weren't looking for it. The faded blue door, slightly ajar, beckoned like a whisper, and the faint chime of a bell above my head announced my arrival. Inside, mismatched furniture crowded the space, each piece with its own story, its own history. A grandmotherly armchair sat beside a sleek, modern table, creating an eclectic charm that enveloped me like a warm hug. I spotted Ethan at the far end, his head bent over a notebook, a pen dancing between his fingers as he scribbled thoughts with an intensity that made my heart flutter.

"Hey, you," I said, sliding into the chair opposite him. He looked up, a smile breaking across his face, lighting up the room more than the sun filtering through the window.

"Did you know coffee tastes better in places like this?" he asked, tapping his pen against the notebook. "I swear, it's the ambiance."

"Or maybe it's just the caffeine talking," I replied, grinning as I glanced around. The café hummed with life, laughter mingling with the soft melodies wafting from an unseen speaker.

"True," he admitted, leaning back, his relaxed posture making me feel at ease. "But this place has character, don't you think? Like each cup of coffee is brewed with a story."

I couldn't help but agree. "I love how every corner feels like a different chapter."

Ethan's eyes sparkled with mischief. "And I bet you'd read every single one."

"Guilty as charged," I laughed, allowing myself to indulge in the moment, the warmth of his presence weaving through my thoughts. I watched as he took a sip of his coffee, a momentary silence stretching between us.

"Tell me more about this book you're working on," he prompted, leaning forward, his elbows resting on the table, interest etched on his face.

"It's a bit of a mess, really," I confessed, feeling the familiar flutter of anxiety. "I'm trying to weave in themes of love and loss, but I can't quite seem to capture the emotion I want."

"Why not write about us?" he suggested, a playful glint in his eye. "You've got a front-row seat to this blossoming friendship—or romance, perhaps?"

"Ethan!" I exclaimed, my cheeks flushing. "That's too personal! What if it flops?"

"Ah, but what if it doesn't?" he countered, his tone serious yet playful. "Sometimes the best stories come from real experiences. You just have to be brave enough to write them."

His words struck a chord, resonating deep within me. As we delved into a conversation about storytelling, I couldn't shake the warmth spreading through my chest. Our friendship had grown like a delicate vine, twisting and turning, each conversation a new branch reaching for the sun.

After a few more cups of coffee, we decided to leave the cozy confines of the café. As we stepped out, the cool breeze greeted us, swirling leaves around our feet like tiny dancers. The sky overhead was painted in hues of soft gold and rose, the perfect backdrop for our stroll.

"Where to next?" I asked, a thrill of anticipation sparking in my veins.

"There's a vintage bookstore just a few blocks away. They say it's magical, filled with hidden treasures," he said, his enthusiasm contagious.

"Magic, huh? Lead the way," I replied, matching his energy, my heart light and carefree.

We wandered through the streets, each step igniting a sense of discovery. Ethan's laughter echoed against the brick walls, a melody I wanted to capture and replay in my mind. The bookstore stood like an enchanted castle, its door adorned with whimsical illustrations of characters from forgotten tales.

As we entered, the musty scent of old pages enveloped me, transporting me to a world of stories waiting to be uncovered. Shelves towered above us, crammed with dusty tomes and dog-eared paperbacks, their spines telling tales of love, adventure, and everything in between.

"Let's find the most ridiculous title," Ethan declared, his eyes twinkling with mischief.

I giggled, scanning the shelves. "How about 'The Secret Life of Socks'?" I suggested, pulling out a book with a cover that looked like it had seen better days.

"Classic," he said, nodding in mock seriousness. "I hear it's a gripping tale."

"Must be a real page-turner," I quipped, enjoying the easy banter that flowed between us.

As we continued our playful quest, I felt an undeniable connection growing. Each laugh, each shared glance, wrapped us tighter in an invisible thread. Yet, lurking beneath the surface was a gnawing uncertainty. The weight of our budding romance felt precarious, like a house of cards teetering on the edge of a table, ready to collapse with the slightest breeze.

Ethan's gaze shifted to a small, tucked-away section labeled "Local Authors." My heart quickened. "You should check this out," he said, motioning toward a shelf filled with names that felt familiar yet distant. "You could be here one day."

"Maybe," I replied, my voice barely above a whisper. The thought filled me with both hope and dread. Would my stories resonate? Would they matter?

"Hey," he said softly, sensing the shift in my mood. "No matter what, I believe in you."

His words wrapped around me, grounding me in a moment where doubt threatened to drown me. As we left the bookstore, a promise lingered in the air—one of dreams and possibilities, of navigating the space between friendship and something more profound.

With each step into the unknown, I felt the fragile threads of our connection strengthening, weaving a tapestry of moments that sparkled with potential. The world felt alive around us, each heartbeat syncing with the rhythm of a story yet to unfold.

The sun dipped lower in the sky, casting a warm golden hue over the town, as Ethan and I strolled along the cobblestone streets. The chatter of nearby pedestrians blended with the distant sound of a busker strumming an acoustic guitar, creating a soundtrack for our little adventure. My heart raced with the exhilaration of the day, an unspoken bond between us pulsating like a gentle heartbeat.

Ethan nudged me with his shoulder. "You know, I think we might just be the best team this town has ever seen," he said, his voice light and teasing. "First, we conquer coffee, then vintage books. What's next? Local art?"

"Only if we can make fun of it," I replied, grinning. "I'm not above critiquing poorly executed landscapes."

His laughter rang out, bright and infectious. "Deal! Let's see if we can find a masterpiece that leaves us questioning the very fabric of artistic integrity."

As we meandered toward the art gallery, we playfully critiqued the eclectic collection displayed in the shop windows. One piece—a surreal canvas splashed with neon pink and green—evoked a spirited debate. "I think it's a statement on modern chaos," Ethan said, crossing his arms as he studied it intently.

"Or an artist's unfortunate misadventure with paint and a hangover," I countered, chuckling. "Either way, it's giving me a headache."

"You have a keen eye for art, you know," he said, grinning. "Not many can identify a hangover-induced masterpiece."

As we entered the gallery, the scent of fresh paint and varnish enveloped us, the walls adorned with vibrant works that seemed to pulse with life. Each piece sparked a conversation, and we drifted from one exhibit to another, our discussion evolving from jest to earnest appreciation. I watched him as he stood before a canvas depicting a turbulent sea, his brow furrowed in thought.

"It's beautiful," he said softly, his gaze lost in the waves captured in strokes of deep blue and white. "It feels alive, like it's about to swallow you whole."

"Or rescue you," I countered, stepping closer. "It's all about perspective."

He turned to me, a spark of understanding in his eyes. "Isn't that the essence of life? How we choose to see things?"

I felt a jolt, the conversation nudging at something deeper, a layer I hadn't anticipated exploring. "That's profound, Mr. Philosophical," I teased, nudging him back playfully. "Are you sure you're not just a writer masquerading as a coffee aficionado?"

He chuckled, shaking his head. "Just a guy trying to make sense of the world—one cup of coffee at a time."

As we moved through the gallery, we encountered a series of portraits that made me stop in my tracks. The eyes in one painting seemed to follow me, capturing a storm of emotion that made my chest tighten.

"What do you see?" Ethan asked, his voice barely above a whisper, as if not to break the spell.

"It's like they're pleading," I said, my breath hitching. "There's so much longing there, and yet... sadness. It's haunting."

He stepped closer, studying the piece as if it were a riddle begging to be solved. "I see it too. It's like the artist poured their heart into it, leaving their pain bare for the world to see."

The weight of his words settled between us, drawing a delicate thread of vulnerability. In that moment, the gallery felt like a sanctuary where we could expose our raw emotions without fear of judgment.

"Maybe that's what art is meant to do," I said softly, turning to him. "To connect us, to remind us we're not alone in our struggles."

"Exactly," he said, meeting my gaze. "And maybe that's what we're doing too—connecting over coffee, books, and this strange thing called friendship."

A gentle silence enveloped us, and I realized how much I cherished these moments. With each shared laugh and heartfelt conversation, the walls I'd built around myself began to crack. Yet, the lingering doubts about our fragile relationship loomed in the background, threatening to dampen my spirit.

"Let's find something lighter," I suggested, steering us away from the depths of the portraits. "I need a palate cleanser after that emotional rollercoaster."

Ethan laughed, his eyes brightening. "Agreed! How about a painting of a cat doing yoga? I hear those are all the rage."

"Now that," I replied, "I can get behind. Cat yoga sounds like a masterpiece in the making."

As we wandered deeper into the gallery, we stumbled upon a series of whimsical landscapes—vibrant colors, playful brushstrokes, and scenes that seemed to dance across the canvas. I pointed to one that depicted a field of wildflowers, swaying under a cartoonish sun. "This feels like a slice of happiness," I said, a genuine smile spreading across my face.

"Now that's a mood," Ethan said, mirroring my expression. "I'd hang that in my living room just to remind me to embrace the lighter side of life."

"You? Embracing anything lighter than your usual philosophical musings? I'm skeptical," I teased, raising an eyebrow.

"Hey! I have layers, you know. Just like an onion. Or a parfait," he replied, mock indignation in his voice. "There's more to me than deep thoughts and coffee preferences."

"You do make a compelling case," I said, trying to suppress my laughter. "But I reserve the right to call you out on your existential dread next time we discuss art."

"Fair enough," he conceded, a playful glint in his eyes.

As we exited the gallery, the sun was beginning its descent, painting the sky in hues of orange and pink. The streets buzzed with life, couples wandering hand in hand, laughter mingling with the chatter of friends gathering for the evening. I could feel the warmth of the day slipping away, leaving a gentle chill in the air.

"Let's grab dinner," Ethan suggested, a hint of mischief returning to his voice. "I know a place with the best pasta this side of town. You'll thank me later."

"Is that a challenge?" I shot back, intrigued.

"Always," he replied, flashing a confident grin that sent a thrill racing through me.

As we walked, the spaces between us began to close, our shoulders brushing against each other with a frequency that felt electrifying. The evening air was laced with the promise of something more, each glance exchanged simmering with unspoken words. I could sense it—this uncharted territory we were traversing felt precarious yet exhilarating.

My heart raced, each step bringing us closer to the edge of something beautiful yet terrifying. The unsteady ground beneath us was ripe with possibility, and I found myself caught in a whirlwind of excitement and fear. Would we survive the leap, or would the fall unravel everything we'd built?

The restaurant was a cozy haven tucked away on a quiet street, its exterior charmingly adorned with twinkling fairy lights that beckoned us closer. As we entered, the warm glow from the wooden beams and the smell of garlic and rosemary wrapped around us like a comforting embrace. Soft Italian music floated through the air, a gentle backdrop to the sound of clinking glasses and quiet laughter.

"Welcome to La Bella Notte," Ethan said, gesturing grandly as if he were unveiling a hidden gem. "Best pasta in town, and the ambiance? Perfect for a first date. Or a second, if you play your cards right."

"Look at you, all suave and sophisticated," I teased, nudging him playfully. "What's next, a tuxedo?"

He feigned shock. "I only reserve tuxedos for very special occasions—like birthdays or world-ending events. A casual dinner like this? I'd just embarrass myself."

"Good to know," I said, laughing as we settled into a corner booth. The menu boasted a delightful selection of dishes, and as I browsed, I felt an undeniable warmth spreading through me. This was more than just a meal; it felt like a celebration of our newfound connection, a shared secret tucked away from the rest of the world.

"I'm going to order the fettuccine alfredo," Ethan announced, leaning back, his confidence radiating. "You can't go wrong with creamy pasta. It's like a warm hug for your soul."

"Or a delicious excuse to avoid adulting," I quipped, my eyes dancing with mischief. "I'm torn between that and the seafood linguine. I do love a good shrimp moment."

"Then get the shrimp moment! I'll try a bite and we can have a little taste test. Teamwork makes the dream work, right?"

"Such a charmer," I replied, shaking my head with a grin. "Fine, shrimp it is. But you better deliver on that bite!"

As we placed our orders, the waiter flashed us a knowing smile, as if he sensed the spark crackling between us. I could feel the tension lingering in the air, a gentle reminder of everything that remained unsaid, a tightrope walk over a vast chasm of uncertainty.

"So, tell me more about your writing," Ethan said, leaning forward with genuine curiosity. "What's your latest obsession?"

With each word, the passion ignited within me. "I'm working on a story about a woman who discovers a hidden talent for painting when she inherits her grandmother's old art supplies. It's about finding beauty in unexpected places, overcoming doubt—"

"Wow, sounds like a metaphor for your life right now," he interrupted, his expression serious yet playful. "Are you secretly writing about us?"

"Only if you promise to read the final draft," I shot back, half-joking. "You might not like the character based on you, though."

"Oh? Why's that?"

"Let's just say he's prone to excessive philosophizing and has a habit of disappearing at the most inconvenient times," I replied, trying to suppress a grin.

"Hey now, that's unfair! I can be very present. Look, I'm here, in the flesh!"

"True, but are you here, mentally?" I teased, raising an eyebrow. "Sometimes you feel a little… aloof."

"Aloof? Me?" he laughed, shaking his head. "You're just trying to distract me from the fact that I'm winning this conversation."

"Winning? In what world?" I feigned offense, putting my hand to my heart dramatically.

Just then, our food arrived, steam wafting from the dishes like a fragrant invitation. I dug in, savoring the creamy sauce as it coated the pasta, every bite a testament to the chef's mastery.

"This is incredible!" I exclaimed, relishing the flavors. "I might have to come here every week just for this."

"Glad you're enjoying it," Ethan replied, focusing on his own plate. "But fair warning, the more you love it, the more likely you'll turn into a pasta snob."

"Is that so?" I asked, a playful smirk on my face. "So what's your pasta rating system?"

"I rate it on a scale of 'fabulous' to 'I'll propose to the chef.'"

"Ah, so this is at least a 'fabulous' then?"

"Oh, easily," he said, raising an eyebrow. "But it could become a 'chef proposal' if it keeps up this level of deliciousness."

We bantered back and forth, laughter echoing around our little corner. But beneath the lightheartedness, an undercurrent of tension tugged at me, reminding me of the thin line we were walking. Each shared laugh drew me closer to him, but the deeper we ventured into our connection, the more I felt the stakes rising.

After dinner, as we stepped back into the cool night air, a sudden chill swept through me, more than just the temperature. The stars twinkled above, distant and mysterious, and for a moment, I felt both exhilarated and anxious.

"Want to go for a walk?" Ethan asked, tilting his head towards the nearby park.

"Sure, but no more philosophical discussions. I can only handle so much depth in one night," I replied, trying to sound nonchalant, even as my heart raced at the thought of being alone with him.

"Deal. Let's keep it light," he said, matching my pace as we strolled along the tree-lined path. The soft crunch of leaves underfoot echoed in the stillness, a soothing rhythm that enveloped us.

"What if I asked you a serious question?" he asked after a moment, the tone of his voice shifting.

"Okay, hit me," I said, my pulse quickening.

"Where do you see this going?"

My breath caught in my throat. The weight of his question hung heavy in the air, and for a heartbeat, the world around us faded away. I wanted to answer, to share the wild hopes swirling in my heart, but the fear of vulnerability gripped me.

"I..." I began, my voice faltering.

Just then, a flash of movement caught my eye—a figure emerging from the shadows at the edge of the park. A man, his face obscured, took a few steps toward us, his posture rigid. My stomach tightened, an instinctive fear surging through me.

"Ethan, do you see that?" I whispered, my heart racing as the figure approached.

He turned, his brow furrowing as he noticed the stranger. "Yeah, I see him. Stay close to me."

The man drew closer, the moonlight revealing a tense expression, and I felt the air shift, charged with an energy that sent a shiver down my spine. My heart pounded in my chest, the looming uncertainty swallowing the warmth of the evening whole.

"What do you want?" Ethan called out, his voice steady yet laced with caution.

The man paused, a hint of something unreadable in his eyes. "I need to talk to you," he said, his voice low and gravelly.

A chill crept up my spine as the words hung in the air, a portent of something I couldn't yet understand. My instincts screamed at me to flee, to escape the unknown that loomed before us, and I could feel the fragile thread of our evening unraveling before my eyes.

"Who are you?" I demanded, stepping slightly behind Ethan, my heart pounding louder than ever.

The man took another step forward, and everything shifted in an instant, the world tilting on its axis, leaving me teetering on the edge of something dark and unknown.

Chapter 15: Breaking Point

The air hummed with tension, a static electricity crackling just beneath the surface of my carefully constructed world. I stood in front of the mirror, fixing the loose strands of hair that seemed intent on framing my face like a chaotic halo. My reflection showed a woman who had clawed her way back from the brink, who had learned to take up space and stand tall, yet the memory of who I used to be lingered like an unwelcome ghost. Just as I thought I'd exorcised those demons, the door swung open, and in walked Julian, a tempest in a tailored suit.

"Surprise, darling!" he exclaimed, his voice a silky baritone that was both infuriating and intoxicating. The smile he wore was equal parts charming and cocky, the kind that had once made me feel special and now felt like a slap to the face. "Didn't expect to see me, did you?"

I pivoted slowly, arms crossing defensively over my chest. "What are you doing here, Julian?" The words tumbled from my mouth, coated in disbelief and something like dread. My heart raced—not with excitement, but with a visceral instinct to protect what I'd built since he had last barged into my life, leaving wreckage in his wake.

"Business, mostly," he replied, his eyes glimmering with mischief. "But I'd be lying if I said I wasn't hoping to see you." His gaze lingered too long, drawing me back into memories that had faded but never disappeared. The intoxicating blend of ambition and charm he carried wrapped around him like a well-fitted coat, reminding me of summer nights spent chasing dreams that always felt just out of reach.

"Business," I echoed, raising an eyebrow. "And I suppose it has nothing to do with the fact that I'm finally happy without you?"

"Ah, happiness. A slippery thing, isn't it?" He chuckled, but there was an edge to his laughter, a challenge that made my skin prickle. "Besides, you can't expect me to believe that. We both know I was the reason for most of those happy moments."

I fought the urge to roll my eyes, a gesture that would have made me seem less mature than I'd fought so hard to be. Instead, I allowed the corners of my mouth to curve into a half-smile, feigning nonchalance. "I think you're confusing happy with 'what could have been.' There's a big difference."

Before he could respond, the door swung open again, and in walked Ethan. He was everything I needed, a steady force that balanced out the chaotic whirlwind that was Julian. The warmth of his presence was like sunlight breaking through a gloomy sky. But as he stepped into the room, I could see the shift in his expression—the way his brows knitted together, creating lines of tension that hadn't been there a moment before.

"Julian," Ethan said, his tone even but laced with an underlying current that crackled with possessiveness. "Didn't know you were back in town."

The way Ethan's jaw tightened was not lost on me. I could feel the air grow thick with unspoken words, the temperature of the room rising as I desperately searched for a way to navigate this minefield I hadn't anticipated. "Just catching up with an old friend," I offered, my voice almost a whisper. But the way Ethan's gaze darted between us felt like a countdown to an explosion.

"Right," Julian said, a grin spreading across his face that sent a chill down my spine. "Your 'old friend' is back to shake things up. I was just telling her how I've missed our late-night brainstorming sessions."

Ethan's eyes narrowed, the depths of his anger simmering beneath a calm facade. "Sounds like you have quite the agenda." His voice was low, barely above a murmur, but I could hear the warning woven into it. I needed to defuse this before it spiraled out of control.

"Julian's here to launch his line," I interjected, forcing a casualness that felt so very forced. "He's looking for inspiration, and I just happen to be one of the best minds in the industry."

Ethan crossed his arms, an unmistakable protective gesture that sent a jolt of both comfort and anxiety through me. "Inspiration? Or a distraction?" His tone was sharp, cutting through the air with the precision of a knife.

"Why can't it be both?" Julian quipped, leaning back casually, as if he had all the time in the world. "You know, sometimes the best ideas come from unexpected encounters. Isn't that right, Harper?" His gaze locked onto mine, the challenge flickering in his eyes.

I took a deep breath, feeling the weight of both men's attention like a spotlight blazing down. I needed to show that I was strong enough to withstand this storm. "Unexpected encounters can lead to some pretty awful ideas too," I replied, attempting to inject a lightness into my voice, though my heart thudded wildly. "Like the time you thought we could sell beach sand as 'exotic' in winter. Remember that?"

Ethan smirked, the tension easing just a fraction, and for a moment, I felt like I could juggle both men, keeping them at bay with wit and a well-timed memory. But Julian wasn't done yet.

"Is that how you see me now? As a memory?" He leaned forward, his expression shifting from playful to something more earnest, and I felt my resolve falter. "I don't want to be just a memory, Harper. I want to be part of your future."

A knot twisted in my stomach, an emotional tug-of-war threatening to unravel the careful threads I'd woven since he'd left. But the promise of a future with Ethan shimmered brightly in my mind, a beacon of everything I'd fought for. I had to choose.

"Julian," I began, my voice steady but my heart racing, "the past is the past for a reason. I'm not that girl anymore."

Ethan's expression softened at my words, but Julian wasn't backing down. "Maybe not, but what if you could have the best of both worlds?" His charm, that insufferable charisma, wrapped around me like a warm blanket, but I knew it was a mirage.

"No," I said firmly, stepping back from the emotional ledge I could feel myself teetering on. "I can't go back to the way things were. I've worked too hard to build something new."

As the silence stretched between us, I realized that I was at a breaking point, caught between the shimmering past and a hopeful future that felt fragile but real. I glanced at Ethan, who stood resolute, a fortress in the storm, and in that moment, I made my choice.

The conversation hung heavy in the air, like the oppressive heat before a summer storm. I could feel Ethan's gaze piercing through me, a mix of concern and confusion swirling behind those deep brown eyes. I had just declared my allegiance to the present, but Julian, ever the opportunist, wasn't about to let that slip away without a fight.

"Come on, Harper. You can't honestly tell me you're happier now than when we were together," Julian taunted, leaning in slightly, his voice dropping to a conspiratorial whisper, as if sharing a delicious secret. The faint scent of his cologne wafted toward me, a bittersweet reminder of late nights filled with ambition and reckless dreams.

Ethan's jaw clenched tighter, the muscles there working like a clock winding up for a strike. "Actually, I can," he countered, his tone flat, devoid of the warmth he usually reserved for me. "Happiness isn't measured in late-night brainstorming sessions or flashy business ideas, Julian." The emphasis on the word "business" sent a chill through the room, reminding me of all the ways we had danced around our shared history.

"Maybe," Julian replied, shrugging as though the exchange was just a casual debate. "But you can't deny we had something special, something... electric."

"Electricity can spark fires," I retorted, crossing my arms, but the confidence in my voice faltered. I was fighting a battle I hadn't prepared for, my instincts clashing with the remnants of old feelings.

Ethan stepped closer, grounding me with his presence. "What you had was a distraction, Julian. Just like you are now." The words rolled off his tongue like a sharp-edged compliment, cutting through the tension thickening the air.

"I see you've become quite the protector," Julian shot back, a smirk playing on his lips. "It's cute, really."

I shifted uncomfortably between them, acutely aware of the way my heart raced, torn between nostalgia and the visceral need to protect my new beginning. "This isn't helping," I said, my voice rising slightly. "We're not kids anymore, Julian. I've moved on."

Julian's expression shifted, the charming facade cracking ever so slightly. "Moved on? Or just buried the past beneath a pile of responsibilities and a man who's not me?"

"Does it matter?" Ethan snapped, frustration evident in his tone. "She doesn't need you to validate her choices."

Julian stepped back as if struck, but I could see the fire in his eyes igniting again, fueled by the challenge. "You can't seriously think this is over, can you? You think he's really what you want?" His gaze landed on Ethan, eyes narrowing. "He's safe. But safe is boring."

"Safe is what keeps me from falling apart," I replied, surprised at the steel in my voice. "I'm not looking for fireworks, Julian. I'm looking for stability."

Julian's laughter rang out, a sharp sound that echoed through the room. "Stability? That's just code for settling."

My heart raced as the air shifted, a tension I hadn't anticipated coiling tightly around us. "You don't know anything about me now.

You can't judge my life from the sidelines." I took a deep breath, channeling my newfound resolve. "This isn't a game anymore."

"Isn't it?" Julian leaned back against the doorframe, casual but intense. "You think you can just push me away, and I'll disappear? You and I have unfinished business, Harper."

Ethan's hands balled into fists at his sides. "This isn't a negotiation. Harper made her choice."

"Choices can be swayed, my dear Ethan," Julian retorted, and I could see the glimmer of triumph in his eyes. "She's just one invitation away from remembering all the good times. Who knows? You might even become a mere footnote in her story."

I shot Ethan a glance, searching for reassurance in the depths of his gaze. There was a flicker of hurt there, a brief crack in his otherwise composed demeanor. "You know this isn't true," he said softly, but the tension lay heavy between us.

Julian stepped closer, a predatory gleam in his eyes. "You want to know the truth? She's the best thing that ever happened to me, and she'll always be that girl in the back of my mind. Always."

"Stop it!" I shouted, feeling the weight of his words like stones. "This isn't a pissing contest over who I loved more."

"Isn't it?" Julian pressed, an insistent challenge laced through his words. "You can pretend all you want, but deep down, you know what you feel."

I was drowning in the past, the way it beckoned to me, shimmering with all the allure of dreams unfulfilled. But I had clawed my way out of that darkness, fought tooth and nail to emerge whole. "I'm not that girl anymore, Julian," I insisted, my voice steadier now. "And you can't just waltz back in and expect me to revert to old habits."

Ethan's expression shifted from anger to something softer, a mixture of admiration and concern. "Harper, are you sure about this?" His voice was low, soothing, grounding me as I stood on the precipice of uncertainty.

"I am," I said, and this time, I believed it. "I've built a life I love. And I won't let you tear that down."

Julian opened his mouth to retort, but before he could unleash whatever words had been bubbling at the back of his throat, a commotion outside the window caught our attention.

"Harper! You won't believe this!" A voice called out, bright and cheerful, slicing through the tension like a hot knife through butter. It was Lily, my best friend and the embodiment of sunshine, striding into the room without a care for the storm brewing around us.

"Lily, not now," I pleaded, but her infectious energy pulled me from the brink.

She beamed at us, her enthusiasm filling the space like an explosion of color in a monochrome world. "I have news! You're going to want to hear this!"

Julian's face soured at the interruption, but I felt a rush of gratitude toward Lily. She had a talent for defusing situations with her relentless optimism.

"What is it?" I asked, unable to hide my curiosity as I stepped away from the charged atmosphere.

"The event at the gallery tomorrow night? It's going to be amazing! And guess who's headlining?" She leaned in, eyes sparkling.

"Who?" I asked, the tension easing slightly as I embraced the distraction.

"Carter! He's back in town and performing! We have to go!"

"Carter?" Julian echoed, clearly uninterested, but Ethan's interest piqued, his brows lifting ever so slightly.

"Yes! We have to support him! This could be our chance to celebrate!" She grabbed my hand, pulling me toward the door. "And you know what that means—a little fun, some music, and a break from all this heaviness!"

I glanced back at Ethan, who looked both relieved and amused. "I suppose we could use a break," he said, a hint of a smile dancing on his lips.

Before I could respond, Julian interrupted, his voice dripping with sarcasm. "Oh, please, don't let me stop you. Enjoy your little soiree. Just remember, I'll still be here, waiting for you to wake up from your little fantasy."

I took a step forward, ready to fire back, but Lily interjected. "Come on, Julian! You can't bring down the vibe with your shadowy past. You need to come too! Live a little!"

"Lily," I warned, but she was relentless, her enthusiasm brighter than the noonday sun.

"I'm not going to let you sulk in your bad mood! Let's make this a night to remember!"

With her infectious energy enveloping us, I found myself caught in a whirlwind of possibilities, of laughter and light breaking through the encroaching shadows. The choice between two worlds hung like a pendulum, swinging ever so slowly as I felt the warmth of Ethan's hand brush against mine.

"Alright," I conceded, feeling a cautious smile spreading across my face. "But only if Julian promises to be good."

He scoffed, but there was an underlying respect in the way he nodded. "I'll be on my best behavior, for you."

I could feel the tension dissipate as we stepped into the unknown, leaving behind the weight of the past, if only for a night. And as we exited into the world beyond, I couldn't shake the feeling that perhaps, just perhaps, the dawn would rise brighter tomorrow.

The night unfurled with the vibrant energy of anticipation, bright lights flickering overhead like stars falling from the heavens. The gallery buzzed with life, a tapestry of art and laughter, and I felt my heart beat in rhythm with the pulse of the crowd. Lily's excitement was infectious as she tugged me through the throng, her laughter mingling with the music drifting through the air. The hum of conversation wrapped around us, filling the space with an electric buzz that promised an escape from the storm of emotions I had left behind.

"Look at this place!" she exclaimed, gesturing wildly at the artwork adorning the walls. "It's alive! It's like walking into a painting!" She spun in place, arms wide as if to embrace the world around her.

"Your enthusiasm could power a small city," I chuckled, grateful for her ability to sweep me up and distract me from the tensions I'd left simmering behind. The vibrant colors splashed across the canvas seemed to reflect the tumult in my heart, each stroke a reminder of the chaos Julian had ignited within me.

"Who needs power when we have wine?" she shot back with a grin, guiding me toward the bar nestled in a cozy corner. The bartender flashed us a bright smile as he poured generous glasses of red, the rich aroma swirling around us like a comforting embrace.

"Two glasses of your finest, please!" Lily called out, her voice cutting through the ambient noise like a cheerful siren. "Tonight is about celebration, not introspection!"

"Or the ghost of your past," I muttered, half-joking, half-worried.

"Oh, don't start," she replied, rolling her eyes with dramatic flair. "Just for tonight, let's leave the baggage behind. We'll pick it up on the way out, okay?"

"Fine," I conceded, clinking my glass against hers, the sound ringing like a bell. I took a deep sip, letting the warmth seep into my bones, temporarily numbing the lingering dread of Julian's presence.

As we wandered through the gallery, I marveled at the array of talent on display. Each piece seemed to tell its own story, vibrant and alive, capturing emotions I could hardly put into words. I felt an urge to connect with each canvas, to explore the layers hidden beneath the paint, just as I had learned to peel back the layers of my own life.

"Look at that one!" Lily exclaimed, pointing at a striking piece dominated by bold strokes of red and blue, clashing yet harmonizing in a chaotic dance. "It's so raw! I love it!"

"Reminds me of my life," I replied wryly, and we both laughed, the tension momentarily forgotten as we continued our exploration. The noise of the crowd faded into a gentle murmur, a background hum that felt almost comforting. I let myself get lost in the moment, my worries melting away, if only for a little while.

But the feeling was fleeting. As I turned toward a particularly striking painting, my heart dropped. There, across the room, stood Julian, laughing and engaging with a group of admirers, his charisma as magnetic as ever. The way he drew people in reminded me of how he used to dominate every room, how he effortlessly became the center of attention. I felt a knot form in my stomach, a mixture of anxiety and irritation.

"Uh-oh," Lily said, following my gaze. "Looks like the ghost of your past is stalking you in real time."

"More like haunting," I muttered, forcing a smile that didn't quite reach my eyes. I tried to focus on the art, but the prickling sensation of being watched sent my heart racing. I was hyper-aware of the space around me, the whispers of memories dancing in the shadows, and suddenly the vibrant gallery felt stifling.

"Let's go over there," Lily suggested, nodding toward a quieter corner. "I need a break from all this... drama."

As we stepped away, I spotted Ethan across the room, deep in conversation with a friend, his presence a soothing balm amidst the chaos. Just seeing him made my heart swell, and I could feel my worries dissipate as if they had never existed. I took a deep breath, ready to make my way toward him, but Julian's laughter cut through the air, pulling my attention back.

"Look who's come to join the party!" Julian's voice was smooth and inviting, like a well-aged whiskey, and it set my nerves on edge.

"Ugh," I hissed under my breath. "Why is he everywhere?"

"Maybe the universe wants to stir the pot," Lily whispered conspiratorially, squeezing my arm in solidarity. "Just go talk to Ethan. You're not alone in this."

I nodded, steeling myself as I approached Ethan, who caught my eye and smiled, the warmth of his expression making my heart flutter. "There you are," he said, his voice like honey, rich and smooth. "I was starting to think I'd have to rescue you from your past."

"More like I was hoping you'd come save me from this mess," I replied, my voice teasing. "How's the conversation? Are you winning?"

Ethan chuckled, the sound deep and inviting. "Well, the guy keeps trying to sell me a new investment strategy, so I'd say I'm winning by not throwing my drink in his face."

"I appreciate your restraint," I said, glancing over my shoulder to catch Julian's eye. He smirked, his gaze lingering on us with an intensity that made my stomach churn.

"What's wrong?" Ethan's expression shifted as he noticed my unease. "Is it Julian?"

I hesitated, weighing my words carefully. "It's just... he's been... Julian. You know? Charming and infuriating all at once."

Ethan's jaw tightened, and I could see the flicker of jealousy in his eyes, a dark cloud shadowing the warmth they usually held. "I get that. Just remember, he doesn't have a claim on you anymore. You're not that girl."

"Right," I said, forcing a smile that felt more like a grimace. "I'm not. I'm here with you."

"Then let's enjoy ourselves," Ethan suggested, his tone brightening as he took my hand, weaving us through the crowd toward the dance floor. The rhythm pulsed beneath our feet, and as the music enveloped us, I felt the tension of the evening begin to dissolve.

But just as I began to lose myself in the moment, a familiar voice rang out from behind us. "Harper, there you are! I've been looking for you!"

I turned, my stomach sinking at the sight of Julian cutting through the crowd, his confident stride unyielding as he approached.

"Great," I muttered under my breath, half-laughing at the absurdity of it all. "The universe really loves a dramatic entrance, doesn't it?"

Ethan's expression hardened, a wall of protective instinct rising as he faced Julian, but I stepped forward, determined to diffuse the tension. "Julian, this isn't the time—"

"Oh, come on," he interrupted, a devilish grin on his face. "You can't hide away forever. Let's show everyone what they're missing!"

He reached for my hand, the contact sending a jolt through me, igniting old memories I desperately wanted to forget. But before I could respond, Ethan's grip tightened around my waist, pulling me protectively closer. "She's not going anywhere with you."

The air crackled with tension, every gaze in the room suddenly fixed on us as the music faded into the background. My heart raced as I caught glimpses of the crowd's interest—a tableau of intrigue, a moment hanging delicately in the balance.

"Ethan—" I began, but the words caught in my throat. Julian leaned in closer, his voice low and taunting. "You really think you can keep her from living her life? Just because you're her safety net doesn't mean you're her choice."

"Stop," I said firmly, feeling the weight of their stares like a heavy cloak. I turned to face Ethan, searching for understanding in his eyes. "I—"

But Julian stepped forward, leaning into the growing tension. "What's it going to be, Harper? Do you want to stay in this little bubble of safety, or are you ready to embrace the chaos?"

The choice hung before me like a flickering flame, its glow enticing yet dangerous. I could feel the weight of the room pressing in, the expectations and emotions colliding in a whirlwind that threatened to pull me under.

In that moment, everything slowed, the music fading into silence as I stood at the precipice of my past and future. I was torn between the allure of familiarity and the promise of something new, caught in a web of desire and fear.

And then, as if summoned by the intensity of my indecision, the lights above flickered, plunging us momentarily into darkness. A gasp rippled through the crowd, and as the emergency lights kicked in, illuminating the room in a harsh glow, the world around me twisted into a swirl of chaos.

The room erupted into panic. People began to shout, and I felt Ethan's grip slip as he turned toward the noise.

"What's happening?" he asked, a mix of concern and confusion on his face.

Julian stepped closer, a smirk playing on his lips, eyes glinting in the dim light. "Looks like the universe has other plans for you, Harper."

Before I could process his words, a loud crash reverberated through the gallery, sending shockwaves of fear rippling through the crowd

Chapter 16: The Color of Fear

The sun dipped low on the horizon, casting a warm glow over the cluttered chaos of my studio. It was a sanctuary of fabric swatches and half-finished garments, but today it felt more like a prison, its walls closing in on me with each passing moment. I'd always found solace in creation, but lately, my sketches seemed to mock me with their emptiness. Each line I drew felt like a hollow echo of what I once poured into my designs—where once there had been vibrancy and passion, now there was only a faint whisper of color, a reminder of the turbulence that had seeped into every corner of my life.

I could hear Clara's voice in my head, a persistent reminder that communication was key, like the punchline to a joke I didn't quite understand. "You need to talk to Ethan," she had urged, her brow furrowing in that way that made it clear she wouldn't let me off easy. "You can't just let it fester." But what did she know about it? She wasn't the one battling demons of self-doubt, her heart a mess of unresolved feelings. I couldn't just wave a magic wand and conjure the perfect words to mend the growing chasm between us.

As the light began to fade, I settled onto my worn-out stool, its surface marked with the stains of past projects, a testament to my creativity—or perhaps my chaos. I picked up a pencil and began to sketch, letting the tip glide over the paper, hoping to reclaim some semblance of control. But instead of flowing lines, I found jagged edges, an erratic representation of my state of mind. Frustration bubbled beneath my skin, and I pressed harder against the page, nearly tearing it as I tried to force clarity from confusion.

Then my phone buzzed, breaking through the haze of my thoughts like a sudden clap of thunder. The screen lit up with Ethan's name, and my heart jumped, then plummeted as uncertainty washed over me. The text was simple, almost painfully so. Can we meet?

I stared at the message, the letters swimming in a sea of possibilities. There was hope tangled with fear, a mix that left me feeling both exhilarated and hollow. I set my phone down as if it were a live grenade, its potential for destruction weighing heavily in the air around me. What did he want? Did he miss me, or was he just as lost as I was, seeking some kind of resolution to our mess?

The shadows deepened in the room, and with each passing second, my anxiety climbed higher. I took a deep breath, trying to channel Clara's unwavering confidence. Maybe she was right. Maybe talking could heal the rifts that had formed between us. But what if I opened my mouth and nothing came out? What if the conversation turned into a battlefield, with emotions flying like arrows, leaving us both wounded?

I forced myself to stand and clean up my workspace, each movement mechanical as I tucked away the evidence of my struggles. I wasn't just tidying; I was stalling, allowing my thoughts to spiral out of control. As I moved from one corner to another, I felt the weight of doubt settle on my shoulders, a cloak of uncertainty I couldn't quite shake off.

Finally, I grabbed my coat and stepped outside, the crisp evening air biting at my cheeks. The world had transformed into a canvas of deep blues and vibrant oranges, a stark contrast to the turmoil within me. The stars began to peek through the velvety sky, tiny beacons of light in a vast expanse, reminding me that even in the darkest moments, there was still beauty to be found.

I made my way to the café where we'd shared countless cups of coffee, laughter, and dreams. It felt surreal to return to a place that once symbolized warmth and connection, now heavy with the weight of my fears. As I entered, the familiar aroma of roasted beans and pastries enveloped me, a bittersweet reminder of what was, mingling with the uncertainty of what was to come.

Ethan was already there, seated at a small table tucked away in a corner, his fingers drumming anxiously against the wood. He looked up as I approached, his expression a cocktail of hope and apprehension. It was in his eyes—those stormy depths I had once found so comforting—that I saw the reflection of my own inner turmoil.

"Hey," I said, trying to sound casual, though my heart raced like a startled rabbit.

"Hey," he replied, his voice barely above a whisper.

The silence stretched between us, thick and charged, like the moment before a storm breaks. I sat down, suddenly acutely aware of every detail—the way the light caught the strands of his hair, the slight furrow in his brow, the nervous twitch of his lip. We were both suspended in time, teetering on the edge of a cliff with no clear path down.

"I've missed you," he said, and I could hear the sincerity lacing his words, but they felt like a fragile bridge over turbulent waters, easily swept away by the currents of our unresolved issues.

"I've missed you too," I managed, though it felt like admitting to a crime I hadn't committed. It wasn't just about missing him; it was about missing us—the laughter, the intimacy, the shared moments that had become a distant memory.

"I wanted to talk about everything," he said, leaning in slightly, as if the gravity of his words might pull me closer. "Things have been... complicated, and I hate feeling this distance between us."

And there it was—the truth, raw and unfiltered, hanging between us like a fragile thread.

Ethan's words hung in the air, and I could feel the tension weave itself into the very fabric of our shared space. His gaze pierced through my defenses, and for a moment, I felt as if I were being stripped bare, left to grapple with the swirling emotions that threatened to overtake me. "It's complicated?" I echoed, my voice steadier than my heart. "That's a charming way to put it. I'd say it's a bit more like navigating a minefield blindfolded."

A ghost of a smile flickered across his lips, and I noted the warmth in his expression as he leaned back slightly, taking a breath as if to gather his thoughts. "You're not wrong. I just... I didn't expect things to spiral like this. One minute we're perfect, and the next, it's like we're speaking different languages."

"And I'm fluent in 'avoidance,'" I shot back, feeling a spark of defiance. "What do you want me to say? That I don't feel like I can reach you anymore? That I've started to think my sketches might actually listen better than you do?"

He winced, but there was a lightness in his eyes, a flicker of recognition that made me feel a little less isolated in my storm of emotions. "Fair point. My listening skills have been less than stellar." He rubbed the back of his neck, a gesture I knew all too well. It was his way of revealing vulnerability, a slip in his armor that made him more human, more relatable. "I just want to understand what happened. I want to fix it."

Fix it. The words resonated with a sense of possibility that I hadn't dared to consider. My heart fluttered in response, but I quickly doused that flicker of hope. "And what if I don't know how to fix it? What if it's beyond repair?" The question slipped from my lips, heavy with the weight of the truth I had been avoiding.

He opened his mouth to respond but hesitated, his brows knitting together as he thought. "What if it's not about fixing? What if it's about rebuilding?"

The idea sat with me, lingering like a stubborn fly buzzing around my head. Rebuilding. The word had a certain ring to it, like the first notes of a song I had forgotten but longed to hear again. "You mean we could just—start over?" I asked, uncertainty lacing my words.

"Why not?" he said, a hint of a grin tugging at the corners of his mouth. "Maybe we could go back to the basics, the way we used to. No pretenses, just... us."

The image stirred something deep within me, a flicker of nostalgia tinged with yearning. I remembered the late-night talks over pizza, the spontaneous drives to nowhere, the laughter that felt like a soundtrack to our lives. "And how do you suggest we do that? You think a 'Let's be best friends again' campaign is going to magically erase all the awkwardness?"

"Not quite. But we can start with honesty. I think I've been too caught up in my head, and maybe you have, too." He paused, his eyes softening as he continued. "I don't want to lose you, and I need you to know that."

My heart twisted at his admission, the sincerity of his words wrapping around my chest like a vice. I had never doubted his feelings for me, but the distance between us had made those feelings feel like a distant memory, a shadow of what once was. "Okay," I replied, feeling a cautious spark ignite within me. "Let's try it. But I can't promise it will be easy."

"Easy is overrated," he chuckled, his voice lightening the heaviness of our conversation. "We'll take it one step at a time. You'll guide me through the minefield, and I'll do my best not to blow us both up."

With each word, the tension in my shoulders began to ease, and I felt a weight lifting ever so slightly. There was still a long road ahead, but perhaps we could navigate it together, hand in hand.

"So, what's first on our list?" I asked, playing along with the lightheartedness of the moment. "Shall we exchange friendship bracelets? Or maybe do an awkward dance-off to bond?"

Ethan laughed, a rich sound that resonated deep within me, and for the first time in weeks, I felt a genuine smile break through the surface of my anxiety. "I think I'd rather go for coffee first, actually. A classic 'us' move."

"Ah, yes, the sacred ritual of caffeine. How could I forget?" I teased, standing up and motioning for him to follow. "Lead the way, my guide through the minefield."

As we exited the café, the cool night air wrapped around us, and the stars shone brightly overhead, casting a celestial glow that felt like a promise of new beginnings. We strolled side by side, the silence between us now comfortable, the tension dissolving into something lighter.

"I've been thinking about that fabric store we loved," I said as we walked. "The one with the outrageous prints that made us laugh? We should definitely go back."

"The one where you insisted on making that horrendous pillow that looked like a disco ball?" he shot back, his eyes sparkling with mischief.

"Hey, that pillow had character! It was a statement piece!" I countered, laughing at the memory of our fabric adventures.

"More like a cry for help," he teased, nudging me playfully.

The banter felt like a balm, soothing the raw edges of my insecurities. In that moment, I realized that maybe rebuilding wasn't as daunting as I had thought. Perhaps we could recreate our connection, stitch by stitch, until we had woven something beautiful again.

As we neared the fabric store, I felt a sudden rush of excitement, a childlike thrill at the thought of rediscovering our spark amidst the bolts of colorful fabric. The door chimed as we entered, and the familiar scent of cotton and thread enveloped me. The chaos of colors and textures ignited a spark of creativity that had long been dulled by my worries.

"Okay, let's find something truly outrageous," I declared, my spirit lifting with each passing moment. "I'm thinking a fabric so loud it could wake the neighbors."

"Why stop there? Let's go for something that could single-handedly cause an earthquake."

His eyes twinkled with mischief, and as we dove into the piles of fabric, I felt a renewed sense of hope. Maybe this was the first step toward rekindling not just our relationship, but also the vibrant life I had been missing. I watched as he ran his fingers over the materials, each one sparking a memory, a promise that perhaps the color of fear could be transformed into the palette of love once more.

Surrounded by the riot of colors and textures, I could feel the familiar thrill of inspiration surging through me as I and Ethan navigated the narrow aisles of the fabric store. Each bolt of fabric held a story, and I was suddenly acutely aware that we were on the precipice of writing a new chapter together. He picked up a bolt with a garish neon print, holding it up against his torso with a bemused expression.

"This would definitely make a statement," he said, his voice dripping with sarcasm. "I'm thinking we could blind our neighbors with this one."

"Exactly! It's not just fabric; it's a conversation starter," I replied, biting back a laugh as I watched him dramatically drape it over his shoulders. "You'd be the talk of the town, or at least the local gossip circle."

He struck a pose, one hand on his hip, the other flinging the fabric over his shoulder as if it were a glamorous cape. "Fear me, for I am the Neon Phantom! What do you think?"

"Honestly? I think I'm impressed. You've captured my soul right there," I said, chuckling at his antics. The tension that had clung to us like a heavy fog began to lift, revealing the underlying warmth and laughter that had once defined our connection.

Just as I reached for a rich emerald green fabric, a voice broke through our playful banter. "Ethan? Is that you?"

I turned to see a woman approaching, her auburn hair catching the light as she moved. It was someone I recognized—Lila, his ex-girlfriend. She radiated confidence, the kind that made the air crackle with intensity. My heart sank into my stomach, an unwelcome twist of jealousy sparking to life. I could feel Ethan stiffen beside me, a subtle shift that betrayed his discomfort.

"Uh, hey Lila," he said, the warmth in his tone suddenly replaced with a guarded edge. "What are you doing here?"

"I just came to pick up some fabric for a new project," she replied, her eyes darting between us with a curious glimmer. "Looks like you've found a little creative partner there."

"Yeah, we're just... browsing," I said, forcing a smile that felt stretched and false. I glanced at Ethan, who was shifting on his feet, clearly caught off guard. The spark of joy I had felt moments before dimmed, overshadowed by an unwelcome wave of insecurity.

"Oh, good to see you've moved on," Lila said, her tone dripping with something I couldn't quite place—was it disdain? Was it genuine curiosity? "I always thought you two would make a cute couple."

Ethan coughed lightly, an awkward sound that only served to intensify the discomfort. "We're just—"

"Just experimenting with some outrageous fabrics," I interrupted, wanting to steer the conversation back to safer waters. "This one here," I gestured to the neon fabric he had draped over himself, "is definitely a fashion risk."

"Risky, indeed," Lila replied, arching an eyebrow. "But sometimes risks pay off."

I forced a laugh, but it came out more strained than I intended. "Or they blow up in your face. Either way, it's an adventure."

Ethan's gaze flicked between us, and I could see the wheels turning in his mind, trying to navigate this unexpected turn of events. "Well, I should probably get back to—" he started, but Lila cut him off.

"Come on, Ethan. It's been ages since we caught up. Let's grab a coffee after this."

I felt a tightening in my chest, a knot of apprehension coiling tighter with each word that left her lips. I turned to Ethan, searching his expression for any hint of what he might say next. "Uh, I—" he stammered, glancing back at me, caught in the middle of a precarious balancing act.

Before I could interject, Lila continued, her voice bright with enthusiasm. "Just the two of us. We could reminisce about old times, you know? Like that trip to the lake."

I felt the air grow thick, a pressure cooker of unsaid words simmering just below the surface. "Ethan and I were just about to—"

He stepped in, his tone firm yet gentle. "I appreciate the offer, Lila, but I'm with someone now. We have plans."

The words hung in the air, a fragile lifeline thrown into the turbulence of our interaction. Lila's smile faltered for just a second, but then it returned, like the sun peeking out from behind clouds. "Oh, of course. I didn't mean to interrupt."

"Not at all," I said, forcing a smile as I crossed my arms defensively. "Just keeping our options open, right? You know how it is."

"Sure," she said, her gaze narrowing slightly as if evaluating the dynamics between us. "Well, it was nice to see you, Ethan. Take care."

As she walked away, I exhaled a breath I hadn't realized I was holding, the tension in my shoulders easing slightly. But the moment was short-lived, as Ethan turned to me, a storm brewing behind his eyes.

"Sorry about that," he said, running a hand through his hair, the gesture betraying his own unease. "That was... unexpected."

"Understatement of the year," I replied, my tone sharper than I intended. "Is she always this... intrusive?"

He opened his mouth to respond, then closed it again, searching for the right words. "I didn't know she'd be here. We've been trying to keep things amicable, but it's not always easy."

"I see that." I tried to keep my tone light, but the edges of my voice were fraying with uncertainty. "It's just... I didn't realize she would pop up like a bad sequel."

"Believe me, I'd prefer an entirely different genre." He paused, his gaze softening. "Look, I want to focus on us. This was supposed to be our day."

The sincerity in his eyes pierced through the uncertainty I felt, yet I couldn't shake off the unease that lingered in the aftermath of Lila's sudden appearance. "Maybe we should just go," I suggested, my heart heavy. "It might be better to do something else."

"Like what?" he asked, his brows knitting together in concern.

"Maybe we could find somewhere quieter? I'm suddenly craving an ice cream that will drown out my insecurities."

"Sounds like a plan."

As we left the fabric store behind, the air outside felt charged, as if the universe had tipped ever so slightly on its axis. We walked in silence for a few moments, the tension from the encounter still lingering, but Ethan's presence was a soothing balm, a reminder that we were in this together.

Just as we rounded the corner, the distant sounds of laughter caught my attention, and I turned to see a group of kids playing a game of tag, their joy spilling into the air like confetti. I smiled at the sight, but my amusement faded when I noticed a figure standing on the fringes of the group, their eyes locked onto us with an intensity that sent a shiver racing down my spine.

"Ethan," I whispered, pointing toward the figure, my heart racing as recognition hit me like a cold wave.

He turned, his expression shifting from curiosity to disbelief. "What the hell?"

Before we could react, the figure took a step closer, and I felt my pulse quicken, a sinking sensation clawing at my insides. "We need to talk," the stranger said, their voice low and urgent.

A chill rippled through the air as they stepped into the light, and my stomach dropped at the sight of the familiar face. It was someone I hadn't seen in years, someone I had hoped to leave behind.

My breath caught in my throat, and I turned to Ethan, my heart racing with a mix of dread and confusion. "What do they want?"

The uncertainty loomed over us like a dark cloud, the once vibrant colors of the day fading into a palette of fear and anticipation. In that moment, I realized that the fragile progress we had made might hang in the balance, teetering on the edge of an unexpected confrontation.

Chapter 17: Finding Our Way

The air crackled with unspoken words as I stood in the dimly lit café, my heart thudding against my ribcage like a frantic drummer. The scent of freshly brewed coffee swirled around me, mingling with the sweet notes of pastries that lay temptingly on the counter, yet I couldn't focus on anything but the figure seated at the far end. Ethan. His dark hair tousled in a way that seemed effortless, yet I knew him well enough to see the tension in the way he gripped the mug cradled in his hands. The faintest trace of a frown etched across his brow told me he was as unsettled as I was.

As I approached, the familiar warmth of his presence pulled me closer, like a moth to a flame. But beneath that warmth lay an icy current of uncertainty that sent chills racing down my spine. I slid into the seat across from him, the distance between us feeling both monumental and painfully intimate. "Hey," I managed, my voice barely above a whisper, laden with emotions that swirled within me like storm clouds.

"Hey." He met my gaze, those deep-set eyes flickering with a mix of longing and fear. "I wasn't sure you'd come."

A quiet laugh escaped me, tinged with bitterness. "Neither was I, but here we are." I shifted in my seat, the wooden chair creaking beneath me, a stark reminder of the weight of our unresolved past. "I needed to talk to you."

His jaw clenched slightly, and I could see the internal battle raging within him. "About us?" he asked, his voice low and measured, as if each word was carefully selected to avoid the landmines between us.

I nodded, feeling the heaviness of my admission settle in the space between us. "Yes. I... I can't keep pretending everything's fine." My heart raced as I laid it bare, feeling vulnerable and raw under the intensity of his gaze. "There's a part of me that's still trapped in everything that happened before. I don't want to drag you down with me, Ethan."

For a moment, silence stretched like an elastic band ready to snap. He leaned forward, his eyes narrowing, studying me as if trying to decipher the puzzle I had become. "You're not dragging me down. I just… I'm scared," he confessed, the honesty in his voice slicing through the air like a hot knife through butter.

"Scared of what?" I asked, my curiosity piqued.

"Scared of losing you," he admitted, his voice a low murmur, laced with vulnerability. "It feels like every time I think we're getting somewhere, something else pulls us apart." His hands tightened around the mug, the knuckles pale against the dark ceramic.

"Believe me, I get it," I replied, the walls I had built around my heart beginning to tremble. "I've been running from everything, even from myself." The heat of the café enveloped me, but the chill of my past lingered, making me feel exposed. "I've been so afraid of being hurt again that I didn't realize how much I was pushing you away."

His expression softened, the lines of worry etched across his forehead beginning to ease. "I want to be here for you, but you have to let me in."

The earnestness in his tone made my chest tighten with a mixture of longing and fear. "How do I do that? I don't even know where to start."

Ethan shifted closer, the distance that had felt insurmountable moments ago now evaporating. "Start by trusting me," he urged, the intensity in his voice igniting something deep within me. "We can face whatever's out there together. You don't have to carry this alone."

I took a shaky breath, the vulnerability of the moment crashing over me like a wave. "I want to trust you, but—"

"No 'buts,'" he interrupted gently, his eyes locking onto mine with fierce determination. "We've both been through hell. It's okay to be scared, but we owe it to ourselves to fight for this, for each other."

His words hung in the air, heavy and beautiful, a promise waiting to be fulfilled. I felt the weight of my past pressing down, but there was also a flicker of hope, a spark igniting the darkness that had threatened to consume me.

"Okay," I finally said, my voice steadying as a sense of clarity washed over me. "I'll try. I'll try to let you in."

Ethan's face broke into a tentative smile, the kind that lit up his entire being, revealing the man I had fallen in love with—the man who had always been there beneath layers of confusion and hurt. "That's all I ask," he replied, his tone brightening.

The café buzzed around us, the clinking of cups and low hum of conversation fading into the background. We were in our own world, one that felt fragile yet promising. In that moment, I realized that this was the turning point I had desperately needed. We could shed the weight of our past and walk forward, hand in hand, navigating the complexities of love and vulnerability together.

"I think I've been waiting for the right moment," I said, allowing a smile to bloom on my lips. "And it turns out, it was right here all along."

Ethan chuckled, his eyes sparkling with mischief. "So, what's next? Ice cream? A duet of terrible karaoke?"

I laughed, the tension in my shoulders easing as I considered the possibilities. "Only if you promise to sing off-key."

"Deal," he grinned, the atmosphere shifting to something lighter, more playful. "But I'm going to hold you to that."

And just like that, the world outside faded, leaving only the promise of new beginnings, laughter, and the exhilarating thrill of finding our way back to one another.

The warmth of the café clung to us like a favorite old sweater, comfortable and familiar, yet there was an electric charge between us that felt entirely new. As Ethan and I settled into our conversation, laughter began to weave its way through our words, creating a tapestry of shared moments that felt like sunlight breaking through clouds. The banter was easy, filled with the sharpness that had always been our trademark. I leaned back in my chair, arms crossed, a smile dancing on my lips as I challenged him, "So, karaoke night, huh? Do you think the universe can handle that level of bad?"

"Only one way to find out," he shot back, a wicked grin stretching across his face. "But I have to warn you, I have a reputation to uphold as the worst singer in the tri-county area."

"Tri-county?" I raised an eyebrow, feigning shock. "What, did you lose a bet or something?"

"Maybe," he said, his voice dropping to a conspiratorial whisper. "But mostly, it was an unfortunate school talent show incident involving an inflatable guitar and a power outage. Let's just say, I'll never live it down."

I couldn't help but laugh, picturing him as a kid, standing there in all his awkward glory. "You should consider charging admission to relive that moment."

"Tempting, but I don't think my dignity could take another hit," he replied, his tone light, but I could sense the underlying seriousness that still lingered. The laugh faded slightly, leaving a moment of stillness between us, a reminder of the weight of our earlier conversation.

"Do you really think we can do this?" I asked, the vulnerability creeping back in. "I mean, I want to believe it, but the past feels like an anchor sometimes, pulling me under."

Ethan's expression shifted from playful to earnest. "I think we can. But it'll take work—on both sides." He paused, looking into my eyes as if searching for something. "I'm willing to put in the effort. You just have to trust me."

Trust. The word hung heavy in the air, and I felt a flicker of doubt threaten to snuff out the warmth we had ignited. "It's not that simple, Ethan. I've been burned before, and it's hard to just switch that off."

"I get it," he replied softly, leaning in closer, his voice a soothing balm against my anxiety. "But this is different. You and I... we've fought to be here. We owe it to ourselves to at least try."

"Okay," I breathed, the word a reluctant agreement that tasted both sweet and bitter. "I'll try."

The moment of clarity transformed the energy around us. The café, once a simple backdrop, became our sanctuary, each clink of a coffee cup echoing the quiet commitment we were forging.

But just as I began to feel a sense of optimism wrapping around my heart like a warm embrace, a loud crash shattered the atmosphere. The front door of the café swung open with a dramatic flourish, a gust of chilly air following a figure cloaked in a heavy coat. It was Miranda, my roommate, with her hair wild and her cheeks flushed, as though she had been sprinting through a snowstorm.

"Thank God I found you!" she exclaimed, her eyes wide, darting between Ethan and me. "I've been trying to track you down for ages!"

"What's wrong?" I asked, instantly alert, the unease creeping back in.

"Did you hear?" she said breathlessly, grabbing the back of my chair as she steadied herself. "There's been a fire in the building next to ours. It's huge, and they're evacuating people! I thought you were still at home!"

A chill raced down my spine, freezing the warmth that had been blossoming between us. "Is everyone okay?" I asked, dread pooling in my stomach.

"I think so," she replied, her voice steadying. "But the firefighters are everywhere. I thought you might want to check it out, just in case."

Ethan's expression shifted to one of concern as he reached for my hand, grounding me. "I'll go with you," he said, his voice firm.

"No," I said quickly, shaking my head. "I can handle this. You stay here. I need to figure this out on my own."

"Are you sure?" he asked, searching my face. "You don't have to do this alone."

"I appreciate that, but I need to see it for myself. If something happened to our place...." My voice trailed off, the weight of possibility pressing heavily on my chest.

He studied me for a long moment, then nodded slowly. "Okay, but promise you'll call me when you get there."

"I will," I promised, feeling the heat of his concern wrap around me like a lifeline. I stood, pushing my chair back, and glanced at Miranda. "Let's go."

The streets outside were abuzz with chaos, the usual serenity of the neighborhood replaced by the wail of sirens and the clamor of voices. As we rushed through the throng of onlookers, my heart pounded against my ribs, fear knotting in my stomach. The sight of the fire, flames licking at the sky like angry tongues, sent a wave of nausea crashing over me.

"Is that our building?" I asked, panic rising as we got closer. The acrid smell of smoke clawed at my throat, and I struggled to catch my breath.

Miranda's eyes were wide, scanning the chaos. "I can't tell. Just stay close."

The sight of firefighters, their faces grim and focused, felt surreal. I strained to catch a glimpse of our home, the place where I had poured my dreams, my laughter, and yes, my heartache.

Just then, a familiar voice cut through the noise. "Is that you, Sam?"

I turned to see Mr. Jenkins, our elderly neighbor, making his way through the crowd, his face lined with worry. "I was just at the grocery store when I saw the smoke. I thought I'd better come back and check on you."

"We're okay, Mr. Jenkins," I assured him, my heart thudding in my chest. "But our building...."

"Nothing to worry about, dear," he said, trying to smile, but his eyes betrayed his anxiety. "I've seen worse. Just keep your distance, alright?"

As I stood there, flanked by my roommate and my neighbor, the warmth of earlier faded away, replaced by the sharp sting of reality. The flames danced menacingly, casting flickering shadows that flickered over the crowd, mirroring the turmoil roiling within me. Just as quickly as I had felt hope blossoming in my heart, it was replaced by the fear of uncertainty.

Ethan's voice echoed in my mind—trust. And as I watched the firemen work, my heart clenched. Maybe trust meant not just believing in the good times, but also in the midst of chaos, allowing others to support you, to be there when everything felt like it was crumbling.

The chaos around us felt surreal, a stark contrast to the warmth that had enveloped Ethan and me just moments ago. As we edged closer to the throng of people, my heart raced with a mixture of fear and determination. I glanced at Miranda, who kept shooting worried glances back at me, her anxiety palpable. The crowd buzzed like a disturbed hive, every whisper a reminder of the danger looming just a few blocks away.

"Do you think our place is okay?" I asked, my voice barely breaking through the din. Each time I asked, the response always felt like a prayer, something I needed to say to keep the gnawing worry at bay.

"I hope so," she said, biting her lip, her brow furrowing in concern. "It's right next to that bakery. If the fire spreads…."

The thought of my small sanctuary going up in flames made my stomach twist. "Let's just focus on the here and now," I said, trying to sound braver than I felt. "We can't change what's happening, but we can be here for each other."

Miranda squeezed my hand, a gesture of solidarity that gave me a fleeting sense of comfort. "You're right. We'll get through this. Together."

The sharp crackling of flames drew my attention back to the scene unfolding before us. Firefighters worked tirelessly, their movements precise and coordinated, battling the inferno that threatened to engulf everything in its path. The acrid smell of smoke clung to my clothes, mingling with the sweet scent of melting pastries from the nearby café, a cruel juxtaposition that made my heart ache.

As I stood there, the weight of uncertainty pressed down on me. I wanted to believe in our strength, in the notion that we could handle anything life threw our way, but the reality of the moment felt heavy.

"What's that?" Miranda suddenly shouted, pointing towards a figure emerging from the haze of smoke and chaos. I squinted, my heart quickening as the figure stumbled forward, swaying on unsteady legs.

"Is that…?" My breath caught as I recognized the familiar silhouette.

"Ethan!" I shouted, the word bursting from my lips like a lifeline. He was pushing through the crowd, his face streaked with soot and his expression grim.

"Sam!" He called, relief flooding his voice as he made his way to me. The moment he reached my side, he enveloped me in a tight embrace, grounding me in the whirlwind of anxiety and fear. "Are you okay? I was worried when you didn't call."

"I'm fine," I said, pulling back to look into his eyes. "What are you doing here? I told you to stay at the café."

"I couldn't just sit there and do nothing," he replied, running a hand through his hair, the movement making the soot smudge across his forehead. "I had to come find you."

The warmth of his concern ignited something inside me, pushing back against the icy fingers of dread that had wrapped around my heart. "You didn't have to come. I would've been okay," I insisted, my voice softer, but the fear clung to me like a shadow.

"Not a chance," he said, his voice steady, determination etched on his face. "You mean too much to me to let you face this alone."

Before I could respond, the ground beneath us trembled, and a loud crack echoed through the air as a piece of the building crumbled, sending debris flying into the street. My heart raced as I instinctively reached for Ethan, drawing him closer. "What just happened?"

"Everyone back!" a firefighter shouted, waving his arms and directing the crowd away from the chaos. "Stay back! We need space!"

"Let's move," I urged, pulling Miranda with me as we stepped back, instinctively retreating from the growing danger. Ethan remained close, his presence a steady anchor against the turmoil surrounding us.

"What are we going to do?" Miranda asked, her voice shaky. "We can't just stand here!"

"I think we should head to the community center," I suggested, remembering it was a safe gathering place for displaced residents. "They'll have information and resources for everyone."

"Good idea," Ethan said, his tone supportive. "Let's stick together."

As we turned to make our way through the crowd, I felt a pang of fear ripple through me. The adrenaline of the moment was fading, and reality was sinking in. We were facing the unknown, and my heart pounded in time with the anxiety churning in my stomach.

The community center was only a few blocks away, but every step felt heavier than the last. The distant sound of sirens wailed like a mournful song, and I couldn't shake the feeling that we were leaving behind something precious, something that might never be the same again.

"Sam, wait!" Miranda's voice cut through my thoughts. I turned to see her pointing toward a commotion near the edge of the crowd. "What's going on over there?"

I followed her gaze, and my breath hitched in my throat. A group of people was gathered around a young woman, her face pale and eyes wide with panic. "Help! Someone help!" she cried, her voice shrill as she clutched a small child in her arms, who appeared to be unconscious.

Ethan and I exchanged worried glances before rushing toward the scene. My heart raced as I knelt beside the woman, who was clearly in distress. "What happened?" I asked, my voice gentle yet urgent.

"I don't know!" she sobbed, her fingers trembling as she stroked the child's hair. "We were inside when the smoke started. I—I thought I could get out in time, but...." Her voice trailed off into a choked sob.

The sight of the child, limp and unresponsive, made my stomach twist. "Can someone call an ambulance?" I shouted, glancing at the growing crowd. "We need medical help!"

Ethan crouched beside me, his face set in grim determination. "Stay calm," he said, his voice steady. "We're going to help. Just focus on your child."

I felt the weight of the world resting on my shoulders, but the fire in my chest ignited something primal—a fierce need to help, to do something. "Is there anyone trained in first aid?" I called out, my heart pounding as I scanned the crowd.

"I am!" a man stepped forward, pushing through the throng. He dropped to his knees beside us, a determined expression on his face. "Let me take a look."

As the man assessed the child, I glanced at Ethan, who was watching intently. "What if it's too late?" I whispered, dread clawing at my insides.

"Don't think that way," he urged, his grip on my hand tightening. "We're doing everything we can."

But as the man began to administer care, a growing unease settled over me. The child lay motionless, and I felt the walls closing in, the air thickening with uncertainty. The crowd watched with bated breath, the reality of the situation stark and unforgiving.

Suddenly, another loud crack echoed through the air, and the ground trembled beneath us. My heart raced as I looked back at the building, dread washing over me. "Ethan, we need to get out of here!"

In an instant, the world seemed to shift. The sound of cracking timber echoed, and I barely had time to react before debris began to rain down, sending people screaming and scrambling in all directions. Panic surged through me as I pulled Ethan and Miranda away from the chaos, adrenaline flooding my veins.

But just as we turned to run, I caught sight of the woman with the child, frozen in fear. "Get out!" I screamed, my voice desperate as I reached for her.

And then, the unthinkable happened. As we dashed for safety, a massive beam broke free from the structure, crashing down toward us in a terrifying arc. My heart lurched, and time seemed to stretch as I realized there was no way to escape the impending disaster.

"Sam!" Ethan shouted, his voice cutting through the cacophony, but all I could see was the inevitable chaos bearing down on us, a world of fire and debris that threatened to erase everything in its path. The last thing I felt was the crushing weight of fate bearing down on us, and then—darkness enveloped me like a shroud.

Chapter 18: Threads of Trust

Each stitch of fabric felt like a heartbeat, pulsing with the vibrant energy that had taken over my life in recent weeks. I stood in Clara's boutique, surrounded by an array of textiles that shimmered under the soft lights like whispers of untold stories. The air was thick with the scent of fresh linen and the faint, intoxicating notes of lavender from a candle flickering in the corner. With renewed determination, I dove headfirst into designing a new collection, a labor of love infused with the passion I had found alongside Ethan.

Ethan. Just thinking his name sent a cascade of warmth through me, a steady reminder that I was not alone in this endeavor. He had become my sounding board, my inspiration, and, if I dared to admit it, the one who made my heart flutter with a joy I hadn't anticipated. Our evenings together had morphed into a symphony of creativity and laughter, each idea we tossed back and forth a note in our shared melody. I remembered our late-night brainstorming sessions, hunched over sketches and swatches, our words blending like paint on a palette, creating something entirely new. The thrill of it all was electric, igniting something deep within me, something I had long thought extinguished.

The boutique itself was a treasure trove, filled with the kind of garments that made you feel alive just by touching them. A soft cotton dress with delicate floral prints hung to my left, the colors reminiscent of a sunset, while a bold silk blouse sparkled under the lights, its rich navy hues speaking of ocean depths. I walked among them, fingers trailing along the fabric, imagining how each piece would evolve into something special, something that could make someone's day a little brighter.

"Hey, are you going to just stare at the fabric, or are we actually going to make magic happen?" Ethan's voice broke through my reverie, teasing but laced with an affectionate undertone that made me smile. He stood by the cutting table, his dark hair slightly tousled, the hint of a playful grin tugging at his lips.

"Magic, huh? I thought we were crafting a collection, not pulling rabbits out of hats," I shot back, my tone light yet teasing, grateful for the comfortable banter that had developed between us.

"Why not both? A little enchantment never hurt anyone." He leaned back, arms crossed, eyes glinting with mischief. "What do you have in mind for today? I hope it's not another collection of basic tees."

I rolled my eyes, stifling a laugh. "You mean, 'vintage-inspired graphic tees'?" I asked, throwing in a dramatic flair for effect. "Because that's all the rage right now."

"Only in a parallel universe where taste is optional." He feigned shock, a hand pressed dramatically to his chest, his laughter ringing through the boutique like a joyous bell. I loved this side of him—the witty banter, the playful jabs that made the day brighter.

"Fine, I'll come up with something more... avant-garde," I declared, pulling a rich emerald green fabric from the rack, its texture a soft whisper against my skin. I could envision it transforming into a chic dress, a statement piece that would turn heads.

"Now you're talking! I can see it—an asymmetrical cut with those delicate sleeves. Maybe a daring plunge in the back?" Ethan suggested, stepping closer, his enthusiasm infectious.

"Wow, getting bold there, aren't we?" I shot back, playful disbelief lacing my tone. "What happened to the guy who thought my last collection was a tad too... 'colorful'?"

He shrugged, feigning nonchalance. "I've seen the light. Or perhaps it's just the spark in your eyes when you talk about your designs."

As we brainstormed, the connection between us deepened, weaving a tapestry of trust that felt both exhilarating and terrifying. I realized, with each moment shared, that I was not just trusting him with fabric and designs, but also with pieces of myself that I had guarded so fiercely. With every laugh and shared idea, I was weaving my heart into this collection, a reflection of our experiences, our late-night talks, and the quiet moments that lingered long after the laughter faded.

"Okay, let's sketch this out before I get distracted by how cute you look when you're in creative mode," Ethan said, his tone shifting slightly, sincerity cutting through the playfulness. I caught the glint in his eyes, the warmth that seemed to radiate from him, and for a moment, the air felt charged with something unspoken.

"Don't flatter me too much; I might just design something ridiculous," I replied, feeling my cheeks warm.

"Ridiculous or not, I'm all in," he grinned, and we settled into a rhythm, the sound of pencils scratching against paper filling the air as we collaborated. Each line I drew felt like a promise, each shape a testament to our growing bond.

As the hours flew by, laughter punctuated our work, the lightness of our shared creativity wrapping around us like a warm embrace. The world outside faded away, leaving just us—two souls stitching together a vision, a dream. I felt more alive than I had in years, the thrill of possibility electrifying the air between us. I was falling, not just for the designs we were creating, but for the man standing beside me, whose laughter lit up the room and whose unwavering support made me believe in love's duality—exhilarating yet steady, wild yet secure.

"Alright, let's take a break," I suggested, glancing at the clock, surprised to see how much time had slipped away. The boutique felt like a cocoon, a sanctuary where I could explore both my creativity and the burgeoning feelings I had for Ethan. "We deserve some fresh air."

"Fresh air sounds good," he agreed, and as we stepped outside, the cool breeze brushed against my skin, invigorating and alive, much like the moments we had shared. The world felt vibrant, every color more vivid, every sound more pronounced, as if echoing the possibilities we were crafting together.

In that moment, as I stood beside him, the threads of trust weaving through our lives, I realized that I was ready to embrace whatever came next.

The sun dipped below the horizon, casting a golden hue over the city and filling Clara's boutique with a warm, inviting glow. I had stepped outside for a moment, seeking the crispness of the evening air to clear my head and refocus. As I leaned against the storefront, the bustling sounds of the street wrapped around me like an old friend. Laughter, snippets of conversation, and the distant melody of a street musician strumming a soft tune created a soundtrack that felt alive, vibrant.

"Do you always take breaks to ponder life's mysteries in the middle of a workday?" Ethan's voice broke through my thoughts, laced with a playful curiosity. I turned to find him standing there, hands stuffed casually into the pockets of his jeans, a mischievous grin spreading across his face. The soft evening light danced in his eyes, making them sparkle with a warmth that sent a flutter through my stomach.

"Only when I'm pondering how to make you do my bidding," I shot back, the banter rolling off my tongue effortlessly. "But it appears you've discovered my secret."

"Ah, yes. You should really work on your stealth. You're not as subtle as you think," he teased, taking a step closer, his playful energy wrapping around me like a cozy blanket.

"Subtlety? That's a word you won't find in my dictionary," I replied, rolling my eyes, but I couldn't help the smile creeping onto my face. "What's on your mind, oh wise one?"

He leaned against the wall, mirroring my pose, his expression shifting to something more serious. "I was just thinking about how much we've accomplished in such a short time. It's impressive. I mean, we're practically a creative powerhouse."

"Creative powerhouse, huh? So, what are we now—an unstoppable design duo? A fashion phenomenon?" I replied, mimicking his tone and gesturing dramatically, savoring the silliness of it all.

"Why not? We could even have matching capes." His laughter filled the air, and I found myself lost in the moment, the world around us fading as I soaked in the genuine connection we shared.

"What would our capes be made of? Something fabulous, I hope. No polyester allowed." I pretended to consider our fabric choices, tapping my chin in mock seriousness.

"Of course, only the finest silk. We can't let the fashion world down," he responded, a glint of mischief in his eyes. "I can see it now—'Ethan and [Your Name]'—a name that strikes fear in the hearts of mediocre designers everywhere."

Our laughter faded, leaving a comfortable silence that felt charged with something deeper. I looked up at him, really looked, and in that moment, the playful facade slipped away, revealing a shared understanding that both thrilled and terrified me. There was a connection blooming between us, a fragile flower in a garden of uncertainty, and I wasn't sure I was ready to tend to it.

"Okay, let's not get too carried away. We need to focus on making this collection something people will actually want to wear," I said, shaking off the sudden weight of my thoughts. "It's time to put our genius to work."

"Genius, yes. But let's not forget about the sheer hard work that goes into it," Ethan replied, his tone softening. "And maybe a little bit of magic."

"Alright, Mr. Magic, how do you propose we infuse some enchantment into our designs?" I challenged, feeling a spark of inspiration ignite within me.

"Easy," he said, his voice dropping to a conspiratorial whisper. "We combine our styles. You, with your elegant lines and romantic touches, and me, with my... well, I guess I'll just have to think of something."

"Confidence is key, Ethan. Own your style," I encouraged, a smile tugging at my lips. "But let's make sure you're not trying to pass off a Hawaiian shirt as high fashion."

His eyes widened in mock horror. "That was one time! I thought it was a bold statement!"

"Bold? More like a crime against fashion," I teased, nudging him playfully.

As we returned to the boutique, the atmosphere shifted. The laughter hung in the air, but there was an undercurrent of tension—a spark that seemed to buzz just beneath the surface. I felt it in the way our shoulders brushed as we moved past each other, in the charged pauses between our words. The creative brainstorming that had once flowed easily began to waver, the rhythm shifting as I wrestled with my own feelings.

"Let's try something different," Ethan suggested, gesturing to a nearby table filled with fabric remnants. "Why not mix and match? Take a chance? After all, fashion is about breaking boundaries, right?"

I nodded, even as my heart raced. "Right, but what if we mix the wrong colors? What if our 'bold statements' turn out to be fashion disasters?"

"Then we'll have a hilarious story to tell at parties," he shot back, his laughter infectious. "But I believe in us. I know we can create something extraordinary."

With renewed determination, I dove into the challenge, fabric swatches flying as we experimented. Hours melted away in a haze of color and texture, ideas sparking and colliding. The boutique transformed into a whirlwind of creativity, a kaleidoscope of possibilities that mirrored the chemistry crackling between us.

"Look at this," I exclaimed, holding up a combination of deep burgundy and soft cream, a daring clash of colors that somehow worked. "It's bold and beautiful—like us."

"Maybe just beautiful," Ethan replied, laughter dancing in his voice. "But I'm here for the journey. Even if we crash and burn, at least we'll go down in style."

"Crash and burn? I don't think I can handle the pressure!" I feigned panic, clutching my chest in exaggerated dismay.

"You can handle it, trust me," he said, stepping closer, his gaze steady and reassuring. "You've already come so far. You've built something amazing here."

The sincerity in his voice sent a rush of warmth through me, a wave of affection that swept away the lingering insecurities I had kept hidden. Maybe I could trust him with this part of my heart, this fear that had always held me back. Perhaps this collection was more than just a business venture; it was a tapestry woven from the threads of trust, love, and creativity we were cultivating together.

As the night wore on and the stars peeked through the window, I realized we were creating not just a collection but a foundation for something far greater. And as I glanced over at Ethan, his eyes lit with the spark of creativity and mischief, I couldn't shake the feeling that this was only the beginning of our story.

The boutique was a vibrant whirlpool of color and creativity, each corner bursting with the evidence of our collaboration. The walls echoed with our laughter, a sweet symphony that filled the air like the heady scent of blooming flowers. I stepped back, surveying the scattered fabrics and sketches sprawled across the tables, my heart swelling with pride. We had turned chaos into a tapestry of potential, a world crafted from our shared dreams and daring aspirations.

Ethan was engrossed in the next design, his brow furrowed in concentration, a pencil dancing across the page with fervor. I watched him, my heart fluttering with a mix of admiration and something deeper. The way he dedicated himself to our project, to me, sparked a warmth in my chest that I had never known before. "You know," I said, a playful lilt to my voice, "if we keep this up, we might need to hire an assistant just to manage our brilliance."

He looked up, feigning shock. "An assistant? I think you underestimate my multitasking skills. Besides, I have to keep an eye on your 'brilliant' ideas. Wouldn't want you to design something too avant-garde and scare away our customers."

I crossed my arms, tilting my head in mock indignation. "Avant-garde? Is that what you call my genius? Because I call it fashion-forward."

"Let's just agree to call it... interesting," he shot back, a grin breaking through his mock seriousness. "But speaking of genius, I was thinking we should incorporate a theme for this collection. Something that resonates with the current season, maybe."

"Theme?" I echoed, intrigued. "What did you have in mind? Spring is all about renewal and rebirth, after all. We could play with colors that evoke that feeling—soft pastels, floral patterns. Something light and airy."

"Or," he countered, leaning closer, his excitement palpable, "we could do the unexpected. Darker colors, rich fabrics—embracing the shadows and contrasts of life. There's beauty in the depth."

I paused, considering the idea. It was bold, almost unsettling in its deviation from the norm. "You want to go dark? Like a fashion noir?"

"Exactly! Imagine flowing silhouettes that capture elegance and mystery, garments that tell a story. It would be a departure from what people expect, and isn't that what makes fashion truly exciting?" His eyes sparkled with passion, and I felt a rush of adrenaline at the thought of breaking the mold.

"Okay, I'm in. Let's weave some drama into this collection!" I exclaimed, the idea electrifying. We dove into the task, brainstorming a palette that blended the whimsical with the profound. The room thrummed with our energy, the air crackling as we bounced ideas off each other, layering creativity like fabric on a dress form.

Hours slipped away unnoticed. We shifted between sketches and swatches, the creative process flowing like water—fluid and unstoppable. I felt exhilarated, the thrill of our collaboration fueling my spirit. With every design, I poured my heart into the fabric, stitching not just seams but memories, emotions, and the trust that had bloomed between us.

As the night wore on, the boutique transformed under the soft glow of fairy lights, the shadows creating a magical atmosphere. But as I glanced at the clock, a flicker of anxiety passed through me. "We've been at this for a while. Are we even remotely close to a cohesive collection?"

"Cohesive? That's overrated," he quipped, throwing a playful wink my way. "What we're doing is crafting art. Sometimes art doesn't follow a straight line. It twists and turns, just like life."

"You make a compelling argument, but I'm pretty sure art doesn't involve so many coffee cups scattered around," I replied, gesturing at the evidence of our long night. The remnants of caffeine-fueled creativity lay everywhere, a testament to our passion.

"Coffee is an essential tool of the trade," he said, mock seriousness in his tone, before suddenly breaking into laughter. "Besides, it fuels genius, and we wouldn't want to run out of that, would we?"

I joined in the laughter, feeling a sense of comfort wash over me. The night was slipping away, and I was glad to share it with him, but as I moved closer to him, a shadow crossed my mind—one of uncertainty. What if this feeling we were cultivating was just a fleeting moment, a spark that would fade as quickly as it ignited?

Suddenly, a loud crash from the back of the boutique shattered my thoughts. We both jumped, eyes wide, hearts racing as we turned toward the source of the noise. The sound of something heavy falling echoed ominously, followed by the faint tinkle of glass shattering.

"What was that?" Ethan exclaimed, his playful demeanor instantly shifting to one of concern.

"Let's find out," I said, trying to steady my voice even as my pulse quickened. Together, we moved cautiously toward the back room, the air thick with tension. My heart pounded in my chest, the thrill of creativity replaced by a gnawing uncertainty.

As we rounded the corner, the sight before us made my stomach drop. A tall shelving unit had toppled over, spilling its contents across the floor like a spilled treasure chest. Glass jars filled with buttons and trinkets lay shattered, their colorful contents scattered like confetti.

"Oh no," I gasped, stepping closer. "The vintage collection! What if it's all ruined?"

Ethan was already kneeling, carefully picking up the shards of glass. "We need to clean this up quickly before anyone gets hurt. Grab the dustpan," he ordered, and I rushed to help, but my mind was racing, questions swirling like the chaos around us.

How had this happened? Was it just an accident, or was something more sinister lurking in the shadows? As we worked side by side, the uneasy feeling settled deeper in my gut. There was more to this than just a toppled shelf, a sense of impending change looming like a storm cloud.

Just as we began to restore order, a voice echoed from the entrance, freezing us in our tracks. "Well, well, what do we have here?"

I turned slowly, heart thundering in my chest, to see Clara standing there, arms crossed and an unreadable expression on her face. The shadows in her eyes hinted at a depth I hadn't noticed before, and in that moment, I knew that everything was about to change.

Chapter 19: The Weight of Secrets

The morning sun filtered through the gauzy curtains of my bedroom, painting the walls in a warm, golden hue. It was one of those idyllic days when the world outside felt like a dream—birds chirping, leaves rustling gently in the light breeze, and the scent of freshly baked pastries wafting in from the café below. I had taken to my window sill, perched like a bird ready to take flight, watching the small town of Maplewood wake up. Life felt almost perfect, the kind of perfect you only see in postcards or those cheesy romantic comedies where the girl always ends up with the charming guy despite the odds.

Ethan had become my anchor, his laughter a balm to my soul. We had found a rhythm, a harmonious dance that made the mundane feel extraordinary. The way his eyes crinkled when he laughed was a melody I wanted to hear every day, and our stolen moments—coffee at dawn, long walks through the park, and impromptu dinners at his place—had woven a tapestry of joy around us. It was blissful, but like all good things, it felt a bit too fragile, a bit too close to breaking.

As I reached for my phone, the sudden buzz jolted me from my reverie. It was a message, but the name on the screen sent a cold shiver down my spine. Claire. The name alone was a ghost from a time I had tried desperately to bury. We had been inseparable once, two wild spirits unafraid of the world, but life, with its cruel twists, had severed that bond. My heart raced as I hesitated, fingers hovering over the screen. Should I open it? Was this truly a message I wanted to read?

With a deep breath, I pressed my thumb against the glass, and the message unfurled like a dark ribbon: "Hey, I know it's been a while, but I really need to talk. Can we meet?" There it was, the past calling me back with a siren's song, luring me into waters I thought I had long since navigated.

A cacophony of emotions surged through me—fear, confusion, and a familiar sense of nostalgia that wrapped around my heart like a vine, choking out the sunlight. What could she possibly want? Part of me wanted to ignore it, to dismiss her as an unwelcome memory, but another part—the part that still remembered our adventures, our secrets—yearned to know what had driven her to reach out now.

I scrolled through our old messages, a trove of shared dreams and laughter, of summer nights spent under the stars whispering promises that felt eternal. Memories flooded my mind, tinged with bittersweetness. I had built a life here, a life filled with hope and the promise of love. Did I really want to jeopardize that?

With a determined exhale, I decided to reply. "Okay. When?" My heart raced as I hit send, a rush of adrenaline coursing through me. Moments later, my phone buzzed again: "Can we meet at the old diner? Tomorrow at noon?"

The old diner. It was a place steeped in our history, where we had shared fries and dreams in equal measure. How could I say no? Even if it was just to tell her to leave me alone, to remind her that the girl she once knew was gone. I typed a quick reply, trying to mask the growing knot in my stomach. "Sure. I'll be there."

As I made my way to the café later that morning, the aroma of rich coffee and sweet pastries enveloped me, momentarily distracting me from the looming confrontation. Ethan was behind the counter, his face lighting up when he saw me. He was everything I had needed and more—his kindness was a fortress I had never anticipated finding.

"Hey there, beautiful," he said, his voice warm as melted chocolate. I felt my cheeks flush as he leaned over the counter, brushing his lips against my cheek, sending delightful tingles racing through me. "What's got you looking so pensive today?"

"Just...thinking," I replied, trying to hide the turmoil beneath my smile. I couldn't burden him with Claire's reemergence, not now, not when everything felt so delicate. "But I think I need a slice of your best chocolate cake to help with that."

He chuckled, an infectious sound that made my heart swell. "Coming right up! You know I can't resist a challenge." He moved to the back, leaving me with a flutter of excitement mixed with unease. I couldn't help but feel that the calm before the storm was too good to last.

After finishing my slice of heaven, I returned home, my mind racing with the anticipation of the next day. The old diner, the shadows of memories flickering behind me like fireflies. I had to know what secrets Claire harbored, but at what cost?

The next day, I approached the diner with a heavy heart, every step weighted with uncertainty. Inside, the familiar clatter of dishes and the murmur of conversations enveloped me, yet my focus was solely on the booth in the back where Claire sat, her back turned to me. It was as if time had folded in on itself, transporting me back to our youth.

When she turned, the years slipped away, leaving the girl I once knew—still wild, still fierce, but with shadows in her eyes that hadn't been there before. "You came," she said, her voice a mix of surprise and relief.

"I did," I replied, my throat dry, heart pounding. "What's going on, Claire? Why now?"

She shifted uneasily, her fingers twisting the edge of the tablecloth. "I didn't know how to reach you. I just... there's something you need to know."

And in that moment, as she opened her mouth to speak, I felt the ground beneath me shift, the weight of her words poised to shatter my carefully constructed world.

The words hung in the air between us, a fragile thread waiting to snap. Claire's gaze bore into me, her expression a blend of vulnerability and resolve. I could see the familiar spark of mischief in her eyes, but it was overshadowed by something deeper—something that hinted at trouble. "You're scaring me, Claire. Just tell me what's going on," I urged, my voice steadier than I felt.

She took a deep breath, and for a moment, I thought she might crumble under the weight of whatever she carried. "It's about Jake," she said, and the name struck me like a cold wave. Jake had been our best friend—a whirlwind of charm and laughter, but also of chaos and heartbreak. I hadn't thought of him in years, not since that night when everything went sideways and tore us apart.

"What about him?" I asked, heart racing. I felt like I was diving back into waters I hadn't traversed in ages. "I thought we were done with that chapter."

Claire winced, a shadow crossing her face. "I thought so too, but... I ran into him a few weeks ago. He was in town, and we ended up talking. He told me something. Something about you."

The air felt charged, thick with unsaid things. My stomach twisted as I processed her words. "What did he say?" I whispered, already fearing the answer.

"That you're not who you think you are," Claire replied, her eyes searching mine for understanding. "He said there are things about your past that you don't remember, things that could change everything."

A wave of disbelief washed over me. How could Jake know anything about my life now? I had spent years reconstructing myself, piece by painstaking piece, burying the past and all its ugly remnants. "You can't seriously believe that," I shot back, but my voice wavered.

"I didn't want to believe it either," Claire said, her fingers tapping nervously against the table. "But he mentioned your family. Your mom, the accident... and then he said something about a secret. Something you've been hiding."

The room felt smaller, the walls pressing in around me. I forced myself to breathe, to pull back from the brink of panic. "Jake has always been a master of embellishment. He loved to stir the pot," I countered, but even I could hear the uncertainty in my voice.

Claire leaned in closer, her voice dropping to a conspiratorial whisper. "What if he's not lying? What if there's more to your story than you've been told?"

I shook my head, fighting against the waves of doubt crashing over me. "I don't want to hear this," I said, voice thick with emotion. The last thing I wanted was to dig up old bones, especially ones that had the potential to shatter the fragile life I'd built.

"Then maybe you should," she said softly. "Because the way he said it... it didn't feel like a joke. He seemed genuinely concerned, like he was trying to warn me."

"What kind of warning?" I pressed, though I was already wary of where this conversation was heading.

Claire hesitated, glancing around the diner as if checking for eavesdroppers, but there were only a few patrons, absorbed in their own worlds. "He said that there are people who want to keep the past buried—people who would do anything to protect the secret. That maybe even your happiness is at stake."

A chill ran down my spine, and the air around us thickened with unspoken threats. The diner felt suddenly claustrophobic, as if it were closing in on me, and I had to get out. "I don't need this right now. I'm happy. I've worked so hard to build a life here," I said, trying to keep my voice steady, even as my heart raced.

"I know, but you deserve to know the truth," Claire insisted, a fire igniting in her eyes. "If there's something out there that could take away your happiness, don't you think you should face it head-on? Maybe it's not just about you anymore."

Her words hung in the air, and I felt a flutter of unease. I was living for myself, yes, but there was Ethan to consider too. His laughter, his warmth—they had wrapped around me like a protective blanket. But what would happen if this secret tore through that warmth, exposing me to the cold reality of my past?

"I can't just waltz back into the past, Claire. I left it for a reason," I said, my voice edged with frustration. "Jake is a ghost. He shouldn't be haunting me."

Claire opened her mouth to respond, but I raised a hand, cutting her off. "I need to think. I can't process this right now."

"Just promise me you'll think about it," she urged, her tone softening. "I know we've had our differences, but I wouldn't be here if I didn't care. You're still my friend."

I nodded, feeling the weight of her concern pressing down on me like a heavy stone. As we parted ways, the weight of her words lingered, echoing in the back of my mind. What if there was a truth I had buried so deep that it had begun to rot at the edges of my carefully constructed life?

Back home, the sun was dipping low in the sky, casting long shadows across the living room. I sank onto the couch, my mind racing, replaying Claire's revelation like a broken record. Every creak of the floorboards felt amplified, echoing the secrets I'd buried. I could almost hear Jake's voice whispering through the cracks, taunting me, teasing me with possibilities that sent chills down my spine.

Just as I was about to lose myself in a spiral of what-ifs, a knock at the door startled me. My heart raced, and I could hardly catch my breath. I wasn't ready for visitors, especially not with the tempest swirling inside me. I rose cautiously, peeking through the peephole, and my heart did a little somersault.

Ethan stood on the doorstep, his smile bright enough to light the dimness that had enveloped me. He was like a breath of fresh air, a soothing balm against the storm raging within. But as I opened the door, that joy faltered, the weight of my unresolved thoughts pressing heavily against my chest.

"Hey! I thought I'd surprise you with dinner," he said, holding up a takeout box, the enticing smell of Italian food wafting in. "You okay? You look a little... off."

I forced a smile, trying to mask the turmoil behind my eyes. "Just a long day, that's all."

"Long days call for pasta," he declared, stepping inside and setting the box on the table. "Come on, let's eat. You know I make the best garlic bread this side of the Mississippi."

As he chatted on, my heart sank. I wanted to bask in his light, to drown in his laughter, but shadows loomed at the edges of my happiness, threatening to consume us both. Would I ever be able to fully embrace this happiness, knowing the past was a breath away? The weight of secrets pressed down on me, heavier than ever, and I felt the delicate strands of my life begin to unravel.

The scent of garlic and herbs wafted through the room as Ethan set the takeout containers on the table, his smile infectious despite the tumult swirling inside me. He had a way of bringing light into even the darkest corners of my mind. I wanted to be present, to enjoy the comfort of his company, but every time I tried to immerse myself in the moment, the specter of Claire's revelations loomed, casting a long shadow over my thoughts.

"Are you sure you're okay?" Ethan asked, his brows furrowing as he watched me pick at my food, the pasta untouched on my plate. "You seem a million miles away."

"Just thinking about work," I lied, a practiced smile plastered on my face, hoping he wouldn't see the cracks forming underneath. "You know how it gets sometimes."

He nodded, but the concern didn't leave his eyes. "Well, I'm here if you want to vent. Or we can just sit in comfortable silence and eat pasta. I can be quiet. I promise!"

I chuckled softly, the warmth of his presence wrapping around me like a familiar blanket. "Comfortable silence sounds lovely. But I do have to say, that garlic bread does deserve an audience."

"Good to hear," he said, feigning a deep bow as he reached for a slice. "For a moment there, I thought you were going to turn into a pensive statue. I've never met a woman who could frown at pasta before."

"Trust me, I'm the first," I said, the banter flowing as easily as the wine he poured. It was moments like these, filled with laughter and teasing, that made me forget the unease shadowing my heart. But as we ate, I felt each bite heavier, each laugh punctuated by the weight of secrets pressing down.

After dinner, we moved to the couch, Ethan flipping on the television to find some mindless show to fill the space between us. I nestled into him, trying to lose myself in the comfort of his warmth, but my mind kept drifting back to Claire's words. The idea that something hidden could come crashing into my carefully constructed life was like a storm on the horizon, dark and threatening.

"Okay, spill it," Ethan said suddenly, turning to me with a knowing smile. "You're still lost in your thoughts, and I can't take it. You're like a cat in a room full of rocking chairs—too much potential for disaster."

I laughed, appreciating his attempt to lighten the mood, but I felt the words bubbling up, yearning for release. "It's just... I ran into an old friend today," I said carefully, gauging his reaction.

"Old friend, huh? One of those who shows up, shakes things up, and then disappears into the shadows?" His playful tone masked genuine concern, a glimmer of jealousy lurking just beneath the surface.

"Something like that," I replied, feeling a pang of guilt at the deception. "She just... reminded me of some things I thought I had left behind."

"What kind of things?" he asked, his voice low and steady, a steadying force against my rising anxiety.

I hesitated, caught between the urge to share and the instinct to protect him from the storm brewing inside me. "Just some personal stuff. Nothing to worry about," I finally said, forcing a smile that felt more like a grimace.

He studied me for a moment, his brow creased in thought. "Okay, but remember, I'm not just some guy you can hide things from. I'm here to help. If it's weighing you down, you can tell me."

"I know, and I appreciate that," I replied, leaning into him, desperately wanting to trust him, to let him in. "I'm just not ready to unpack it all yet. It's... complicated."

"Complicated seems to be my middle name," he joked, but his expression shifted, and for a brief moment, I saw a flicker of vulnerability in his eyes. "Just promise me you'll talk to me when you're ready. You don't have to face this alone."

I nodded, grateful for his patience, but I still felt like a dam ready to burst. My heart raced, torn between the safety of his embrace and the storm brewing in my past.

As the evening wore on, we settled into a comfortable silence, the TV flickering in the background while I wrestled with my thoughts. My phone buzzed on the table, and I glanced at the screen, my stomach twisting at the sight of Claire's name lighting up the display.

"Do you need to get that?" Ethan asked, noticing my sudden tension.

"Um, no. It's just a friend," I said, forcing myself to smile as I silenced the phone. But the truth was that Claire's message loomed larger than ever, a dark cloud hovering over my happiness. The knot in my stomach tightened, an impending sense of doom threading through my mind.

"Hey, I've been thinking..." Ethan began, breaking through my internal turmoil. "What if we have a little adventure this weekend? You, me, the great outdoors? Hiking? A picnic? Anything to get you out of this funk?"

I managed a genuine smile, grateful for his unwavering positivity. "That actually sounds wonderful. I could use some fresh air. And food. Always food."

"Then it's a plan! I'll even make you my famous sandwiches," he declared with mock bravado, his eyes sparkling with excitement.

I felt a rush of affection as I looked at him, but just as quickly, that familiar sense of foreboding crept back in. What if I had to confront my past before our weekend getaway?

Just as I was about to voice my concerns, my phone buzzed again, this time more insistent. I glanced at it, and my heart plummeted as I read the message. "I'm in town. We need to talk. Tonight."

My breath hitched, and I felt as if the ground beneath me had shifted. Claire's message pulsed with urgency, the weight of her words crashing into me like a tidal wave. I felt the room closing in, a tightness gripping my chest.

Ethan's eyes were on me, concern etched across his face. "You okay?"

"I... I need to step outside for a minute," I stammered, scrambling to my feet. My heart raced as I made my way to the door, the air thick with tension.

"Hey, wait! What's going on?" he called after me, his voice laced with worry.

"Just a quick breath of fresh air," I said, forcing a smile even as my heart sank. I stepped outside, the cool night air hitting my skin like a splash of ice water.

The stars twinkled overhead, but their beauty felt far away, overshadowed by the darkness creeping in around me. I leaned against the door frame, the weight of my choices pressing heavily on my chest. Could I really face Claire again? And what if the truth she held was something I couldn't bear to hear?

As I stared into the depths of the night, a sense of foreboding enveloped me. I felt like a ship caught in a storm, tossed between the waves of my past and the safety of my present. My phone buzzed in my pocket again, and I pulled it out, the glow illuminating my face.

"Please. I can't wait any longer."

The message was urgent, demanding my attention. I closed my eyes, battling the whirlpool of emotions inside. I could feel Ethan's presence behind me, a tether to reality that pulled me back from the brink.

With one last glance at the stars, I turned, ready to face whatever lay ahead. But as I opened the door, I was met with the sight of Ethan standing there, his expression a mixture of concern and something darker—something that hinted he had overheard more than I'd intended to reveal.

"What's really going on?" he asked, his voice steady yet filled with the weight of uncertainty.

And in that moment, I knew my world was about to tilt on its axis, my carefully constructed life unraveling before me like a thread pulled too tightly.

Chapter 20: Whispers of the Past

The bell above the café door jingled as I pushed it open, and the comforting aroma of roasted coffee beans and freshly baked pastries enveloped me like an old sweater. The sun poured through the large bay windows, casting playful shadows on the wooden floor, and I spotted Clara sitting at our usual table in the back corner. The mismatched chairs—one a vibrant blue, the other a soft green—had become a testament to our years of laughter, whispered secrets, and countless plans that never quite made it beyond those walls.

"Look at you," Clara teased, her eyes sparkling like the surface of the nearby lake on a sunny day. "You actually made it out of bed before noon!"

I rolled my eyes, sliding into the chair opposite her. "You know me, the queen of all things procrastination. I practically live in my pajamas."

Clara chuckled, taking a sip of her latte, the foam forming a perfect heart on top. "Well, I'm glad to see you've dressed for the occasion. We have serious matters to discuss." Her tone turned serious, and a weight settled between us, more substantial than the chipped ceramic mugs that rested before us.

As I picked up my own cup, the warmth seeped through my fingers, grounding me in the moment. "It's about Julian," I blurted, the name tasting foreign on my tongue, like a bittersweet piece of candy I hadn't anticipated. I had thought I could keep this part of my life locked away, a dusty relic tucked beneath the floorboards of my memory. But Clara had always had a knack for unearthing truths, even when I wasn't ready to share.

"Of course it is," she replied, leaning in closer, her brow furrowed with concern. "What did he want? Did he even tell you he misses you?"

"No, not exactly," I admitted, my heart pounding like the bass in a club. "He wants to meet. He... he sent me a message saying he's back in town, and he needs to talk."

Clara's expression morphed from curiosity to empathy. "I can see why that would rattle you. What do you think he wants? Closure? A second chance?"

"Honestly? I don't know." My voice trembled slightly as I spoke. The past felt like a thick fog rolling in from the ocean, obscuring everything in its path. "I left him, Clara. I walked away, and it was the hardest thing I've ever done. But now—"

"Now the shadows of your past are knocking at your door," she finished for me, her voice soft. "And it's up to you to decide if you're ready to let them in."

I stared into my latte, the swirls of brown and cream blurring together like my memories of Julian. It was as if a tidal wave of emotions was crashing over me, each wave threatening to pull me under. I had thought I was done with that chapter of my life, that I had buried it deep enough that it wouldn't resurface. But life, as it often does, had other plans.

"What am I even supposed to say?" I mused aloud, tapping my finger against the edge of the cup. "Hi, remember me? The one who left you because I was terrified of commitment?"

"Maybe start with the truth," Clara suggested, her voice steady. "Tell him how you felt back then and how you feel now. You're not the same person you were when you left."

The thought of laying bare my heart and fears made my stomach churn. "And what if he's changed? What if he's moved on?"

"Then you'll know, won't you?" Clara said, a hint of challenge in her tone. "But if you don't meet him, you'll always wonder."

I sighed, the weight of indecision pressing heavily on my chest. "It's just—what if he's still the same Julian? The one who couldn't handle my dreams or my ambition? The one who saw my life as something to be fixed instead of cherished?"

"People can surprise you," Clara countered gently, her gaze unwavering. "And sometimes, they're not the ones who need to change. Maybe it's you who has to find closure."

Her words hung in the air, resonating like a song I couldn't quite place. Perhaps the past wasn't just a ghost that haunted me; maybe it was a teacher, waiting for me to learn the lessons it had to offer. "I'll think about it," I said finally, though part of me felt like a tightrope walker, teetering precariously on the edge of something unknown.

"Good. And remember, no matter what happens, you have me," she said, raising her cup as if toasting to our friendship, the light catching the steam swirling upwards. "Now, let's order something sweet to fuel your bravery. You'll need it."

Just then, the door swung open, and a gust of autumn air rushed in, causing the scent of cinnamon to dance around us. My heart skipped as I glanced over, only to find a stranger, tall and brooding, stepping inside. He scanned the room, and for a brief moment, our eyes met. There was an intensity in his gaze that sent a shiver down my spine. Before I could decipher the connection, he turned, slipping past the tables and disappearing into the crowd.

I shook my head, attempting to shake off the strange feeling that lingered like the last notes of a haunting melody. "It's nothing," I assured Clara, who raised an eyebrow, clearly unconvinced.

"Nothing or something?" she teased. "You know, I've read that often the past comes back to taunt us right when we're on the verge of moving forward."

I laughed, a nervous sound that echoed through the café, but beneath it, I felt a glimmer of truth. As we ordered our pastries and engaged in light-hearted banter, the weight of Julian's impending return loomed in the background, a whisper of unresolved emotions ready to emerge from the shadows. I couldn't escape the feeling that the universe was conspiring to push me towards a reckoning—one I was not entirely sure I was ready to face.

I spent the rest of the day in a haze, each hour stretching and warping as my thoughts spun around the specter of Julian. The sun had dipped low, casting golden hues across the sky when I finally returned home, but the light did little to soothe the tempest brewing in my chest. My apartment was eerily quiet, the kind of silence that could swallow you whole if you weren't careful. It was an unsettling contrast to the warm buzz of the café, where laughter mingled with the clatter of cups. Here, the air felt thick with unspoken words and unresolved feelings.

I dropped my bag onto the sofa, its leather thudding against the cushions. As I moved to the kitchen, the familiar aroma of fresh herbs and spices wafted from the small windowsill garden I'd nurtured over the past few months. The basil plants seemed to sway slightly, as if beckoning me to ground myself in their vibrancy. I pulled a few leaves, their fragrance sharp and invigorating, and tossed them into a sizzling pan with olive oil. Cooking was my sanctuary, a way to distract my restless mind. As the vegetables began to soften, the vibrant colors brightening against the darkened room, I let the rhythm of chopping and stirring calm me, even if only a little.

But the moment I sat down to eat, a knot formed in my stomach. The weight of Julian's message loomed over me, the echoes of Clara's words ringing in my ears. Closure. It felt like a heavy, elusive thing, as though it were a prize dangling just out of reach. What if confronting him only stirred the ashes of a fire I had hoped was long extinguished? I picked at my food, each bite feeling like a deliberate decision I wasn't ready to make.

The clock ticked loudly on the wall, the second hand a relentless reminder of the minutes slipping away. I could practically hear Clara's voice urging me to decide. Was I ready to face the past? To confront Julian and the memories that danced like phantoms in my mind? I let out a frustrated sigh, the steam from my plate mingling with the cool air of the room, and leaned back in my chair, eyes fixed on the flickering candle on the table.

Just as I pushed my plate away, my phone buzzed on the counter, startling me out of my reverie. I reached for it, half-expecting another message from Clara. Instead, it was from Julian.

Can we meet tomorrow? I need to talk.

The simplicity of his words made my heart race, but my mind quickly spiraled into chaos. What did he need to talk about? What if he had changed? What if he hadn't? I bit my lip, grappling with a thousand questions, each one more daunting than the last. A part of me craved to see him, to know if he still carried the same spark in his eyes, if his laugh still had the power to make the world feel lighter. But the other part screamed at me to run, to avoid the possibility of reopening old wounds.

With a deep breath, I set my phone down and decided to seek refuge in a distraction. I rifled through my bookshelf, my fingers brushing against the spines of countless novels. Their stories had provided solace in times of need, a welcome escape into worlds where problems could be neatly wrapped up in a few hundred pages. I settled on a light romantic comedy, hoping for something to pull me from my spiraling thoughts. But as the characters flitted through their own delightful dilemmas, my mind continued to drift back to Julian, the voice of my heart whispering questions I was too afraid to answer.

Sleep came fitfully that night, dreams punctuated by flashes of laughter and warmth mixed with shadows of doubt and regret. When morning broke, the sun poured through my curtains, illuminating the mess of blankets I had twisted around myself in the night. I dragged myself to the bathroom, splashing cold water on my face, trying to shake off the remnants of slumber and the lingering weight of impending decisions.

As I dressed, my heart raced with a mixture of anticipation and fear. A part of me wanted to cancel, to stay buried in the safety of my routine, but another part—a braver part—urged me to embrace whatever lay ahead. I chose a simple yet chic outfit, a dark blue dress that hugged my figure without clinging too tightly, paired with a light cardigan. The soft fabric felt like a hug, a comforting reminder that I was more than just my past.

With each step towards the café, I could feel the electric pulse of the city around me, the chatter of pedestrians blending with the soft rustle of leaves. The crisp air was invigorating, stirring a sense of possibility within me. What if today was a turning point? What if this meeting brought clarity, a new beginning, or perhaps even a closure I had been unknowingly craving?

As I entered the café, the familiar bell chimed overhead, and my gaze immediately landed on Julian. He was seated at a corner table, looking every bit as handsome as I remembered, with that tousled hair and those deep, expressive eyes that seemed to hold the weight of the world. My breath caught in my throat, and for a brief moment, the bustling café faded away, leaving only the two of us suspended in a bubble of time.

He looked up, our eyes locking, and an unexpected warmth flooded through me, igniting the flicker of memories I had tried so hard to forget. I approached slowly, my heart racing as I took in the nuances of his expression—a mixture of hope, nervousness, and something else that I couldn't quite decipher.

"Hey," I said, forcing a casualness into my tone that I certainly didn't feel.

"Hey," he replied, his voice low and steady, sending a ripple of familiarity down my spine.

We sat in silence for a moment, the hum of the café swirling around us like a chaotic symphony. The air was thick with unspoken words, each second stretching between us as we both searched for the right way to begin. Finally, he broke the silence, his brow furrowing slightly as he leaned forward. "Thanks for meeting me."

"Of course," I replied, my voice steadier than I felt. "You said you needed to talk."

"I do," he began, his gaze unwavering. "But first, I want to know how you've been. How's life treating you?"

And just like that, the walls I had built around my heart began to crack, letting a sliver of vulnerability seep through. The past was a complicated puzzle, but sitting here with him, I realized I wasn't just confronting it; I was choosing to reshape it.

His question hung in the air like a tender note suspended in a symphony, inviting yet laden with the weight of past experiences. I shifted slightly in my chair, the rough wood pressing against my back, grounding me in the moment even as my thoughts danced with memories I had tried to confine. "I've been... okay, I guess," I replied, forcing a smile that didn't quite reach my eyes. "Busy with work, keeping my plants alive, you know, the usual adulting struggles."

Julian's lips quirked up in that familiar half-smile that used to send butterflies fluttering in my stomach. "You always did have a way with plants. I think you could probably coax a cactus to bloom if you put your mind to it."

The nostalgia washed over me, bringing with it the bittersweet taste of memories that felt both comforting and agonizing. "Well, I can't say the same for relationships," I quipped lightly, though the truth hung heavy between us. "Those have been more... complicated."

His expression shifted, the humor fading into something deeper, more contemplative. "Complicated is one way to put it," he said, his voice dropping an octave as he leaned in, clearly sensing the weight of my words. "I've missed you, you know. Things haven't been the same since you left."

"Have they ever been the same?" I shot back, surprising myself with the edge in my tone. It was a question I had asked myself countless times since I'd walked away.

"I've spent a lot of time thinking about that," he replied, running a hand through his hair, the familiar gesture drawing me into a whirlwind of emotions. "After you left, everything felt... muted. Like the color had been drained from my life. I didn't realize how much you added to it until you were gone."

The vulnerability in his voice tugged at something buried deep within me. I had always known Julian had a knack for introspection, but hearing him articulate his feelings made the reality of our shared history palpable. "It's easy to miss things when they're gone," I said, more softly this time, the tension in my shoulders easing just a fraction.

"And harder to change," he admitted, his gaze piercing through the haze of unresolved feelings swirling around us. "I wanted to reach out so many times, but I didn't know how to face you. I wasn't the person you needed back then. I was so wrapped up in my own issues that I didn't see what was right in front of me."

A part of me wanted to tell him that it was too late, that I had built a life without him and learned to find joy in my independence. But that very independence felt precarious in this moment, like a fragile thread stretched too tight. "You were in your own world, Julian. We both were," I replied, trying to steady my voice. "But it's different now. I'm different."

"Different how?" he pressed, leaning forward, the earnestness in his eyes both exhilarating and terrifying.

"I'm not the scared girl who ran away anymore," I confessed, the words spilling out before I could stop them. "I've faced challenges and built something for myself. But I don't know if that means I can just dive back into whatever this is—whatever we had."

He was silent for a moment, the weight of my confession hanging between us like an invisible thread, drawing us closer. "Then let's take it slow," he offered. "No expectations. Just... see where this goes."

A flicker of hope ignited in my chest, but it was quickly doused by a flash of doubt. "You think it's that simple?" I scoffed lightly, masking my uncertainty with humor. "You can't just shake hands and forget the past. It's like trying to convince a cat to take a bath. It's messy and fraught with claws."

Julian chuckled, the sound warm and soothing, breaking the tension. "Fair enough. But I'd like to try, even if it means navigating a few scratches along the way."

"Is that your idea of romance? To dodge emotional landmines with me?"

"It's either that or go back to pretending we never knew each other," he replied, his eyes twinkling with mischief. "And I'm not sure I could handle that."

Just as I was about to respond, my phone buzzed again, slicing through the moment. I glanced at the screen, my heart leaping as I recognized Clara's name. I could feel Julian's gaze on me, the curiosity palpable. I quickly opened the message, my heart racing as I read her words.

I hope you're okay. I just found out something that might change everything. Meet me at the park after your coffee? It's urgent.

"What's wrong?" Julian asked, the concern etching lines on his forehead.

"I... I don't know yet," I stammered, my mind racing. "It's Clara. She says it's urgent. I should go."

He frowned, but then nodded slowly, understanding flashing across his face. "If you need to go, then you should."

"Thanks for understanding," I said, standing up abruptly. The laughter and warmth of our earlier conversation felt like a distant memory, replaced by the sudden heaviness of uncertainty. "Let's talk later? Maybe after I figure out what this is all about?"

"Absolutely," he replied, his eyes lingering on mine with an intensity that made my heart race. "I'll be waiting."

I turned to leave, my pulse quickening with each step away from him. The café felt stifling as I pushed through the door, the fresh air hitting me like a wave, forcing me to catch my breath. I glanced back at Julian, who was still watching me, a mixture of hope and concern written on his face. My heart fluttered in response, but the nagging worry from Clara's message pulled me onward.

As I hurried towards the park, the world around me blurred into a haze of colors and sounds, the laughter of children playing, the soft rustle of leaves in the breeze. I couldn't shake the feeling that whatever Clara had to share might be life-altering, a revelation that could change everything I thought I knew about my past.

When I finally reached the park, I spotted Clara sitting on a bench, her hands clenched tightly around her coffee cup. She looked up as I approached, her expression grave.

"Julia," she said, urgency lacing her voice. "You need to hear this."

"What is it?" I asked, my heart pounding in my chest.

Before she could respond, I felt a presence behind me, the familiar scent of pine and cologne wafting through the air. I turned slowly, and the ground seemed to shift beneath my feet. There, standing just a few feet away, was Julian, his face a mask of uncertainty and something darker.

"Julian?" I breathed, my voice barely a whisper.

Clara's eyes darted between us, and I felt the weight of the world pressing down. "You both need to hear this together," she said, her tone resolute, as if she were a general preparing to deliver news of a battle lost or won.

My stomach knotted with apprehension, and just as Clara opened her mouth to speak, I felt the air grow thick with tension, the moment stretching like a tightrope between us, daring us to step off into the unknown.

Chapter 21: The Storm Before the Calm

The air was thick with anticipation, a pulse echoing through the charming little boutique I had poured my heart into. Sunlight filtered through the large front windows, casting playful shadows across the sleek displays of vibrant fabric and expertly crafted accessories. Each piece in our new collection was a testament to sleepless nights and endless cups of coffee, yet beneath the fabric's beauty lay a creeping sense of foreboding. I busied myself straightening a row of delicate blouses, but my mind was a tempest, swirling with doubts and lingering echoes of a past that refused to let go.

"Hey, you okay?" Ethan's voice broke through my haze, his brow furrowed with genuine concern. He stood in the doorway, hands shoved deep into the pockets of his jeans, that familiar, boyish charm illuminated by the afternoon light. I loved how he always seemed to radiate warmth, like a cozy fire on a frigid winter night, but today his gaze felt like a spotlight, illuminating every shadow of doubt I tried to conceal.

I offered a smile that didn't quite reach my eyes. "Just getting everything ready for the launch tonight," I replied, my voice bright yet strained, like a note on the verge of cracking.

He stepped closer, the floorboards creaking beneath his weight, and leaned against the counter, studying me with a knowing look. "You've been off lately. It's not just work, is it?"

With a heavy sigh, I turned my attention to a display, rearranging a set of silk scarves. "I just... I have this feeling. Like something's brewing just out of sight. I can't quite put my finger on it." My voice trailed off, the weight of my own words pressing against my chest.

"Trust your instincts," he said softly, his gaze unwavering. "You've built something beautiful here. You can handle whatever comes next."

His faith in me was like a soothing balm, yet the knots in my stomach tightened. If only he knew how much I longed to believe that. I swallowed hard and smiled again, this time more genuinely. "Thanks. I'll be fine. Just... a bit of pre-launch jitters, you know?"

Ethan nodded, but the concern lingered in his eyes, the kind that made me want to unravel my worries to him, to share the heavy history that still clung to my soul like an unwelcome shroud. But I couldn't. Not now, not before the launch that was supposed to be the pinnacle of my hard work. I needed to focus on this moment, the success I had carved out with determination and creativity.

As the day wore on, the excitement in the boutique grew. My team buzzed around me, putting finishing touches on everything from the floral arrangements to the delicate lighting that would cast our designs in the best possible light. The scent of fresh blooms wafted through the air, a mix of lavender and jasmine, creating an inviting atmosphere that made the space feel alive. Laughter echoed as friends and loyal customers filtered in, eager to see our latest offerings.

But just as I felt myself slipping into the joyous rhythm of the evening, a familiar figure stepped through the door, casting an unwelcome shadow. Julian. My heart stuttered, and a cold rush of dread washed over me. He looked impossibly handsome, his tousled hair catching the light in a way that made my stomach churn with an unwanted mixture of nostalgia and anxiety.

"What are you doing here?" The words escaped my lips before I could stop them, sharp and laced with an edge of disbelief.

He flashed a smile, one that could light up a room yet felt like a dagger aimed at my heart. "I heard about the launch and thought I'd check it out. Looks amazing, by the way."

"Thanks," I managed, my voice barely above a whisper. "It's... it's good to see you." The lie hung between us, fragile and transparent.

He stepped further into the boutique, his presence both magnetic and menacing. "It's been a while. I thought maybe we could talk."

Talk. The word hung in the air like a storm cloud, threatening to unleash the chaos I had so carefully kept at bay. I glanced at Ethan, who stood watching from a distance, his expression shifting from concern to something more guarded. The tension between Julian and me crackled like static electricity, a silent battle of wills that felt all too familiar.

"Not here," I said, my voice firm as I took a step back, reclaiming a sliver of control. "We can't do this right now."

"Why not? We need to clear the air, don't you think?" His tone was light, teasing even, but beneath it lay a current of seriousness that made my skin prickle.

The guests mingled around us, laughter and chatter wrapping around me like a comforting embrace, yet Julian's presence felt like an intrusion. I could almost hear the ticking of the clock, each second pulling me closer to a confrontation I wasn't ready for.

"Now's not the time. This is my moment," I said, my voice steadier than I felt. "This is about my work, not our past."

Julian's smile faded, replaced by a shadow of something darker, something I couldn't quite name. "You think I came here to ruin it? I just wanted to see you."

"Too late for that," I shot back, a mix of defiance and desperation fueling my words. "You don't get to waltz in and act like nothing happened."

He stepped closer, the heat of his presence wrapping around me like a thick fog. "I know I messed up, but we need to talk. Just the two of us."

My heart raced, an unwelcome reminder of all the history buried beneath our fragile façade. "You're not welcome here, Julian," I said, and for a fleeting moment, I felt the strength of my resolve. But deep down, a part of me wondered if he was right—if we needed to confront the storm before it swept everything away.

I turned away, my mind racing, as Ethan approached, an anchor amidst the chaos. "You okay?" he asked, his voice low and steady, concern etched on his face.

I forced a nod, but the tension coiled tighter within me. As I glanced back at Julian, I could see the storm brewing in his eyes, and I knew that tonight would change everything.

I turned my back on Julian, my pulse racing as I forced a smile for the guests swirling around me, the laughter and chatter of the boutique filling the space like a warm embrace. Yet, the air crackled with a tension that I couldn't shake. I caught Ethan's eye, and he gave me a subtle nod, a wordless encouragement wrapped in concern. I needed to ground myself, to remember that this was my moment—the culmination of years of hard work, creativity, and the courage to believe in my dreams.

As I moved through the boutique, engaging with customers, my mind wrestled with the sight of Julian lurking in the corner, his gaze never straying far from me. I could almost feel the weight of our shared history hanging between us, thick and suffocating, like a storm cloud ready to unleash its fury. It wasn't just the memories that haunted me; it was the potential for future chaos, a maelstrom of emotions that threatened to spill over if I didn't contain it.

"Can you believe how stunning these designs are?" a customer gushed, lifting a silk blouse to the light, the fabric shimmering like starlight.

"Absolutely! Each piece tells a story," I replied, my voice bright, though my heart felt heavy. I knew this was my moment, a chance to showcase my talent, yet Julian's presence loomed like a dark shadow, threatening to eclipse everything I had built.

"Excuse me, I'll be right back," I said, excusing myself and weaving through the crowd, my eyes flicking back to where Julian stood. He appeared to be engaged in conversation with a couple of guests, his charming demeanor effortlessly drawing them in. It infuriated me to see him in a place he didn't belong, casually mingling as if our past was just a trivial chapter in his life.

"Julia!" Ethan's voice called out, pulling me from my spiraling thoughts. I turned to find him at the bar, pouring himself a drink. "You need to take a breath. Come join me for a second."

"Is that code for 'let's avoid the brooding ex'?" I teased, trying to lighten the mood as I stepped toward him.

He chuckled, his eyes sparkling with mischief. "You caught me. But seriously, you're going to wear a hole in the floor pacing around like that."

I leaned against the bar, letting the cool surface steady me. "It's just… I didn't expect him to show up. Not tonight."

Ethan nodded, his expression shifting to something more serious. "You know you don't have to engage with him if you don't want to. This is your night."

"Right," I replied, feeling a mixture of gratitude and guilt. "But I can't just pretend he's not here. That would be like ignoring a hurricane brewing in the distance."

"True, but maybe you could let the storm blow over without getting swept away?" His smile was warm, but his eyes were keen, watching me as if he could see through the facade I had carefully constructed.

"Maybe," I conceded, but my heart wasn't convinced. The thought of confronting Julian filled me with dread, yet the notion of allowing him to disrupt my night felt equally unbearable.

Just then, the ambient noise of the boutique shifted, laughter bubbling up before fading into whispers. I turned to see what had captured everyone's attention. Julian stood at the center of a small crowd, animatedly gesturing as he shared a story. I couldn't hear the details, but the ease with which he commanded the room twisted something inside me, a reminder of how effortlessly he had once held my heart captive.

"See?" Ethan said, nudging my shoulder gently. "You could just ignore him and focus on the people who actually matter."

I couldn't tear my gaze away from Julian, though. The way he laughed, his voice rich and smooth, sent a shiver down my spine. "I need to talk to him, Ethan. I can't keep dodging him forever."

Ethan sighed, his shoulders dropping slightly. "Just... be careful. I know how he can be."

"I'll be fine." I offered a reassuring smile, though it felt more like a promise I was struggling to keep. Gathering my resolve, I excused myself from Ethan and approached the gathering, my heart thudding loudly in my chest.

As I neared, Julian caught sight of me and smiled, that familiar boyish grin that had once melted my defenses. "Julia! Come join us. I was just telling everyone how fabulous this place is."

The crowd parted slightly, and I stood before him, feeling both powerful and vulnerable. "Thanks," I said, my tone cool as I crossed my arms, hoping to project an air of confidence I didn't entirely feel.

"It really is impressive," Julian continued, unabashed. "You've really turned this place into something special."

"Thanks, Julian. I appreciate the compliment." The words felt like nails on a chalkboard. His charm was grating, reminding me of the days when I had fallen for his flattery, only to discover it came with strings attached.

"I mean it," he said, tilting his head, a hint of sincerity in his gaze. "I didn't come here to cause trouble, I swear. I just wanted to see you, to reconnect."

The word "reconnect" hung in the air like an unwelcome guest. "Reconnect?" I echoed, my voice a mixture of disbelief and irritation. "After everything? You think it's that simple?"

His expression faltered, the flicker of uncertainty crossing his features only for a moment. "I know I messed up. I just thought... maybe we could talk it out. Clear the air, you know?"

"Talk it out? Julian, you walked away without so much as a backward glance." My words were sharper than I intended, but the sting of old wounds resurfaced with every moment spent in his presence.

He stepped closer, the warmth of his body invading my personal space, a gesture both inviting and intrusive. "I thought you'd understand. Things were complicated. I didn't want to hurt you."

I scoffed, shaking my head. "And yet, here we are. You show up at my launch party like everything's fine, as if you didn't leave a wake of chaos behind you."

"Maybe I thought I could help clean up some of that chaos," he replied, a hint of defiance in his tone.

"Help? Or make it worse?" I shot back, the frustration bubbling over.

The crowd had fallen silent, eyes darting between us like spectators at a tennis match, and I felt the heat of their scrutiny. My heart raced, a strange mix of anger and hurt coursing through me. I could almost feel the storm breaking, the tension in the air electrifying.

"Julia," he began, his voice dropping to a more serious note, "I know I don't deserve your forgiveness. But I'm here because I want to make things right."

"Make things right?" I echoed, incredulous. "You can't just stroll in here and expect everything to go back to normal."

Julian opened his mouth to respond, but before he could speak, a loud crash echoed from the back of the boutique. The crowd gasped, all heads turning as a display of delicate ceramic vases toppled to the floor, shattering into a thousand sparkling pieces.

My heart raced as chaos erupted, the laughter turning to startled cries. In that moment of distraction, the storm of emotions between Julian and me was momentarily overshadowed, and I felt a jolt of relief mixed with dread. The night was unraveling before my eyes, and I could only hope that I could pull the pieces together before it was too late.

The sound of shattering pottery jolted me from the storm brewing in my mind. Instinctively, I stepped away from Julian, my heart racing. The guests' gasps echoed in the space, a symphony of surprise and dismay that pulled me back to the present. I glanced over to see a young intern, her face flushed with embarrassment, standing over the wreckage of what had once been an elegant display.

"Uh-oh," Julian muttered, attempting to mask his amusement. "Looks like chaos really does have a knack for timing."

"Now's not the time, Julian," I shot back, my eyes still trained on the scene unfolding before us. "We need to help her."

He raised an eyebrow, a hint of a smirk playing on his lips. "You know, if you wanted to distract me, you could've just mentioned that vase was an antique."

Ignoring his quip, I rushed toward the intern, my heart still pounding in response to the unexpected drama. "Are you okay?" I asked, kneeling beside her as she blinked rapidly, her eyes wide with shock.

"I— I didn't mean to," she stammered, her voice trembling. "I was just trying to rearrange them for a better view, and then they just..."

"It's alright. Accidents happen." I offered her a reassuring smile. "Let's get this cleaned up. I'll help."

As I gathered the shards of porcelain, a flurry of thoughts raced through my mind. Julian's presence felt like a constant distraction, his dark charisma tangling with my emotions like strands of thread in a knot. I could hear him behind me, chatting with the other guests, his laughter cutting through the air, but it only fueled my resolve to keep the focus on the launch party.

"Really, Julia, you're a lifesaver," the intern said, her voice steadier now as she collected herself. "I didn't think it would be such a disaster."

I shook my head, dismissing her worry. "You've got enough on your plate without adding this to it. Let's make sure everything else stays intact, alright?"

With her nod of agreement, we worked in tandem, gathering the shattered pieces and carefully setting aside the intact vases. I felt a rush of gratitude toward the intern, her eagerness to help contrasting sharply with the turbulence in my heart. In a way, it reminded me that while life was unpredictable, the small victories were what kept us grounded.

Once the mess was cleared, I stood up, brushing my hands on my skirt and taking a deep breath. But before I could return to the crowd, Julian sauntered over, an unmistakable glint of mischief in his eyes.

"Didn't know you had a hidden talent for cleaning up after disasters," he said, his tone light, though I detected an undercurrent of something more serious.

"Life skills, Julian. Maybe you should try some." I kept my tone teasing, but my insides churned. The earlier tension had only been amplified by the interruption, and now it loomed over us like an impending downpour.

He took a step closer, his expression shifting to something softer, more earnest. "You know, I really am here to make amends. I can't help but feel I owe you that much."

I scoffed, shaking my head. "And what, exactly, do you think making amends looks like? A bouquet of flowers? A heartfelt apology?"

"Honestly? I was thinking more like a drink after this chaos dies down."

I crossed my arms, a mix of disbelief and curiosity flaring within me. "You think I'd want to sit down with you, after everything?"

"Why not?" he challenged, an eyebrow raised. "You're the one who keeps saying we need to talk. I figured a quiet moment away from the chaos could do us good."

The sincerity in his eyes was disarming, and a part of me ached to believe that we could find some kind of resolution. "You think you can just charm your way back into my life?"

"I'd say it's more of a process," he replied, a playful smile teasing his lips. "But you have to admit, I'm rather good at it."

I rolled my eyes, but beneath my irritation lay a flicker of interest. "So you want me to be charmed into ignoring the past? What makes you think that would work?"

"Because we had something real, Julia. And it's worth exploring if you're open to it."

His words hung in the air, a tantalizing invitation wrapped in layers of history. My heart raced, not just from the confrontation but from the undercurrents of old feelings that threatened to bubble back to the surface.

Before I could respond, the boutique doors swung open, a gust of wind sweeping through the room as a group of latecomers entered, laughter spilling out into the night. It brought a welcome distraction, a reminder of the joy that was still present, despite the tension.

"Let's go mingle," I suggested, trying to steer the conversation away from the precipice it felt like we were teetering on. "You can help me greet the newcomers."

Julian chuckled, falling into step beside me. "I can see you're trying to avoid that talk."

"Maybe I'm just trying to keep the focus on my work tonight. Something you seem to excel at—making everything about you."

"Touché," he replied, a grin spreading across his face. "But you can't blame me for wanting to get your attention."

We moved through the crowd, the chatter and laughter enveloping us. I smiled and greeted friends and customers, but my mind remained split between the buoyant atmosphere and the storm brewing within me.

As we reached the new arrivals, I felt a renewed sense of purpose wash over me. I was here to showcase my work, to celebrate the fruits of my labor, and nothing—especially not Julian—would take that away from me.

Just as I began to feel the tension dissipate, a loud crash came from the back of the boutique, drawing our attention. This time it was the wine station, the table overturned, bottles rolling across the floor, splattering crimson liquid everywhere like a scene from a drama.

"Oh, come on!" I exclaimed, rushing toward the mess with Julian close behind. "This is turning into a complete disaster!"

As I bent to help clean up the glass and wine, I felt Julian's presence beside me, his arm brushing against mine as we worked to contain the chaos. It was a simple gesture, yet it ignited a spark of electricity between us, a reminder of the undeniable chemistry that had always existed.

"Maybe we're just not cut out for celebrations," he quipped, tossing a towel in my direction.

"Or maybe we should just stick to lemonade next time," I shot back, my mood brightening despite the mayhem.

As we continued to clean, laughter mingled with the chatter, creating an oddly comforting backdrop. Yet, beneath the surface, I felt the storm of unresolved feelings swirling between us, a tempest waiting for the right moment to break.

Just then, the front door swung open again, and in walked a figure that froze my heart in place. There stood a woman, striking and confident, with an air of familiarity that made my breath catch. She was undeniably beautiful, her smile radiant, yet it was the way she looked directly at Julian that sent a ripple of anxiety through me.

"Hey, everyone!" she called, her voice bright and cheerful, cutting through the chaos like a knife. "I heard there was a party, and I couldn't resist crashing it!"

In that moment, as she made her way toward Julian, I felt the ground shift beneath my feet. The storm that had been brewing was no longer just about me and my past. It was about to become a whirlwind, and I was right in the eye of it, teetering on the brink of chaos as the pieces of my carefully constructed world began to crumble.

Chapter 22: Confrontation

The air in the gallery buzzes with the kind of electric excitement that seems to pulse through the very fabric of our creations. Dazzling hues of turquoise, vermilion, and ochre twist and dance in vibrant displays, each piece a story yearning to be told. Guests swirl about in laughter, glasses clinking like a melodic symphony celebrating our success. It should have been a night of unbridled joy, yet a weight pulls at my chest, anchoring me to a turbulent sea of memories that surge up as I spot him: Julian, gliding through the throng like a specter summoned from my past.

His presence has the uncanny ability to drain the color from the room, the laughter fading to a dull hum in my ears. I've spent months weaving my life back together, brick by painstaking brick, a mosaic of self-empowerment and fierce independence. But here he is, a wild card, tossing my fragile equilibrium into chaos once more. I grip the edge of the table, grounding myself against the sudden rush of old emotions, reminding myself of the promise I made to never again be a victim of his whims.

"Fancy seeing you here," he says, his voice smooth, almost too smooth, as if he's rehearsed the line. The corner of his mouth lifts in a smirk that makes my stomach churn.

I arch an eyebrow, crossing my arms in a defensive posture. "The invitation was open to all, wasn't it? Or do you think the universe revolves around you?"

His gaze sharpens, and for a fleeting moment, I wonder if I've struck a nerve. But the confidence in his eyes betrays any sign of uncertainty. "Come now, don't be like that. We both know I had as much right to be here as anyone else. I'm just here to support you."

"Support? Is that what you call it?" I can feel the heat rising in my cheeks, a mixture of anger and something more vulnerable.

"You supported my dreams right into the ground last time we met. Remember that?"

The laughter around us feels muted, as if the crowd has become a distant echo, leaving us in our own pocket of tension. The vibrant colors of the gallery swirl into a haze, and I struggle to keep my thoughts from spiraling back to all the ways he shattered my trust, how I gave him everything only to be left with nothing.

He steps closer, the familiar scent of his cologne—woodsy, warm, intoxicating—wraps around me, trying to coax me back to a time when the world felt simpler. "You've done well for yourself, I'll admit that. But you can't deny that I played a part in your success."

I scoff, shaking my head as if to physically rid myself of his poison. "You mean the part where you walked away and left me to pick up the pieces? Your influence ended the moment you decided to prioritize your own needs over mine. Don't twist this into something it's not."

Julian's expression shifts, frustration cracking the facade of cool indifference. "I never intended for it to end that way. You know me better than that."

"Do I?" My heart pounds in my ears as I lean in, my voice a sharp whisper, cutting through the ambient noise of the celebration. "You were never the man I thought you were, Julian. You turned into a ghost, one I didn't ask for, and yet here you are, haunting my moment."

"Haunting? Is that how you see me?" He laughs, but there's an edge to it, a brittle note that feels like a warning. "You've always had a flair for the dramatic, haven't you? Why can't you just see this for what it is? An opportunity for us to reconnect?"

"Reconnect?" The word feels foreign, a sharp blade against my heart. "You think we can just pretend like everything's fine? Like I can erase the hurt you caused with a few kind words? It doesn't work that way."

I start to turn away, needing to escape this suffocating confrontation, but his hand wraps around my wrist, a hold both familiar and unsettling. "Wait. Can't we at least talk? Just for a moment?"

I look at him, really look at him, and in the depths of his hazel eyes, I see something—regret, perhaps? Or maybe it's just desperation. "We've already talked, Julian. And every time we do, it's just another round in a game where I never wanted to play."

His grip loosens, and I pull away, wrapping my arms around myself as if I can shield my heart from the onslaught of emotions he incites. The chaos of the party swells around us, vibrant and inviting, but all I can focus on is the void he creates in my carefully constructed world.

Ethan stands at the edge of the gathering, watching us, his brow furrowed in concern. His gaze meets mine, a steadying presence amid the storm. I see pride in his eyes, mingled with the protective spark that flares whenever Julian steps too close. The thought grounds me, pulling me back to the present.

"You know, Julian, for someone who claims to support me, you sure have a funny way of showing it," I say, my voice stronger now. "I'm not the girl you once knew. I've grown. I've fought to reclaim my life, my dreams. I refuse to let you disrupt that."

His mouth opens, but I cut him off, feeling the fire within me surge. "I deserve better than what you offered before, and I won't allow you to pull me back into the shadows. So, if you'll excuse me, I have a celebration to attend, and it doesn't involve you."

With that, I turn on my heel, the weight of his gaze burning into my back. Each step I take feels like a victory, a reclaiming of my strength. I weave through the crowd, laughter and light enveloping me once more. I can feel Ethan's presence close behind, his warmth a comforting balm against the chill Julian leaves in his wake.

As I rejoin the festivities, my heart thuds in my chest, a reminder of the confrontation and the triumph that followed. I'm not just surviving; I'm thriving. And for the first time in a long while, I believe I have the strength to keep moving forward.

The music thrums in the background, a lively rhythm that dances through the air and wraps itself around the laughter spilling from lips. Yet the moment I step back into the crowd, a shadow lingers behind me, a reminder of the confrontation that nearly unraveled my evening. I scan the gallery, my pulse still quickening at the echo of Julian's words, the weight of our exchange still pressing against my chest like an unwelcome visitor. But I refuse to be tethered to that moment; I've clawed my way to this celebration, and I'll be damned if I let him steal my joy.

Ethan catches my eye again, his easy smile piercing through the fog of uncertainty lingering in my mind. He's a breath of fresh air, a steady presence amid the swirling chaos, and I find my resolve fortifying in his gaze. I weave through the throng of guests, my fingertips grazing the smooth surfaces of our designs, each one a testament to hard work and resilience. The fabric feels like magic beneath my touch, a reminder of the late nights spent stitching dreams into reality, and I can't help but smile as I take in the vibrant chaos that surrounds me.

"Hey, you!" Ethan calls out, his voice cutting through the noise as I reach for a glass of champagne. "Look at you! This place is incredible."

I lift my glass to him, the bubbly liquid catching the light as I step closer. "Not bad for a night I nearly ruined, huh?"

He chuckles, a deep, warm sound that curls around me like a soft blanket. "Please. You've been nothing short of spectacular. You deserve every bit of this." His gaze flickers momentarily toward the other side of the room, where Julian still lingers like a storm cloud, but he quickly refocuses on me, his expression playful. "So, tell me, how does it feel to be the belle of the ball? Are you ready for your royal debut?"

"Oh, you know," I say with a wink, "just waiting for my fairy godmother to show up and whisk me away to a land free of ex-boyfriends."

Ethan raises his glass, a knowing look in his eyes. "To fairy godmothers and the end of haunting memories, then."

We clink our glasses, and for a moment, the tension lifts, the laughter of our friends creating a buoyant atmosphere around us. I catch a glimpse of myself in the mirrored wall behind him, and the reflection reminds me of how far I've come. This dress, a deep emerald, hugs my curves in all the right places, a manifestation of the confidence I've fought to reclaim. I remember the nights I spent doubting whether I would ever feel like this again—alive, vibrant, and full of potential.

"Seriously, though," Ethan says, leaning closer, the warmth of his body radiating a comfort that momentarily pushes away the shadows. "If you need me to be your knight in shining armor tonight, just say the word. I'm not above saving damsels in distress."

I laugh, a sound that feels genuine and free, fluttering from my lips like a breath of fresh air. "You'd make a terrible knight, you know. You'd probably forget the sword and show up with a bouquet of flowers instead."

His eyes sparkle, the corners crinkling with delight. "What can I say? I'm a lover, not a fighter."

"Perfectly stated. I'm convinced that's exactly what you want on your résumé." I take a sip of champagne, savoring the effervescence, and let the moment settle into a comfortable rhythm. The stress of the confrontation fades, replaced by the buoyant energy of those around us.

As we laugh and mingle, the buzz of the party envelops us, but Julian's presence still looms like a specter in the background. Every now and then, I feel his eyes on me, a prickling sensation that sends shivers down my spine. I want to dismiss him, to believe I've moved past his shadow, but the way my heart quickens reminds me of the fight that still lingers within me.

"Are you okay?" Ethan's voice cuts through my thoughts, his brow furrowed with genuine concern. "I noticed you tensing up back there. Did he say something?"

I shrug, trying to shake off the weight of it all. "Just the same old song and dance. He thinks he can waltz back into my life, and I should just forget everything. It's exhausting."

His expression hardens, a protective flicker sparking in his eyes. "You're stronger than that. You've built this whole new life. Don't let anyone, especially him, take that away from you."

"Thanks for the pep talk, Captain Obvious." I smirk, lightening the mood. "But really, you're right. I won't let him pull me under again. I've worked too hard for that."

Ethan's smile softens, a gentle warmth that makes my heart flutter unexpectedly. "I admire that about you. Your strength is infectious."

Before I can respond, the lights dim momentarily, casting an enchanting glow over the gallery. The crowd buzzes with excitement as the host announces a surprise performance—a local band I've always wanted to see. The rich strains of music fill the space, a delightful distraction that draws us all closer together.

"Come on, let's dance!" Ethan nudges me playfully, his eyes alight with mischief. "What better way to celebrate than to let loose?"

"Dance? In this dress? You must have a death wish." But the infectious energy of the music swirls around us, wrapping me in a bubble of exhilaration that's impossible to resist.

Before I can protest, he takes my hand, leading me toward the makeshift dance floor, the rhythm pulsing through the air like a heartbeat. The crowd sways, a mass of colorful fabric and laughter, and I can't help but grin as Ethan spins me around.

We lose ourselves in the music, moving together with a fluidity that feels both exhilarating and freeing. I watch as the world blurs around us, the vibrant colors merging into a tapestry of light and sound. Laughter bubbles between us as we sway and twirl, a dance of joy that ignites something deep within my soul. In this moment, I am not defined by my past but rather by the possibilities that stretch out before me.

But amid the joyous chaos, a flash of movement catches my eye, and I glance back toward the edge of the dance floor. Julian stands there, arms crossed, a frown marring his otherwise handsome features. The sight sends a jolt through me, and suddenly, the carefree laughter feels a touch hollow. The weight of his gaze is a reminder of the unresolved conflict, and I can't help but feel that the battle isn't quite over.

Ethan follows my line of sight, his expression shifting into something darker. "Ignore him. This is your night."

"Easier said than done," I murmur, the tension coiling back into my chest. I want to shake it off, to dance the night away without a care, but Julian's presence is a shadow I can't quite escape.

And yet, as Ethan pulls me closer, his grip steady and reassuring, I find solace in the moment. I won't let fear dictate my joy, not now, not ever. The music envelops us, a balm against the past, and as I lean into Ethan, I remind myself that every step forward is a testament to my strength—a promise that I will not be defined by those who try to pull me back into their darkness.

As the music swells, I lose myself in the rhythm, letting the pulse of the beat guide me away from the specter of Julian. The lights twinkle like stars above us, creating a dreamy ambiance that lures me into a moment of pure bliss. With Ethan by my side, the world transforms, the weight of my past feeling lighter with every twirl and step. We move seamlessly, our bodies swaying together, laughter spilling between us like sparkling champagne.

"Who knew you could bust a move like this?" Ethan teases, a playful glint in his eye as he spins me around again, the hem of my dress fluttering around my legs. "I'm not sure if I should be impressed or terrified."

"Both, obviously!" I laugh, feeling a freedom that almost makes me giddy. The way he twirls me back into his embrace ignites something electric between us. "Just wait until I break out my signature move. It involves a lot of flailing and possibly knocking someone out."

"Flailing? I've seen better moves from my grandma at her weekly bingo night," he counters, feigning seriousness as he throws his hands up in mock defense. "Please, don't go all Broadway on me!"

I can't help but burst into laughter, the sound bubbling up like the finest of wines. Ethan is a refreshing presence, the kind that makes me feel like I can breathe without fear. Yet as I lose myself in this fleeting happiness, a shadow flickers at the corner of my vision, and for a moment, the bright lights dim. I glance over my shoulder, my heart dropping when I spot Julian standing in the doorway, his expression a blend of annoyance and something darker.

"What is it with him? Can't he take a hint?" I mutter, my good mood faltering slightly.

"Hey," Ethan says softly, gently cupping my chin and turning my face toward him. "You're not going to let him ruin this, are you?"

"No, of course not. It's just... hard to ignore him." The conviction in my voice wavers as I watch Julian step further into the room, his posture exuding an arrogance that's impossible to overlook. "He's like a bad penny that keeps showing up."

"Then let's give him a reason to look elsewhere." Ethan grins, and before I can respond, he pulls me closer, our bodies fitting together in a way that feels both natural and exciting. The music shifts to something slower, a sweet melody that calls for intimacy rather than exuberance. "Let's show him what he's missing."

And just like that, we sway together, our movements synchronized to the rhythm of the moment. I feel a warmth blossoming in my chest as I gaze into Ethan's eyes, the playful banter transforming into something deeper. "You really think so?" I whisper, trying to mask the tremor of vulnerability in my voice.

"Absolutely," he replies, his tone serious now, yet still infused with warmth. "You're a force of nature, and he's too blind to see that. Just look at you, shining like a diamond."

As we move together, the world around us fades, but I can't shake the sensation of being watched. Julian's presence feels like a dark cloud looming just out of reach. I steal another glance, and our eyes lock for a heartbeat—a flash of recognition followed by something jagged and sharp. I shiver, and for a moment, I'm back in that old place where fear mingled with love, where I was lost to his charms.

"What is it?" Ethan asks, his brow furrowed with concern.

"Nothing, I—" I hesitate, weighing the words carefully. "Just a little déjà vu, that's all. I'm fine."

But I can feel the storm brewing inside me, the tension of unresolved feelings swirling beneath the surface. Just when I think I've escaped the darkness, there it is again, taunting me, waiting for a moment of weakness. I shake it off, determined to stay present, to focus on this enchanting moment with Ethan.

"Let's get out of here," I say suddenly, a reckless spark igniting in my chest. "I don't want to spend another second worrying about him."

Ethan raises an eyebrow, a playful challenge lighting his gaze. "Are you suggesting we abandon this glorious soirée? Think of all the delicious hors d'oeuvres and fancy drinks we'll miss!"

"Food and drinks can wait. I want to do something spontaneous, something that makes me feel alive."

His eyes widen with intrigue, and for a second, the playful mask slips, revealing an intensity that sends shivers down my spine. "I like the sound of that. What do you have in mind?"

"Let's sneak out and find that rooftop terrace I heard about. I've always wanted to see the city skyline at night." The idea bubbles up from within me, fueled by the exhilaration of the moment. "And besides, I could use a little fresh air."

"Lead the way, then," he says, his smile wide as he takes my hand. "Just promise you won't go all flailing on me again. I might drop you over the edge."

"Just try to keep up, slowpoke!" I tease, and together we weave through the crowd, laughter spilling from our lips like a shared secret.

As we slip out of the gallery, the cool night air envelops us, a refreshing reprieve from the stuffiness inside. The skyline stretches out before us, a glittering tapestry of lights twinkling against the velvet sky. I take a deep breath, inhaling the mingled scents of the city—fresh rain on pavement, the distant aroma of street food, and something indescribably sweet.

"Wow," I breathe, awestruck by the view. "It's even more beautiful than I imagined."

Ethan steps beside me, his presence warm and grounding. "It really is. But I think you might be the most beautiful thing here." He glances sideways at me, mischief dancing in his eyes. "What's your secret? Is it the dress, or did you steal the moonlight?"

I laugh, a soft blush creeping up my cheeks. "Please, it's definitely the dress. The moonlight just makes it sparkle a bit more."

"Glad to see you've still got your sense of humor. That's a key ingredient in a perfect night." He nudges me playfully, but then his expression shifts, growing serious. "You know, you don't have to pretend with me. I get that tonight hasn't been easy."

"Yeah, well, it's easier to laugh it off than to dwell on the mess he made," I reply, a hint of bitterness creeping into my voice. "But I'm tired of letting him have any power over me."

"Then let's make a pact," he suggests, his tone earnest. "No more letting the past dictate our present. Tonight is ours. Let's leave all that behind and just... be here."

"Deal." I extend my pinky finger, and he chuckles, linking it with his own. "Now, what's next on our adventure? Should we pretend to be superheroes and jump off this roof?"

Ethan laughs, the sound buoyant against the night sky. "Only if I can wear a cape. I've always wanted to be the guy in the background, saving the day while looking fabulous."

"Fabulous is an understatement. You'd be a legend in the cape-wearing community."

Just as I'm about to suggest we take a selfie against the skyline, a chill races up my spine, a sensation so intense it stops me mid-laugh. I turn, heart pounding, and see Julian standing at the entrance to the terrace, his expression unreadable. The vibrant energy of the night dims, replaced by a sense of foreboding that wraps around me like a heavy cloak.

Ethan tenses beside me, instinctively shifting closer. "He followed us."

"Why can't he just take a hint?" I mutter, fury igniting within me, battling the fear that threatens to creep back in. "I thought I was done with him."

Julian steps forward, eyes blazing with something that looks like determination—or is it desperation? "Can we talk? Please? Just for a minute."

"No." The word escapes my lips before I can think, firm and unwavering.

Ethan moves protectively in front of me, his posture radiating strength. "You don't get to dictate how this night goes, Julian. You had your chance, and you blew it."

"Ethan—" I start, but the tension crackles between us like static electricity.

"I'm not going to let him intimidate you again," he says, a fierce determination in his voice.

Julian scoffs, an ugly sneer twisting his handsome features. "This isn't about you. It's about her. You think you're some knight in shining armor, but you don't know what you're getting into."

I can feel my heart hammering in my chest, a mixture of anger and confusion spiraling within me. "What do you mean by that?"

But before Julian can respond, a flash of movement catches my eye. I turn just in time to see something glinting in the light—something sharp. My breath hitches as I realize the threat is much closer than I ever anticipated.

"Ethan, look out!" I shout, adrenaline surging as I reach for him. But before I can warn him, the world erupts into chaos, and I'm left standing at the precipice of danger, with everything I've fought for hanging in the balance.

Chapter 23: A Fragile Peace

With Julian gone, a fragile peace settled over the boutique, wrapping around me like the gentle embrace of a familiar cashmere sweater. Sunlight streamed through the large front windows, igniting the racks of clothes in a warm glow, highlighting the vibrant hues of summer dresses and the soft pastels of the spring collection. I stood behind the register, idly folding a display of silk scarves, my fingers brushing against the delicate fabric, the rich colors reminiscent of sunsets I used to watch with my grandmother. It was in this moment of tranquility that I noticed the sound of laughter and chatter rising from the dressing rooms, where Clara was helping a group of customers choose their outfits. Her voice rang out, cheerful and infectious, like the first notes of a favorite song, filling the air with joy.

Ethan entered, a breeze of fresh air following him as he stepped inside. He always carried that peculiar scent—citrus and musk, an aroma that lingered long after he left. Today, he wore a fitted navy shirt that accentuated his lean frame, the sleeves rolled up to reveal toned forearms. I caught myself stealing glances, marveling at the way he moved with an easy grace, as though he belonged to a world where every moment was an invitation to dance.

"Hey there, superstar," he said, a playful smirk dancing on his lips as he leaned against the doorframe. "Looks like you've been working hard."

I waved my hand dismissively, a smile tugging at the corners of my mouth. "It's just the usual chaos. The world of fashion waits for no one, not even for a moment of respite."

He approached the counter, leaning over it, our faces close enough that I could see the faint freckles dotting his nose. "And how is our little kingdom holding up without its king?" The question hung between us, unspoken yet heavy with meaning. Julian had been the enigmatic force behind the collection, a whirlwind of creativity and charisma, leaving an indelible mark that was difficult to forget.

I sighed, my shoulders dropping slightly. "It's... peaceful. But there's a lingering shadow, you know? It's like I'm waiting for the other shoe to drop."

Ethan's expression shifted, a flicker of understanding passing between us. "You're stronger than you think. I mean, you've built this place from the ground up. Don't let one person's departure shake your foundation."

His words wrapped around me like a warm blanket, offering comfort in their simple truth. I'd spent so long carving my path in this industry, defying expectations and standing tall against the tide of doubt. But with Julian's absence came an unsettling realization; I was no longer tethered to someone who often overshadowed my accomplishments. "I know, but it's hard not to feel... lost. He was a part of everything—my vision, my dreams. Without him, it feels like I'm steering this ship alone."

"Maybe it's time to chart your own course." His eyes sparkled with mischief. "Let's have an adventure."

The idea sparked a flicker of excitement within me, igniting the embers of hope that had dimmed in Julian's wake. "Adventure? You mean, like setting off to conquer the fashion world one spontaneous trip at a time?"

"Why not? A little getaway could be just what you need. Think of it as a chance to rediscover your spark, your vision. I could help. We could hit the markets, find inspiration—just the two of us."

"Just the two of us?" I repeated, my heart racing slightly at the thought. The prospect of spending more time with Ethan filled me with warmth, but the flutter of uncertainty swirled in my stomach. It felt thrilling and terrifying all at once. "What about Clara?"

"Clara can hold down the fort. Besides, it's a business trip. A chance for you to explore the latest trends, meet designers. It'll be great!"

His enthusiasm was infectious, and I felt myself drawn into the orbit of his plans. The idea began to bloom in my mind, unfurling like a delicate flower seeking the sun. "You really think I can do this without Julian?"

"Of course you can. And who says you need him? You have an incredible vision and a great team. This boutique is your creation, not his."

The weight of his words sank in, grounding me in the realization that I could carve my own path without depending on anyone else's brilliance. My heart quickened, and I leaned closer, feeling the magnetic pull between us, as if the world had narrowed to just this moment. "You really believe in me, don't you?"

"Absolutely. I wouldn't be here if I didn't." His sincerity wrapped around me, and for a brief moment, the shadows of doubt were pushed aside.

"I'll think about it," I said, trying to play it cool, but inside, the excitement bubbled. "When do we leave?"

"Tomorrow morning?" he suggested, a grin lighting up his face. "I'll arrange everything. We'll hit the road, find inspiration, and see where the adventure takes us."

Before I could think better of it, I nodded, my mind racing with possibilities. The thrill of uncertainty danced along my spine, pulling me into its embrace. "Okay, let's do it."

He chuckled, his laughter warm and rich like dark chocolate. "That's the spirit! Now, let's make sure you look fabulous while you're doing it."

As we spent the rest of the day strategizing, I felt the echoes of Julian fade further into the background, replaced by the thrill of what lay ahead. Each idea we tossed around, each dream we dared to voice, added layers to the burgeoning bond between Ethan and me. In those moments of laughter and collaboration, the once-feared silence transformed into a canvas awaiting our strokes of brilliance, daring us to paint a future uniquely our own.

The morning light spilled through the windows like liquid gold, illuminating the boutique in a soft, inviting glow. I stood in front of the mirror, adjusting the collar of a crisp white shirt, the fabric cool against my skin. My heart raced with a mix of excitement and nerves. Today was the day Ethan and I would embark on our impromptu adventure, leaving behind the familiar confines of the boutique for the unknown. It was exhilarating and terrifying all at once. The thought of trading routine for spontaneity made my breath quicken, each exhale tinged with the thrill of possibility.

Ethan arrived with a bounce in his step, the door chiming as he pushed it open, a canvas bag slung over his shoulder. "Ready to take the fashion world by storm?" His grin was infectious, radiating a confidence that seemed to wrap around me like a protective cloak.

"Only if you promise not to lose me in the chaos," I replied, a playful challenge in my tone. I felt lighter, more like myself, as I joined him at the door.

"Chaos? Please, I thrive in chaos." He winked, and I felt a rush of warmth spread through me. "Just follow my lead, and we'll have a great time. Plus, you'll get to meet some fantastic people."

"Fantastic people or fantastically eccentric?" I asked, raising an eyebrow as we stepped out into the bustling street. The morning air was brisk, a refreshing contrast to the warmth of the boutique, invigorating my senses as we walked side by side.

"Eccentric, for sure. But isn't that part of the charm?" He nudged my shoulder with his, an effortless camaraderie blooming between us as we made our way to the car.

The drive was filled with laughter and spirited banter, the kind that made the miles melt away. The scenery outside shifted from urban grit to rolling hills, the landscapes unfolding like a painter's canvas splashed with vibrant greens and the occasional burst of wildflowers. I turned to look at Ethan, the sunlight catching the strands of his dark hair, creating an ethereal halo around him. It was hard to believe that just days ago, I was lost in a fog of uncertainty. Now, I felt alive, my spirit soaring with each passing moment.

As we pulled into the quaint town of Maplewood, a place teeming with boutiques and artisan shops, I felt a familiar thrill. It was a vibrant hub where creativity thrived, and inspiration seemed to waft through the air like the scent of fresh coffee from the nearby café. "This place is adorable," I remarked, scanning the storefronts lined with colorful displays.

"I thought you'd like it. This little gem is a hotspot for emerging designers. We'll meet some up-and-coming talents today." Ethan's eyes twinkled with enthusiasm, his passion for fashion evident in the way he spoke.

Our first stop was a tiny shop tucked away on a side street, its window adorned with whimsical designs and handmade jewelry. Inside, the air buzzed with creativity, the walls covered in sketches and vibrant fabric swatches. A young woman with bright pink hair greeted us, her smile wide and inviting. "Welcome to The Stitchery! I'm Clara, and you must be the fashionistas everyone's been talking about."

"Guilty as charged," Ethan said, stepping forward. "We're here to soak in all the inspiration we can find."

Clara's eyes sparkled with mischief. "Then you've come to the right place! I have a collection that's going to blow your mind." She led us deeper into the shop, and as we wandered through the labyrinth of fabric and design, my senses ignited. The vibrant colors, the textures that begged to be touched, it was all overwhelming in the best possible way.

As Clara showcased her latest creations, I felt a rush of inspiration surging through me. Each piece told a story, whispering secrets of creativity and daring. "This one," Clara said, holding up a dress that shimmered like a summer sunset, "is inspired by my grandmother's garden."

"It's beautiful," I breathed, captivated. "I can see the blossoms in the colors."

Clara beamed, her passion palpable. "That's exactly what I was going for! The world needs more beauty, don't you think?"

"Absolutely," I replied, feeling a kinship with her vision. A glance at Ethan revealed he was equally captivated, his gaze intent on Clara's creations.

As the conversation flowed, I felt the walls I'd built around myself start to crumble. Here, in this space filled with creativity and like-minded souls, my insecurities seemed to fade. I shared snippets of my journey, how the boutique was a manifestation of my dreams, a canvas on which I painted my aspirations. To my surprise, I found myself talking about Julian—how he had once been a guiding force but now felt more like a fleeting shadow.

"You're doing it on your own now," Ethan said softly, his voice threading through the moment. "That's a victory in itself."

His words hung in the air, a lifeline tossed into the sea of my thoughts. "I guess I needed to hear that," I admitted, glancing at him. "It's easy to forget my own strength when I'm caught up in what was."

Clara chimed in, her enthusiasm unwavering. "You're both remarkable. The industry needs fresh perspectives, and from what I see, you're on your way to making waves."

Ethan leaned closer, mischief twinkling in his eyes. "Just wait until she unveils her next collection. It's going to be legendary."

I laughed, a genuine sound that bubbled up from my core. "Now you're putting a lot of pressure on me."

"That's the point. You're capable of greatness. Just embrace it," he replied, his tone teasing yet earnest.

The day unfolded like a beautifully woven tapestry, each interaction adding another thread to my burgeoning sense of self. We explored boutique after boutique, soaking in the energy of the designers, exchanging ideas and insights, each moment cementing the bond between Ethan and me. With each passing hour, I felt the confidence within me swell, fueling the fire of creativity that had once flickered in the shadow of self-doubt.

But just as I began to feel untouchable, a nagging thought crept into the corners of my mind, whispering reminders of Julian's influence, of the intricate dance between reliance and independence that I had yet to master. The fleeting sense of freedom was sweet, but the echo of the past lingered, threatening to pull me back into the depths of uncertainty.

The sun dipped low in the sky, casting a warm golden hue over Maplewood as Ethan and I strolled down the bustling streets, our bags laden with treasures gathered from our day of exploration. The quaint charm of the town had seeped into my bones, wrapping around me like a cozy blanket. Laughter spilled from nearby cafés, mingling with the aroma of fresh pastries and strong coffee, creating an atmosphere that felt alive with potential.

"I can't believe how many incredible designers we met today," I said, my voice tinged with excitement as we stopped to admire a window display showcasing eclectic accessories. "Each one had a unique story, a vision that sparked inspiration in me."

Ethan leaned closer, studying the display. "You have a way of connecting with people, you know? It's like you draw their creativity out of them." His compliment wrapped around me like a silk ribbon, brightening my mood even further.

"Maybe I should add 'inspiration whisperer' to my résumé," I teased, nudging him playfully. "But I'll need to perfect my mystical aura first."

He chuckled, a rich sound that made my heart flutter. "No need for that. You're already magical without any tricks."

His words lingered in the air, igniting something deep within me. I realized how refreshing it felt to be seen for who I was, not just as a reflection of someone else's vision. It was a heady feeling, and I found myself wanting to explore this burgeoning connection between us further. "What's next on our adventure?" I asked, eager to prolong our time together.

Ethan looked thoughtful for a moment. "How about we grab a bite at that little bistro we passed? I hear their pastries are to die for."

"Pastries? I'm in," I said, unable to hide my grin. We made our way to the bistro, the bell above the door jingling cheerfully as we stepped inside. The atmosphere was cozy, with rustic wooden tables and an inviting display of treats behind the glass counter. The sweet scent of fresh bread and sugar enveloped us, making my stomach rumble in anticipation.

We settled at a small table near the window, the warm light bathing us in a golden glow. As I perused the menu, I couldn't help but steal glances at Ethan, whose enthusiasm for life made my heart race. "What's your favorite here?" I asked, unable to resist his captivating energy.

"The lemon tarts are life-changing. You'll thank me later," he replied, his eyes sparkling with mischief.

"Life-changing? You know how to sell a pastry, I'll give you that." I laughed, settling on the tart and a cup of coffee. As we placed our orders, I felt a comfortable rhythm between us, a dance of playful banter and easy conversation.

Over coffee and pastries, we delved deeper into our aspirations. Ethan spoke about his dreams of starting his own fashion line, the challenges he faced, and how he longed to push the boundaries of creativity. His passion was contagious, igniting my own desire to explore new horizons. "You know," I said, my voice barely above a whisper, "I've always dreamed of hosting a fashion show. One that highlights local talents and brings the community together."

"Now that sounds like a brilliant idea!" Ethan leaned forward, his eyes wide with excitement. "We could showcase the designs we discovered today, give those designers a platform. It would be like a celebration of creativity!"

"Exactly! It would be a way to unite everyone in the spirit of collaboration. I can already picture the venue, the atmosphere." My mind raced with possibilities, the vision crystallizing in my thoughts.

"Then let's make it happen," Ethan said, his tone filled with determination. "I'll help you every step of the way."

My heart swelled with gratitude, but just as quickly, doubt crept back in. "But what if it fails? What if no one shows up?" The fear spilled from my lips before I could catch it, a reminder of the vulnerability that lurked beneath my newfound confidence.

"Hey," he said softly, reaching across the table to grasp my hand. "What if it's a smashing success? You can't let fear dictate your dreams. You owe it to yourself to try."

His touch sent a thrill coursing through me, grounding me while lifting me at the same time. "You're right. I just need to keep pushing forward."

As we finished our pastries and coffee, I felt an exhilarating blend of hope and trepidation swirling inside me. The more I shared my vision, the clearer it became; this was my chance to step out of Julian's shadow and carve my own path.

After we left the bistro, we wandered through the nearby park, the soft rustling of leaves a soothing backdrop to our conversation. "I can't believe how inspired I feel," I confessed, glancing at Ethan, whose presence felt like a guiding light. "Today has reignited a fire in me that I thought had gone out."

"It's only going to get brighter from here." He flashed that charming grin, and I felt a rush of warmth. "We'll set a date, plan everything meticulously. I can already picture the invite—glamorous, chic, just like you."

As the sun began to dip below the horizon, casting long shadows over the park, I caught a glimpse of a figure in the distance. My heart raced as the familiar silhouette grew closer. Julian.

He walked with an air of confidence, but there was something in his gaze—a mix of determination and regret. I felt a jolt of uncertainty ripple through me, the fragile peace I'd cultivated suddenly feeling threatened.

"What's wrong?" Ethan noticed my change in demeanor, concern etched on his face.

"Look," I whispered, my eyes fixed on Julian. "It's him."

"Do you want me to handle this?" Ethan's protective instinct kicked in, a sharp edge to his tone.

"No, let me talk to him." I drew a deep breath, bracing myself for the encounter. I hadn't expected to see him here, not after everything that had transpired. As he approached, I felt the weight of unfinished business hovering in the air, an unresolved tension that threatened to unravel the progress I had made.

"Hey," Julian said, his voice low and steady. "Can we talk?"

The world around us seemed to fade, leaving only the three of us in an unsteady triangle, each moment pregnant with anticipation. My heart raced, and I could feel Ethan's gaze on me, a steadying force. But as I prepared to respond, my mind raced with thoughts of all I'd gained, all I stood to lose.

"Sure," I replied, my voice steady despite the turmoil churning inside me. "We can talk."

As I took a step closer, I couldn't shake the feeling that the fragile peace I had found was about to be tested in ways I could never have anticipated.

Chapter 24: Breaking the Surface

The soft hum of the vintage shop's doorbell announced Clara's arrival, breaking the early morning silence that hung in the air like a fog. Sunlight streamed through the dusty windows, illuminating the delicate fabrics and shimmering baubles that adorned the boutique. I turned my back to the mirror where I'd been adjusting my hair, my reflection a whirlwind of emotions—a blend of determination and lingering vulnerability. The scent of fresh coffee wafted in from the small kitchenette, grounding me. Clara stepped in, her vibrant personality almost palpable, her laughter dancing in the space between us.

"Good morning! I come bearing caffeine and gossip," she declared, her eyes sparkling mischievously. She held out a steaming cup, steam curling up like wisps of secrets waiting to be unveiled. I accepted the coffee, the warmth seeping into my palms, soothing the slight tremor of anxiety that had begun to build since the previous night.

As I took a sip, the rich flavor enveloped my senses, but the moment was short-lived. Clara's expression shifted, her playful demeanor melting away like morning mist under the sun. "We need to talk. It's about Julian," she said, her tone suddenly serious.

The mention of his name sent a chill through me, like ice water poured over a hot flame. Julian and I shared a past that felt more like a series of unfortunate events than a romance. The mere thought of him had a way of igniting that old flame of anger. "What about him?" I asked, bracing myself for the inevitable storm.

"I heard some things," Clara continued, leaning closer, lowering her voice. "He's been saying some really awful things about you. Rumors that could hurt your business." Her words hung in the air, heavy and unyielding, like a dark cloud gathering before a storm.

I set my coffee down, the porcelain clinking against the wooden table, a stark contrast to the turmoil within. "What kind of things?" I demanded, my heart racing.

"Nothing specific—just that you're not the person you pretend to be. He's painting a picture of you that's far from the truth." Clara's eyes were fierce, unwavering in their resolve. "He's trying to undermine everything you've worked for."

My mind whirled. Julian, with his charming smile and smooth words, had always possessed a knack for manipulation. I thought I had left him behind, buried beneath the layers of self-reinvention I had painstakingly built since moving to this quaint town. Yet here he was, like a specter, haunting my every effort to rise above my past. "Why would he do this?"

Clara took a deep breath, her expression softening with concern. "He's jealous, obviously. You've created something beautiful here, and he can't stand it. But we can't let him win."

I nodded, my heart pounding as a plan began to form in my mind. "You're right. We need to show everyone the truth. Let's launch a positive PR campaign for the boutique. Highlight our work, the community we've built. Make it clear who I really am."

Clara's face lit up, enthusiasm radiating from her like sunlight breaking through a canopy of trees. "Exactly! We'll showcase our new collection with a launch party. Invite everyone—the locals, bloggers, anyone who can spread the word."

A swell of determination rose within me, replacing the initial shock. "And we'll feature the stories behind each piece, how they reflect our journey and the heart of this place."

"Let's make it unforgettable," Clara added, her voice brimming with excitement. "We'll share the laughter, the late-night brainstorming sessions, and the mistakes that brought us here. People love authenticity."

Our conversation sparked a fire that chased away the shadows of doubt. Ideas flowed between us, painting a vivid picture of what our campaign could look like—colorful invitations, a social media blitz, and local partnerships that would showcase the true spirit of our work. As we planned, laughter punctuated our discussions, weaving a tapestry of camaraderie and resilience.

But just as I felt the tide turning, the door creaked open again, and I turned to find Julian standing there, his presence a storm cloud in our sunlit sanctuary. He wore that infuriating smirk, the kind that made my skin crawl. "Fancy seeing you here," he drawled, his tone dripping with faux charm.

"What do you want?" I shot back, my voice steady despite the storm brewing inside me. Clara stepped slightly in front of me, a protective barrier.

"Just checking in on my favorite designer. Heard you've been having some trouble." He leaned casually against the doorframe, arms crossed, as if he were a spectator in a drama he had scripted.

I met his gaze with all the ferocity I could muster. "I'm not interested in your games, Julian. If you're here to spread more rumors, you can leave."

He chuckled, the sound devoid of warmth, almost echoing in the silence of the boutique. "Oh, come now. I'm just trying to look out for you. You know how people talk in this town. It's like a soap opera."

"Your soap opera," Clara interjected, her voice sharp and unwavering. "You think this is funny? You're toying with someone's reputation."

His smirk faltered for just a heartbeat, revealing a glimpse of the uncertainty beneath his bravado. "Maybe I'm just trying to remind you that life isn't all sunshine and roses. You can't escape your past, no matter how hard you try."

I held my ground, refusing to let his words wound me. "You're right. I can't escape it, but I can redefine it. You've underestimated me, Julian, and that's a mistake you won't make again."

As he stepped back, a flicker of something—fear, perhaps?—crossed his face before he masked it with that infuriating grin again. "We'll see about that." With one last lingering glance, he turned and walked away, the door closing behind him with a finality that reverberated through the room.

The moment he was gone, I exhaled, tension releasing like a coiled spring. Clara and I exchanged a glance, a silent understanding passing between us. "He thinks he can intimidate you?" she said, disbelief etched across her features.

"Not anymore," I replied, my voice stronger now, filled with a newfound purpose. "Let's get to work. We have a boutique to protect."

With that, we dove headfirst into our plans, the shadows of doubt pushed aside by the vibrant colors of possibility, and the knowledge that together, we could turn the tide against Julian's darkness.

The sunlight poured into the boutique, casting a golden hue across the polished wooden floors and glinting off the array of colorful fabrics. Clara and I stood amidst our preparations, buzzing with energy as we crafted our PR campaign. We had transformed our initial shock into something constructive, a joint mission pulsing with purpose. As I unfurled swatches of vibrant textiles, Clara busily typed on her laptop, her fingers dancing across the keyboard like a pianist composing a symphony.

"This is going to be epic," she said, her eyes shining with excitement. "I'm thinking we can set up a series of 'Behind the Design' videos. People love that kind of stuff. It's personal, relatable. We can show them the real story behind each piece."

I nodded, feeling the weight of her enthusiasm. "Yes! And we should incorporate testimonials from our regulars. The ones who have turned our little shop into their sanctuary. Their voices matter; they are part of our journey."

Just then, the bell above the door chimed again, breaking our rhythm. I turned, a smile ready to greet yet another patron, only to find Lucy—my neighbor and perhaps the most colorful character in our small town—bursting through the threshold. Her wild curls bounced with every step, and she wore a bright floral dress that seemed to laugh in the sunshine.

"Did I hear something about testimonials?" she chirped, her voice as effervescent as her personality. "Because if you need a glowing recommendation, look no further! I would fight a bear for your designs. Well, maybe not a bear. I'd probably just bribe it with snacks instead."

Clara and I exchanged amused glances, her antics often an unexpected source of joy in our daily lives. "We might just take you up on that, Lucy," I said, grinning at her theatrics. "But you'll have to make it sound like you're not actually fighting a bear. We don't want to scare off potential customers."

"Oh, darling, I would never let a bear ruin your reputation," she replied, placing a hand dramatically on her heart. "Besides, I have a way with words. People listen when I speak. I could charm a cactus to bloom if I tried."

Clara giggled, and I couldn't help but feel a wave of gratitude wash over me. Lucy's spirit was infectious; it fueled the fire within us to rise above Julian's cruel taunts. "Okay, so let's get you on camera. We'll film your testimonial this afternoon."

"Perfect! I'll bring props!" she exclaimed, her excitement palpable. "Maybe a glitter cannon for added effect? Or just some really fabulous fabric swatches to wave around. You know, something to keep it classy yet chaotic."

"Classy yet chaotic should definitely be our tagline," I said, laughing as I imagined the scenes Lucy would create. "If it doesn't make the viewers smile, what's the point?"

With plans swirling around us like autumn leaves caught in a gust of wind, we settled into the day. Clara took charge of the social media strategy, devising catchy captions while I sorted through our newest designs, each piece bursting with creativity and passion. The rhythmic tapping of her keys blended seamlessly with my fabric rustling, creating a melody of productivity that resonated within the walls of our boutique.

As the sun dipped lower in the sky, painting the room in warm shades of orange and pink, I felt a sense of calm settling over me. We were doing something meaningful, something that honored our hard work and dedication. This wasn't just about fighting Julian's rumors; it was about celebrating our journey—the friendships forged, the late nights spent dreaming, and the resilience that had brought us to this moment.

Clara leaned back in her chair, stretching her arms overhead, a satisfied smile on her face. "I think we're ready for our launch party. The community will love what we've created together. I can already picture the energy."

"Absolutely! And I'm thinking we could add a little live music to the event," I suggested, the idea sparking excitement within me. "A local band could draw a crowd and set the perfect atmosphere."

"Oh, I know just the group! The Sweetwater Trio—they're phenomenal. And one of them happens to be my cousin. I can pull some strings."

"Look at you, the ultimate insider," I teased, nudging her playfully. "With connections like that, we might just become the social hub of the town."

"Wouldn't that be delightful?" Clara replied, her laughter ringing out like a bell. "Imagine it—a sea of happy faces, surrounded by our creations. Just think of all the 'oohs' and 'aahs' when they see our pieces."

"Now you've got me daydreaming," I admitted, leaning back against the counter, a wistful smile gracing my lips. The dream of a thriving boutique filled with laughter and life was within reach, the shadows of Julian's treachery fading like a bad memory.

Yet, just as the optimism swelled, my phone buzzed insistently on the countertop. I reached for it, glancing at the screen, my heart stuttering when I saw Julian's name flash across it. A pit formed in my stomach, a reminder of the undercurrent of tension that still lurked beneath our plans.

"Are you going to answer that?" Clara asked, her voice low, sensing the shift in my demeanor.

I hesitated, staring at the phone, a swirling mixture of dread and curiosity. "Should I? What could he possibly want?"

"Maybe it's an apology?" she suggested, her tone dripping with sarcasm. "Or a heartfelt invitation to tea? Either way, I'd grab popcorn for this show."

With a resigned sigh, I tapped the screen, bringing the phone to my ear. "Julian," I said, my voice firm but controlled.

"Hello, darling," he replied, his tone as smooth as silk, but I could hear the underlying edge, the hint of something darker. "I just wanted to check in. Heard you're planning quite the event."

"Is that why you're calling? To gloat?" I shot back, the anger bubbling beneath my surface, barely contained.

"Oh, come now, I'm just curious," he said, feigning innocence. "I can't help but wonder if you'll still be able to pull off your little PR stunt now that the truth is out there."

"What truth? Your lies? You think people will believe you over what they see with their own eyes?"

A pause stretched between us, heavy and fraught with tension. "You're more naïve than I thought, but good luck. I'll be watching closely," he said before hanging up, leaving only the echo of his laughter behind.

I clenched my jaw, fury boiling beneath my skin. "He's insufferable. The audacity to think he can intimidate me."

Clara placed a hand on my shoulder, grounding me. "You know what you need to do? Focus on your vision. We're not giving him the satisfaction of reacting."

"You're right," I said, taking a deep breath, feeling the weight of his words lift ever so slightly. "I won't let him ruin this. We have too much at stake."

With renewed resolve, we returned to our plans, pouring every ounce of creativity into our campaign. Each moment spent creating was a step further from Julian's grasp, a way to break free from the past that sought to ensnare me. Together, we were more than a boutique—we were a force, and no rumor could dim the light we had begun to shine.

The evening sun dipped below the horizon, casting a warm glow through the boutique's windows, illuminating the vibrant colors of our latest collection. Clara and I stood amidst the flurry of preparations for the upcoming launch party, the air thick with excitement and the unmistakable scent of fresh flowers we'd arranged earlier. Each petal held a promise, a whisper of what was to come, and I found solace in the beauty that surrounded us.

As Clara hung a string of fairy lights, her fingers deftly weaving the delicate bulbs, I meticulously arranged the garments on display, each piece a reflection of the hard work and heart we had poured into our creations. The thought of Julian's taunts still lingered like a cloud overhead, but it was becoming less potent, overshadowed by the thrill of what lay ahead.

"Do you think we have enough snacks?" Clara mused, her brow furrowed as she inspected the towering trays of treats we had prepared. "I mean, I want the guests to have a sugar rush, but not so much that they start bouncing off the walls."

I chuckled, picturing our local guests with sugar-fueled energy, running amok through the boutique. "A few sugar highs could liven up the place. Besides, it'll be fun to watch Lucy try to wrangle them," I replied, amusement dancing in my eyes.

"True! She'll probably hand out cupcakes like a carnival barker. 'Step right up and try the best treats this side of the river!'" Clara laughed, her infectious spirit easing the tension that had crept in since Julian's last phone call.

Just then, the door swung open, the bell tinkling like a herald of excitement, and in walked Lucy, decked out in an outfit even more flamboyant than usual—floral patterns clashing with polka dots in a way only she could pull off. "I hope you both are ready for a night of glitz and glamour! I brought my props!"

With a flourish, she revealed a bag brimming with glittering accessories and confetti poppers. "I couldn't resist! We need to give this place some pizzazz. What's a launch party without a little sparkle?"

"Or a lot of sparkle!" Clara quipped, and together, they dived into a playful debate over how much glitter was too much.

As their banter filled the air, I felt a rush of gratitude for these two women in my life—partners in creativity and mischief. They made the daunting task of overcoming Julian's influence feel manageable, even enjoyable. I was ready to embrace the night, to showcase not just our products but our story—the triumphs and the struggles, all woven together like the threads of the fabrics we designed.

As dusk settled outside, we finished our preparations, arranging the space into a cozy yet vibrant oasis that felt alive with anticipation. Clara took charge of the music, curating a playlist that combined our favorite indie artists with a dash of classic charm. Meanwhile, I set up a makeshift photo booth with props that Lucy had brought, ready to capture the joy of our guests.

The first few attendees began to trickle in—friends, loyal customers, and even some curious onlookers. The atmosphere buzzed with excitement as laughter and chatter filled the boutique, mingling with the warm scents of baked goods and blooming flowers. I welcomed each guest, my heart swelling with pride as they admired our work, their compliments like honey sweetening my resolve.

"Your designs are breathtaking," one woman said, holding a delicate dress that seemed to shimmer in the light. "You must be so proud."

"I am," I replied, my voice warm with sincerity. "Each piece tells a story. It's not just fashion; it's a reflection of who we are."

As the evening unfolded, I felt more at home within my creations than ever before. Clara flitted from group to group, engaging everyone with her characteristic charm, while Lucy snapped candid photos, capturing the laughter and joy that blossomed around us.

Yet, just as I began to lose myself in the warmth of the night, I noticed a figure lingering at the edge of the crowd—a familiar silhouette that sent an icy tendril of dread slithering down my spine. Julian stood there, his presence like a dark cloud eclipsing the warmth of our celebration. He leaned against the wall, arms crossed, an unsettling smirk plastered across his face as he observed the scene.

"Why does he have to show up now?" I muttered under my breath, the joyous atmosphere around me suddenly tinged with unease.

"Who?" Clara asked, following my gaze. Her expression shifted, morphing from delight to concern as she recognized him. "Ugh. Of all the places he could have chosen, why here?"

"I don't know, but I'm not going to let him ruin this," I asserted, forcing my voice to remain steady. "Let's keep the focus on our guests."

But as the minutes passed, Julian's smirk only deepened, his eyes darting around the room, searching for an opening. He seemed to relish the tension, feeding off it like a moth drawn to flame. And then, just as I was about to turn away and refocus on the guests, he strolled forward, his presence suddenly consuming the air around us.

"Quite the gathering you've got here," he said, his voice dripping with mock admiration. "I didn't realize you were so... popular."

I squared my shoulders, ready to respond with a sharp retort, but Clara interjected before I could speak. "What do you want, Julian? We're busy."

"Just wanted to see what all the fuss was about," he replied, feigning innocence. "And, of course, to congratulate you on your little comeback."

"Enough with the games. You're not welcome here," I snapped, my patience wearing thin.

He chuckled, his gaze sweeping across the room as if assessing a battlefield. "You know, it's interesting how you've tried to paint this lovely little picture of yourself. But it's all a façade, isn't it?"

My breath hitched, fury coursing through my veins. "You have no idea what you're talking about."

"Oh, I think I do," he replied, his voice low and smooth, the confidence oozing from him. "Everyone here will soon see that. You can only hold up a façade for so long."

Before I could retort, Lucy stepped forward, eyes blazing with protectiveness. "You need to leave, Julian. You're ruining the vibe. We're here to celebrate, not entertain your twisted little games."

He turned his gaze to her, a flicker of surprise crossing his face, as if he hadn't expected such defiance. "Cute, but I'm not going anywhere. I'm just getting started."

And with that, he stepped closer, an unsettling grin spreading across his face. I felt the air grow thick with tension, the joyous atmosphere suddenly fracturing like a glass dropped onto a stone floor.

"Julian, don't," I warned, my voice barely above a whisper, sensing the shift in his demeanor.

"I think it's time everyone knew the truth," he said, and just as the room fell silent, anticipation crackling in the air, he pulled out his phone, the screen glowing ominously in the dim light.

I knew then that whatever he was about to reveal would shatter the fragile peace we had built. My heart raced, dread creeping in, but before he could press the button, the door swung open again, and in walked someone I hadn't expected to see—a figure from my past, someone whose presence could change everything.

The collective gasp of the crowd echoed in the air, and I felt my stomach drop as recognition settled in. As the familiar face turned towards me, a storm of emotions swirled within, leaving me breathless, caught between the ghosts of what had been and the impending chaos that loomed just ahead.

Chapter 25: The Tides of Change

The sun dipped below the horizon, casting a golden hue over the bustling streets of our little town, where the air was laced with the scent of fresh pastries and blooming jasmine. I stood in the heart of my boutique, the fabric swatches and sketches strewn across the work table like the aftermath of a vibrant art class. Each design represented not just a garment but a piece of my soul, stitched together with threads of ambition and a sprinkle of whimsy.

Ethan leaned against the doorframe, arms crossed, the light behind him framing his silhouette like a sunbeam caught in a photograph. His presence brought a warmth that wrapped around me, soothing the flutters of anxiety in my stomach. "Are you ready for this?" he asked, a teasing smile playing on his lips, his deep voice laced with playful mischief. I turned to face him, attempting to channel my nerves into something more formidable.

"Ready as I'll ever be," I replied, shaking my head with a half-hearted laugh, attempting to mask the tremors of anticipation. The invitation from the bridal magazine had arrived like a thunderstorm on an otherwise sunny day—unexpected and electrifying. A feature, a spread, an opportunity to showcase not just my creations but the story behind them.

Ethan straightened, pushing off from the doorframe with a sudden urgency. "You've worked too hard to shy away now. This is your moment, Rebecca. Don't let the shadows of doubt creep in." His voice was steady, but I could see the way his brow furrowed slightly, a hint of concern glimmering in his gaze. It was a reminder of the internal battle I fought daily—the fear of inadequacy juxtaposed against the bright spark of potential.

The boutique was alive with the soft rustle of fabrics and the faint music drifting from a nearby café. Each design hung like a whispered secret, the delicate lace and satin shimmering under the warm lights. I moved among them, fingertips grazing the fabrics, feeling the stories each thread held. My heart swelled as I thought of all the couples who would wear my creations, their laughter, their tears, their promises sewn into the very seams of the gowns.

But with the rising tide of success came the nagging worry about Julian, the shadow of my past that lingered like a ghost I couldn't quite shake. We had danced around each other like strangers in a crowded room, his presence both alluring and unsettling. The thought of him lurking in the corners of my newfound happiness was a chilling reminder of the control he once held over my life. I had fought so hard to break free from his grasp; the last thing I wanted was to invite him back into my world.

Ethan, sensing the shift in my mood, stepped closer, his eyes searching mine. "You're not alone in this, you know. I'm right here. Whatever happens, I'm in your corner." The sincerity in his voice made my heart flutter, a sensation that had become all too familiar. He reached for my hand, the warmth of his skin grounding me. I took a deep breath, inhaling the mingled scents of fabric and flowers, letting them fill my lungs and clear my mind.

"Okay, let's do this," I declared, determination blooming within me. I turned towards the mirror that graced the back wall, catching a glimpse of my reflection. The girl staring back at me was no longer the timid designer afraid of her own shadow; she was a woman ready to reclaim her narrative.

The day of the shoot arrived with a crispness in the air that hinted at autumn's approach. The team bustled around the boutique, transforming my workspace into a dazzling display of lights and cameras. I watched as models twirled in my designs, the flowing fabric catching the light, creating an ethereal glow that enveloped them. Every spin, every smile brought the visions I had crafted to life, and I could hardly contain the joy bubbling inside me.

"Rebecca! Come here!" the photographer called, gesturing animatedly. I moved toward him, heart racing with excitement and nerves. "I want you to interact with the models. Your passion is what makes these gowns sing!"

As I stepped into the frame, the world around me melted away, and for a moment, it was just me, the models, and the exquisite creations that had emerged from my mind. I guided them, sharing stories about each design, weaving my narrative into theirs. Laughter rang out, echoing against the walls, and for the first time in a long while, I felt the weight of Julian's influence lift, replaced by the thrill of creation and connection.

"Who knew you had such a flair for this?" Ethan quipped from the sidelines, a glint of admiration in his eyes. "You're a natural!"

"Only because you're here to remind me of what I'm capable of," I shot back, my voice light but my heart full. The chemistry between us was undeniable, a simmering tension that crackled in the air, hinting at something deeper than mere friendship.

The shoot flowed seamlessly, laughter intertwining with the sounds of shuffling feet and camera clicks. I lost track of time, entirely absorbed in the moment, until a familiar figure entered the frame—a figure I had not seen for years but had not forgotten. Julian stood in the doorway, his presence slicing through the joy like a knife. My heart sank, the warmth in my chest replaced by an icy grip of dread.

"Why am I not surprised?" he drawled, a sly smile curving his lips, his eyes scanning the scene with a mix of disdain and interest. The room felt smaller, the air thickening with tension as I felt the weight of his gaze on me, an unsettling reminder of a past I had fought so hard to escape.

My heart raced, caught in a whirlwind of emotions as Julian's familiar smirk cut through the air like a blade. It was surreal to see him here, in a place where joy and creativity had flourished—his presence a stark contrast to the vibrant atmosphere that had enveloped me just moments before. Models in shimmering gowns paused, their laughter stilled, and I felt the weight of their curious glances shift toward the unwelcome intrusion.

"Nice to see you've turned your little dreams into a reality," he remarked, his tone dripping with a mix of mockery and intrigue. "Though I have to say, it seems a bit too... quaint for someone of your talent." His words hung in the air, each one sharp and calculated, aiming to pierce the newfound confidence I had begun to embrace.

"Julian, what are you doing here?" I managed, forcing the words out as I steadied myself against the wall. I could feel Ethan's presence at my back, a reassuring force in the midst of the brewing storm.

"Just passing by, and what a delightful surprise to find you playing dress-up with your little creations," he said, waving a dismissive hand toward the models. The disdain dripped from his voice, and I could feel the heat rising in my cheeks. It was as if he had come to siphon the joy from the room, replacing it with an all-too-familiar dread.

Ethan stepped forward, muscles tensing as he approached Julian. "This is Rebecca's moment. You should respect that." His words were calm, yet there was a steely edge beneath them, a protective instinct flaring to life.

"Ah, the new boyfriend? How charming," Julian replied, feigning enthusiasm. "You must feel like a knight in shining armor, swooping in to save the day. But don't be fooled, my friend. She's always been better at hiding behind fabric than facing the truth."

"Why do you always have to make everything a competition?" I shot back, my voice sharper than I intended. "This isn't about you."

His expression shifted slightly, the smug veneer cracking just enough for me to glimpse the insecurities he typically cloaked in arrogance. "You know I'm right. You've always struggled to stand out without me. I was the talent, and you were just... the sidekick."

The air felt thick and electric, the atmosphere charged with the tension of old wounds reopening. I took a step closer to him, feeling Ethan's presence solid behind me, grounding me in a way I hadn't anticipated. "I'm not your sidekick anymore, Julian. I'm building something here. Something real. And you can't take that away from me."

A smirk danced across Julian's lips as he leaned closer, his voice low and conspiratorial. "But can you truly say you're happy? Or is it just the thrill of a new toy?"

Before I could respond, Ethan interjected, his voice steady and unyielding. "Why don't you leave? You're not welcome here."

Julian's eyes flickered with surprise before a laugh escaped him, harsh and cold. "You think you can dictate who stays and who goes? How quaint." He turned to me, a dark glint in his eye. "Just remember, Rebecca, it's not just about the clothes. It's about who's wearing them."

With that, he turned on his heel, striding out of the boutique as quickly as he had entered, leaving behind an atmosphere thick with unspoken words and unrelenting tension. The models exchanged nervous glances, their excitement for the shoot replaced by an uneasy silence.

Ethan stepped beside me, his expression a mixture of concern and frustration. "You okay?"

I nodded, though the tremor in my voice betrayed my bravado. "I didn't think I'd see him again. Not like this."

"Does he always know how to ruin a moment?" Ethan's tone was light, but I could sense the undercurrent of anger.

"Apparently," I replied, forcing a smile. "But let's not dwell on that. I want to get back to the shoot."

"Are you sure?" he asked, studying my face. "I can call it a day if you need some space."

"No," I insisted, shaking my head firmly. "This is important to me, and I won't let him steal that."

With a shared nod of understanding, we turned back to the set. I tried to focus on the colors, the textures, the way the light danced across the gowns, but Julian's words echoed in my mind like a sinister melody. I shook my head, pushing aside the doubt that threatened to seep in.

As the shoot resumed, I found myself directing with renewed vigor, letting the energy of the moment fill the space. The laughter returned, models twirling and posing as I reveled in the beauty of my creations. I was grateful for Ethan's unwavering support, his quiet strength bolstering my resolve.

After the final shot was captured, I breathed a sigh of relief. The tension had dissipated, replaced by the buzz of accomplishment and the scent of success hanging in the air like the heady perfume of blooming flowers. I stepped away from the chaos, seeking a moment of solace in the back room, the soft hum of the air conditioner providing a comforting backdrop.

Ethan followed me, closing the door behind him. "You did it, Rebecca. You handled him like a pro."

"I didn't feel like a pro," I admitted, rubbing my temples as the adrenaline began to fade. "I felt like a kid again, lost in his shadow."

He stepped closer, placing a hand on my shoulder, grounding me. "That's not who you are anymore. You've fought too hard to become this version of yourself. Don't let him pull you back."

"Sometimes I wonder if I'm just pretending," I confessed, the vulnerability creeping into my voice. "What if he's right? What if I'm still that girl who needed his approval?"

"Stop," he interrupted, his gaze steady and unwavering. "You're not that girl. You're the woman who built a boutique from the ground up, who turned her dreams into reality. You have every right to celebrate that."

I swallowed hard, the weight of his words sinking in. "You're right. I can't let him define me anymore."

"Exactly," he said, a warm smile breaking through the tension. "Now, let's get back out there and show them what you're made of."

With renewed determination, I took a deep breath and nodded. "Let's do this."

As we stepped back into the boutique, the lights brightened, and laughter filled the air once more. I was ready to embrace my future—one that was undeniably mine, stitched together with the threads of my own making. The warmth of Ethan's support wrapped around me like a comforting embrace, a reminder that I wasn't alone in this fight.

The atmosphere buzzed with renewed energy as we returned to the set. The models resumed their playful poses, laughter erupting like confetti around the boutique. I felt a surge of excitement course through me, the earlier encounter with Julian slowly fading into the background, overshadowed by the vibrancy of creativity that enveloped us. Each dress I had designed came alive in the light, transforming not just into fabric but into dreams waiting to be worn.

Ethan took a step back, letting me dive into the moment fully, and as I watched the fabric swirl and shimmer, I couldn't help but smile. The soft hum of conversations mingled with the click of cameras, a delightful cacophony that wrapped around me like a warm blanket. "Okay, ladies, let's show them what love looks like!" I called out, a playful challenge hanging in the air.

"Love and a whole lot of tulle!" one of the models shot back, twirling dramatically, the layers of her gown expanding like a blooming flower. I chuckled, savoring the lighthearted banter that felt so natural among this team. We were not just creating; we were celebrating, and in that moment, I felt invincible.

As the session progressed, I lost myself in the rhythm of creation, pouring every ounce of passion into my designs. I twirled alongside the models, adding flourishes to their poses, adjusting hemlines, and fluffing skirts. Each detail mattered, a testament to the love and care I had stitched into every seam. The sound of laughter and compliments filled the room, and I basked in the warmth of camaraderie.

Yet, amidst the joy, I could feel an undercurrent of uncertainty lurking at the edges of my mind, a reminder that my world had shifted. Just as I was savoring this sweet moment, a sharp knock echoed through the boutique. The door swung open, and in walked a figure I hadn't anticipated—a woman with striking features and an air of confidence that seemed to demand attention. Her presence was electric, and the chatter among the models quieted as she approached.

"Rebecca? I'm Charlotte," she said, extending a hand. "I'm the fashion editor for that bridal magazine you've been in talks with." Her smile was warm, yet I could sense a steely determination behind it.

"Hi, yes! It's so nice to finally meet you!" I responded, shaking her hand, but the warmth of her smile didn't quite reach her eyes.

"I just wanted to see the magic in person," she said, glancing around the boutique with a discerning eye. "I must say, I'm impressed by the energy here."

"Thank you! We're just having a bit of fun," I replied, attempting to keep the tone light despite the sudden shift in atmosphere.

Charlotte nodded, but I could tell her mind was racing. "I've been following your work, and I think you have something special. However, I'm concerned about your previous association."

"Julian?" The name slipped from my lips before I could catch myself.

"Yes, I know he was quite influential in your early career," she said, her tone shifting slightly. "But this feature is about showcasing your talent—without the shadows of the past."

I felt a knot tighten in my stomach, the thought of Julian lingering like a dark cloud. "I understand. I'm not letting him define my work anymore."

Charlotte raised an eyebrow, her gaze piercing. "That's good to hear, but I must stress the importance of focusing on your vision, free from any distractions."

"Believe me, I'm all about distractions today," I replied with a nervous laugh, but Charlotte didn't return the smile.

"Good. Just make sure it stays that way," she said, a hint of warning in her tone before she turned and walked away, her heels clicking against the polished floor.

The models resumed their chatter, but I felt a weight settling on my shoulders. "What was that about?" Ethan asked, stepping closer.

"Just the fashion editor setting expectations," I said, forcing a smile. "You know how it is."

"Yeah, but it sounded more like a warning than a pep talk." His brow furrowed with concern, and I could see he wasn't entirely convinced.

"I'm fine. Really." I brushed off his worry, though I could feel the seeds of doubt sprouting in my mind. The conversation with Charlotte had stirred something I hadn't quite anticipated—the fear that perhaps Julian's influence could still seep into my life despite my best efforts to distance myself.

"Let's focus on the shoot," I said, redirecting the energy in the room. "We've got some stunning gowns to showcase!"

Ethan nodded, though I could see the tension in his jaw. As the models resumed their playful poses, I forced myself to focus, guiding them through the shots, trying to ignore the creeping sense of foreboding that threatened to eclipse the joy of the moment.

But the afternoon wore on, the sun dipping lower in the sky, and just as we wrapped up, a familiar voice echoed through the boutique. "Well, well, what a cozy little gathering we have here."

Julian stepped back into the space, his confidence palpable, and I could feel the atmosphere shift once more. The models froze, uncertainty etched across their faces.

"What do you want, Julian?" I asked, my voice steadier than I felt.

"I just came to check in on my favorite designer," he said, an insincere grin plastered on his face. "You know, I wouldn't want you to slip up and lose your footing."

"Get out," I snapped, frustration bubbling to the surface.

"Oh, but I can't resist a good show," he replied, his gaze sweeping across the room, lingering on Ethan. "And it seems like the circus is in full swing. Such a shame if something were to... disrupt the performance."

Ethan moved closer to me, a protective stance taking shape. "You need to leave, Julian. Now."

Julian chuckled, a low, menacing sound. "But why would I? This is too entertaining to miss." He stepped further into the room, the tension thickening like fog, stifling the air around us.

"Listen, I'm done with your games," I said, forcing the words out with a strength I didn't entirely feel. "I've built something here, and you're not a part of it anymore."

"Oh, sweet Rebecca," he said, his tone dripping with sarcasm. "You really think you can just erase me?"

As the last word left his mouth, the power suddenly flickered and went out, plunging the boutique into darkness. Gasps erupted from the models, and I felt my heart race.

"What just happened?" Ethan's voice cut through the darkness, filled with urgency.

Before I could respond, a loud crash echoed from the back of the boutique, followed by an eerie silence that seemed to stretch endlessly. I clutched Ethan's arm, fear coursing through me.

"Stay close," he whispered, his voice steady as he led me toward the sound.

With the soft glow of emergency lights flickering to life, we stepped cautiously into the chaos, the boutique transformed into a stage for something dark and unpredictable. And just as we reached the source of the crash, a figure loomed in the shadows, their face obscured.

"Don't move," the voice commanded, sending chills down my spine.

My heart thundered as I glanced at Ethan, who stood beside me, tension radiating from him. In that moment, everything I had built felt precarious, teetering on the edge of an unforeseen danger.

Chapter 26: Rising Waters

The vibrant streets of New York thrummed with energy as I stepped into the whirlpool of fashion week preparation. Each bustling corner seemed to pulse with possibilities, a symphony of fabric swishing, heels clicking, and the soft hum of whispered dreams. The invitation to showcase my designs felt like a spark of magic dropped into my life, igniting a fire I thought had long flickered out. As the reality of it settled in, I could barely contain the storm of emotions swirling inside me.

The sun had begun its lazy descent, casting a golden hue across the city, which was my favorite time to wander. I found myself at a quaint café on the Upper West Side, nestled between towering buildings and chic boutiques. Clara was already there, her table strewn with sketches and fabric swatches, the chaos of creativity erupting like a blossoming flower. She looked up, her smile a beacon of encouragement amidst my swirling doubts.

"Ready for this?" she asked, her eyes sparkling with mischief. She had that uncanny ability to read me like a book, and today, the pages were riddled with anxiety.

"Define 'ready,'" I replied, forcing a laugh, even as my heart thudded in my chest like a rebellious drummer. "I'm pretty sure my designs have a better chance of surviving in a tornado than I do on that runway."

"Oh, please! Your designs are like poetry in fabric form. It's the perfect blend of elegance and edge," Clara said, her enthusiasm infectious. "Besides, you're not just a designer anymore; you're the designer. Look at this opportunity as a chance to spread your wings."

I took a sip of my coffee, letting the warmth seep into me, the rich aroma wrapping around my senses. Clara always knew how to lift me up, and yet, despite her words, I felt a gnawing apprehension at the back of my mind. What if I stumbled? What if my vision faltered under the scrutiny of the fashion elite?

With every passing day, the reality of my dreams seemed closer yet achingly out of reach. The showcase loomed like a tidal wave, and just when I thought I'd found my footing, the shadow of Julian entered the scene. News spread like wildfire that he would be debuting his new line at the same event, a fact that sent my insecurities swirling in a dizzying spiral. The last time we'd crossed paths, it had felt like a lifetime of unspoken words hung heavy between us, layered with both admiration and bitterness.

"Julian is talented, but you have something he doesn't," Clara said, breaking into my thoughts. "You've got heart. He's all surface and shine."

"Yeah, well, sometimes the surface is all people see," I muttered, unable to shake the memory of his charming smile and sharp tongue. "What if everyone prefers his glitzy show over my... whatever it is I create?"

"Stop! You're amazing. You're real," she insisted, her voice a firm anchor against my rising tide of doubt. "And honestly, what do you think he's feeling? Probably as nervous as you are. It's a competition, sure, but it's also an opportunity to show who you are, unfiltered. Remember the passion behind your work?"

The weight of her words settled in, grounding me momentarily. I took a deep breath, letting the scent of fresh pastries and coffee envelop me. "You're right," I admitted, my pulse steadier now. "I just need to focus on the art, not the noise."

"Exactly! You're going to shine, and I'll be right there cheering you on." She grinned, her enthusiasm radiating around us like sunlight.

As the days drifted by, I immersed myself in the preparations, the hum of sewing machines and rustling fabric becoming my soundtrack. Ethan, ever my steady rock, devoted countless hours to helping me refine my collection. With every late-night design session, we forged a rhythm that felt as natural as breathing.

"Do you really think they'll like this?" I asked one evening, anxiety creeping back as I draped a new garment over a mannequin.

"Like it? They'll love it," Ethan replied, stepping back to admire my work. "It's different, it's you, and it tells a story. Every stitch, every seam, it's a piece of your heart."

His words wrapped around me like a warm blanket, banishing the lingering chill of doubt. There was a comfort in our partnership, an electric connection that sparked with every glance. In his presence, I found a refuge from the looming storm of competition and my own insecurities.

Yet, even as I nestled deeper into this cocoon of love and support, the thought of facing Julian hung like a storm cloud, dark and threatening. I could almost hear the echo of his laughter from our last encounter, his smirk cutting through the noise of my confidence. But then I'd remind myself of Clara's words, and I'd clutch onto the hope that perhaps Julian wasn't the only one growing.

The day of the showcase dawned with an exhilarating rush of anticipation. The city seemed to buzz with excitement, the air thick with promise. I stood before the mirror, taking in my reflection—the fierce determination in my eyes, the confidence that came from the support surrounding me. As I dressed, I slipped on a piece from my collection, feeling the fabric cling to me like a second skin, whispering secrets of dreams and aspirations.

"Ready?" Ethan appeared at my side, his eyes gleaming with pride.

"Let's do this," I replied, my voice steady as I linked my arm with his. Together, we stepped into the heartbeat of the fashion world, ready to confront whatever waves might rise before us.

The venue buzzed with an electric energy as I stepped into the grand hall, a sprawling expanse transformed into a dazzling showcase of talent. Brilliant lights danced across the ceiling, illuminating an array of stunning designs that seemed to shimmer in anticipation. Models flitted about, their elegant forms gliding effortlessly in and out of fitting rooms, while stylists fussed over hair and makeup with the precision of surgeons. I stood there, heart racing, amidst the whirlwind, feeling like a fragile leaf caught in the powerful gusts of autumn.

"Are you ready to make a splash?" Clara's voice pierced through the din, her infectious enthusiasm radiating as she bounded toward me, a bright flash of color in her floral dress. She wore a confidence that I envied, and for a moment, her joy felt like a buoy to my sinking spirit.

"I'm ready to sink," I joked, forcing a laugh despite the tight knot of anxiety in my stomach. "What if I trip over my own fabric on the runway?"

"Then you trip in style, darling," she quipped back, her laughter brightening the moment. "Just think of it as an avant-garde performance art piece. People pay top dollar for that kind of drama."

"Ah yes, fashion as interpretive dance. I can see the headlines now," I replied, my voice laced with playful sarcasm. Clara's laughter echoed through the hall, and for a moment, the weight of my fears lifted.

But as we made our way through the chaos, the bright colors and jubilant energy around me began to dim with each step. I caught sight of him—Julian, standing tall and imposing near a group of stylists. His dark hair glistened under the bright lights, and his piercing gaze scanned the room like a hawk searching for prey. My heart fluttered, not from excitement but from the tidal wave of insecurities crashing over me. How could I possibly compete with that kind of magnetism?

"Keep your chin up," Clara whispered, nudging me with her elbow. "You're the star of this show, remember?"

"I'm trying to channel my inner Beyoncé," I replied, taking a deep breath to steady myself. "But I feel more like a backup dancer."

Clara's eyes twinkled with mischief. "Just remember, you don't have to outshine anyone else. Just shine in your own light. The right people will notice."

We moved deeper into the venue, the air thickening with anticipation and the faint scent of high-end perfume and polished wood. My collection was draped elegantly along the makeshift display area, each piece a reflection of my journey, my struggles, and my triumphs. I had poured my heart into every stitch, and it was time to unveil the depths of my soul wrapped in silk and chiffon.

As I turned to take a closer look, a familiar voice cut through the air like a knife. "Well, if it isn't my favorite little fashionista."

I spun around to find Julian leaning against a nearby column, a casual elegance about him that made my stomach knot in an unsettling mix of excitement and dread. He wore a perfectly tailored suit that accentuated his athletic build, and that infuriatingly charming smile played on his lips.

"Julian," I managed, my voice steady even as my heart raced. "Fancy seeing you here."

"Of course. Where else would I be?" He stepped closer, his gaze lingering on my collection. "I have to say, it looks quite... ambitious."

"Ambition is my middle name," I shot back, a hint of bravado spilling forth to mask my unease. "But don't worry, I won't take all the attention away from your precious designs."

"Oh, please. The spotlight will suit you just fine," he retorted, a teasing glint in his eye. "But really, I can't wait to see how you handle the pressure. You always did have a flair for the dramatic."

"Right back at you, Julian. I'm sure the crowd will love your theatrics, too," I replied, crossing my arms defensively.

The tension between us crackled in the air, a fierce battle of wills wrapped in layers of past grievances and unresolved feelings. He had a way of pushing my buttons, igniting the embers of insecurity that lay just beneath the surface.

"Can I offer you a word of advice?" he said, his tone turning serious as he leaned closer, his breath warm against my ear. "Don't let the competition scare you. Everyone's fighting their own battles. Just focus on your vision. It's the only way to stand out."

I blinked, caught off guard by his sincerity. The Julian I remembered was all bravado and swagger, not this unexpected moment of genuine advice. "Thanks for the tip, but I think I'll manage without your help," I replied, trying to keep the edge in my voice.

"Suit yourself," he replied, flashing that infuriatingly charming smile before stepping away. "But I'll be watching."

As he sauntered off, I fought against the tide of emotions swirling inside me. Was he genuinely being supportive, or was this just another game for him? I shook my head, pushing the thoughts aside. This wasn't the time to dwell on old ghosts. I had my own journey to navigate, and I couldn't afford to get lost in his shadow.

"Are you okay?" Clara asked, her eyes narrowing as she observed my change in demeanor.

"Just peachy," I replied, forcing a smile. "Julian is... well, he's Julian."

"You can handle him. I believe in you," she said firmly, her confidence washing over me like a balm.

The backstage area began to fill with voices as the final preparations took shape, and I lost myself in the rhythm of it all. Stylist after stylist flitted past, models lined up, each one a vision of beauty and poise. I felt a rush of adrenaline pulse through me, reminding me that I was part of something extraordinary.

As the minutes ticked down, I stood with Ethan, my heartbeat synchronized with the frantic energy surrounding us. He leaned in, his voice low and comforting. "You've got this. Remember to breathe, and let your passion shine through."

I nodded, drawing strength from his presence. "With you by my side, how could I not?"

As the lights dimmed for the first show, a hush fell over the crowd. I caught my breath, my heart pounding against my ribs as I stepped into the limelight, ready to share my vision with the world. The spotlight felt blinding, but as I began to walk, I found clarity in the chaos, embracing the thrill of this moment as I stepped onto the runway, my dreams finally unfolding beneath my feet.

The runway stretched out before me like a shimmering ribbon, the glaring lights casting sharp shadows that danced across the polished floor. I stood at the edge, the flutter of anticipation mingling with the clench of anxiety in my stomach. The atmosphere buzzed, a collective breath held tight, ready to explode into applause. My heart raced as I prepared to unveil the culmination of my dreams, each piece a reflection of my journey, each fabric telling a story of resilience and hope.

"Just remember, you're not just showcasing clothes. You're telling a story," Ethan whispered, his voice a low hum against the cacophony around us. He stood close, his presence a reassuring anchor amidst the swirling chaos. I looked up at him, the warmth of his gaze grounding me, and nodded, swallowing the lump in my throat.

As the first model stepped onto the runway, a wave of admiration swept over me. She wore one of my creations—a flowing gown that danced with every step, the fabric capturing the light like a waterfall of color. My heart swelled with pride, a rush of warmth cascading through me as I watched my vision come to life, each movement echoing the rhythm of my heartbeat.

Then came another model, and another, each strutting confidently in designs that reflected my passion and creativity. Clara stood at the end of the runway, her hands clasped in anticipation, her face glowing with pride. I couldn't help but mirror her enthusiasm, my nerves easing with each confident stride of my models. This was what I had dreamed of, the applause of an audience filling my heart with hope.

But just as I began to lose myself in the moment, the door at the far end swung open, and Julian stepped onto the runway. My breath hitched in my throat, a jolt of recognition crashing over me like a rogue wave. Dressed in a sharply tailored suit that clung to his frame, he radiated charisma, and the crowd responded with a roar that echoed through the hall. It was as if the universe had conspired to throw me off balance, reminding me that I was not the only one here to stake a claim.

The juxtaposition was striking; my ethereal designs flowed like whispers while his garments screamed confidence. My heart raced with a mix of admiration and resentment. Here was the man who had once inspired me to chase my dreams, now standing as my fiercest competitor, and I felt the wind of his success stirring up insecurities I thought I'd conquered.

"Don't let him rattle you," Ethan murmured, his hand slipping into mine. "You're more than capable of holding your own. Focus on your work, not his."

I took a deep breath, trying to channel the strength of his words. "Right. Just breathe and be me," I whispered, even as my heart thudded a frantic rhythm.

As the show progressed, I lost myself in the flow of creativity, each model gliding effortlessly across the runway, their poise illuminating the garments draped upon them. The applause reverberated around me, and I felt the adrenaline course through my veins, igniting the spark of determination deep within. I was doing this, and for every ounce of doubt that lurked in the shadows, there was a corresponding thrill of achievement that drowned it out.

But as I glanced back at Julian, I noticed something that sent a chill down my spine. He had turned his gaze toward me, a knowing smile playing at the corners of his lips, as if he relished in the very competition that threatened to unhinge me. My stomach twisted, and a wave of apprehension washed over me, threatening to overshadow the moment I had worked so hard for.

"Don't look at him," Clara urged, her voice a tight whisper as she stepped closer. "You're the one with the vision. Remember that."

I nodded, forcing my attention back to the runway. The models finished their walk, and I felt the applause crescendo into a roar, washing over me like a warm tide. My heart swelled with pride as I stepped forward, joining my models for a final bow. The cheers filled the air, a cacophony of support that made my head spin.

And then, the moment of glory turned, the spotlight suddenly shifting as Julian's final model strode out, his designs striking a powerful chord with the audience. Gasps filled the hall, and I felt the atmosphere change, the energy crackling with excitement. The crowd erupted into applause, a wave of adoration that washed over him, pulling my dreams momentarily into the undertow.

"Julian's collection is incredible," Clara said, her voice barely audible over the clamor. "But you can't let that distract you. You've done something amazing here, and it's not over yet."

But as I stepped off the runway, a sense of unease began to settle in the pit of my stomach. There was something lurking behind Julian's smile, a tension in the air that I couldn't quite shake. I could see him mingling with influential figures, laughter bubbling up around him, and it felt as though he was pulling the strings of fate, weaving them around my efforts.

"Let's get a drink," Ethan suggested, wrapping an arm around my shoulders. "You need to celebrate what you've accomplished. You've come so far."

"Yeah, I think I need that," I said, allowing him to lead me toward the bar area, where a mix of excitement and nervous energy lingered. Yet, the unease gnawed at me, refusing to dissipate even as I sipped my drink, the fizzy bubbles tickling my throat.

But then the evening took a turn I hadn't anticipated. A sudden commotion erupted at the far end of the bar, voices rising in alarm. I turned to look, only to find Julian at the center of it, his expression shifting from charming to something dark and intense. I watched as he exchanged heated words with a prominent designer, the tension palpable, crackling like static in the air.

"What's going on?" I whispered, glancing up at Clara, who had joined me at the bar.

"I'm not sure, but it doesn't look good," she replied, her brow furrowing in concern.

As I leaned closer, trying to catch snippets of the conversation, Julian's voice cut through the noise, sharp and accusatory. "You think you can just push me out? You'll regret it."

A collective hush fell over the crowd, and I felt my heart race in response. What was happening? The air crackled with tension, and suddenly I was struck by a wave of realization—this was more than just a competition; it was a battle of wills, and Julian was fighting for something far more significant than he let on.

"Should we intervene?" Clara asked, her eyes darting around the room.

"Maybe we should just stay out of it," I suggested, my instincts urging caution. But curiosity gnawed at me, pulling me closer to the fray.

The atmosphere shifted again as another figure stepped into the fray—someone I recognized. It was a high-profile fashion editor known for her sharp critique and even sharper tongue. The way she held herself, the cold glint in her eye, spoke volumes. She looked straight at Julian, her expression a blend of amusement and contempt.

"What's this? A little drama before the show even wraps?" she said, her tone dripping with sarcasm.

Before Julian could respond, she continued, "You really think you can challenge the established order with your little tantrum?"

My heart raced, tension coiling tightly in my chest. I glanced at Ethan, who was watching with a mix of fascination and apprehension. This wasn't just a moment of competition; it was the unveiling of a conflict that threatened to engulf us all.

The crowd held its breath, and I found myself standing at the precipice of an unfolding storm. Would Julian's battle affect my chance at success? The night was still young, and as the drama unfolded, I realized that the true challenge was only just beginning. The echoes of Julian's words reverberated in my mind, and I felt a chill run down my spine. What secrets lay behind those dark eyes? Would the rising waters of ambition consume us all?

Chapter 27: Navigating the Rapids

The vibrant lights of the runway flickered like stars reborn, casting a golden glow across the faces of the audience. Each flash was a heartbeat in the throbbing pulse of fashion week, where dreams strutted confidently alongside relentless ambition. The hum of chatter mingled with the rich scent of expensive perfumes and freshly polished wood. I stepped onto the runway, my heart a wild drum echoing the rhythm of my hopes and fears. Each footfall felt monumental, the click of my heels punctuating the silence as I transitioned from the chaos backstage to the intensity of the spotlight.

Draped in a gown that wrapped around my body like the embrace of an old friend, I felt the fabric whisper secrets of grace and power. A cascade of silk and chiffon swirled around my legs, catching the light and reflecting it back like a shimmering cascade of stars. Each design was a piece of me—a narrative woven from late nights of sewing, coffee-stained sketches, and the bittersweet notes of my journey. With each stride, I released my fears, channeling every ounce of my passion into the fabric that danced around me.

But then I saw him. Julian. He sat there, a stark silhouette against the vibrant crowd, his presence as unnerving as it was magnetic. His dark hair fell over his forehead in that effortlessly stylish way that made him look both approachable and untouchable. The tight line of his lips told a story I was all too familiar with, a mixture of scrutiny and judgment. My pulse quickened, an involuntary response to the memories etched into my heart—days filled with laughter and moments that left an indelible mark of longing.

In that electric moment, my confidence wavered like the flickering lights overhead. The rhythm of the music morphed into an erratic beat, each note mirroring the uncertainty bubbling in my chest. Doubts whispered like deceitful little demons in my ear. Did

I truly belong here? Was I merely playing dress-up in a world where I would never fit? The harshness of his gaze felt like an icy wind, seeping through my carefully crafted façade, threatening to unravel everything I had worked so hard to achieve.

But then, from the shadows, I spotted Ethan. His warm, encouraging smile cut through the haze of anxiety like a sunbeam breaking through a heavy cloud. I was reminded of our late-night brainstorming sessions, where we poured over sketches, laughed at terrible ideas, and celebrated every tiny victory. He had seen me at my worst and still believed I was capable of soaring high above the doubts that clung to me now. I squared my shoulders, shaking off the uncertainty as I met his gaze. The silent encouragement felt like a lifeline, anchoring me to the purpose that had propelled me to this moment.

With a deep breath, I returned to the rhythm of the show, my feet finding their stride once more. Each step was a declaration, each twirl an affirmation of my resolve. I recalled the late nights in my studio, the stubborn insistence that beauty could be born from chaos, and that passion could illuminate even the darkest corners of self-doubt. As I glided past the front row, I felt the energy shift. The audience was no longer just faces—each one transformed into a canvas eager to absorb my art, to feel the emotions stitched into every seam.

The music swelled, and I channeled the energy around me, letting it fuel my performance. I focused on the intricate details of my creations—the delicate embroidery that told stories of resilience, the vibrant colors reflecting my journey, each hue a note in the symphony of my aspirations. I twirled, allowing the gown to sweep around me like a soft wave, feeling the fabric kiss my skin as I lost myself in the moment.

The applause erupted like a warm wave, washing over me, infusing me with strength. My heart soared, buoyed by the voices that rose in appreciation. They saw me, not as a girl lost in a sea of doubt, but as an artist pouring her soul onto the canvas of the runway. I caught sight of Julian again, and this time, I held his gaze. There was something in his eyes—a flicker of respect, perhaps. I refused to be defined by his perceptions. I was more than a reflection of someone else's expectations; I was the architect of my own narrative.

As I turned to face the exit of the runway, I felt an unfamiliar thrill—a cocktail of fear and exhilaration that tasted like freedom. This was my moment, and I refused to let it slip away. With one final twirl, I let the last vestiges of my anxiety dissipate into the atmosphere, allowing the energy of the night to infuse me with courage. I stepped back into the shadows, and the moment I did, Ethan was there, wrapping me in a tight embrace that felt like home.

"You were amazing!" he exclaimed, his eyes sparkling with pride. "You owned that runway!"

I laughed, a sound bubbling with relief and joy. "I almost didn't make it. Did you see Julian?"

His expression shifted, eyes narrowing in thought. "Yeah, I did. But who cares what he thinks? You were incredible, and everyone saw it."

"Right. Everyone except him," I said, my voice tinged with a mock pout, though the warmth of Ethan's support banished the lingering doubts.

"Forget him. Let's celebrate! You did this—this is your victory!" He grabbed my hand, pulling me toward the thrumming heart of the after-party, where laughter mingled with the clinking of glasses, and the air was thick with possibility.

As we stepped into the vibrant chaos, the world around us blurred into a whirl of colors and sounds. I felt the weight of the evening lift, replaced by an electrifying sense of anticipation. This was just the beginning, and I was ready to navigate the rapids of whatever came next.

The vibrant pulse of the after-party enveloped me as Ethan and I navigated through a sea of laughter and glimmering champagne flutes. The air was thick with the scent of fresh blooms and extravagant perfumes, a heady mixture that made my heart race with exhilaration. Each laugh and shout formed a symphony, an undercurrent of celebration flowing around us, filling the space with warmth and energy.

Ethan leaned in close, his voice a conspiratorial whisper. "Okay, spill it. What's the first thing you're going to do with your newfound fame? Start a clothing line? Write a memoir titled Confessions of a Runway Queen?"

"Only if I get a reality show deal," I teased, rolling my eyes dramatically. "I can already picture it—me, in a tiny apartment, frantically sewing as my cat critiques my designs. Riveting television."

His laughter was infectious, drawing a few curious glances our way, but I didn't care. For the first time in a long while, I felt weightless, untethered from the doubts that had held me hostage. We pushed through the crowd, weaving between clusters of fashionistas and photographers, all eager to capture the glamour of the evening.

"Let's get you a drink," Ethan suggested, and before I could argue, he had steered me toward a bar draped in gold and glimmering lights. As we approached, the bartender, a whirlwind of charm and skill, mixed drinks with a flourish, tossing bottles into the air and catching them with grace.

"What do you want?" he asked, flashing a dazzling smile.

"Something bubbly, with a hint of mischief," I replied, feeling my confidence swell like the fizz in the glass he poured.

"Perfect choice for a runway star," Ethan said, nudging me playfully. "So, what's next? You'll be dressing celebs in no time."

"Let's not get ahead of ourselves. I'm still figuring out how to dress myself without tripping," I said, gesturing toward the towering stilettos on my feet. They were beautiful but had proven treacherous during rehearsals.

"Just don't trip on the way to the top," he quipped, raising his glass as if making a toast. I clinked my own against his, the sound sharp and bright. We both took a sip, and I savored the effervescence dancing on my tongue, a reflection of the evening's magic.

As the party swirled around us, I felt a sudden tug at my sleeve. I turned to find a petite woman with an electrifying aura, her platinum hair contrasting sharply against her deep green gown. She had eyes that sparkled like jewels, and a smile that hinted at secrets.

"Congratulations!" she exclaimed, her voice warm and inviting. "You were spectacular on the runway! I'm Vivienne, by the way."

"Thank you so much! It means a lot to hear that from you," I replied, genuinely touched. "Your designs were incredible too. I've seen your work—absolutely breathtaking."

Vivienne's laughter rang out, rich and melodious. "Oh, darling, flattery will get you everywhere. But really, you have an eye for beauty. I could see it in every step you took. What's next for you?"

"Honestly? I'm still figuring that out," I admitted, the honesty refreshing. "It's all a bit overwhelming, to be honest."

"Good!" she said, a mischievous glint in her eyes. "Embrace it. That feeling of being lost means you're on the brink of something spectacular. And if you need help navigating this world, I'd love to offer my guidance. Connections matter."

Ethan raised an eyebrow at me, his intrigue evident. "What do you say? Should we take her up on that offer?"

I grinned at Vivienne. "I'd love that! Any advice on how to avoid the pitfalls of this industry would be invaluable."

"Pitfalls? Honey, there are chasms!" she replied, her laugh infectious. "But let's save that for another time. Tonight, you celebrate. You've earned it!"

The conversation flowed like the champagne, each word sparkling with possibility. Vivienne's charisma made the world around us dim, her presence intoxicating. She shared stories of her own struggles, the missteps that had led her to find her voice, and the beautiful chaos that characterized the fashion world. As she spoke, I couldn't help but lean in closer, captivated by her tales of triumph and failure, each one echoing my own journey.

"Just remember, darling, this industry can be as fickle as a cat on a hot tin roof. One moment you're the star, and the next, you're a ghost," she cautioned, her tone suddenly serious. "So keep your friends close and your enemies closer."

"Sounds like a fashion week survival guide," I said, trying to lighten the mood, but her intensity was infectious.

"Precisely! And don't forget—your passion is your greatest asset. Never let anyone dim your light," she said, her gaze locking onto mine, unwavering. "You have talent, and the world deserves to see it."

"Thank you, Vivienne. That means more than you know," I said, my heart swelling with gratitude.

As the night wore on, we found ourselves lost in a flurry of conversations and laughter, spinning tales of the runway and dreams yet to be realized. I felt a kinship growing between us, the kind that was rare and precious. She introduced me to a few other designers, each one a unique thread in the vibrant tapestry of fashion, each with their own stories of resilience and reinvention.

But amidst the laughter, the shadows of self-doubt began to creep back. Julian's presence lingered like an unwelcome specter, a reminder of the insecurities I fought so hard to overcome. I excused myself from the group, needing a moment to breathe, to regain my focus.

I stepped outside onto the terrace, the cool night air wrapping around me like a comforting blanket. The stars shimmered overhead, each one a reminder of the dreams I dared to chase. But the tranquility was short-lived. I turned, and there he was—Julian, leaning casually against the wall, his expression unreadable.

"Enjoying the party?" he asked, his tone casual, yet the weight behind the words felt heavy.

"Very much, thank you," I replied, crossing my arms defensively. "What about you? Didn't peg you for a post-runway celebration."

"I'm here for the connections," he admitted, his eyes boring into mine. "You put on a good show. I'll give you that. But I know you. This isn't just about fashion for you, is it?"

I straightened, the fire of determination igniting within me. "What I do is about passion. You should know that better than anyone."

He chuckled, the sound deep and rich, but it felt hollow. "You always were the dreamer. Just remember, it's a tough world out there. Not everyone is going to root for you."

"Maybe not, but that won't stop me," I shot back, my voice stronger than I felt. "I'm done letting fear dictate my journey."

For a moment, the tension crackled between us like electricity, the air thick with unsaid words and unhealed wounds. Then, just as quickly, he turned, stepping back into the party, leaving me standing alone on the terrace, the night air heavy with the scent of impending change.

The cool night air had calmed the feverish pulse of the party, but the remnants of Julian's unexpected appearance lingered in my mind like an unwelcome shadow. I took a moment on the terrace, the city sprawling beneath me in a glittering mosaic of lights, a breathtaking reminder of everything I was fighting for. It was a world full of possibilities, but right now, it felt like a battleground, and Julian was an obstacle I hadn't anticipated.

As I turned to rejoin the celebration, I caught sight of Ethan animatedly conversing with Vivienne and a couple of other designers, their laughter rising like bubbles in a freshly poured glass of champagne. The camaraderie felt intoxicating, grounding me in this whirlwind of ambition and artistry. I stepped back inside, letting the warmth of the party wrap around me like a cocoon, attempting to shake off the heaviness that Julian had left in his wake.

"Look who decided to rejoin us!" Ethan exclaimed, his eyes sparkling with delight. "I thought we lost you to the night."

I feigned a dramatic sigh. "Oh, just having a deep philosophical conversation with my inner critic. You know, the usual."

Vivienne raised an eyebrow, clearly intrigued. "Care to share any gems of wisdom?"

"Mostly just the part where it tells me I should have worn flats instead of these lethal weapons," I joked, lifting a foot to display the towering stilettos. The group burst into laughter, the lightness of the moment dispelling the remnants of my earlier encounter.

"Flats are overrated," Vivienne declared, dismissing the idea with a wave of her hand. "But you? You need to own those heels. You strut like you mean it."

I grinned, buoyed by her confidence in me. The evening continued to unfold like a vivid tapestry, each interaction adding threads of connection and creativity. We moved from one cluster of attendees to another, discussing the intricacies of design, the ebb and flow of inspiration, and the small triumphs that kept us all afloat.

Yet, as the night wore on, the gleam of success was tinged with a nagging sense of unease. I couldn't shake Julian's words or his piercing gaze from my mind. They played like a broken record, reminding me of the critical side of this industry, the relentless scrutiny that came with being a designer.

Suddenly, the atmosphere shifted. The clamor of voices dimmed as whispers fluttered through the crowd like startled birds. I glanced around, sensing that something was brewing beyond the usual party chatter. Ethan noticed my furrowed brow and leaned in closer. "What's happening?"

"Not sure. But it feels like the calm before a storm," I said, scanning the room. Just then, a prominent figure in the fashion world stepped onto a makeshift stage at the far end of the terrace, his silhouette framed against the dazzling lights.

"Ladies and gentlemen," he boomed, capturing everyone's attention. "We have a special announcement tonight that may change the landscape of fashion week!"

The excitement in the air thickened, and I felt the buzz ripple through the crowd, drawing us closer to the stage. I exchanged glances with Ethan, curiosity igniting a spark in my chest.

"Could it be a new collaboration?" he speculated, bouncing on his heels. "Maybe an exclusive line with a big-name celebrity?"

"Or perhaps a surprise guest?" I added, feeling the energy electrify my skin. The crowd hushed, the anticipation palpable as we awaited the revelation.

The speaker smiled, his eyes glimmering with mischief. "I'm pleased to announce the launch of a new award—The Rising Star in Fashion Design! This prestigious accolade will honor one talented designer whose work embodies creativity, innovation, and resilience. The winner will be revealed at the closing gala of fashion week!"

Gasps echoed through the audience, a wave of excitement crashing over us. My heart raced, each beat resonating with the potential of such an opportunity. I felt a fierce determination igniting within me. I had fought to be seen, to be acknowledged, and this was the moment that could catapult my dreams into reality.

"Think you could be the one?" Ethan asked, his eyes wide with encouragement.

"I can't even think that far ahead," I admitted, trying to temper the wild flutter of hope that took flight in my chest. "There are so many incredible designers here."

"Yeah, but you just rocked the runway! You belong in that conversation," he insisted, his voice firm. "Go for it. This is your moment."

The crowd began to disperse, buzzing with excitement, but I remained rooted in place, my thoughts racing. The prospect of the award felt monumental, a tidal wave crashing against the shore of my aspirations.

Suddenly, I spotted Julian again, hovering at the edge of the crowd, watching me. A knot tightened in my stomach. Did he think I was chasing dreams too big for me? The thought was suffocating, and I could feel his presence like a weight pressing down on my shoulders.

"Excuse me for a moment," I said to Ethan, needing a brief reprieve from the whirlwind of emotions. I slipped away, weaving through the throngs of people, the music blaring in the background, pulling me further from the comfort of my friends.

I found myself in a quieter corner of the terrace, clutching my drink, gazing at the city below. The view was breathtaking, a sea of lights twinkling like stars scattered across the horizon. I took a deep breath, trying to find my center amidst the chaos.

But then, just as I was about to turn back to the party, I heard a familiar voice—Julian's voice—low and earnest. "You don't have to prove anything to anyone, you know."

I froze, my heart racing as I turned slowly to face him. His expression was softer, almost vulnerable, the sharp edges of our previous conversation smoothed over by the distance of time and perspective. "What do you mean?" I asked, cautious yet intrigued.

"You've always had talent. But sometimes, it's the pressure that makes you second-guess yourself," he said, his tone surprisingly gentle. "I've seen it happen to so many."

"Are you trying to make me feel better or just point out my insecurities?" I shot back, crossing my arms defensively.

"Maybe a bit of both," he admitted, his lips quirking into a half-smile. "But honestly, I don't want to see you falter because of doubts. You're stronger than that."

I opened my mouth to retort, but the sincerity in his gaze stopped me. It was as if the barriers we had erected were beginning to crumble, the space between us narrowing. For a heartbeat, I considered his words, the fragile line between our histories woven with past misunderstandings and lingering emotions.

"Why do you care?" I finally managed, the question hanging heavy in the air between us. "You left all of this behind."

"Because I can see the fire in you, and I know what it's like to let fear extinguish it," he replied, his eyes searching mine. "Don't let it happen to you. Fight for what you believe in, for who you are."

Just then, the atmosphere shifted again, a crackle of energy igniting in the crowd. The sound of applause erupted, drawing our attention back toward the stage where a familiar figure stepped up to make another announcement.

"Sorry to interrupt this poignant moment," the speaker said, a playful glint in his eye, "but we have one more surprise for tonight."

My heart sank; I knew I should step back, return to the safety of my friends, but Julian's words lingered, igniting a flicker of hope. I hesitated, caught in the storm of conflicting emotions swirling inside me, when the speaker continued, "We have a surprise guest! Please welcome the legendary fashion designer, Eloise Duval!"

Gasps filled the air, a collective wave of excitement crashing over us. I felt Julian's presence beside me, his warmth comforting yet unsettling. All eyes turned toward the entrance as a striking figure walked in, an aura of elegance and power radiating from her.

But before I could process the weight of her arrival, a loud crash echoed from somewhere inside the venue, snapping the crowd's focus. The moment felt suspended in time, the air thick with confusion as I turned toward the commotion.

In the blink of an eye, everything shifted. The atmosphere shattered, and chaos erupted, sending shockwaves through the crowd. My heart pounded in my chest as I caught a glimpse of something—someone—darting through the crowd, urgency written all over their face.

"Did you see that?" I gasped, my voice barely a whisper, as I turned to Julian. But he had already taken a step forward, a fierce determination in his eyes.

"Stay here," he commanded, and before I could argue, he was gone, lost in the sea of bodies.

I stood frozen, the vibrant night transforming into a whirlwind of uncertainty. Fear clutched at my throat, the pulse of the party fading into an echo as the crowd surged. Whatever was happening felt like the harbinger of something monumental, and I had a sinking feeling it was just the beginning.

Chapter 28: The Watershed Moment

The evening air buzzed with the electric hum of excitement, the vibrant colors of the party swirling like confetti in the spotlight of a thousand glowing chandeliers. As the applause echoed around me, I stood momentarily frozen, caught in the delicate web of triumph and impending treachery. My heart raced, not from the exhilaration of our successful show but from a gnawing anxiety that Julian would retaliate. I could feel his presence like a shadow lingering at the edge of my thoughts, a specter of doubt that refused to be exorcised.

Surrounded by laughter and clinking glasses, I made my way through the throng of guests, the fabric of my sequined dress shimmering with every step. The scent of vanilla and sandalwood lingered in the air, mingling with the sweet notes of champagne, but all I could focus on was the knot tightening in my stomach. Whispers floated like feathers in the breeze, but they were sharp, each one a dagger aimed directly at my success.

"Did you hear about the new production?" one voice tittered, all too familiar.

"Rumor has it Julian's not done yet," another responded, dripping with smug satisfaction.

I caught snippets of conversations as I maneuvered through the crowd, every whispered threat a reminder that victory could be fleeting. With each step, I replayed the finale in my mind—the climactic moment of our performance when the stage had burst to life with color, energy, and the ecstatic roars of an audience that had genuinely connected with our vision. We had done it; we had captured their hearts. But now, it felt as though that victory was a flame flickering dangerously close to the wind.

"Are you alright?" Clara appeared beside me, her voice cutting through the haze of my thoughts. Her warm brown eyes shimmered with concern, and the golden curls framing her face seemed to glow under the soft lights of the room.

"Not sure yet," I admitted, casting a wary glance over the partygoers. "I overheard something about Julian. I think he's planning something—something to undermine us."

Clara's expression hardened, a mix of determination and disbelief. "We won't let him. You've worked too hard to let him ruin this. We need a plan."

Ethan, always the pragmatist, joined us, his brow furrowing with a blend of worry and focus. "What's he up to this time? We need to outmaneuver him before he makes his move. We can't allow his negativity to overshadow our success."

His straightforwardness grounded me, his presence a reassuring anchor amid the chaotic waves of uncertainty. Ethan, with his perpetually tousled hair and an insatiable curiosity that matched my own, had a knack for seeing through the fog of drama.

"Maybe we should get ahead of the rumors," I proposed, my pulse steadying with each word. "If we address them head-on, we can redirect the conversation back to our achievements. Let's share our successes, spotlight the hard work we've put in, and showcase the impact we've had."

"Exactly," Clara chimed in, her enthusiasm sparking like fire in dry grass. "Let's create a buzz that's so big, Julian's whispers will seem like a distant echo. We can set up a series of interviews, highlight our vision moving forward, and make it clear that we're just getting started."

Ethan nodded, the gears in his mind visibly turning. "We should craft a message that emphasizes our unity. If the three of us stand strong together, we can showcase how much we value collaboration and the contributions of every team member. It'll be hard for Julian to attack that."

As we formulated our strategy, the murmurs around us began to fade, replaced by a collective sense of purpose. Each detail fell into place, and for the first time since the show, I felt a flicker of hope against the encroaching darkness. We would rise, unyielding and resolute, and Julian would find that undermining our success would only backfire.

"Let's make sure to keep our energy high," Clara said, determination radiating from her. "We need to show everyone that we are confident and focused. Our enthusiasm will be infectious; people will want to be part of what we're building."

In that moment, surrounded by laughter and the echoes of success, I understood that our journey was about more than just a performance; it was about creating something lasting—a community where creativity thrived, nurtured by trust and shared vision. Together, we would navigate the treacherous waters of jealousy and ambition, emerging stronger than ever.

The evening continued to whirl around us, laughter mingling with soft music, the room a kaleidoscope of bright faces and lively chatter. Yet, despite the gaiety, my thoughts remained tethered to Julian. He had never been one to shy away from manipulation, and as much as I hoped to stave off his antics, the reality was that he had a talent for sowing discord.

"I just wish he would step back and realize that collaboration is the key," I mused aloud, frustration bubbling to the surface. "He doesn't have to see us as competition."

Ethan shot me a quizzical look, his eyebrows raised. "You really think he sees it that way? He's always been driven by a need to prove himself, to be the best, regardless of who he steps on to get there."

"True," Clara chimed in, her tone softening. "But we have something he doesn't: genuine connection and passion for what we do. That's our advantage. No matter how he tries to tear us down, we'll always have that."

We exchanged resolute glances, our spirits buoyed by the camaraderie that had defined our journey thus far. The evening continued to hum with life, but a sense of urgency now coursed through me, igniting a fire that had been stifled by Julian's looming shadow. Together, we would confront whatever challenges lay ahead, uniting our strengths against his machinations. I could feel the tide turning in our favor, a fresh breeze pushing against the weight of uncertainty.

With Clara and Ethan at my side, we stepped deeper into the throng, ready to reclaim our narrative and stand strong against whatever storm Julian sought to unleash.

The air was thick with an intoxicating blend of laughter and ambition, each voice layered like a rich tapestry woven from the threads of our shared success. I felt buoyed by the sheer energy of the crowd, but every burst of joy was tempered by an unsettling current that whispered warnings. I spotted Clara animatedly discussing our plans with a group of newcomers, her gestures as vibrant as her personality. Ethan leaned against the bar, nursing a drink, his eyes scanning the room like a hawk searching for prey. It was comforting to know that I wasn't alone in this; we were a trio bound by mutual respect and shared goals.

As I made my way over to them, the laughter bubbled around me like champagne, sparkling and effervescent, but there was a heaviness beneath it all that I couldn't ignore. "You'd think we just won an Oscar the way they're celebrating," I remarked, slipping in beside Clara, who greeted me with a bright smile that cut through the tension.

"Just wait until the after-after-party," Clara replied, her eyes dancing with mischief. "That's when the real fun begins. You know, the one where we let our hair down and unleash our inner wildlings."

Ethan smirked. "I'm sure that includes a lot of questionable dance moves and terrible karaoke. Count me out."

"Dance moves? You haven't seen my interpretive salsa," Clara teased, nudging him with her elbow. "And I have the video evidence to prove it. You'll regret that when I release it to the world."

"Please don't," Ethan groaned, feigning horror as he raised his glass to ward off any potential footage. The lighthearted banter felt like a salve against the anxiety clawing at me. The world could wait for Julian's next move; right now, I needed this moment of levity.

As the laughter faded into the background, I steered the conversation back to the business at hand. "How do we tackle this?" I asked, glancing around to ensure no one was eavesdropping. "We need to be proactive about Julian's whispers. I can't let him taint what we've built."

"Agreed," Clara said, her tone shifting from playful to serious in an instant. "We can leverage social media to showcase our successes. Maybe a series of posts highlighting individual contributions and behind-the-scenes magic?"

Ethan nodded. "We should also consider hosting an open Q&A session. If we're transparent, people will see the truth. Let them ask questions; we'll answer them honestly. It'll make it harder for Julian to twist the narrative."

My heart raced at the thought. "What if he tries to sabotage that, too? What if he shows up and tries to spin his own story?"

Clara crossed her arms, her chin lifting defiantly. "Let him try. We're not going to hide. We're not going to be intimidated. If he shows up, we'll confront him head-on. Together."

The fire in her eyes ignited something within me. We were stronger than his petty tactics; we just had to believe it. "Okay, let's map this out. I'll start drafting a press release, something that emphasizes our unity and accomplishments."

"Good," Ethan replied. "And let's keep the communication lines open. If we hear anything new about Julian, we need to know. We can't be caught off guard."

As we continued to brainstorm, the atmosphere around us began to shift. Conversations swirled like leaves caught in a sudden gust, and I noticed a cluster of familiar faces gathering near the edge of the dance floor. Curiosity piqued, I drifted toward them, drawn by the spark of recognition.

"Is that—?" Clara began, her eyes widening as she leaned closer to me.

"Julian," I confirmed, my stomach twisting. There he was, impeccably dressed, with that disarming smile that had once charmed its way into the hearts of so many. He exuded confidence, but it was tainted by a hint of malice that sent a shiver down my spine.

"I thought he was going to lay low for a while," Clara murmured, her gaze narrowed in suspicion.

"More like plotting our demise," I muttered, feeling the weight of his presence like an anchor pulling me under.

Before I could register my next move, Julian caught sight of me, a predatory glint sparking in his eyes. "Ah, the stars of the evening! Or should I say, the fallen stars?" His tone dripped with sarcasm, and a nervous tension crackled in the air.

"Enjoying the show?" I shot back, determination mingling with the rising tide of unease.

"Always," he replied smoothly, leaning against the bar with an air of casual arrogance. "But I couldn't help but overhear some interesting chatter. You know how it is in this industry—everyone loves a good rumor, especially when it's about a supposed 'rising star.'" His gaze flickered toward Ethan and Clara, assessing, calculating.

"Funny, I thought rising stars burned the brightest," Clara said, her voice laced with defiance. "It's the falling stars that tend to fizzle out."

Julian chuckled, the sound low and unsettling. "You've got spirit, I'll give you that. But remember, even the brightest stars can be snuffed out."

"What's your point, Julian?" I challenged, stepping closer, refusing to back down.

He leaned forward, his voice dropping to a conspiratorial whisper that sent chills racing along my spine. "Just a friendly warning. This industry is ruthless, and sometimes, it's easier to watch others crumble than to build something yourself. I'd hate to see all your hard work go to waste."

Ethan stepped in, his posture shifting to protectively flank me. "We're not afraid of you or your games. Our success is built on talent and hard work, not manipulation."

Julian straightened, his smile faltering for a moment, revealing the cracks beneath his polished exterior. "We'll see, won't we?" With that, he turned, blending back into the crowd, leaving a trail of unease in his wake.

I took a deep breath, steadying my pulse as the reality of the confrontation settled around us. "What a charmer," I remarked, my voice tinged with sarcasm. "Did he really think he could intimidate us with his theatrics?"

"Don't let him get to you," Clara reassured me, her hand resting lightly on my shoulder. "He's just trying to rattle you, but it won't work. We have a plan, and we're moving forward."

"Right," I replied, though uncertainty clung to my thoughts like a stubborn shadow. Julian's words echoed, an unsettling mantra that warned of danger. We had to be vigilant. With him lurking in the background, every step forward felt precarious.

Yet, beneath the unease, a flicker of determination ignited. We would not let him dictate our story. As long as we stood together, we could face whatever tempest he conjured. In the face of uncertainty, we had each other—and that was worth fighting for.

The night dripped with tension as I stood beside Clara and Ethan, watching the crowd pulse with excitement, laughter mingling with the clinking of glasses. Julian had woven his dark thread into the fabric of our celebration, but I refused to let his presence taint the colors we had so carefully painted. The vibrant chatter was punctuated by laughter that rang like music, but there was a heaviness beneath it all, a lurking sense of dread that made me feel as if the walls were closing in.

"Do you think he'll try something tonight?" Clara asked, her brow furrowing as she scanned the room, searching for Julian's unmistakable silhouette among the guests.

"Not if we keep our guard up," I replied, summoning a confidence I didn't quite feel. "If he knows we're aware of his game, he might think twice."

Ethan, leaning casually against the bar, shook his head. "Julian thrives on chaos. He'll strike when we least expect it. We have to stay one step ahead."

The thought of him plotting made my skin crawl, but I pushed the unease aside, focusing on the task at hand. "Let's use this party as a platform. Showcase what we've accomplished. If we share our wins loud enough, maybe it will drown out whatever nonsense he's spreading."

Clara's eyes sparkled with excitement, her creative spirit igniting. "We can set up a photo booth! Capture the fun and success of tonight. A visual celebration that tells our story. Let's get everyone involved!"

"Great idea," Ethan replied, his enthusiasm matching Clara's. "We can also gather testimonials from guests about their experiences working with us. Real people telling real stories; it will be hard for anyone to dispute that."

As the night unfolded, the three of us strategized with a fervor that made me forget the weight of Julian's looming threat. We rallied friends and colleagues, spreading the word about our impromptu photo booth and inviting everyone to share their success stories. I was heartened to see people gravitate toward us, their smiles brightening the room. Together, we created a mosaic of joy that was both infectious and necessary.

The laughter flowed, punctuated by flashes from the camera capturing our shared moments, a stark contrast to the creeping sense of impending doom. I watched Clara charm guests with her infectious energy while Ethan held court, his witty repartee keeping everyone engaged. For a moment, I felt the tightness in my chest ease, the knot of tension unfurling as I immersed myself in the celebration.

But as the evening wore on, the laughter around me began to dull. I caught sight of Julian again, lurking at the edge of the festivities, his demeanor like a storm cloud on the horizon. He leaned against a pillar, observing with that infuriatingly smug smile that made my stomach churn. I felt the hair on the back of my neck rise, the warning bells ringing louder in my ears.

"Focus," I murmured to myself, reminding my racing heart to steady. I was here to shine, to show everyone the truth of our work and the bonds we'd built. Julian was just a shadow; he wouldn't dim our light.

As I turned back to the party, Clara appeared beside me, her brow creased with concern. "Did you see him? He's not even trying to hide. I think he's plotting something."

"Then let's make sure we keep the spotlight on us," I insisted, forcing a smile. "We'll keep the momentum going."

Just as I began to relax, the atmosphere shifted again. A hush fell over the crowd, and I turned to see what had caused the stir. Julian had climbed onto a makeshift stage, a microphone in hand, his charismatic grin lighting up his face as he surveyed the room.

"Hello, everyone!" he called out, his voice smooth and inviting. "What an amazing evening we've had. But I think we should take a moment to reflect on some truths."

The room quieted, the weight of his words heavy in the air. I felt the collective tension rise, my stomach twisting as he continued. "We've seen some incredible talent on display tonight, but as we all know, not everything is as it seems. Behind every success story, there's often a tangled web of competition and betrayal."

Gasps rippled through the crowd, and my heart raced as he locked eyes with me. I felt exposed, raw under his scrutiny. "Isn't that right, Samantha?"

Before I could react, Clara squeezed my arm, a surge of solidarity radiating between us. "He's just trying to intimidate you," she whispered fiercely. "Don't let him."

"Thank you for that wonderful introduction, Julian," I called out, raising my voice to cut through the tension. "But I'd like to remind everyone that this evening is about celebrating our achievements, not tearing each other down."

The crowd shifted, some nodding in agreement, others unsure how to react. "We've worked hard to create something special," I continued, my voice steadying. "And that success is built on collaboration, trust, and mutual respect."

Julian chuckled, his gaze unwavering. "Collaboration? Respect? Oh, Samantha, you do make it sound so noble. But don't you think it's a little disingenuous to gloss over the fact that some of us have had to claw our way to the top?"

"Claw? Really?" Ethan shouted from the crowd, his voice a clarion call of support. "You've got to be kidding me. This is about our passion and dedication, not petty rivalries."

Julian's smile faltered for just a heartbeat, but he recovered quickly, feeding off the energy of the audience. "Passion, yes! But isn't it interesting how some people will do whatever it takes to stay relevant? It's all about perception, isn't it?"

I could feel the tide turning, the murmur of uncertainty echoing through the crowd as they began to question what was unfolding. My pulse quickened, fear and anger warring within me. "You're just trying to stir up trouble," I retorted, standing my ground. "And we won't let you."

"Ah, but trouble has a way of finding you, doesn't it?" Julian replied, his voice silky smooth, yet laced with a threat that sent shivers down my spine. "Perhaps you should ask yourself who your real friends are in this industry."

Suddenly, a ripple of unease swept through the crowd. I glanced around, catching Clara's anxious expression, and the world around me began to blur. Julian was playing a dangerous game, and I could sense the stakes rising higher with each word he spoke.

As the tension reached a boiling point, I felt a strange compulsion to counter his bravado. "If anyone's interested in genuine collaboration, we'll be at the back, celebrating the people who truly matter—those who uplift us, who support us through thick and thin."

Julian raised an eyebrow, a smirk playing on his lips. "Support? That's rich coming from someone so desperate to defend her position."

Just then, a figure broke through the crowd, a woman with striking red hair and a determined expression. She stormed toward the stage, and for a moment, I felt hope flaring in my chest—could this be the ally we needed?

"Excuse me!" she shouted, her voice cutting through the murmur of disbelief. "I don't know who you think you are, but you've crossed a line. We're not here to tear each other down; we're here to build each other up."

A gasp rippled through the crowd as Julian's face morphed from amusement to anger. "And who are you to lecture me?"

"I'm someone who believes in the power of community!" she shot back, her voice unwavering. "And I'm not afraid to stand up to bullies like you."

I felt a rush of admiration for this woman, whose bravery seemed to set the room ablaze. Julian's eyes narrowed, and a tension thick enough to cut with a knife filled the space.

As the crowd murmured in surprise, I realized we had a chance to turn the tide, to unite against the darkness he represented. But then, just as I felt the momentum shifting, Julian's voice rose above the din once more.

"Let's see how strong your community really is, shall we? I have a little surprise that will change everything."

A chill ran down my spine, and as he stepped back, the stage lights dimmed, plunging us into an unsettling darkness. The laughter, the camaraderie, the spirit of unity we'd fought so hard to create—all of it teetered on the brink of collapse.

As the anticipation thickened, I exchanged worried glances with Clara and Ethan. The air crackled with tension, and my heart raced. What had Julian planned?

Then, with a flicker, the lights surged back to life, revealing a massive screen behind Julian. As the first images flashed across the screen, my breath caught in my throat. What I saw was beyond anything I had prepared for.

The room fell silent, the revelry replaced by a heavy dread that seemed to wrap around us like a noose. I could feel my heart pounding in my ears, drowning out the whispers, the gasps, and the nervous shuffles of the crowd.

Julian's smile stretched wider, a wolfish grin filled with satisfaction, as the screen showcased a series of videos—each one revealing secrets, moments of vulnerability, and unguarded discussions that had taken place in our planning meetings.

I felt the world tilt, the ground beneath me shifting as reality slipped through my fingers like sand.

And just like that, everything I had built began to crumble.

Chapter 29: Resilience in the Face of Adversity

The clattering of heels echoed against the polished marble floor of my studio, a symphony of sound punctuated by the occasional swish of fabric as Clara flitted from one corner to another, draping shimmering silks over the racks. The intoxicating scent of fresh paint mingled with the earthy aroma of vintage wood, creating a heady atmosphere of creativity and determination. Sunlight streamed through the large windows, casting a warm glow on the chaos we had embraced as our new normal, a testament to our fervor and the whirlwind of excitement that followed fashion week.

"Do you think we should add a pop of red to the collection?" Clara's voice was bright, brimming with possibility, as she held up a bolt of crimson satin that gleamed like a ripe cherry. Her auburn hair, twisted into a messy bun, held a few rebellious strands that danced around her face, echoing her spirited personality. She was a whirlwind of energy, and I couldn't help but smile at her enthusiasm, even amidst the storm of rumors swirling outside our sanctuary.

"Maybe," I mused, tilting my head as I considered the idea. "But I'm worried it might overshadow the subtlety we're aiming for. Our pieces should whisper elegance, not shout for attention." I picked up a delicate lace overlay, its intricate patterns reminiscent of an artist's brushstrokes, and imagined it cascading down the runway, telling a story of love and resilience.

Just then, Ethan entered, his tall frame blocking the sunlight for a moment before he stepped into the room with an air of purpose. "I have an idea," he announced, his deep voice slicing through the chatter like a knife. His charcoal-grey suit contrasted sharply with the vibrant chaos around him, and his dark hair was slightly tousled, as if he'd just emerged from a brainstorming session with the universe itself. "We need to fight back. Julian thinks he can smear our name? Let's turn this into an opportunity."

I exchanged a glance with Clara, her eyes sparkling with intrigue. "What do you have in mind?" I asked, leaning forward, sensing the tide of creativity rising once more.

"A campaign that emphasizes our journey. The authenticity behind each design, the love we pour into this," Ethan said, pacing slowly as if the words were forming themselves in the air. "We showcase our inspiration—the stories, the late nights, the laughter and the tears. This isn't just about clothes; it's about who we are."

I felt a rush of warmth at his words, a flicker of hope igniting within me. "Yes! Let's show them why we started this. Why every stitch is a piece of our soul." My voice trembled with the energy that surged through me. "We'll share behind-the-scenes footage, snippets of our lives, the friendships that sustain us."

As I spoke, I could almost see it—the vibrant colors of our journey unfurling like petals in the sun, each moment more beautiful than the last. Clara nodded vigorously, her enthusiasm palpable. "And we can invite people to share their stories too! Let's make this personal. Show how our designs resonate with their lives. Everyone has a story worth telling."

With the plan solidifying around us, we sprang into action, a whirlwind of creativity fueled by determination. Days melted into nights as we poured ourselves into the campaign, creating content that spoke to the heart of our brand. Clara's infectious laughter filled the studio as she filmed snippets of our brainstorming sessions, while I played around with mood boards, layering fabric swatches that told a story of resilience and authenticity.

But the shadows loomed, a reminder of the battles we faced. Each notification from social media was a gamble—would it be support or another malicious whisper from Julian? Despite the anxiety that prickled at my skin, I pressed on, pouring my heart into the campaign with every ounce of my being. The thought of giving in was unbearable. Each design was a testament to our struggles, our triumphs, and the bond that kept us afloat amid the chaos.

As the days turned into a blur of fabric, laughter, and the occasional tears of frustration, the response began to trickle in. Support flooded our feeds, messages of encouragement lighting up the dim corners of my doubt. "I can't believe how much I relate to your story," one follower wrote. "Your designs are more than just clothes; they're a piece of who you are."

Each comment felt like a balm, soothing the raw edges of my fraying confidence. With every like and share, the whispers of Julian's disparagement began to fade into the background, eclipsed by the resonance of our truth. We were not just fighting for a name; we were standing up for our dreams, our identities woven into the very fabric we created.

The tension between us and Julian simmered beneath the surface, a storm waiting to be unleashed. He wasn't going to let this go quietly. I could feel it in the air, a charged electricity that made my heart race whenever I thought about the confrontation that felt inevitable. But for now, we were riding the wave of momentum, our spirits buoyed by the community that embraced us.

As I stood in the studio one late evening, the city skyline twinkling like a million stars beyond the glass, I felt a surge of gratitude for Clara and Ethan. They were more than friends; they were my chosen family. We were bound by a shared vision, a determination to rise above the noise, and a fierce loyalty that anchored us amid the storm.

With a deep breath, I turned back to the fabric, ready to weave our story into the tapestry of our designs. I could almost hear the applause of the runway, feel the fabric fluttering in the wind as it celebrated our resilience. We were more than just designers; we were dreamers, warriors, and storytellers, and together, we were unstoppable.

The moment I stepped into the studio that morning, the vibrant chaos felt almost electric. Clara was already at it, her laughter ringing out like a bell as she twirled between fabric swatches and mood boards, an effervescent reminder that joy could still thrive amidst adversity. Her hands danced through the air, punctuating her thoughts as she spoke, and I couldn't help but marvel at her unyielding spirit. I'd been through the wringer, but Clara and Ethan were my lifebuoys in this turbulent sea of rumors and mischief, always ready to buoy my spirits just when I needed it most.

"Okay, so how about we feature the behind-the-scenes of our design process?" Clara suggested, her auburn hair swirling as she gestured animatedly. "Let's show the world the blood, sweat, and glitter that goes into each piece." Her eyes sparkled with enthusiasm, like she'd just struck gold.

"Blood? I'm not sure we need to go that far," I shot back, rolling my eyes playfully as I sifted through a pile of sketches. "But the glitter part? Absolutely."

Ethan leaned against the doorframe, arms crossed, a smirk playing on his lips as he observed us. "You know, if we're going to capture all that blood, sweat, and glitter, we might need to hire a medic for the next photoshoot." His voice was rich with humor, the kind that made even the most mundane moments feel lighter.

"Oh please, if anything, we need a fire extinguisher for Clara's brilliance," I quipped back, causing her to feign offense with a dramatic hand to her heart.

"Excuse me, I'll have you know that my brilliance is entirely contained!" she replied, a mock-serious expression crossing her face before breaking into another smile. It felt good to laugh, to let the weight of Julian's threats drift away for just a moment.

But beneath the surface of our playful banter lay an undercurrent of tension. I could feel it—a constant reminder of Julian's insidious whispers, his attempts to sabotage everything we had worked so hard to build. Each notification on my phone felt like a roll of the dice. Would it be a supportive message from a client or another bitter barb aimed at tarnishing my name?

Our campaign took shape over the next few days, a wild tapestry of shared stories and images that highlighted the heart and soul behind our designs. We compiled videos of late-night brainstorming sessions where Clara spilled coffee over her sketches and Ethan debated the merits of polka dots versus stripes. Every moment was infused with a love that transcended mere fabric; we were stitching together a narrative that was as much about us as it was about the clothes we created.

On the eve of our launch, we gathered in the studio, the air thick with anticipation. "Okay, so what's the game plan?" Ethan asked, eyes glimmering with determination as we stood amidst a sea of fabric and creativity.

I inhaled deeply, the scent of freshly cut fabric mingling with the lingering aroma of coffee. "We go live tomorrow morning, showcasing our video series across social media. But more importantly, we're going to engage with our audience. I want to hear their stories, their experiences. It's not just about us; it's about creating a community."

Clara nodded enthusiastically. "We'll ask them to share their journeys with our designs. Let's turn this campaign into a two-way street! People love connecting over shared experiences."

Ethan clapped his hands together, a decisive gesture that seemed to galvanize us. "Then it's settled. We're not just showcasing our talent; we're inviting the world to join us."

As the night deepened, we worked side by side, fueled by takeout and caffeine, stitching our dreams into reality. Each video we edited, each post we crafted, was like weaving a thread into a larger tapestry, vibrant and full of life. I felt the weight of Julian's negativity begin to lift, replaced by a buoyant optimism. Maybe we could turn this tide in our favor, reclaim our narrative.

But just as we finished our final edits and began to celebrate, my phone buzzed violently against the table, sending a shiver of dread through me. I glanced down, the screen illuminating with a notification that made my stomach drop.

Julian had posted.

"Hey, look at this!" I called out, and Clara and Ethan crowded around, their excitement evaporating as they read the words scrawled across Julian's latest post like a dark cloud eclipsing our sunny moment. "The so-called 'designers' can't handle the truth. This is what happens when amateur hour collides with the world of fashion."

"Ugh, this guy is relentless," Clara scoffed, her brows knitting together in frustration.

Ethan clenched his jaw, the air thick with tension as he read further. "This isn't just a jab; it's a full-on attack. He's trying to paint you as some talentless hack."

"Because that's what real professionals do," I muttered, bitterness lacing my words. The urge to fight back flared within me, but I knew better than to let anger dictate my actions.

"We're better than this," I asserted, determination setting my jaw as I swiped away the post. "Let's not stoop to his level. We'll let our work speak for itself."

Clara squeezed my arm, her eyes shining with support. "We've got this. Let's just stay focused on our launch and share our stories."

"Exactly. Let's put our energy into the campaign," Ethan added, his voice steady as he turned back to his laptop. "We'll show the world who we really are."

The following morning dawned with an explosion of light, the sun spilling through the windows like warm honey. We gathered around a table laden with pastries and coffee, the scent of fresh croissants wafting through the air. A sense of calm enveloped us as we prepared for the launch, adrenaline mixing with excitement.

As the clock struck ten, we hit "post," and the response was immediate. Notifications buzzed and pinged like fireworks going off, a celebration of our resilience and creativity. The community we had longed for began to coalesce around us, their voices lifting us higher.

With every comment and share, I felt a flicker of hope ignite within me. We were not just fighting against Julian's negativity; we were building something beautiful, a testament to our hard work, determination, and unwavering spirit. And as I glanced at Clara and Ethan, their faces aglow with the thrill of our endeavor, I realized this journey was not just about overcoming adversity. It was about forging connections, sharing our stories, and creating a legacy that was undeniably ours.

The response to our campaign was like a tidal wave, overwhelming yet exhilarating, sweeping us off our feet. Notifications poured in, each one a burst of color on our screens—hearts, likes, and comments filled the digital landscape, a cacophony of support that drowned out Julian's venomous whispers. Clara was practically bouncing off the walls, her laughter infectious as we celebrated our small victories. "Look at this!" she exclaimed, pointing to a message that read, "Your designs changed my life!"

"Do we need to start an official fan club?" Ethan joked, leaning back in his chair, a satisfied grin plastered across his face. "Maybe we can sell T-shirts with 'We survived Julian' printed on them."

"Only if they come in sequins," Clara chimed in, her eyes sparkling with mischief. The energy in the room was electric, buoyed by the realization that we were creating something meaningful. Our designs resonated with people, transcending mere aesthetics and becoming part of their stories.

But beneath our laughter lurked an undercurrent of tension. I was acutely aware that Julian wouldn't take this lying down. He had a way of lurking in the shadows, plotting his next move. The thought of him made my skin crawl. I refused to let his negativity seep into our newfound joy, but a knot of anxiety twisted in my stomach.

As we dove deeper into the campaign, we planned live sessions, interactive Q&As, and even pop-up events that invited our community into our world. We wanted to share the heart behind each design, the passion that fueled our creativity. It felt invigorating, like we were carving out a space where our voices mattered. Yet, each click of the mouse, each word typed, felt like a step closer to an impending confrontation.

On one particularly lively afternoon, we gathered around a large table littered with sketches and mood boards. The sun streamed in, casting a warm glow across our workspace, illuminating the vibrant colors of fabric that surrounded us. "Let's do a live session next week," I suggested, feeling a spark of inspiration ignite within me. "We can showcase our latest designs and share the stories that inspired them. Let's really engage with our audience."

"Love it!" Clara exclaimed, her enthusiasm infectious. "But what if we throw in a little surprise element? Something that'll keep them on their toes."

Ethan nodded, his eyes narrowing thoughtfully. "Like a giveaway? Maybe a piece from our collection?"

"Or a behind-the-scenes tour of the studio!" Clara chimed in, her excitement palpable. "We could show them the chaos that goes into creating something beautiful."

"Now you're talking," I said, feeling the adrenaline rush through me. "Let's give them a glimpse of the madness behind the magic."

As we plotted our live session, the buzz in the studio grew. Ideas bounced around like confetti, each one more creative than the last. We were riding the high of our success, but the sense of impending confrontation loomed ever closer.

The night before our live event, I found myself restless, sleep slipping through my fingers like grains of sand. I sat curled up in my favorite chair, a steaming cup of chamomile cradled between my hands, the soft glow of my laptop illuminating the room. I scrolled through our campaign's social media feed, the positivity washing over me like a warm blanket. Yet, just as I began to relax, my heart sank at the sight of Julian's latest post.

He had shared a photo of one of our designs, but not in the way I had hoped. "Imitation is the highest form of flattery," he had captioned it, his words dripping with sarcasm. "But beware of counterfeit artists." The comments that followed were a mix of confusion and disdain, some defending my work while others fed into Julian's narrative, questioning my originality.

The anger surged within me, boiling like a pot left unattended. I couldn't let him do this. I wouldn't. I quickly typed out a response, my fingers flying across the keyboard. "Art is subjective, Julian. You should know that better than anyone. But I won't let your jealousy dictate my journey."

Just as I hit send, the screen flickered, and a new message popped up, one that froze me in place. "What do you think you're doing?" It was from Julian. The simple text was a dagger to my heart, and suddenly, I felt like I was back in the ring, ready for a fight.

The room felt suffocating as I stared at the screen, the words swimming before my eyes. My pulse quickened, and I felt a mix of dread and anticipation. "I'm doing my job, Julian," I typed back, my resolve hardening. "Creating beautiful things and sharing my passion with the world."

The seconds stretched like hours before his reply came, each ping a reminder of the battle brewing. "You'll regret this," he shot back.

My breath caught in my throat. The weight of his words hung in the air, heavy and oppressive. Clara and Ethan had been right; this was escalating, and the stakes were higher than I had imagined.

Just as I was about to put my phone down, a knock echoed through the studio, sharp and unexpected. Clara opened the door, her face flushed with excitement. "You're not going to believe this! We're trending!"

But the joy was short-lived as I caught a glimpse of the anxiety etched across her features. "But... there's something else."

"What?" I asked, my heart pounding in my chest, suddenly aware that the atmosphere had shifted again.

"There's a rumor going around that Julian is planning a counter-campaign to discredit us. He's mobilizing some serious firepower."

Panic bubbled within me, but I forced myself to take a breath. "What does that mean? Are we talking about another smear campaign?"

"Worse," she replied, her voice trembling slightly. "He's got connections. People who could really damage our reputation. This could be bigger than anything we've faced so far."

Ethan stepped forward, his expression grim. "We need to prepare ourselves for whatever he throws at us. This is just the beginning."

A chill ran down my spine as the reality settled in. I could feel the shadows closing in around us, and I knew Julian was not done. The stakes were higher, and the fight was only just beginning.

"Alright," I said, a fierce determination igniting within me. "Let's show him what we're made of." But as I spoke, I could almost hear the echoes of Julian's earlier words: "You'll regret this." The air was thick with uncertainty, the tension mounting like a coiled spring.

Just as I turned to Clara and Ethan, the lights in the studio flickered ominously, plunging us into darkness. A distant sound echoed from the front of the building, the unmistakable thud of footsteps approaching. My heart raced as dread settled in. I could feel it in my bones: something was coming, and I couldn't shake the feeling that the real battle had only just begun.

Milton Keynes UK
Ingram Content Group UK Ltd.
UKHW020756231024
450026UK00001B/61

Stitching Fate

Emmeline Rivers

Published by Emmeline Rivers, 2024.

This is a work of fiction. Similarities to real people, places, or events are entirely coincidental.

STITCHING FATE

First edition. October 9, 2024.

Copyright © 2024 Emmeline Rivers.

ISBN: 979-8227840639

Written by Emmeline Rivers.